CONTENTS

INDIAN WHY STORIES: SPARKS FROM WAR EAGLE'S LODGE-FIRE

Introduction

It was the moon when leaves were falling, for Napa had finished painting them for their dance with the North wind. Just over the ragged mountain range the big moon hung in an almost starless sky, and in shadowy outline every peak lay upon the plain like a giant pattern. Slowly the light spread and as slowly the shadows stole away until the October moon looked down on the great Indian camp—a hundred lodges, each as perfect in design as the tusks of a young silver-tip, and all looking ghostly white in the still of the autumn night.

Back from the camp, keeping within the ever-moving shadows, a buffalo-wolf skulked to a hill overlooking the scene, where he stopped to look and listen, his body silhouetted against the sky. A dog howled occasionally, and the weird sound of a tom-tom accompanying the voice of a singer in the Indian village reached the wolf's ears, but caused him no alarm; for not until a great herd of ponies, under the eyes of the night-herder, drifted too close, did he steal away.

Near the center of the camp was the big painted lodge of War Eagle, the medicine-man, and inside had gathered his grandchildren, to whom he was telling the stories of the creation and of the strange doings of Napa, the creator. Being a friend of the old historian, I entered un-hindered, and with the children listened until the hour grew late, and on the lodge-wall the dying fire made warning shadows dance.

What a splendid lodge it was, and how grand War Eagle looked leaning against his back-rest in the firelight! From the tri-pod that supported the back-rest were suspended his weapons and his medicine-bundle, each showing the wonderful skill of the maker. The quiver that held the arrows was combined with a case for the bow, and colored quills of the porcupine had been deftly used to make it a thing of beauty. All about the lodge hung the strangely painted linings, and the fire-light added richness to both color and design. War Eagle's hair was white, for he had known many snows; but his eyes were keen and bright as a boy's, as he gazed in pride at his grand-children across the lodge-fire. He was wise, and had been in many battles, for his was a warlike tribe. He knew all about the world and the people in it. He was deeply religious, and every Indian child loved him for his good-ness and brave deeds.

About the fire were Little Buffalo Calf, a boy of eleven years; Eyes-in-the-Water, his sister, a girl of nine; Fine Bow, a cousin of these, aged ten, and Bluebird, his sister, who was but eight years old.

Not a sound did the children make while the old warrior filled his great pipe, and only the snapping of the lodge-fire broke the stillness. Solemnly War Eagle lit the tobacco that had been mixed with the dried inner bark of the red willow, and for several minutes smoked in silence, while the children's eyes grew large with expectancy. Finally he spoke:

Why The Chipmunk's Back Is Striped
"Napa, Old-man, is very old indeed. He made this world, and all that is on it. He came out of the south, and traveled toward the north, making the birds and animals as he passed. He made the perfumes for the winds to carry about, and he even made the war-paint for the people to use. He was a busy worker, but a great liar and thief, as I shall show you after I have told you more about him. It was Old-man

who taught the beaver all his cunning. It was Old-man who told the bear to go to sleep when the snow grew deep in winter, and it was he who made the curlew's bill so long and crooked, although it was not that way at first. Old-man used to live on this world with the animals and birds. There was no other man or woman then, and he was chief over all the animal-people and the bird-people. He could speak the language of the robin, knew the words of the bear, and understood the sign-talk of the beaver, too. He lived with the wolves, for they are the great hunters. Even today we make the same sign for a smart man as we make for the wolf; so you see he taught them much while he lived with them. Old-man made a great many mistakes in making things, as I shall show you after a while; yet he worked until he had everything good. But he often made great mischief and taught many wicked things. These I shall tell you about some day. Everybody was afraid of Old-man and his tricks and lies—even the animal-people, before he made men and women. He used to visit the lodges of our people and make trouble long ago, but he got so wicked that Manitou grew angry at him, and one day in the month of roses, he built a lodge for Old-man and told him that he must stay in it forever. Of course he had to do that, and nobody knows where the lodge was built, nor in what country, but that is why we never see him as our grand-fathers did, long, long ago.

"What I shall tell you now happened when the world was young. It was a fine summer day, and Old-man was traveling in the forest. He was going north and straight as an arrow—looking at nothing, hearing nothing. No one knows what he was after, to this day. The birds and forest-people spoke politely to him as he passed but he answered none of them. The Pine-squirrel, who is always trying to find out other people's business, asked him where he was going, but Old-man wouldn't tell him. The woodpecker hammered on a dead tree to make him look that way, but he wouldn't. The Elk-people and the Deer-people saw him pass, and all said that he must be up to some mischief or he would stop and talk a while. The pine-trees murmured, and the bushes whispered their greeting, but he kept his eyes straight ahead and went on traveling.

"The sun was low when Old-man heard a groan" (here War Eagle groaned to show the children how it sounded), "and turning about he saw a warrior lying bruised and bleeding near a spring of cold water. Old-man knelt beside the man and asked: 'Is there war in this country?'

"'Yes,' answered the man. 'This whole day long we have fought to kill a Person, but we have all been killed, I am afraid.'

"'That is strange,' said Old-man; 'how can one Person kill so many men? Who is this Person, tell me his name!' but the man didn't answer—he was dead. When Old-man saw that life had left the wounded man, he drank from the spring, and went on toward the north, but before long he heard a noise as of men fighting, and he stopped to look and listen. Finally he saw the bushes bend and sway near a creek that flowed through the forest. He crawled toward the spot, and peering through the brush saw a great Person near a pile of dead men, with his back against a pine-tree. The Person was full of arrows, and he was pulling them from his ugly body. Calmly the Person broke the shafts of the arrows, tossed them aside, and stopped the blood flow with a brush of his hairy hand. His head was large and fierce-looking, and his eyes were small and wicked. His great body was larger than that of a buffalo-bull and covered with scars of many battles.

"Old-man went to the creek, and with his buffalo-horn cup brought some water to the Person, asking as he approached:

"'Who are you, Person? Tell me, so I can make you a fine present, for you are great in war.'

"'I am Bad Sickness,' replied the Person. 'Tribes I have met remember me and always will, for their bravest warriors are afraid when I make war upon them. I come in the night or I visit their camps in daylight. It is always the same; they are frightened and I kill them easily.'

" 'Ho!' said Old-man, 'tell me how to make Bad Sickness, for I often go to war myself.' He lied; for he was never in a battle in his life. The Person shook his ugly head and then Old-man said:

" 'If you will tell me how to make Bad Sickness I will make you small and handsome. When you are big, as you now are, it is very hard to make a living; but when you are small, little food will make you fat. Your living will be easy because I will make your food grow everywhere.'

"'Good,' said the Person, 'I will do it; you must kill the fawns of the deer and the calves of the elk when they first begin to live. When you have killed enough of them you must make a robe of their skins. Whenever you wear that robe and sing—"now you sicken, now you sicken," the sickness will come— that is all there is to it. '

"'Good,' said Old-man, 'now lie down to sleep and I will do as I promised.'

"The Person went to sleep and Old-man breathed upon him until he grew so tiny that he laughed to see how small he had made him. Then he took out his paint sack and striped the Person's back with black and yellow. It looked bright and handsome and he waked the Person, who was now a tiny animal with a bushy tail to make him pretty.

"'Now,' said Old-man, 'you are the Chipmunk, and must always wear those striped clothes. All of your children and their children, must wear them, too.'

"After the Chipmunk had looked at himself, and thanked Old-man for his new clothes, he wanted to know how he could make his living, and Old-man told him what to eat, and said he must cache the pine-nuts when the leaves turned yellow, so he would not have to work in the winter time.

"'You are a cousin to the Pine-squirrel,' said Old-man, 'and you will hunt and hide as he does. You will be spry and your living will be easy to make if you do as I have told you.'

"He taught the Chipmunk his language and his signs, showed him where to live, and then left him, going on toward the north again. He kept looking for the cow-elk and doe-deer, and it was not long before he had killed enough of their young to make the robe as the Person told him, for they were plentiful before the white man came to live on the world. He found a shady place near a creek, and there made the robe that would make Bad Sickness whenever he sang the queer song, but the robe was plain, and brown in color. He didn't like the looks of it. Suddenly he thought how nice the back of the Chipmunk looked after he had striped it with his paints. He got out his old paint sack and with the same colors made the robe look very much like the clothes of the Chipmunk. He was proud of the work, and liked the new robe better; but being lazy, he wanted to save himself work, so he sent the South-wind to tell all the doe-deer and the cow-elk to come to him. They came as soon as they received the message, for they were afraid of Old-man and always tried to please him.

When they had all reached the place where Old-man was he said to them:

"'Do you see this robe?'

"'Yes, we see it,' they replied.

"'Well, I have made it from the skins of your children, and then painted it to look like the Chipmunk's back, for I like the looks of that Person's clothes. I shall need many more of these robes during my life; and every time I make one, I don't want to have to spend my time painting it; so from now on and forever your children shall be born in spotted clothes. I want it to be that way to save me work. On all the fawns there must be spots of white like this (here he pointed to the spots on Bad Sickness's robe) and on all of the elk-calves the spots shall not be so white and shall be in rows and look rather yellow.' Again he showed them his robe, that they might see just what he wanted.

"'Remember,' he said, 'after this I don't want to see any of your children running about wearing plain clothing, because that would mean more painting for me. Now go away, and remember what I have said, lest I make you sick. '

"The cow-elk and the doe-deer were glad to know that their children's clothes would be beautiful, and they went away to their little ones who were hidden in the tall grass, where the wolves and mountain-lions would have a hard time finding them; for you know that in the tracks of the fawn there is no scent, and the wolf cannot trail him when he is alone. That is the way Manitou takes care of the weak, and all of the forest-people know about it, too.

"Now you know why the Chipmunk's back is striped, and why the fawn and elk-calf wear their pretty clothes.

"I hear the owls, and it is time for all young men who will some day be great warriors to go to bed, and for all young women to seek rest, lest beauty go away forever. Ho!"

How The Ducks Got Their Fine Feathers

Another night had come, and I made my way toward War Eagle's lodge. In the bright moonlight the dead leaves of the quaking-aspen fluttered down whenever the wind shook the trees; and over the village great flocks of ducks and geese and swan passed in a never-ending procession, calling to each other in strange tones as they sped away toward the waters that never freeze.

In the lodge War Eagle waited for his grand-children, and when they had entered, happily, he laid aside his pipe and said:

"The Duck-people are traveling tonight just as they have done since the world was young. They are going away from winter because they cannot make a living when ice covers the rivers.

"You have seen the Duck-people often. You have noticed that they wear fine clothes but you do not know how they got them; so I will tell you tonight.

"It was in the fall when leaves are yellow that it happened, and long, long ago. The Duck-people had gathered to go away, just as they are doing now. The buck-deer was coming down from the high ridges to visit friends in the lowlands along the streams as they have always done. On a lake Old-man saw the Duck-people getting ready to go away, and at that time they all looked alike; that is, they all wore the same colored clothes. The loons and the geese and the ducks were there and playing in the sunlight. The loons were laughing loudly and the diving was fast and merry to see. On the hill where Old-man stood there was a great deal of moss, and he began to tear it from the ground and roll it into a great ball. When he had gathered all he needed he shouldered the load and started for the shore of the lake, staggering under the weight of the great burden. Finally the Duck-people saw him coming with his load of moss and began to swim away from the shore.

"'Wait, my brothers!' he called, 'I have a big load here, and I am going to give you people a dance. Come and help me get things ready.'

"'Don't you do it,' said the gray goose to the others; 'that's Old-man and he is up to something bad, I am sure.'

"So the loon called to Old-man and said they wouldn't help him at all.

"Right near the water Old-man dropped his ball of moss and then cut twenty long poles. With the poles he built a lodge which he covered with the moss, leaving a doorway facing the lake. Inside the lodge he built a fire and when it grew bright he cried:

"'Say, brothers, why should you treat me this way when I am here to give you a big dance? Come into the lodge,' but they wouldn't do that. Finally Old-man began to sing a song in the duck-talk, and keep time with his drum. The Duck-people liked the music, and swam a little nearer to the shore, watching for trouble all the time, but Old-man sang so sweetly that pretty soon they waddled up to the lodge and went inside. The loon stopped near the door, for he believed that what the gray goose had said was true, and that Old-man was up to some mischief. The gray goose, too, was careful to stay close to the door but the ducks reached all about the fire. Politely, Old-man passed the pipe, and they all smoked with him because it is wrong not to smoke in a person's lodge if the pipe is offered, and the Duck-people knew that.

"'Well,' said Old-man, 'this is going to be the Blind-dance, but you will have to be painted first.

"'Brother Mallard, name the colors—tell how you want me to paint you.'

"'Well,' replied the mallard drake, 'paint my head green, and put a white circle around my throat, like a necklace. Besides that, I want a brown breast and yellow legs: but I don't want my wife painted that way.'

"Old-man painted him just as he asked, and his wife, too. Then the teal and the wood-duck (it took a long time to paint the wood-duck) and the spoonbill and the blue-bill and the canvasback and the goose and the brant and the loon—all chose their paint. Old-man painted them all just as they wanted him to, and kept singing all the time. They looked very pretty in the firelight, for it was night before the painting was done.

"'Now,' said Old-man, 'as this is the Blind-dance, when I beat upon my drum you must all shut your eyes tight and circle around the fire as I sing. Every one that peeks will have sore eyes forever.'

"Then the Duck-people shut their eyes and Old-man began to sing: 'Now you come, ducks, now you come—tum-tum, tum; tum-tum, tum.'

"Around the fire they came with their eyes still shut, and as fast as they reached Old-man, the rascal would seize them, and wring their necks. Ho! things were going fine for Old-man, but the loon peeked a little, and saw what was going on; several others heard the fluttering and opened their eyes, too. The loon cried out, 'He's killing us—let us fly,' and they did that. There was a great squawking and quacking and fluttering as the Duck-people escaped from the lodge. Ho! but Old-man was angry, and he kicked the back of the loon-duck, and that is why his feet turn from his body when he walks or tries to stand. Yes, that is why he is a cripple today.

"And all of the Duck-people that peeked that night at the dance still have sore eyes— just as Old-man told them they would have. Of course they hurt and smart no more but they stay red to pay for peeking, and always will. You have seen the mallard and the rest of the Duck-people. You can see that the colors Old-man painted so long ago are still bright and handsome, and they will stay that way forever and forever. Ho!"

Why The Kingfisher Always Wears A War-Bonnet
Autumn nights on the upper Missouri river in Montana are indescribably beautiful, and under their spell imagination is a constant companion to him who lives in wilderness, lending strange, weird echoes to the voice of man or wolf, and unnatural shapes in shadow to commonplace forms.

The moon had not yet climbed the distant mountain range to look down on the humbler lands when I started for War Eagle's lodge; and dimming the stars in its course, the milky-way stretched across the jeweled sky. "The wolf's trail," the Indians call this filmy streak that foretells fair weather, and tonight it promised much, for it seemed plainer and brighter than ever before.

"How — how!" greeted War Eagle, making the sign for me to be seated near him, as I entered his lodge. Then he passed me his pipe and together we smoked until the children came.

Entering quietly, they seated themselves in exactly the same positions they had occupied on the previous evenings, and patiently waited in silence. Finally War Eagle laid the pipe away and said: "Ho! Little Buffalo Calf, throw a big stick on the fire and I will tell you why the Kingfisher wears a war-bonnet."

The boy did as he was bidden. The sparks jumped toward the smoke-hole and the blaze lighted up the lodge until it was bright as day-time, when War Eagle continued:

"You have often seen Kingfisher at his fishing along the rivers, I know; and you have heard him laugh in his queer way, for he laughs a good deal when he flies. That same laugh nearly cost him his life once, as you will see. I am sure none could see the Kingfisher without noticing his great head-dress, but not many know how he came by it because it happened so long ago that most men have forgotten.

"It was one day in the winter-time when Old-man and the Wolf were hunting. The snow covered the land and ice was on all of the rivers. It was so cold that Old-man wrapped his robe close about himself and his breath showed white in the air. Of course the Wolf was not cold; wolves never get cold as men do. Both Old-man and the Wolf were hungry for they had traveled far and had killed no meat.

Old-man was complaining and grumbling, for his heart is not very good. It is never well to grumble when we are doing our best, because it will do no good and makes us weak in our hearts. When our hearts are weak our heads sicken and our strength goes away. Yes, it is bad to grumble.

"When the sun was getting low Old-man and the Wolf came to a great river. On the ice that covered the water, they saw four fat Otters playing.

"'There is meat,' said the Wolf; 'wait here and I will try to catch one of those fellows.'

"'No!--No!' cried Old-man, 'do not run after the Otter on the ice, because there are air-holes in all ice that covers rivers, and you may fall in the water and die.' Old-man didn't care much if the Wolf did drown. He was afraid to be left alone and hungry in the snow — that was all.

"'Ho!' said the Wolf, 'I am swift of foot and my teeth are white and sharp. What chance has an Otter against me? Yes, I will go,' and he did.

"Away ran the Otters with the Wolf after them, while Old-man stood on the bank and shivered with fright and cold. Of course the Wolf was faster than the Otter, but he was running on the ice, remember, and slipping a good deal. Nearer and nearer ran the Wolf. In fact he was just about to seize an Otter, when *splash*!--into an air-hole all the Otters went. Ho ! the Wolf was going so fast he couldn't stop, and *swow*! into the air-hole he went like a badger after mice, and the current carried him under the ice. The Otters knew that hole was there. That was their country and they were running to reach that same hole all the time, but the Wolf didn't know that.

"Old-man saw it all and began to cry and wail as women do. Ho! but he made a great fuss. He ran along the bank of the river, stumbling in the snowdrifts, and crying like a woman whose child is dead; but it was be-cause he didn't want to be left in that country alone that he cried — not because he loved his brother, the Wolf. On and on he ran until he came to a place where the water was too swift to freeze, and there he waited and watched for the Wolf to come out from under the ice, crying and wailing and making an awful noise, for a man.

"Well—right there is where the thing happened. You see, Kingfisher can't fish through the ice and he knows it, too; so he always finds places like the one Old-man found. He was there that day, sitting on the limb of a birch-tree, watching for fishes, and when Old-man came near to Kingfisher's tree, crying like an old woman, it tickled the Fisher so much that he laughed that queer, chattering laugh.

"Old-man heard him and—Ho! but he was angry. He looked about to see who was laughing at him and that made Kingfisher laugh again, longer and louder than before. This time Old-man saw him and *swow*! he threw his war-club at Kingfisher; tried to kill the bird for laughing. Kingfisher ducked so quickly that Old-man's club just grazed the feathers on his head, making them stand up straight.

"'There,' said Old-man, 'I'll teach you to laugh at me when I'm sad. Your feathers are standing up on the top of your head now and they will stay that way, too. As long as you live you must wear a head-dress, to pay for your laughing, and all your children must do the same.

"This was long, long ago, but the King-fishers have not forgotten, and they all wear war-bonnets, and always will as long as there are Kingfishers.

"Now I will say good night, and when the sun sleeps again I will tell you why the curlew's bill is so long and crooked. Ho!"

Why The Curlew's Bill Is Long And Crooked
When we reached War Eagle's lodge we stopped near the door, for the old fellow was singing—singing some old, sad song of younger days and keeping time with his tom-tom. Somehow the music made me sad and not until it had ceased, did we enter.

"How! How!"—he greeted us, with no trace of the sadness in his voice that I detected in his song.

"You have come here tonight to learn why the Curlew's bill is so long and crooked. I will tell you, as I promised, but first I must smoke."

In silence we waited until the pipe was laid aside, then War Eagle began:

"By this time you know that Old-man was not always wise, even if he did make the world, and all that is on it. He often got into trouble but something always happened to get him out of it. What I shall tell you now will show you that it is not well to try to do things just because others do them. They may be right for others, and wrong for us, but Old-man didn't understand that, you see.

"One day he saw some mice playing and went near to watch them. It was spring-time, and the frost was just coming out of the ground. A big flat rock was sticking out of a bank near a creek, and the sun had melted the frost from the earth about it, loosening it, so that it was about to fall. The Chief-Mouse would sing a song, while all the other mice danced, and then the chief would cry 'now!' and all the mice would run past the big rock. On the other side, the Chief-Mouse would sing again, and then say 'now!' — back they would come — right under the dangerous rock. Sometimes little bits of dirt would crumble and fall near the rock, as though warning the mice that the rock was going to fall, but they paid no attention to the warning, and kept at their playing. Finally Old-man said:

"'Say, Chief-Mouse, I want to try that. I want to play that game. I am a good runner. '

"He wasn't, you know, but he thought he could run. That is often where we make great mistakes — when we try to do things we were not intended to do.

"'No — no!' cried the Chief-Mouse, as Old-man prepared to make the race past the rock. 'No!--No!--you will shake the ground. You are too heavy, and the rock may fall and kill you. My people are light of foot and fast. We are having a good time, but if you should try to do as we are doing you might get hurt, and that would spoil our fun.'

"'Ho!' said Old-man, 'stand back! I'll show you what a runner I am.'

"He ran like a grizzly bear, and shook the ground with his weight. *Swow!*--came the great rock on top of Old-man and held him fast in the mud. My how he screamed and called for aid. All the Mice-people ran away to find help. It was a long time before the Mice-people found anybody, but they finally found the Coyote, and told him what had happened. Coyote didn't like Old-man very much, but he said he would go and see what he could do, and he did. The Mice-people showed him the way, and when they all reached the spot — there was Old-man deep in the mud, with the big rock on his back. He was angry and was saying things people should not say, for they do no good and make the mind wicked.

"Coyote said: 'Keep still, you big baby. Quit kicking about so. You are splashing mud in my eyes. How can I see with my eyes full of mud? Tell me that. I am going to try to help you out of your trouble.' He tried but Old-man insulted Coyote. and called him a name that is not good, so the Coyote said, 'Well, stay there,' and went away.

"Again Old-man began to call for helpers, and the Curlew, who was flying over, saw the trouble, and came down to the ground to help. In those days Curlew had a short, stubby bill, and he thought that he could break the rock by pecking it. He pecked and pecked away without making any headway, till Old-man grew angry at him, as he did at the Coyote. The harder the Curlew worked, the worse Old-man scolded him. Old-man lost his temper altogether, you see, which is a bad thing to do, for we lose our friends with it, often. Temper is like a bad dog about a lodge—no friends will come to see us when he is about.

"Curlew did his best but finally said: 'I'll go and try to find somebody else to help you. I guess I am too small and weak. I shall come back to you.' He was standing close to Old-man when he spoke, and Old-man reached out and grabbed the Curlew by the bill. Curlew began to scream—oh, my—oh, my—oh, my—as you still hear them in the air when it is morning. Old-man hung onto the bill and finally pulled it out long and slim, and bent it downward, as it is today. Then he let go and laughed at the Curlew.

"'You are a queer-looking bird now. That is a homely bill, but you shall always wear it and so shall all of your children, as long as there are Curlews in the world.'

"I have forgotten who it was that got Old-man out of his trouble, but it seems to me it was the bear. Anyhow he did get out somehow, and lived to make trouble, until Manitou grew tired of him.

"There are good things that Old-man did and tomorrow night, if you will come early, I will tell you how Old-man made the world over after the water made its war on the land, scaring all the animal-people and the bird-people. I will also tell you how he made the first man and the first woman and who they were. But now the grouse is fast asleep; nobody is stirring but those who were made to see in the dark, like the owl and the wolf. Ho!"

Old-Man Remakes The World

The sun was just sinking behind the hills when we started for War Eagle's lodge.

"Tomorrow will be a fine day," said Other-person, "for grandfather says that a red sky is always the sun's promise of fine weather, and the sun cannot lie."

"Yes," said Bluebird, "and he said that when this moon was new it traveled well south for this time of year and its points were up. That means fine, warm weather."

"I wish I knew as much as grandfather," said Fine-bow with pride.

The pipe was laid aside at once upon our entering the lodge and the old warrior said:

"I have told you that Old-man taught the animals and the birds all they know. He made them and therefore knew just what each would have to understand in order to make his living. They have never forgotten anything he told them—even to this day. Their grandfathers told the young ones what they had been told, just as I am telling you the things you should know. Be like the birds and animals—tell your children and grandchildren what I have told you, that our people may always know how things were made, and why strange things are true.

"Yes—Old-man taught the Beaver how to build his dams to make the water deeper; taught the Squirrel to plant the pine-nut so that another tree might grow and have nuts for his children; told the Bear to go to sleep in the winter, when the snow made hard traveling for his short legs—told him to sleep, and promised him that he would need no meat while he slept. All winter long the Bear sleeps and eats nothing, because Old-man told him that he could. He sleeps so much in the winter that he spends most of his time in summer hunting.

"It was Old-man who showed the Owl how to hunt at night and it was Old-man that taught the Weasel all his wonderful ways— his bloodthirsty ways—for the Weasel is the bravest of the animal-people, considering his size. He taught the Beaver one strange thing that you have noticed, and that is to lay sticks on the creek-bottoms, so that they will stay there as long as he wants them to.

"Whenever the animal-people got into trouble they always sought Old-man and told him about it. All were busy working and making a living, when one day it commenced to rain. That was nothing, of course, but it didn't stop as it had always done before. No, it kept right on raining until the rivers over-ran their banks, and the water chased the Weasel out of his hole in the ground. Yes, and it found the Rabbit's hiding-place and made him leave it. It crept into the lodge of the Wolf at night and frightened his wife and children. It poured into the den of the Bear among the rocks and he had to move. It crawled under the logs in the forest and found the Mice-people. Out it went to the plains and chased them out of their homes in the buffalo skulls. At last the Beavers' dams broke under the strain and that made everything worse. It was bad—very bad, indeed. Everybody except the fish-people were frightened and all went to find Old-man that they might tell him what had happened. Finally they found his fire, far up on a timbered bench, and they said that they wanted a council right away.

"It was a strange sight to see the Eagle sitting next to the Grouse; the Rabbit sitting close to the Lynx; the Mouse right under the very nose of the Bobcat, and the tiny Humming-bird talking to the Hawk in a whisper, as though they had always been great friends. All about Old-man's fire they sat and whispered or talked in signs. Even the Deer spoke to the Mountain-lion, and the Antelope told the Wolf that he was glad to see him, because fear had made them all friends.

"The whispering and the sign-making stopped when Old-man raised his hand-like that" (here War Eagle raised his hand with the palm outward)--"and asked them what was troubling them.

"The Bear spoke first, of course, and told how the water had made him move his camp. He said all the animal-people were moving their homes, and he was afraid they would be unable to find good camping-places, because of the water. Then the Beaver spoke, because he is wise and all the forest-people know it. He said his dams would not hold back the water that came against them; that the whole world was a lake, and that he thought they were on an island. He said he could live in the water longer than most people, but that as far as he could see they would all die except, perhaps, the fish-people, who stayed in the water all the time, anyhow. He said he couldn't think of a thing to do—then he sat down and the sign-talking and whispering commenced again.

"Old-man smoked a long time—smoked and thought hard. Finally he grabbed his magic stone axe, and began to sing his war-song. Then the rest knew he had made up his mind and knew what he would do. *Swow!* He struck a mighty pine-tree a blow, and it fell down. *Swow!* Down went another and another, until he had ten times ten of the longest, straightest, and largest trees in all the world lying side by side before him. Then Old-man chopped off the limbs, and with the aid of magic rolled the great logs tight together. With withes of willow that he told the Beaver to cut for him, he bound the logs fast together until they were all as one. It was a monstrous raft that Old-man had built, as he sang his song in the darkness. At last he cried,

'Ho! Everybody hurry and sit on this raft I have made'; and they did hurry.

"It was not long till the water had reached the logs; then it crept in between them, and finally it went on past the raft and off into the forest, looking for more trouble.

"By and by the raft began to groan, and the willow withes squeaked and cried out as though ghost-people were crying in the night. That was when the great logs began to tremble as the water lifted them from the ground. Rain was falling—night was there, and fear made cowards of the bravest on the raft. All through the forest there were bad noises—noises that make the heart cold—as the raft bumped against great trees rising from the earth that they were leaving forever.

"Higher and higher went the raft; higher than the bushes; higher than the limbs on the trees; higher than the Woodpecker's nest; higher than the tree tops, and even higher than the mountains. Then the world was no more, for the water had whipped the land in the war it made against it.

"Day came, and still the rain was falling.

Night returned, and yet the rain came down. For many days and nights they drifted in the falling rain; whirling and twisting about while the water played with the great raft, as a Bear would play with a Mouse. It was bad, and they were all afraid—even Old-man himself was scared.

"At last the sun came but there was no land. All was water. The water was the world. It reached even to the sky and touched it all about the edges. All were hungry, and some of them were grumbling, too. There are always grumblers when there is great trouble, but they are not the ones who become great chiefs—ever.

"Old-man sat in the middle of the raft and thought. He knew that something must be done, but he didn't know what. Finally he said: 'Ho! Chipmunk, bring me the Spotted Loon. Tell him I want him.'

"The Chipmunk found the Spotted Loon and told him that Old-man wanted him, so the Loon went to where Old-man sat. When he got there, Old-man said:

"'Spotted Loon you are a great diver. Nobody can dive as you can. I made you that way and I know. If you will dive and swim down to the world I think you might bring me some of the dirt that it is made of—then I am sure I can make another world.'

"'It is too deep, this water,' replied the Loon, 'I am afraid I shall drown.'

"'Well, what if you do?' said Old-man. 'I gave you life, and if you lose it this way I will return it to you. You shall live again!'

"'All right, Old-man,' he answered, 'I am willing to try'; so he waddled to the edge of the raft. He is a poor walker—the Loon, and you know I told you why. It was all because Old-man kicked him in the back the night he painted all the Duck-people.

"Down went the Spotted Loon, and long he stayed beneath the water. All waited and watched, and longed for good luck, but when he came to the top he was dead. Everybody groaned—all felt badly, I can tell you, as Old-man laid the dead Loon on the logs. The Loon's wife was crying, but Old-man told her to shut up and she did.

"Then Old-man blew his own breath into the Loon's bill, and he came back to life.

"'What did you see, Brother Loon?' asked Old-man, while everybody crowded as close as he could.

"'Nothing but water,' answered the Loon, 'we shall all die here, I cannot reach the world by swimming. My heart stops working.'

"There were many brave ones on the raft, and the Otter tried to reach the world by diving; and the Beaver, and the Gray Goose, and the Gray Goose's wife; but all died in trying, and all were given a new life by Old-man. Things were bad and getting worse. Everybody was cross, and all wondered what Old-man would do next, when somebody laughed.

"All turned to see what there could be to laugh at, at such a time, and Old-man turned about just in time to see the Muskrat bid goodbye to his wife—that was what they were laughing at. But he paid no attention to Old-man or the rest, and slipped from the raft to the water. *Flip*!--his tail cut the water like a knife, and he was gone. Some laughed again, but all wondered at his daring, and waited with little hope in their hearts; for the Muskrat wasn't very great, they thought.

"He was gone longer than the Loon, longer than the Beaver, longer than the Otter or the Gray Goose or his wife, but when he came to the surface of the water he was dead.

"Old-man brought Muskrat back to life, and asked him what he had seen on his journey. Muskrat said: 'I saw trees, Old-man, but I died before I got to them.'

"Old-man told him he was brave. He said his people should forever be great if he succeeded in bringing some dirt to the raft; so just as soon as the Muskrat was rested he dove again.

"When he came up he was dead, but clinched in his tiny hand Old-man found some dirt— not much, but a little. A second time Old-man gave the Muskrat his breath, and told him that he must go once more, and bring dirt. He said there was not quite enough in the first lot, so after resting a while the Muskrat tried a third time and a third time he died, but brought up a little more dirt.

"Everybody on the raft was anxious now, and they were all crowding about Old-man; but he told them to stand back, and they did. Then he blew his breath in Muskrat's mouth a third time, and a third time he lived and joined his wife.

"Old-man then dried the dirt in his hands, rubbing it slowly and singing a queer song. Finally it was dry; then he settled the hand that held the dirt in the water slowly, until the water touched the dirt. The dry dirt began to whirl about and then Old-man blew upon it. Hard he blew and waved his hands, and the dirt began to grow in size right before their eyes. Old-man kept blowing and waving his hands until the dirt became real land, and the trees began to grow. So large it grew that none could see across it. Then he stopped his blowing and sang some more. Everybody wanted to get off the raft, but Old-man said 'no.'

"'Come here, Wolf,' he said, and the Wolf came to him.

"'You are swift of foot and brave. Run around this land I have made, that I may know how large it is.'

"The Wolf started, and it took him half a year to get back to the raft. He was very poor from much running, too, but Old-man said the world wasn't big enough yet so he blew some more, and again sent the Wolf out to run around the land. He never came back—no, the Old-man had made it so big that the Wolf died of old age before he got back to the raft. Then all the people went out upon the land to make their living, and they were happy, there, too.

"After they had been on the land for a long time Old-man said: 'Now I shall make a man and a woman, for I am lonesome living with you people. He took two or three handfuls of mud from the world he had made, and molded both a man and a woman. Then he set them side by side and breathed upon them. They lived!--and he made them very strong and healthy—very beautiful to look upon. Chippewas, he called these people, and they lived happily on that world until a white man saw an Eagle sailing over the land and came to look about. He stole the woman—that white man did; and that is where all the tribes came from that we know today. None are pure of blood but the two humans he made of clay, and their own children. And they are the Chippewas!

"That is a long story and now you must hurry to bed. Tomorrow night I will tell you another story—Ho!"

Why Blackfeet Never Kill Mice

Muskrat and his grandmother were gathering wood for the camp the next morning, when they came to an old buffalo skull. The plains were dotted with these relics of the chase, for already the hide-hunting white man had played havoc with the great herds of buffalo. This skull was in a grove of cottonwood-trees near the river, and as they approached two Mice scampered into it to hide. Muskrat, in great glee, secured a stick and was about to turn the skull over and kill the Mice, when his grandmother said: "No, our people never kill Mice. Your grandfather will tell you why if you ask him. The Mice-people are our friends and we treat them as such. Even small people can be good friends, you know—remember that."

All the day the boy wondered why the Mice-people should not be harmed; and just at dark he came for me to accompany him to War Eagle's lodge. On the way he told me what his grandmother had said, and that he intended to ask for the reason, as soon as we arrived. We found the other children already there, and almost before we had seated ourselves, Muskrat asked:

"Grandfather, why must we never kill the Mice-people? Grandmother said that you knew."

"Yes," replied War Eagle, "I do know and you must know. Therefore I shall tell you all tonight why the Mice-people must be let alone and allowed to do as they please, for we owe them much; much more than we can ever pay. Yes—they are great people, as you will see.

"It happened long, long ago, when there were few men and women on the world. Old-man was chief of all then, and the animal-people and the bird-people were greater than our people, because we had not been on earth long and were not wise.

"There was much quarrelling among the animals and the birds. You see the Bear wanted to be chief, under Old-man, and so did the

Beaver. Almost every night they would have a council and quarrel over it. Beside the Bear and Beaver, there were other animals, and also birds, that thought they had the right to be chief. They couldn't agree and the quarrelling grew worse as time went on. Some said the greatest thief should be chosen. Others thought the wisest one should be the leader; while some said the swiftest traveler was the one they wanted. So it went on and on until they were most all enemies instead of friends, and you could hear them quarrelling almost every night, until Old-man came along that way.

"He heard about the trouble. I forget who told him, but I think it was the Rabbit. Anyhow he visited the council where the quarrelling was going on and listened to what each one had to say. It took until almost daylight, too. He listened to it all—every bit. When they had finished talking and the quarrelling commenced as usual, he said, 'stop!' and they did stop.

"Then he said to them: 'I will settle this thing right here and right now, so that there will be no more rows over it, forever.'

"He opened his paint sack and took from it a small, polished bone. This he held up in the firelight, so that they might all see it, and he said:

"'This will settle the quarrel. You all see this bone in my right hand, don't you?'

"'Yes,' they replied.

"'Well, now you watch the bone and my hands, too, for they are quick and cunning.'

"Old-man began to sing the gambling song and to slip the bone from one hand to the other so rapidly and smoothly that they were all puzzled. Finally he stopped singing and held out his hands—both shut tight, and both with their backs up.

"'Which of my hands holds the bone now?' he asked them.

"Some said it was in the right hand and others claimed that it was the left hand that held it. Old-man asked the Bear to name the hand that held the bone, and the Bear did; but when Old-man opened that hand it was empty—the bone was not there. Then everybody laughed at the Bear. Old-man smiled a little and began to sing and again pass the bone.

"'Beaver, you are smart; name the hand that holds the bone this time.'

"The Beaver said: 'It's in your right hand. I saw you put it there.'

"Old-man opened that hand right before the Beaver's eyes, but the bone wasn't there, and again everybody laughed—especially the Bear.

"'Now, you see,' said Old-man, 'that this is not so easy as it looks, but I am going to teach you all to play the game; and when you have all learned it, you must play it until you find out who is the cleverest at the playing. Whoever that is, he shall be chief under me, forever.'

"Some were awkward and said they didn't care much who was chief, but most all of them learned to play pretty well. First the Bear and the Beaver tried it, but the Beaver beat the Bear easily and held the bone for ever so long. Finally the Buffalo beat the Beaver and started to play with the Mouse. Of course the Mouse had small hands and was quicker than the Buffalo—quicker to see the bone. The Buffalo tried hard for he didn't want the Mouse to be chief but it didn't do him any good; for the Mouse won in the end.

"It was a fair game and the Mouse was chief under the agreement. He looked quite small among the rest but he walked right out to the center of the council and said:

"'Listen, brothers—what is mine to keep is mine to give away. I am too small to be your chief and I know it. I am not warlike. I want to live in peace with my wife and family. I know nothing of war. I get my living easily. I don't like to have enemies. I am going to give my right to be chief to the man that Old-man has made like himself.'

"That settled it. That made the man chief forever, and that is why he is greater than the animals and the birds. That is why we never kill the Mice-people.

"You saw the Mice run into the buffalo skull, of course. There is where they have lived and brought up their families ever since the night the Mouse beat the Buffalo playing the bone game. Yes—the Mice-people always make their nests in the heads of the dead Buffalo-people, ever since that night.

"Our people play the same game, even today. See," and War Eagle took from his paint sack a small, polished bone. Then he sang just as Old-man did so long ago. He let the children try to guess the hand that held the bone, as the animal-people did that fateful night; but, like the animals, they always guessed wrong. Laughingly War Eagle said:

"Now go to your beds and come to see me tomorrow night. Ho!"

How The Otter Skin Became Great "Medicine"

It was rather late when we left War Eagle's lodge after having learned why the Indians never kill the Mice-people; and the milky way was white and plain, dimming the stars with its mist. The children all stopped to say good night to little Sees-in-the-dark, a brand-new baby sister of Bluebird's; then they all went to bed.

The next day the boys played at war, just as white boys do; and the girls played with dolls dressed in buckskin clothes, until it grew tiresome, when they visited relatives until it came time for us all to go to their grand-father's lodge. He was smoking when we entered, but soon laid aside the pipe and said:

"You know that the otter skin is big medicine, no doubt. You have noticed that our warriors wear it sometimes and you know that we all think it very lucky to wear the skin of the Otter. But you don't know how it came to be great; so I shall tell you.

"One time, long before my grandfather was born, a young-man of our tribe was unlucky in everything. No woman wanted to marry him, because he couldn't kill enough meat to keep her in food and clothes. Whenever he went hunting, his bow always broke or he would lose his lance. If these things didn't happen, his horse would fall and hurt him. Everybody talked about him and his bad luck, and although he was fine-looking, he had no close friends, because of his ill fortune. He tried to dream and get his medicine but no dream would come. He grew sour and people were sorry for him all the time. Finally his name was changed to 'The Unlucky-one,' which sounds bad to the ear. He used to wander about alone a good deal, and one morning he saw an old woman gathering wood by the side of a River. The Unlucky-one was about to pass the old woman when she stopped him and asked:

"'Why are you so sad in your handsome face? Why is that sorry look in your fine eyes?'

"'Because,' replied the young-man, 'I am the Unlucky-one. Everything goes wrong with me, always. I don't want to live any longer, for my heart is growing wicked.'

"'Come with me,' said the old woman, and he followed her until she told him to sit down. Then she said: 'Listen to me. First you must learn a song to sing, and this is it.' Then she sang a queer song over and over again until the young-man had learned it well.

"'Now do what I tell you, and your heart shall be glad some day.' She drew from her robe a pair of moccasins and a small sack of dried meat. 'Here,' she said, 'put these moccasins on your feet and take this sack of meat for food, for you must travel far. Go on down this river until you come to a great beaver village. Their lodges will be large and fine-looking and you will know the village by the great size of the lodges. When you get to the place, you must stand still for a long time, and then sing the song I taught you. When you have finished the singing, a great white Beaver, chief of all the Beavers in the world, will come to you. He is wise and can tell you what to do to change your luck. After that I cannot help you; but do what the white Beaver tells you, without asking why. Now go, and be brave!'

"The young-man started at once. Long his steps were, for he was young and strong. Far he traveled down the river—saw many beaver villages, too, but he did not stop, because the lodges were not big, as the old woman told him they would be in the right village. His feet grew tired for he traveled day and night without resting, but his heart was brave and he believed what the old woman had told him.

"It was late on the third day when he came to a mighty beaver village and here the lodges were greater than any he had ever seen before. In the center of the camp was a monstrous lodge built of great sticks and towering above the rest. All about, the ground was neat and clean and bare as your hand. The Unlucky-one knew this was the white Beaver's lodge—knew that at last he had found the chief of all the Beavers in the world; so he stood still for a long time, and then sang that song.

"Soon a great white Beaver—white as the snows of winter—came to him and asked:

'Why do you sing that song, my brother? What do you want of me? I have never heard a man sing that song before. You must be in trouble.'

"'I am the Unlucky-one,' the young-man replied. 'I can do nothing well. I can find no woman who will marry me. In the hunt my bow will often break or my lance is poor. My medicine is bad and I cannot dream. The people do not love me, and they pity me as they do a sick child.'

"'I am sorry for you,' said the white Beaver—chief of all the Beavers in the world—'but you must find my brother the Coyote, who knows where Old-man's lodge is. The Coyote will do your bidding if you sing that song when you see him. Take this stick with you, because you will have a long journey, and with the stick you may cross any river and not drown, if you keep it always in your hand. That is all I can do for you, myself.'

"On down the river the Unlucky-one traveled and the sun was low in the west on the fourth day, when he saw the Coyote on a hillside near by. After looking at Coyote for a long time, the young-man commenced to sing the song the old woman had taught him. When he had finished the singing, the Coyote came up close and asked:

"'What is the matter? Why do you sing that song? I never heard a man sing it before. What is it you want of me?'

"Then the Unlucky-one told the Coyote what he had told the white Beaver, and showed the stick the Beaver-chief had given him, to prove it.

"'I am hungry, too,' said the Unlucky-one, 'for I have eaten all the dried meat the old woman gave me.'

"'Wait here,' said the Coyote, 'my brother the Wolf has just killed a fat Doe, and perhaps he will give me a little of the meat when I tell him about you and your troubles.'

"Away went the Coyote to beg for meat, and while he was gone the young-man bathed his tired feet in a cool creek. Soon the Coyote came back with meat, and young-man built a fire and ate some of it, even before it was warm, for he was starving. When he had finished the Coyote said:

"'Now I shall take you to Old-man's lodge, come.'

"They started, even though it was getting dark. Long they traveled without stopping — over plains and mountains — through great forests and across rivers, until they came to a cave in the rough rocks on the side of a mighty mountain.

"'In there,' said the Coyote, 'you will find Old-man and he can tell you what you want to know.'

"The Unlucky-one stood before the black hole in the rocks for a long time, because he was afraid; but when he turned to speak to the Coyote he found himself to be alone. The Coyote had gone about his own business — had silently slipped away in the night.

"Slowly and carefully the young-man began to creep into the cave, feeling his way in the darkness. His heart was beating like a tom-tom at a dance. Finally he saw a fire away back in the cave.

"The shadows danced about the stone sides of the cave as men say the ghosts do; and they frightened him. But looking, he saw a man sitting on the far side of the fire. The man's hair was like the snow and very long. His face was wrinkled with the seams left by many years of life and he was naked in the firelight that played about him.

"Slowly the young-man stood upon his feet and began to walk toward the fire with great fear in his heart. When he had reached the place where the firelight fell upon him, the Old-man looked up and said:

"'How, young-man, I am Old-man. Why did you come here? What is it you want?'

"Then the Unlucky-one told Old-man just what he had told the old woman and the white Beaver and the Coyote, and showed the stick the Beaver had given him, to prove it.

"'Smoke,' said Old-man, and passed the pipe to his visitor. After they had smoked Old-man said:

"'I will tell you what to do. On the top of this great mountain there live many ghost-people and their chief is a great Owl. This Owl is the only one who knows how you can change your luck, and he will tell you if you are not afraid. Take this arrow and go among those people, without fear. Show them you are unarmed as soon as they see you. Now go!'

"Out into the night went the Unlucky one and on up the mountain. The way was rough and the wind blew from the north, chilling his limbs and stinging his face, but on he went toward the mountain-top, where the storm-clouds sleep and the winter always stays. Drifts of snow were piled all about, and the wind gathered it up and hurled it at the young-man as though it were angry at him. The clouds waked and gathered around him, making the night darker and the world lonelier than before, but on the very top of the mountain he stopped and tried to look through the clouds. Then he heard strange singing all about him; but for a long time there was no singer in sight. Finally the clouds parted and he saw a great circle of ghost-people with large and ugly heads. They were seated on the icy ground and on the drifts of snow and on the rocks, singing a warlike song that made the heart of the young-man stand still, in dread. In the center of the circle there sat a mighty Owl— their chief. Ho!--when the ghost-people saw the Unlucky-one they rushed at him with many lances and would have killed him but the Owl-chief cried, 'Stop!'

"The young-man folded his arms and said:

'I am unarmed—come and see how a Blackfoot dies. I am not afraid of you.'

"'Ho!' said the Owl-chief, 'we kill no unarmed man. Sit down, my son, and tell me what you want. Why do you come here? You must be in trouble. You must smoke with me.'

"The Unlucky-one told the Owl-chief just what he had told the old woman and the Beaver and the Coyote and Old-man, and showed the stick that the white Beaver had given him and the arrow that Old-man had given to him to prove it.

"'Good,' said the Owl-chief, 'I can help you, but first you must help yourself. Take this bow. It is a medicine-bow; then you will have a bow that will not break and an arrow that is good and straight. Now go down this mountain until you come to a river. It will be dark when you reach this river, but you will know the way. There will be a great cottonwood-tree on the bank of the stream where you first come to the water. At this tree, you must turn down the stream and keep on traveling without rest, until you hear a splashing in the water near you. When you hear the splashing, you must shoot this arrow at the sound. Shoot quickly, for if you do not you can never have any good luck. If you do as I have told you the splasher will be killed and you must then take his hide and wear it always. The skin that the splasher wears will make you a lucky man. It will make anybody lucky and you may tell your people that it is so.

"'Now go, for it is nearly day and we must sleep.'

"The young-man took his bow and arrow and the stick the white Beaver had given him and started on his journey. All the day he traveled, and far into the night. At last he came to a river and on the bank he saw the great cottonwood-tree, just as the ghost Owl had told him. At the tree the young-man turned down the stream and in the dark easily found his way along the bank. Very soon he heard a great splashing in the water near him, and — *zipp* — he let the arrow go at the sound — then all was still again. He stood and looked and listened, but for a long time could see nothing — hear nothing.

"Then the moon came out from under a cloud and just where her light struck the river, he saw some animal floating — dead. With the magic stick the young-man walked out on the water, seized the animal by the legs and drew it ashore. It was an Otter, and the young-man took his hide, right there.

"A Wolf waited in the brush for the body of the Otter, and the young-man gave it to him willingly, because he remembered the meat the Wolf had given the Coyote. As soon as the young-man had skinned the Otter he threw the hide over his shoulder and started for his own country with a light heart, but at the first good place he made a camp, and slept. That night he dreamed and all was well with him.

"After days of travel he found his tribe again, and told what had happened. He became a great hunter and a great chief among us. He married the most beautiful woman in the tribe and was good to her always. They had many children, and we remember his name as one that was great in war. That is all—Ho!"

Old-Man Steals The Sun's Leggings

Firelight—what a charm it adds to story-telling. How its moods seem to keep pace with situations pictured by the oracle, offering shadows when dread is abroad, and light when a pleasing climax is reached; for interest undoubtedly tends the blaze, while sympathy contributes or withholds fuel, according to its dictates.

The lodge was alight when I approached and I could hear the children singing in a happy mood, but upon entering, the singing ceased and embarrassed smiles on the young faces greeted me; nor could I coax a continuation of the song.

Seated beside War Eagle was a very old Indian whose name was Red Robe, and as soon as I was seated, the host explained that he was an honored guest; that he was a Sioux and a friend of long standing. Then War Eagle lighted the pipe, passing it to the distinguished friend, who in turn passed it to me, after first offering it to the Sun, the father, and the Earth, the mother of all that is.

In a lodge of the Blackfeet the pipe must never be passed across the doorway. To do so would insult the host and bring bad luck to all who assembled. Therefore if there be a large number of guests ranged about the lodge, the pipe is passed first to the left from guest to guest until it reaches the door, when it goes back, unsmoked, to the host, to be refilled ere it is passed to those on his right hand.

Briefly War Eagle explained my presence to Red Robe and said:

"Once the Moon made the Sun a pair of leggings. Such beautiful work had never been seen before. They were worked with the colored quills of the Porcupine and were covered with strange signs, which none but the Sun and the Moon could read. No man ever saw such leggings as they were, and it took the Moon many snows to make them. Yes, they were wonderful leggings and the Sun always wore them on fine days, for they were bright to look upon.

"Every night when the Sun went to sleep in his lodge away in the west, he used the leggings for a pillow, because there was a thief in the world, even then. That thief and rascal was Old-man, and of course the Sun knew all about him. That is why he always put his fine leggings under his head when he slept. When he worked he almost always wore them, as I have told you, so that there was no danger of losing them in the daytime; but the Sun was careful of his leggings when night came and he slept.

"You wouldn't think that a person would be so foolish as to steal from the Sun, but one night Old-man — who is the only person who ever knew just where the Sun's lodge was — crept near enough to look in, and saw the leggings under the Sun's head.

"We have all traveled a great deal but no man ever found the Sun's lodge. No man knows in what country it is. Of course we know it is located somewhere west of here, for we see him going that way every afternoon, but Old-man knew everything — except that he could not fool the Sun.

"Yes — Old-man looked into the lodge of the Sun and saw the leggings there — saw the Sun, too, and the Sun was asleep. He made up his mind that he would steal the leggings so he crept through the door of the lodge. There was no one at home but the Sun, for the Moon has work to do at night just as the children, the Stars, do, so he thought he could slip the leggings from under the sleeper's head and get away.

"He got down on his hands and knees to walk like the Bear-people and crept into the lodge, but in the black darkness he put his knee upon a dry stick near the Sun's bed. The stick snapped under his weight with so great a noise that the Sun turned over and snorted, scaring Old-man so badly that he couldn't move for a minute. His heart was not strong — wickedness makes every heart weaker — and after making sure that the Sun had not seen him, he crept silently out of the lodge and ran away.

"On the top of a hill Old-man stopped to look and listen, but all was still; so he sat down and thought.

"'I'll get them tomorrow night when he sleeps again'; he said to himself. 'I need those leggings myself, and I'm going to get them, because they will make me handsome as the Sun.'

"He watched the Moon come home to camp and saw the Sun go to work, but he did not go very far away because he wanted to be near the lodge when night came again.

"It was not long to wait, for all the Old-man had to do was to make mischief, and only those who have work to do measure time. He was close to the lodge when the Moon came out, and there he waited until the Sun went inside. From the bushes Old-man saw the Sun take off his leggings and his eyes glittered with greed as he saw their owner fold them and put them under his head as he had always done. Then he waited a while before creeping closer. Little by little the old rascal crawled toward the lodge, till finally his head was inside the door. Then he waited a long, long time, even after the Sun was snoring.

"The strange noises of the night bothered him, for he knew he was doing wrong, and when a Loon cried on a lake near by, he shivered as with cold, but finally crept to the sleeper's side. Cautiously his fingers felt about the precious leggings until he knew just how they could best be removed without waking the Sun. His breath was short and his heart was beating as a war-drum beats, in the black dark of the lodge. Sweat—cold sweat, that great fear always brings to the weak-hearted—was dripping from his body, and once he thought that he would wait for another night, but greed whispered again, and listening to its voice, he stole the leggings from under the Sun's head.

"Carefully he crept out of the lodge, looking over his shoulder as he went through the door. Then he ran away as fast as he could go. Over hills and valleys, across rivers and creeks, toward the east. He wasted much breath laughing at his smartness as he ran, and soon he grew tired.

"'Ho!' he said to himself, 'I am far enough now and I shall sleep. It's easy to steal from the Sun—just as easy as stealing from the Bear or the Beaver.'

"He folded the leggings and put them under his head as the Sun had done, and went to sleep. He had a dream and it waked him with a start. Bad deeds bring bad dreams to us all. Old-man sat up and there was the Sun looking right in his face and laughing. He was frightened and ran away, leaving the leggings behind him.

"Laughingly the Sun put on the leggings and went on toward the west, for he is always busy. He thought he would see Old-man no more, but it takes more than one lesson to teach a fool to be wise, and Old-man hid in the timber until the Sun had traveled out of sight. Then he ran westward and hid himself near the Sun's lodge again, intending to wait for the night and steal the leggings a second time.

"He was much afraid this time, but as soon as the Sun was asleep he crept to the lodge and peeked inside. Here he stopped and looked about, for he was afraid the Sun would hear his heart beating. Finally he started toward the Sun's bed and just then a great white Owl flew from off the lodge poles, and this scared him more, for that is very bad luck and he knew it; but he kept on creeping until he could almost touch the Sun.

"All about the lodge were beautiful linings, tanned and painted by the Moon, and the queer signs on them made the old coward tremble. He heard a night-bird call outside and he thought it would surely wake the Sun; so he hastened to the bed and with cunning fingers stole the leggings, as he had done the night before, without waking the great sleeper. Then he crept out of the lodge, talking bravely to himself as cowards do when they are afraid.

"'Now,' he said to himself, 'I shall run faster and farther than before. I shall not stop running while the night lasts, and I shall stay in the mountains all the time when the Sun is at work in the daytime!'

"Away he went—running as the Buffalo runs—straight ahead, looking at nothing, hearing nothing, stopping at nothing. When day began to break Old-man was far from the Sun's lodge and he hid himself in a deep gulch among some bushes that grew there. He listened a long time before he dared to go to sleep, but finally he did. He was tired from his great run and slept soundly and for a long time, but when he opened his eyes— there was the Sun looking straight at him, and this time he was scowling. Old-man started to run away but the Sun grabbed him and threw him down upon his back.

My! but the Sun was angry, and he said:

"'Old-man, you are a clever thief but a mighty fool as well, for you steal from me and expect to hide away. Twice you have stolen the leggings my wife made for me, and twice I have found you easily. Don't you know that the whole world is my lodge and that you can never get outside of it, if you run your foolish legs off? Don't you know that I light all of my lodge every day and search it carefully? Don't you know that nothing can hide from me and live? I shall not harm you this time, but I warn you now, that if you ever steal from me again, I will hurt you badly. Now go, and don't let me catch you stealing again!'

"Away went Old-man, and on toward the west went the busy Sun. That is all.

"Now go to bed; for I would talk of other things with my friend, who knows of war as I do. Ho! "

Old-Man And His Conscience

Not so many miles away from the village, the great mountain range so divides the streams that are born there, that their waters are offered as tribute to the Atlantic, Pacific, and Arctic Oceans. In this wonderful range the Indians believe the winds are made, and that they battle for supremacy over Gunsight Pass. I have heard an old story, too, that is said to have been generally believed by the Blackfeet, in which a monster bull-elk that lives in Gunsight Pass lords it over the winds. This elk creates the North wind by "flapping" one of his ears, and the South wind by the same use of his other. I am inclined to believe that the winds are made in that Pass, myself, for there they are seldom at rest, especially at this season of the year.

Tonight the wind was blowing from the north, and filmy white clouds were driven across the face of the nearly full moon, momentarily veiling her light. Lodge poles creaked and strained at every heavy gust, and sparks from the fires inside the lodges sped down the wind, to fade and die.

In his lodge War Eagle waited for us, and when we entered he greeted us warmly, but failed to mention the gale. "I have been waiting," he said. "You are late and the story I shall tell you is longer than many of the others." Without further delay the story-telling commenced.

"Once Old-man came upon a lodge in the forest. It was a fine one, and painted with strange signs. Smoke was curling from the top, and thus he knew that the person who lived there was at home. Without calling or speaking, he entered the lodge and saw a man sitting by the fire smoking his pipe. The man didn't speak, nor did he offer his pipe to Old-man, as our people do when they are glad to see visitors. He didn't even look at his guest, but Old-man has no good manners at all. He couldn't see that he wasn't wanted, as he looked about the man's lodge and made himself at home. The linings were beautiful and were painted with fine skill. The lodge was clean and the fire was bright, but there was no woman about.

"Leaning against a fine back-rest, Old-man filled his own pipe and lighted it with a coal from the man's fire. Then he began to smoke and look around, wondering why the man acted so queerly. He saw a star that shone down through the smoke-hole, and the tops of several trees that were near the lodge. Then he saw a woman—way up in a tree top and right over the lodge. She looked young and beautiful and tall.

"'Whose woman is that up there in the tree top?' asked Old-man.

"'She's your woman if you can catch her and will marry her,' growled the man; 'but you will have to live here and help me make a living.'

"'I'll try to catch her, and if I do I will marry her and stay here, for I am a great hunter and can easily kill what meat we want,' said Old-man.

"He went out of the lodge and climbed the tree after the woman. She screamed, but he caught her and held her, although she scratched him badly. He carried her into the lodge and there renewed his promise to stay there always. The man married them, and they were happy for four days, but on the fifth morning Old-man was gone—gone with all the dried meat in the lodge—the thief.

"When they were sure that the rascal had run away the woman began to cry, but not so the man. He got his bow and arrows and left the lodge in anger. There was snow on the ground and the man took the track of Old-man, intending to catch and kill him.

"The track was fresh and the man started on a run, for he was a good hunter and as fast as a Deer. Of course he gained on Old-man, who was a much slower traveler; and the Sun was not very high when the old thief stopped on a hilltop to look back. He saw the man coming fast.

"'This will never do,' he said to himself. 'That queer person will catch me. I know what I shall do; I shall turn myself into a dead Bull-Elk and lie down. Then he will pass me and I can go where I please.'

"He took off his moccasins and said to them: 'Moccasins, go on toward the west. Keep going and making plain tracks in the snow toward the big-water where the Sun sleeps. The queer-one will follow you, and when you pass out of the snowy country, you can lose him. Go quickly for he is close upon us.'

"The moccasins ran away as Old-man wanted them to, and they made plain tracks in the snow leading away toward the big-water. Old-man turned into a dead Bull-Elk and stretched himself near the tracks the moccasins had made.

"Up the hill came the man, his breath short from running. He saw the dead Elk, and thought it might be Old-man playing a trick. He was about to shoot an arrow into the dead Elk to make sure; but just as he was about to let the arrow go, he saw the tracks the moccasins had made. Of course he thought the moccasins were on Old-man's feet, and that the carcass was really that of a dead Elk. He was badly fooled and took the tracks again. On and on he went, following the moccasins over hills and rivers. Faster than before went the man, and still faster traveled the empty moccasins, the trail growing dimmer and dimmer as the daylight faded. All day long, and all of the night the man followed the tracks without rest or food, and just at day-break he came to the shore of the big-water. There, right by the water's edge, stood the empty moccasins, side by side.

"The man turned and looked back. His eyes were red and his legs were trembling. 'Caw — caw, caw,' he heard a Crow say. Right over his head he saw the black bird and knew him, too.

"'Ho! Old-man, you were in that dead Bull-Elk. You fooled me, and now you are a Crow. You think you will escape me, do you? Well, you will not; for I, too, know magic, and am wise.'

"With a stick the man drew a circle in the sand. Then he stood within the ring and sang a song. Old-man was worried and watched the strange doings from the air over-head. Inside the circle the man began to whirl about so rapidly that he faded from sight, and from the center of the circle there came an Eagle. Straight at the Crow flew the Eagle, and away toward the mountains sped the Crow, in fright.

"The Crow knew that the Eagle would catch him, so that as soon as he reached the trees on the mountains he turned himself into a Wren and sought the small bushes under the tall trees. The Eagle saw the change, and at once began turning over and over in the air. When he had reached the ground, instead of an Eagle a Sparrow-hawk chased the Wren. Now the chase was fast indeed, for no place could the Wren find in which to hide from the Sparrow-hawk. Through the brush, into trees, among the weeds and grass, flew the Wren with the Hawk close behind. Once the Sparrow-hawk picked a feather from the Wren's tail — so close was he to his victim. It was nearly over with the Wren, when he suddenly came to a park along a river's side. In this park were a hundred lodges of our people, and before a fine lodge there sat the daughter of the chief. It was growing dark and chilly, but still she sat there looking at the river. The Sparrow-hawk was striking at the Wren with his beak and talons, when the Wren saw the young-woman and flew straight to her. So swift he flew that the young-woman didn't see him at all, but she felt something strike her hand, and when she looked she saw a bone ring on her finger. This frightened her, and she ran inside the lodge, where the fire kept the shadows from coming. Old-man had changed into the ring, of course, and the Sparrow-hawk didn't dare to go into the lodge; so he stopped outside and listened.

This is what he heard Old-man say:

"'Don't be frightened, young-woman, I am neither a Wren nor a ring. I am Old-man and that Sparrow-hawk has chased me all the day and for nothing. I have never done him harm, and he bothers me without reason.'

"'Liar — forked-tongue,' cried the Sparrow-hawk. 'Believe him not, young-woman. He has done wrong. He is wicked and I am not a Sparrow-hawk, but conscience. Like an arrow I travel, straight and fast. When he lies or steals from his friends I follow him. I talk all the time and he hears me, but lies to himself, and says he does not hear. You know who I am, young-woman, I am what talks inside a person.'

"Old-man heard what the Sparrow-hawk said, and he was ashamed for once in his life. He crawled out of the lodge. Into the shadows he ran away — away into the night, and the darkness — away from himself!

"You see," said War Eagle, as he reached for his pipe," Old-man knew that he had done wrong, and his heart troubled him, just as yours will bother you if you do not listen to the voice that speaks within yourselves. Whenever that voice says a thing is wicked, it is wicked — no matter who says it is not. Yes — it is very hard for a man to hide from himself. Ho!"

Old-Man's Treachery

The next afternoon Muskrat and Fine Bow went hunting. They hid them-selves in some brush which grew beside an old game trail that followed the river, and there waited for a chance deer.

Chickadees hopped and called, "chick-a-de-de-de" in the willows and wild-rose bushes that grew near their hiding-place; and the gentle little birds with their pretty coats were often within a few inches of the hands of the young hunters. In perfect silence they watched and admired these little friends, while glance or smile conveyed their appreciation of the bird-visits to each other.

The wind was coming down the stream, and therefore the eyes of the boys seldom left the trail in that direction; for from that quarter an approaching deer would be unwarned by the ever-busy breeze. A rabbit came hopping down the game trail in believed perfect security, passing so close to Fine Bow that he could not resist the desire to strike at him with an arrow. Both boys were obliged to cover their mouths with their open hands to keep from laughing aloud at the surprise and speed shown by the frightened bunny, as he scurried around a bend in the trail, with his white, pudgy tail bobbing rapidly.

They had scarcely regained their compo-sure and silence when, "*snap!*" went a dry stick. The sharp sound sent a thrill through the hearts of the boys, and instantly they became rigidly watchful. Not a leaf could move on the ground now—not a bush might bend or a bird pass and escape being seen by the four sharp eyes that peered from the brush in the direction indicated by the sound of the breaking stick. Two hearts beat loudly as Fine Bow fitted his arrow to the bowstring. Tense and expectant they waited—yes, it was a deer—a buck, too, and he was coming down the trail, alert and watchful—down the trail that he had often traveled and knew so well. Yes, he had followed his mother along that trail when he was but a spotted fawn—now he wore antlers, and was master of his own ways. On he came—nearly to the brush that hid the hunters, when, throwing his beautiful head high in the air, he stopped, turning his side a trifle.

Zipp—went the arrow and, kicking out behind, away went the buck, crashing through willows and alders that grew in his way, until he was out of sight. Then all was still, save the chick-a-de-de-de, chick-a-de-de-de, that came constantly from the bushes about them.

Out from the cover came the hunters, and with ready bow they followed along the trail. Yes—there was blood on a log, and more on the dead leaves. The arrow had found its mark and they must go slowly in their trailing, lest they lose the meat. For two hours they followed the wounded animal, and at last came upon him in a willow thicket—sick unto death, for the arrow was deep in his paunch. His sufferings were ended by another arrow, and the chase was done.

With their knives the boys dressed the buck, and then went back to the camp to tell the women where the meat could be found—just as the men do. It was their first deer; and pride shone in their faces as they told their grandfather that night in the lodge.

"That is good," War Eagle replied, as the boys finished telling of their success. "That is good, if your mother needed the meat, but it is wrong to kill when you have plenty, lest Manitou be angry. There is always enough, but none to waste, and the hunter who kills more than he needs is wicked. Tonight I shall tell you what happened to Old-man when he did that. Yes, and he got into trouble over it.

"One day in the fall when the leaves were yellow, and the Deer-people were dressed in their blue robes—when the Geese and Duck-people were traveling to the country where water does not freeze, and where flowers never die, Old-man was traveling on the plains.

"Near sundown he saw two Buffalo-Bulls feeding on a steep hillside; but he had no bow and arrow with him. He was hungry, and began to think of some way to kill one of the Bulls for meat. Very soon he thought out a plan, for he is cunning always.

"He ran around the hill out of sight of the Bulls, and there made two men out of grass and sage-brush. They were dummies, of course, but he made them to look just like real men, and then armed each with a wooden knife of great length. Then he set them in the position of fighting; made them look as though they were about to fight each other with the knives. When he had them both fixed to suit, he ran back to the place where the Buffalo were calling:

"'Ho! brothers, wait for me—do not run away. There are two fine men on the other side of this hill, and they are quarrelling. They will surely fight unless we stop them. It all started over you two Bulls, too. One of the men says you are fat and fine, and the other claims you are poor and skinny. Don't let our brothers fight over such a foolish thing as that. It would be wicked. Now I can decide it, if you will let me feel all over you to see if you are fat or poor. Then I will go back to the men and settle the trouble by telling them the truth. Stand still and let me feel your sides—quick, lest the fight begin while I am away.'

"'All right,' said the Bulls, 'but don't you tickle us.' Then Old-man walked up close and commenced to feel about the Bulls' sides; but his heart was bad. From his robe he slipped his great knife, and slyly felt about till he found the spot where the heart beats, and then stabbed the knife into the place, clear up to the hilt.

"Both of the Bulls died right away, and Old-man laughed at the trick he had played upon them. Then he gave a knife to both of his hands, and said:

"'Get to work, both of you! Skin these Bulls while I sit here and boss you.'

"Both hands commenced to skin the Buffalo, but the right hand was much the swifter worker. It gained upon the left hand rapidly, and this made the left hand angry. Finally the left hand called the right hand 'dog-face.' That is the very worst thing you can call a person in our language, you know, and of course it made the right hand angry. So crazy and angry was the right hand that it stabbed the left hand, and then they began to fight in earnest.

"Both cut and slashed till blood covered the animals they were skinning. All this fighting hurt Old-man badly, of course, and he commenced to cry, as women do sometimes. This stopped the fight; but still Old-man cried, till, drying his tears, he saw a Red Fox sitting near the Bulls, watching him. 'Hi, there, you—go away from there! If you want meat you go and kill it, as I did.'

"Red Fox laughed—'Ha!--Ha!--Ha!-- foolish Old-man—Ha!--ha!' Then he ran away and told the other Foxes and the Wolves and the Coyotes about Old-man's meat. Told them that his own hands couldn't get along with themselves and that it would be easy to steal it from him.

"They all followed the Red Fox back to the place where Old-man was, and there they ate all of the meat—every bit, and polished the bones.

"Old-man couldn't stop them, because he was hurt, you see; but it all came about through lying and killing more meat than he needed. Yes—he lied and that is bad, but his hands got to quarreling between themselves, and family quarrels are always bad. Do not lie; do not quarrel. It is bad. Ho!"

Why The Night-Hawk's Wings Are Beautiful

I was awakened by the voice of the camp-crier, and although it was yet dark I listened to his message.

The camp was to move. All were to go to the mouth of the Maria's—"The River That Scolds at the Other"—the Indians call this stream, that disturbs the waters of the Missouri with its swifter flood.

On through the camp the crier rode, and behind him the lodge-fires glowed in answer to his call. The village was awake, and soon the thunder of hundreds of hoofs told me that the pony-bands were being driven into camp, where the faithful were being roped for the journey. Fires flickered in the now fading darkness, and down came the lodges as though wizard hands had touched them. Before the sun had come to light the world, we were on our way to "The River That Scolds at the Other."

Not a cloud was in the sky, and the wind was still. The sun came and touched the plains and hilltops with the light that makes all wild things glad. Here and there a jack-rabbit scurried away, often followed by a pack of dogs, and sometimes, though not often, they were overtaken and devoured on the spot. Bands of graceful antelope bounded out of our way, stopping on a knoll to watch the strange procession with wondering eyes, and once we saw a dust-cloud raised by a moving herd of buffalo, in the distance.

So the day wore on, the scene constantly changing as we traveled. Wolves and coyotes looked at us from almost every knoll and hill-top; and sage-hens sneaked to cover among the patches of sage-brush, scarcely ten feet away from our ponies. Toward sundown we reached a grove of cottonwoods near the mouth of the Maria's, and in an incredibly short space of time the lodges took form. Soon, from out the tops of a hundred camps, smoke was curling just as though the lodges had been there always, and would forever remain.

As soon as supper was over I found the children, and together we sought War Eagle's lodge. He was in a happy mood and insisted upon smoking two pipes before commencing his story-telling. At last he said:

"Tonight I shall tell you why the Night-hawk wears fine clothes. My grandfather told me about it when I was young. I am sure you have seen the Night-hawk sailing over you, dipping and making that strange noise. Of course there is a reason for it.

"Old-man was traveling one day in the springtime; but the weather was fine for that time of year. He stopped often and spoke to the bird-people and to the animal-people, for he was in good humor that day. He talked pleasantly with the trees, and his heart grew tender. That is, he had good thoughts; and of course they made him happy. Finally he felt tired and sat down to rest on a big, round stone—the kind of stone our white friend there calls a boulder. Here he rested for a while, but the stone was cold, and he felt it through his robe; so he said:

"'Stone, you seem cold today. You may have my robe. I have hundreds of robes in my camp, and I don't need this one at all.' That was a lie he told about having so many robes. All he had was the one he wore.

"He spread his robe over the stone, and then started down the hill, naked, for it was really a fine day. But storms hide in the mountains, and are never far away when it is springtime. Soon it began to snow—then the wind blew from the north with a good strength behind it. Old-man said:

"'Well, I guess I do need that robe myself, after all. That stone never did anything for me anyhow. Nobody is ever good to a stone. I'll just go back and get my robe.'

"Back he went and found the stone. Then he pulled the robe away, and wrapped it about himself. Ho! but that made the stone angry— Ho! Old-man started to run down the hill, and the stone ran after him. Ho! it was a funny race they made, over the grass, over smaller stones, and over logs that lay in the way, but Old-man managed to keep ahead until he stubbed his toe on a big sage-brush, and fell— *swow!*

"'Now I have you!' cried the stone—'now I'll kill you, too! Now I will teach you to give presents and then take them away,' and the stone rolled right on top of Old-man, and sat on his back.

"It was a big stone, you see, and Old-man couldn't move it at all. He tried to throw off the stone but failed. He squirmed and twisted— no use—the stone held him fast. He called the stone some names that are not good; but that never helps any. At last he began to call:

"'Help!--Help!--Help!' but nobody heard him except the Night hawk, and he told the Old-man that he would help him all he could; so he flew away up in the air—so far that he looked like a black speck. Then he came down straight and struck that rock an awful blow— '*swow!*'—and broke it in two pieces. Indeed he did. The blow was so great that it spoiled the Night-hawk's bill, forever—made it queer in shape, and jammed his head, so that it is queer, too. But he broke the rock, and Old-man stood upon his feet.

"'Thank you, Brother Night-hawk, ' said Old-man, 'now I will do something for you. I am going to make you different from other birds—make you so people will always notice you.'

"You know that when you break a rock the powdered stone is white, like snow; and there is always some of the white powder whenever you break a rock, by pounding it. Well, Old-man took some of the fine powdered stone and shook it on the Night-hawk's wings in spots and stripes—made the great white stripes you have seen on his wings, and told him that no other bird could have such marks on his clothes.

"All the Night-hawk's children dress the same way now; and they always will as long as there are Night-hawks. Of course their clothes make them proud; and that is why they keep at flying over people's heads—soaring and dipping and turning all the time, to show off their pretty wings.

"That is all for tonight. Muskrat, tell your father I would run Buffalo with him tomorrow—Ho!"

Why The Mountain-Lion Is Long And Lean

Have you ever seen the plains in the morning—a June morning, when the spurred lark soars and sings—when the plover calls, and the curlew pipes his shriller notes to the rising sun? Then is there music, indeed, for no bird out-sings the spurred lark; and thanks to Old-man he is not wanting in numbers, either. The plains are wonderful then—more wonderful than they are at this season of the year; but at all times they beckon and hold one as in a spell, especially when they are backed or bordered by a snow-capped mountain range. Looking toward the east they are boundless, but on their western edge superb mountains rear themselves.

All over this vast country the Indians roamed, following the great buffalo herds as did the wolves, and making their living with the bow and lance, since the horse came to them. In the very old days the "*piskun*" was used, and buffalo were enticed to follow a fantastically dressed man toward a cliff, far enough to get the herd moving in that direction, when the "buffalo-man" gained cover, and hidden Indians raised from their hiding places behind the animals, and drove them over the cliff, where they were killed in large numbers.

Not until Cortez came with his cavalry from Spain, were there horses on this continent, and then generations passed ere the plains tribes possessed this valuable animal, that so materially changed their lives. Dogs dragged the Indian's travois or packed his household goods in the days before the horse came, and for hundreds—perhaps thousands of years, these people had no other means of transporting their goods and chattels. As the Indian is slow to forget or change the ways of his father, we should pause before we brand him as wholly improvident, I think.

He has always been a family-man, has the Indian, and small children had to be carried, as well as his camp equipage. Wolf-dogs had to be fed, too, in some way, thus adding to his burden; for it took a great many to make it possible for him to travel at all.

When the night came and we visited War Eagle, we found he had other company—so we waited until their visit was ended before settling ourselves to hear the story that he might tell us.

"The Crows have stolen some of our best horses," said War Eagle, as soon as the other guests had gone. "That is all right—we shall get them back, and more, too. The Crows have only borrowed those horses and will pay for their use with others of their own. Tonight I shall tell you why the Mountain lion is so long and thin and why he wears hair that looks singed. I shall also tell you why that person's nose is black, because it is part of the story.

"A long time ago the Mountain-lion was a short, thick-set person. I am sure you didn't guess that. He was always a great thief like Old-man, but once he went too far, as you shall see.

"One day Old-man was on a hilltop, and saw smoke curling up through the trees, away off on the far side of a gulch. 'Ho!' he said, 'I wonder who builds fires except me. I guess I will go and find out.'

"He crossed the gulch and crept carefully toward the smoke. When he got quite near where the fire was, he stopped and listened. He heard some loud laughing but could not see who it was that felt so glad and gay. Finally he crawled closer and peeked through the brush toward the fire. Then he saw some Squirrel-people, and they were playing some sort of game. They were running and laughing, and having a big time, too. What do you think they were doing? They were running about the fire—all chasing one Squirrel. As soon as the Squirrel was caught, they would bury him in the ashes near the fire until he cried; then they would dig him out in a hurry. Then another Squirrel would take the lead and run until he was caught, as the other had been. In turn the captive would submit to being buried, and so on—while the racing and laughing continued. They never left the buried one in the ashes after he cried, but always kept their promise and dug him out, right away.

"'Say, let me play, won't you?' asked Old-man. But the Squirrel-people all ran away, and he had a hard time getting them to return to the fire.

"'You can't play this game,' replied the Chief-Squirrel, after they had returned to the fire.

"'Yes, I can,' declared Old-man, 'and you may bury me first, but be sure to dig me out when I cry, and not let me burn, for those ashes are hot near the fire.'

"'All right,' said the Chief-Squirrel, 'we will let you play. Lie down,'—and Old-Man did lie down near the fire. Then the Squirrels began to laugh and bury Old-man in the ashes, as they did their own kind. In no time at all Old-man cried: 'Ouch!--you are burning me—quick!--dig me out.'

"True to their promise, the Squirrel-people dug Old-man out of the ashes, and laughed at him because he cried so quickly.

"'Now, it is my turn to cover the captive,' said Old-man, 'and as there are so many of you, I have a scheme that will make the game funnier and shorter. All of you lie down at once in a row. Then I will cover you all at one time. When you cry—I will dig you out right away and the game will be over.'

"They didn't know Old-man very well; so they said, 'all right,' and then they all laid down in a row about the fire.

"Old-man buried them all in the ashes— then he threw some more wood on the fire and went away and left them. Every Squirrel there was in the world was buried in the ashes except one woman Squirrel, and she told Old-man she couldn't play and had to go home. If she hadn't gone, there might not be any Squirrels in this world right now. Yes, it is lucky that she went home.

"For a minute or so Old-man watched the fire as it grew hotter, and then went down to a creek where willows grew and made himself a great plate by weaving them together. When he had finished making the plate, he returned to the fire, and it had burned low again. He laughed at his wicked work, and a Raven, flying over just then, called him 'forked-tongue,' or liar, but he didn't mind that at all. Old-man cut a long stick and began to dig out the Squirrel-people. One by one he fished them out of the hot ashes; and they were roasted fine and were ready to eat. As he fished them out he counted them, and laid them on the willow plate he had made. When he had dug out the last one, he took the plate to the creek and there sat down to eat the Squirrels, for he was hungry, as usual. Old-man is a big eater, but he couldn't eat all of the Squirrels at once, and while eating he fell asleep with the great plate in his lap.

"Nobody knows how long it was that he slept, but when he waked his plate of Squirrels was gone—gone completely. He looked behind him; he looked about him; but the plate was surely gone. Ho! But he was angry. He stamped about in the brush and called aloud to those who might hear him; but nobody answered, and then he started to look for the thief. Old-man has sharp eyes, and he found the trail in the grass where somebody had passed while he slept. 'Ho!' he said, 'the Mountain-lion has stolen my Squirrels. I see his footprints; see where he has mashed the grass as he walked with those soft feet of his; but I shall find him, for I made him and know all his ways.'

"Old-man got down on his hands and knees to walk as the Bear-people do, just as he did that night in the Sun's lodge, and followed the trail of the Mountain-lion over the hills and through the swamps. At last he came to a place where the grass was all bent down, and there he found his willow plate, but it was empty. That was the place where the Mountain-lion had stopped to eat the rest of the Squirrels, you know; but he didn't stay there long because he expected that Old-man would try to follow him.

"The Mountain-lion had eaten so much that he was sleepy and, after traveling a while after he had eaten the Squirrels, he thought he would rest. He hadn't intended to go to sleep; but he crawled upon a big stone near the foot of a hill and sat down where he could see a long way. Here his eyes began to wink, and his head began to nod, and finally he slept.

"Without stopping once, Old-man kept on the trail. That is what counts — sticking right to the thing you are doing — and just before sundown Old-man saw the sleeping Lion. Carefully, lest he wake the sleeper, Old-man crept close, being particular not to move a stone or break a twig; for the Mountain-lion is much faster than men are, you see; and if Old-man had wakened the Lion, he would never have caught him again, perhaps. Little by little he crept to the stone where the Mountain-lion was dreaming, and at last grabbed him by the tail. It wasn't much of a tail then, but enough for Old-man to hold to. Ho!

The Lion was scared and begged hard, saying:

"'Spare me, Old-man. You were full and I was hungry. I had to have something to eat; had to get my living. Please let me go and do not hurt me.' Ho! Old-man was angry — more angry than he was when he waked and found that he had been robbed, because he had traveled so far on his hands and knees.

"'I'll show you. I'll teach you. I'll fix you, right now. Steal from me, will you? Steal from the man that made you, you night-prowling rascal!'

"Old-man put his foot behind the Mountain-lion's head, and, still holding the tail, pulled hard and long, stretching the Lion out to great length. He squalled and cried, but Old-man kept pulling until he nearly broke the Mountain-lion in two pieces — until he couldn't stretch him any more. Then Old-man put his foot on the Mountain-lion's back, and, still holding the tail, stretched that out until the tail was nearly as long as the body.

"'There, you thief—now you are too long and lean to get fat, and you shall always look just like that. Your children shall all grow to look the same way, just to pay you for your stealing from the man that made you. Come on with me'; and he dragged the poor Lion back to the place where the fire was, and there rolled him in the hot ashes, singeing his robe till it looked a great deal like burnt hair. Then Old-man stuck the Lion's nose against the burnt logs and blackened it some—that is why his face looks as it does today.

"The Mountain-lion was lame and sore, but Old-man scolded him some more and told him that it would take lots more food to keep him after that, and that he would have to work harder to get his living, to pay for what he had done. Then he said, 'go now, and remember all the Mountain-lions that ever live shall look just as you do.' And they do, too!

"That is the story—that is why the Mountain-lion is so long and lean, but he is no bigger thief than Old-man, nor does he tell any more lies. Ho!"

The Fire-Leggings

There had been a sudden change in the weather. A cold rain was falling, and the night comes early when the clouds hang low. The children loved a bright fire, and tonight War Eagle's lodge was light as day. Away off on the plains a wolf was howling, and the rain pattered upon the lodge as though it never intended to quit. It was a splendid night for story-telling, and War Eagle filled and lighted the great stone pipe, while the children made themselves comfortable about the fire.

A spark sprang from the burning sticks, and fell upon Fine Bow's bare leg. They all laughed heartily at the boy's antics to rid himself of the burning coal; and as soon as the laughing ceased War Eagle laid aside the pipe. An Indian's pipe is large to look at, but holds little tobacco.

"See your shadows on the lodge wall?" asked the old warrior. The children said they saw them, and he continued:

"Some day I will tell you a story about them, and how they drew the arrows of our enemies, but tonight I am going to tell you of the great fire-leggings.

"It was long before there were men and women on the world, but my grandfather told me what I shall now tell you.

"The gray light that hides the night-stars was creeping through the forests, and the wind the Sun sends to warn the people of his coming was among the fir tops. Flowers, on slender stems, bent their heads out of respect for the herald-wind's Master, and from the dead top of a pine-tree the Yellowhammer beat upon his drum and called 'the Sun is awake—all hail the Sun!'

"Then the bush-birds began to sing the song of the morning, and from alders the Robins joined, until all live things were awakened by the great music. Where the tall ferns grew, the Doe waked her Fawns, and taught them to do homage to the Great Light. In the creeks, where the water was still and clear, and where throughout the day, like a delicate damaskeen, the shadows of leaves that over-hang would lie, the Speckled Trout broke the surface of the pool in his gladness of the coming day. Pine-squirrels chattered gayly, and loudly proclaimed what the wind had told; and all the shadows were preparing for a great journey to the Sand Hills, where the ghost-people dwell.

"Under a great spruce-tree—where the ground was soft and dry, Old-man slept. The joy that thrilled creation disturbed him not, although the Sun was near. The bird-people looked at the sleeper in wonder, but the Pine squirrel climbed the great spruce-tree with a pine-cone in his mouth. Quickly he ran out on the limb that spread over Old-man, and dropped the cone on the sleeper's face. Then he scolded Old-man, saying: 'Get up—get up—lazy one—lazy one—get up—get up.'

"Rubbing his eyes in anger, Old-man sat up and saw the Sun coming—his hunting leggings slipping through the thickets—setting them afire, till all the Deer and Elk ran out and sought new places to hide.

"'Ho, Sun!' called Old-man, 'those are mighty leggings you wear. No wonder you are a great hunter. Your leggings set fire to all the thickets, and by the light you can easily see the Deer and Elk; they cannot hide. Ho! Give them to me and I shall then be the great hunter and never be hungry.'

"'Good,' said the Sun, 'take them, and let me see you wear my leggings.'

"Old-man was glad in his heart, for he was lazy, and now he thought he could kill the game without much work, and that he could be a great hunter—as great as the Sun. He put on the leggings and at once began to hunt the thickets, for he was hungry. Very soon the leggings began to burn his legs. The faster he traveled the hotter they grew, until in pain he cried out to the Sun to come and take back his leggings; but the Sun would not hear him. On and on Old-man ran. Faster and faster he flew through the country, setting fire to the brush and grass as he passed. Finally he came to a great river, and jumped in. Sizzzzzzz— the water said, when Old-man's legs touched it. It cried out, as it does when it is sprinkled upon hot stones in the sweat-lodge, for the leggings were very hot. But standing in the cool water Old-man took off the leggings and threw them out upon the shore, where the Sun found them later in the day.

"The Sun's clothes were too big for Old-man, and his work too great.

"We should never ask to do the things which Manitou did not intend us to do. If we keep this always in mind we shall never get into trouble.

"Be yourselves always. That is what Manitou intended. Never blame the Wolf for what he does. He was made to do such things. Now I want you to go to your fathers' lodges and sleep. Tomorrow night I will tell you why there are so many snakes in the world. Ho!"

The Moon And The Great Snake

The rain had passed; the moon looked down from a clear sky, and the bushes and dead grass smelled wet, after the heavy storm. A cottontail ran into a clump of wild-rose bushes near War Eagle's lodge, and some dogs were close behind the frightened animal, as he gained cover. Little Buffalo Calf threw a stone into the bushes, scaring the rabbit from his hiding-place, and away went bunny, followed by the yelping pack. We stood and listened until the noise of the chase died away, and then went into the lodge, where we were greeted, as usual, by War Eagle. Tonight he smoked; but with greater ceremony, and I suspected that it had something to do with the forthcoming story. Finally he said:

"You have seen many Snakes, I suppose?" "Yes," replied the children, "we have seen a great many. In the summer we see them every day."

"Well," continued the story-teller, "once there was only one Snake on the whole world, and he was a big one, I tell you. He was pretty to look at, and was painted with all the colors we know. This snake was proud of his clothes and had a wicked heart. Most Snakes are wicked, because they are his relations.

"Now, I have not told you all about it yet, nor will I tell you tonight, but the Moon is the Sun's wife, and some day I shall tell you that story, but tonight I am telling you about the Snakes.

"You know that the Sun goes early to bed, and that the Moon most always leaves before he gets to the lodge. Sometimes this is not so, but that is part of another story.

"This big Snake used to crawl up a high hill and watch the Moon in the sky. He was in love with her, and she knew it; but she paid no attention to him. She liked his looks, for his clothes were fine, and he was always slick and smooth. This went on for a long time, but she never talked to him at all. The Snake thought maybe the hill wasn't high enough, so he found a higher one, and watched the Moon pass, from the top. Every night he climbed this high hill and motioned to her. She began to pay more attention to the big Snake, and one morning early, she loafed at her work a little, and spoke to him. He was flattered, and so was she, because he said many nice things to her, but she went on to the Sun's lodge, and left the Snake.

"The next morning very early she saw the Snake again, and this time she stopped a long time—so long that the Sun had started out from the lodge before she reached home. He wondered what kept her so long, and became suspicious of the Snake. He made up his mind to watch, and try to catch them together. So every morning the Sun left the lodge a little earlier than before; and one morning, just as he climbed a mountain, he saw the big Snake talking to the Moon. That made him angry, and you can't blame him, because his wife was spending her time loafing with a Snake.

"She ran away; ran to the Sun's lodge and left the Snake on the hill. In no time the Sun had grabbed him. My, the Sun was angry! The big Snake begged, and promised never to speak to the Moon again, but the Sun had him; and he smashed him into thousands of little pieces, all of different colors from the different parts of his painted body. The little pieces each turned into a little snake, just as you see them now, but they were all too small for the Moon to notice after that. That is how so many Snakes came into the world; and that is why they are all small, nowadays.

"Our people do not like the Snake-people very well, but we know that they were made to do something on this world, and that they do it, or they wouldn't live here.

"That was a short story, but tomorrow night I will tell you why the Deer-people have no gall on their livers; and why the Antelope-people do not wear dew-claws, for you should know that there are no other animals with cloven hoofs that are like them in this.

"I am tired tonight, and I will ask that you go to your lodges, that I may sleep, for I am getting old. Ho!"

Why The Deer Has No Gall

Bright and early the next morning the children were playing on the bank of "The River That Scolds the Other," when Fine Bow said:

"Let us find a Deer's foot, and the foot of an Antelope and look at them, for tonight grandfather will tell us why the Deer has the dew-claws, and why the Antelope has none."

"Yes, and let us ask mother if the Deer has no gall on its liver. Maybe she can show both the liver of a Deer and that of an Antelope; then we can see for ourselves," said Blue-bird.

So they began to look about where the hides had been grained for tanning; and sure enough, there were the feet of both the antelope and the deer. On the deer's feet, or legs, they found the dew-claws, but on the antelope there were none. This made them all anxious to know why these animals, so nearly alike, should differ in this way.

Bluebird's mother passed the children on her way to the river for water, and the little girl asked: "Say, mother, does the Deer have gall on his liver?"

"No, my child, but the Antelope does; and your grandfather will tell you why if you ask him."

That night in the lodge War Eagle placed before his grandchildren the leg of a deer and the leg of an antelope, as well as the liver of a deer and the liver of an antelope.

"See for yourselves that this thing is true, before I tell you why it is so, and how it happened."

"We see," they replied, "and today we found that these strange things are true, but we don't know why, grandfather."

"Of course you don't know why. Nobody knows that until he is told, and now I shall tell you, so you will always know, and tell your children, that they, too, may know.

"It was long, long ago, of course. All these things happened long ago when the world was young, as you are now. It was on a summer morning, and the Deer was traveling across the plains country to reach the mountains on the far-off side, where he had relatives. He grew thirsty, for it was very warm, and stopped to drink from a water-hole on the plains. When he had finished drinking he looked up, and there was his own cousin, the Antelope, drinking near him.

"'Good morning, cousin,' said the Deer. 'It is a warm morning and water tastes good, doesn't it?'

"'Yes,' replied the Antelope, 'it is warm today, but I can beat you running, just the same.'

"'Ha-ha!' laughed the Deer—'you beat me running? Why, you can't run half as fast as I can, but if you want to run a race let us bet something. What shall it be?'

"'I will bet you my gall-sack,' replied the Antelope.

"'Good,' said the Deer, 'but let us run toward that range of mountains, for I am going that way, anyhow, to see my relations.'

"'All right,' said the Antelope. 'All ready, and here we go.'

"Away they ran toward the far-off range. All the way the Antelope was far ahead of the Deer; and just at the foot of the mountains he stopped to wait for him to catch up.

"Both were out of breath from running, but both declared they had done their best, and the Deer, being beaten, gave the Antelope his sack of gall.

"'This ground is too flat for me,' said the Deer. 'Come up the hillside where the gulches cut the country, and rocks are in our way, and I will show you how to run. I can't run on flat ground. It's too easy for me.' Another race with you on your own ground, and I think I can beat you there, too.'

"Together they climbed the hill until they reached a rough country, when the Deer said:

"'This is my kind of country. Let us run a race here. Whoever gets ahead and stays there, must keep on running until the other calls on him to stop.'

"'That suits me,' replied the Antelope, 'but what shall we bet this time? I don't want to waste my breath for nothing. I'll tell you— let us bet our dew-claws.'

"'Good. I'll bet you my dew-claws against your own, that I can beat you again. Are you all ready?--Go!'

"Away they went over logs, over stones and across great gulches that cut the hills in two. On and on they ran, with the Deer far ahead of the Antelope. Both were getting tired, when the Antelope called:

"'Hi, there—you! Stop, you can beat me. I give up.'

"So the Deer stopped and waited until the Antelope came up to him, and they both laughed over the fun, but the Antelope had to give the Deer his dew-claws, and now he goes without himself. The Deer wears dew-claws and always will, because of that race, but on his liver there is no gall, while the Antelope carries a gall-sack like the other animals with cloven hoofs.

"That is all of that story, but it is too late to tell you another tonight. If you will come tomorrow evening, I will tell you of some trouble that Old-man got into once. He deserved it, for he was wicked, as you shall see. Ho!"

Why The Indians Whip The Buffalo-Berries From The Bushes

The Indian believes that all things live again; that all were created by one and the same power; that nothing was created in vain; and that in the life beyond the grave he will know all things that he knew here. In that other world he expects to make his living easier, and not suffer from hunger or cold; therefore, all things that die must go to his heaven, in order that he may be supplied with the necessities of life.

The sun is not the Indian's God, but a personification of the Deity; His greatest manifestation; His light.

The Indian believes that to each of His creations God gave some peculiar power, and that the possessors of these special favors are His lieutenants and keepers of the several special attributes; such as wisdom, cunning, speed, and the knowledge of healing wounds. These wonderful gifts, he knew, were bestowed as favors by a common God, and therefore he revered these powers, and, without jealousy, paid tribute thereto.

The bear was great in war, because before the horse came, he would sometimes charge the camps and kill or wound many people.

Al-though many arrows were sent into his huge carcass, he seldom died. Hence the Indian was sure that the bear could heal his wounds. That the bear possessed a great knowledge of roots and berries, the Indian knew, for he often saw him digging the one and stripping the others from the bushes. The buffalo, the beaver, the wolf, and the eagle — each possessed strange powers that commanded the Indian's admiration and respect, as did many other things in creation.

If about to go to war, the Indian did not ask his God for aid — oh, no. He realized that God made his enemy, too; and that if He desired that enemy's destruction, it would be accomplished without man's aid. So the Indian sang his song to the bear, prayed to the bear, and thus invoked aid from a brute, and not his God, when he sought to destroy his fellows.

Whenever the Indian addressed the Great God, his prayer was for life, and life alone. He is the most religious man I have ever known, as well as the most superstitious; and there are stories dealing with his religious faith that are startling, indeed.

"It is the wrong time of year to talk about berries," said War Eagle, that night in the lodge, "but I shall tell you why your mothers whip the buffalo berries from the bushes. Old-man was the one who started it, and our people have followed his example ever since. Ho! Old-man made a fool of himself that day.

"It was the time when buffalo-berries are red and ripe. All of the bushes along the rivers were loaded with them, and our people were about to gather what they needed, when Old-man changed things, as far as the gathering was concerned.

"He was traveling along a river, and hungry, as he always was. Standing on the bank of that river, he saw great clusters of red, ripe buffalo-berries in the water. They were larger than any berries he had ever seen, and he said:

"'I guess I will get those berries. They look fine, and I need them. Besides, some of the people will see them and get them, if I don't.'

"He jumped into the water; looked for the berries; but they were not there. For a time Old-man stood in the river and looked for the berries, but they were gone.

"After a while he climbed out on the bank again, and when the water got smooth once more there were the berries — the same berries, in the same spot in the water.

"'Ho!--that is a funny thing. I wonder where they hid that time. I must have those berries!' he said to himself.

"In he went again—splashing the water like a Grizzly Bear. He looked about him and the berries were gone again. The water was rippling about him, but there were no berries at all. He felt on the bottom of the river but they were not there.

"'Well,' he said, 'I will climb out and watch to see where they come from; then I shall grab them when I hit the water next time.'

"He did that; but he couldn't tell where the berries came from. As soon as the water settled and became smooth—there were the berries—the same as before. Ho!--Old-man was wild; he was angry, I tell you. And in he went flat on his stomach! He made an awful splash and mussed the water greatly; but there were no berries.

"'I know what I shall do. I will stay right here and wait for those berries; that is what I shall do'; and he did.

"He thought maybe somebody was looking at him and would laugh, so he glanced along the bank. And there, right over the water, he saw the same bunch of berries on some tall bushes. Don't you see? Old-man saw the shadow of the berry-bunch; not the berries. He saw the red shadow-berries on the water; that was all, and he was such a fool he didn't know they were not real.

"Well, now he was angry in truth. Now he was ready for war. He climbed out on the bank again and cut a club. Then he went at the buffalo-berry bushes and pounded them till all of the red berries fell upon the ground— till the branches were bare of berries.

"'There,' he said, 'that's what you get for making a fool of the man who made you. You shall be beaten every year as long as you live, to pay for what you have done; you and your children, too.'

"That is how it all came about, and that is why your mothers whip the buffalo-berry bushes and then pick the berries from the ground. Ho!"

Old-Man And The Fox

I am sure that the plains Indian never made nor used the stone arrowhead. I have heard white men say that they had seen Indians use them; but I have never found an Indian that ever used them himself, or knew of their having been used by his people. Thirty years ago I knew Indians, intimately, who were nearly a hundred years old, who told me that the stone arrowhead had never been in use in their day, nor had their fathers used them in their own time. Indians find these arrow-points just as they find the stone mauls and hammers, which I have seen them use thou-sands of times, but they do not make them any more than they make the stone mauls and hammers. In the old days, both the head of the lance and the point of the arrow were of bone; even knives were of bone, but some other people surely made the arrow-points that are scattered throughout the United States and Europe, I am told.

One night I asked War Eagle if he had ever known the use, by Indians, of the stone arrowhead, and he said he had not. He told me that just across the Canadian line there was a small lake, surrounded by trees, wherein there was an island covered with long reeds and grass. All about the edge of this island were willows that grew nearly to the water, but intervening there was a narrow beach of stones. Here, he said, the stone arrowheads had been made by little ghost-people who lived there, and he assured me that he had often seen these strange little beings when he was a small boy. Whenever his people were camped by this lake the old folks waked the children at daybreak to see the inhabitants of this strange island; and always when a noise was made, or the sun came up, the little people hid away. Often he had seen their heads above the grass and tiny willows, and his grandfather had told him that all the stone arrowheads had been made on that island, and in war had been shot all over the world, by magic bows.

"No," he said, "I shall not lie to you, my friend. I never saw those little people shoot an arrow, but there are so many arrows there, and so many pieces of broken ones, that it proves that my grandfather was right in what he told me. Besides, nobody could ever sleep on that island."

I have heard a legend wherein Old-man, in the beginning, killed an animal for the people to eat, and then instructed them to use the ribs of the dead brute to make knives and arrow-points. I have seen lance-heads, made from shank bones, that were so highly polished that they resembled pearl, and I have in my possession bone arrow-points such as were used long ago. Indians do not readily forget their tribal history, and I have photographed a war-bonnet, made of twisted buffalo hair, that was manufactured before the present owner's people had, or ever saw, the horse. The owner of this bonnet has told me that the stone arrowhead was never used by Indians, and that he knew that ghost-people made and used them when the world was young.

The bow of the plains Indian was from thirty-six to forty-four inches long, and made from the wood of the choke-cherry tree. Sometimes bows were made from the service (or sarvice) berry bush, and this bush furnished the best material for arrows. I have seen hickory bows among the plains Indians, too, and these were longer and always straight, instead of being fashioned like Cupid's weapon. These hickory bows came from the East, of course, and through trading, reached the plains country. I have also seen bows covered with the skins of the bull-snake, or wound with sinew, and bows have been made from the horns of the elk, in the early days, after a long course of preparation.

Before Lewis and Clark crossed this vast country, the Blackfeet had traded with the Hudson Bay Company, and steel knives and lance-heads, bearing the names of English makers, still remain to testify to the relations existing, in those days, between those famous traders and men of the Piegan, Blood, and Blackfoot tribes, although it took many years for traders on our own side of the line to gain their friendship. Indeed, trappers and traders blamed the Hudson Bay Company for the feeling of hatred held by the three tribes of Blackfeet for the "Americans"; and there is no doubt that they were right to some extent, although the killing of the Blackfoot warrior by Captain Lewis in 1805 may have been largely to blame for the trouble. Certain it is that for many years after the killing, the Blackfeet kept traders and trappers on the dodge unless they were Hudson Bay men, and in 1810 drove the "American" trappers and traders from their fort at Three-Forks.

It was early when we gathered in War Eagle's lodge, the children and I, but the story-telling began at once.

"Now I shall tell you a story that will show you how little Old-man cared for the welfare of others," said War Eagle.

"It happened in the fall, this thing I shall tell you, and the day was warm and bright. Old-man and his brother the Red Fox were traveling together for company. They were on a hillside when Old-Man said: 'I am hungry. Can you not kill a Rabbit or something for us to eat? The way is long, and I am getting old, you know. You are swift of foot and cunning, and there are Rabbits among these rocks.'

"'Ever since morning came I have watched for food, but the moon must be wrong or something, for I see nothing that is good to eat,' replied the Fox. 'Besides that, my medicine is bad and my heart is weak. You are great, and I have heard you can do most anything.

Many snows have known your footprints, and the snows make us all wise. I think you are the one to help, not I.'

"'Listen, brother,' said Old-man, 'I have neither bow nor lance — nothing to use in hunting. Your weapons are ever with you — your great nose and your sharp teeth. Just as we came up this hill I saw two great Buffalo-Bulls. You were not looking, but I saw them, and if you will do as I want you to we shall have plenty of meat. This is my scheme; I shall pull out all of your hair, leaving your body white and smooth, like that of the fish. I shall leave only the white hair that grows on the tip of your tail, and that will make you funny to look at. Then you are to go before the Bulls and commence to dance and act foolish. Of course the Bulls will laugh at you, and as soon as they get to laughing you must act sillier than ever. That will make them laugh so hard that they will fall down and laugh on the ground. When they fall, I shall come upon them with my knife and kill them. Will you do as I suggest, brother, or will you starve?'

"'What! Pull out my hair? I shall freeze with no hair on my body, Old-man. No — I will not suffer you to pull my hair out when the winter is so near,' cried the Fox.

"'Ho! It is vanity, my brother, not fear of freezing. If you will do this we shall have meat for the winter, and a fire to keep us warm. See, the wind is in the south and warm. There is no danger of freezing. Come, let me do it,' replied Old-man.

"'Well — if you are sure that I won't freeze, all right,' said the Fox, 'but I'll bet I'll be sorry.'

"So Old-man pulled out all of the Fox's hair, leaving only the white tip that grew near the end of his tail. Poor little Red Fox shivered in the warm breeze that Old-man told about, and kept telling Old-man that the hair-pulling hurt badly. Finally Old-man finished the job and laughed at the Fox, saying: 'Why, you make me laugh, too. Now go and dance before the Bulls, and I shall watch and be ready for my part of the scheme.'

"Around the hill went the poor Red Fox and found the Bulls. Then he began to dance before them as Old-man had told him. The Bulls took one look at the hairless Fox and began to laugh. My! How they did laugh, and then the Red Fox stood upon his hind legs and danced some more; acted sillier, as Old-man had told him. Louder and louder laughed the Bulls, until they fell to the ground with their breath short from the laughing. The Red Fox kept at his antics lest the Bulls get up before Old-man reached them; but soon he saw him coming, with a knife in his hand.

"Running up to the Bulls, Old-man plunged his knife into their hearts, and they died. Into the ground ran their blood, and then Old-man laughed and said: 'Ho, I am the smart one. I am the real hunter. I depend on my head for meat—ha!--ha!-ha!'

"Then Old-man began to dress and skin the Bulls, and he worked hard and long. In fact it was nearly night when he got the work all done.

"Poor little Red Fox had stood there all the time, and Old-man never noticed that the wind had changed and was coming from the north. Yes, poor Red Fox stood there and spoke no word; said nothing at all, even when Old-man had finished.

"'Hi, there, you! What's the matter with you? Are you sorry that we have meat? Say, answer me!'

"But the Red Fox was frozen stiff—was dead. Yes, the north wind had killed him while Old-man worked at the skinning. The Fox had been caught by the north wind naked, and was dead. Old-man built a fire and warmed his hands; that was all he cared for the Red Fox, and that is all he cared for anybody. He might have known that no person could stand the north wind without a robe; but as long as he was warm himself—that was all he wanted.

"That is all of that story. Tomorrow night I shall tell you why the birch-tree wears those slashes in its bark. That was some of Old-man's work, too. Ho!"

Why The Birch-Tree Wears The Slashes In Its Bark

The white man has never understood the Indian, and the example set the Western tribes of the plains by our white brethren has not been such as to inspire the red man with either confidence or respect for our laws or our religion. The fighting trapper, the border bandit, the horse-thief and rustler, in whose stomach legitimately acquired beef would cause colic— were the Indians' first acquaintances who wore a white skin, and he did not know that they were not of the best type. Being outlaws in every sense, these men sought shelter from the Indian in the wilderness; and he learned of their ways about his lodge-fire, or in battle, often provoked by the white ruffian in the hope of gain. They lied to the Indian—these first white acquaintances, and in after-years, the great Government of the United States lied and lied again, until he has come to believe that there is no truth in the white man's heart. And I don't blame him.

The Indian is a charitable man. I don't believe he ever refused food and shelter or abused a visitor. He has never been a bigot, and concedes to every other man the right to his own beliefs. Further than that, the Indian believes that every man's religion and belief is right and proper for that man's self.

It was blowing a gale and snow was being driven in fine flakes across the plains when we went to the lodge for a story. Every minute the weather was growing colder, and an early fall storm of severity was upon us. The wind seemed to add to the good nature of our host as he filled and passed me the pipe.

"This is the night I was to tell you about the Birch-Tree, and the wind will help to make you understand," said War Eagle after we had finished smoking.

"Of course," he continued, " this all happened in the summer-time when the weather was warm, very warm. Sometimes, you know, there are great winds in the summer, too.

"It was a hot day, and Old-man was trying to sleep, but the heat made him sick. He wandered to a hilltop for air; but there was no air. Then he went down to the river and found no relief. He traveled to the timber-lands, and there the heat was great, although he found plenty of shade. The traveling made him warmer, of course, but he wouldn't stay still.

"By and by he called to the winds to blow, and they commenced. First they didn't blow very hard, because they were afraid they might make Old-man angry, but he kept crying:

"'Blow harder—harder—harder! Blow worse than ever you blew before, and send this heat away from the world.'

"So, of course, the winds did blow harder— harder than they ever had blown before.

"'Bend and break, Fir-Tree!' cried Old-man, and the Fir-Tree did bend and break. 'Bend and break, Pine-Tree!' and the Pine-Tree did bend and break. 'Bend and break, Spruce-Tree!' and the Spruce-Tree did bend and break. 'Bend and break, O Birch-Tree!' and the Birch-Tree did bend, but it wouldn't break— no, sir!--it wouldn't break!

"'Ho! Birch-Tree, won't you mind me? Bend and break! I tell you,' but all the Birch-Tree would do was to bend.

"It bent to the ground; it bent double to please Old-man, but it would not break.

"'Blow harder, wind!' cried Old-man, 'blow harder and break the Birch-Tree.' The wind tried to blow harder, but it couldn't, and that made the thing worse, because Old-man was so angry he went crazy. 'Break! I tell you— break!' screamed Old-man to the Birch-Tree.

"'I won't break,' replied the Birch; 'I shall never break for any wind. I will bend, but I shall never, never break.'

"'You won't, hey?' cried Old-man, and he rushed at the Birch-Tree with his hunting-knife. He grabbed the top of the Birch because it was touching the ground, and began slashing the bark of the Birch-Tree with the knife. All up and down the trunk of the tree Old-man slashed, until the Birch was covered with the knife slashes.

"'There! That is for not minding me. That will do you good! As long as time lasts you shall always look like that, Birch-Tree; always be marked as one who will not mind its maker. Yes, and all the Birch-Trees in the world shall have the same marks forever.' They do, too. You have seen them and have wondered why the Birch-Tree is so queerly marked. Now you know.

"That is all—Ho!"

Mistakes Of Old-Man

All night the storm raged, and in the morning the plains were white with snow. The sun came and the light was blinding, but the hunters were abroad early, as usual.

That day the children came to my camp, and I told them several stories that appeal to white children. They were deeply interested, and asked many questions. Not until the hunters returned did my visitors leave.

That night War Eagle told us of the mistakes of Old-man. He said:

"Old-man made a great many mistakes in making things in the world, but he worked until he had everything good. I told you at the beginning that Old-man made mistakes, but I didn't tell you what they were, so now I shall tell you.

"One of the things he did that was wrong, was to make the Big-Horn to live on the plains. Yes, he made him on the plains and turned him loose, to make his living there. Of course the Big-Horn couldn't run on the plains, and Old-man wondered what was wrong. Finally, he said: 'Come here, Big-Horn!' and the Big-Horn came to him. Old-man stuck his arm through the circle his horns made, and dragged the Big-Horn far up into the mountains. There he set him free again, and sat down to watch him. Ho! It made Old-man dizzy to watch the Big-Horn run about on the ragged cliffs. He saw at once that this was the country the Big-Horn liked, and he left him there. Yes, he left him there forever, and there he stays, seldom coming down to the lower country.

"While Old-man was waiting to see what the Big-Horn would do in the high mountains, he made an Antelope and set him free with the Big-Horn. Ho! But the Antelope stumbled and fell down among the rocks. He couldn't man called to the Antelope to come back to him, and the Antelope did come to him. Then he called to the Big-Horn, and said:

"'You are all right, I guess, but this one isn't, and I'll have to take him somewhere else.'

"He dragged the Antelope down to the prairie country, and set him free there. Then he watched him a minute; that was as long as the Antelope was in sight, for he was afraid Old-man might take him back to the mountains.

"He said: 'I guess that fellow was made for the plains, all right, so I'll leave him there'; and he did. That is why the Antelope always stays on the plains, even today. He likes it better.

"That wasn't a very long story; sometime when you get older I will tell you some different stories, but that will be all for this time, I guess. Ho!"

How The Man Found His Mate

Each tribe has its own stories. Most of them deal with the same subjects, differing only in immaterial particulars.

Instead of squirrels in the timber, the Black-feet are sure they were prairie-dogs that Old-man roasted that time when he made the mountain-lion long and lean. The Chippewas and Crees insist that they were squirrels that were cooked and eaten, but one tribe is essentially a forest-people and the other lives on the plains—hence the difference.

Some tribes will not wear the feathers of the owl, nor will they have anything to do with that bird, while others use his feathers freely.

The forest Indian wears the soft-soled moccasin, while his brother of the plains covers the bottoms of his footwear with rawhide, because of the cactus and prickly-pear, most likely.

The door of the lodge of the forest Indian reaches to the ground, but the plains Indian makes his lodge skin to reach all about the circle at the bottom, because of the wind.

One night in War Eagle's lodge, Other-person asked: "Why don't the Bear have a tail, grandfather?"

War Eagle laughed and said: "Our people do not know why, but we believe he was made that way at the beginning, although I have heard men of other tribes say that the Bear lost his tail while fishing.

"I don't know how true it is, but I have been told that a long time ago the Bear was fishing in the winter, and the Fox asked him if he had any luck.

"'No,' replied the Bear, 'I can't catch a fish.'

"'Well,' said the Fox, 'if you will stick your long tail down through this hole in the ice, and sit very still, I am sure you will catch a fish.'

"So the Bear stuck his tail through the hole in the ice, and the Fox told him to sit still, till he called him; then the Fox went off, pretending to hunt along the bank. It was mighty cold weather, and the water froze all about the Bear's tail, yet he sat still, waiting for the Fox to call him. Yes, the Bear sat so still and so long that his tail was frozen in the ice, but he didn't know it. When the Fox thought it was time, he called:

"'Hey, Bear, come here quick—quick! I have a Rabbit in this hole, and I want you to help me dig him out.' Ho! The Bear tried to get up, but he couldn't.

"'Hey, Bear, come here—there are two Rabbits in this hole,' called the Fox.

"The Bear pulled so hard to get away from the ice, that he broke his tail off short to his body. Then the Fox ran away laughing at the Bear.

"I hardly believe that story, but once I heard an old man who visited my father from the country far east of here, tell it. I remembered it. But I can't say that I know it is true, as I can the others.

"When I told you the story of how Old-man made the world over, after the water had made its war upon it, I told you how the first man and woman were made. There is another story of how the first man found his wife, and I will tell you that.

"After Old-man had made a man to look like himself, he left him to live with the Wolves, and went away. The man had a hard time of it, with no clothes to keep him warm, and no wife to help him, so he went out looking for Old-man.

"It took the man a long time to find Old-man's lodge, but as soon as he got there he went right in and said:

"'Old-man, you have made me and left me to live with the Wolf-people. I don't like them at all. They give me scraps of meat to eat and won't build a fire. They have wives, but I don't want a Wolf-woman. I think you should take better care of me.'

"'Well,' replied Old-man, 'I was just waiting for you to come to see me. I have things fixed for you. You go down this river until you come to a steep hillside. There you will see a lodge. Then I will leave you to do the rest. Go!'

"The man started and traveled all that day. When night came he camped and ate some berries that grew near the river. The next morning he started down the river again, looking for the steep hillside and the lodge. Just before sundown, the man saw a fine lodge near a steep hillside, and he knew that was the lodge he was looking for; so he crossed the river and went into the lodge.

"Sitting by the fire inside, was a woman. She was dressed in buckskin clothes, and was cooking some meat that smelled good to the man, but when she saw him without any clothes, she pushed him out of the lodge, and dropped the door.

"Things didn't look very good to that man, I tell you, but to get even with the woman, he went up on the steep hillside and commenced to roll big rocks down upon her lodge. He kept this up until one of the largest rocks knocked down the lodge, and the woman ran out, crying.

"When the man heard the woman crying, it made him sorry and he ran down the hill to her. She sat down on the ground, and the man ran to where she was and said:

"'I am sorry I made you cry, woman. I will help you fix your lodge. I will stay with you, if you will only let me.'

"That pleased the woman, and she showed the man how to fix up the lodge and gather some wood for the fire. Then she let him come inside and eat. Finally, she made him some clothes, and they got along very well, after that.

"That is how the man found his wife—Ho!"

Dreams

As soon as manhood is attained, the young Indian must secure his "charm," or "medicine." After a sweat-bath, he retires to some lonely spot, and there, for four days and nights, if necessary, he remains in solitude. During this time he eats nothing; drinks nothing; but spends his time invoking the Great Mystery for the boon of a long life. In this state of mind, he at last sleeps, perhaps dreams. If a dream does not come to him, he abandons the task for a time, and later on will take another sweat-bath and try again. Sometimes dangerous cliffs, or other equally uncomfortable places, are selected for dreaming, because the surrounding terrors impress themselves upon the mind, and even in slumber add to the vividness of dreams.

At last the dream comes, and in it some bird or animal appears as a helper to the dreamer, in trouble. Then he seeks that bird or animal; kills a specimen; and if a bird, he stuffs its skin with moss and forever keeps it near him. If an animal, instead of a bird, appears in the dream, the Indian takes his hide, claws, or teeth; and throughout his life never leaves it behind him, unless in another dream a greater charm is offered. If this happens, he discards the old "medicine" for the new; but such cases are rare.

Sometimes the Indian will deck his "medicine-bundle" with fanciful trinkets and quill-work At other times the "bundle" is kept forever out of the sight of all uninterested persons, and is altogether unadorned. But "medicine" is necessary; without it, the Indian is afraid of his shadow.

An old chief, who had been in many battles, once told me his great dream, withholding the name of the animal or bird that appeared therein and became his "medicine."

He said that when he was a boy of twelve years, his father, who was chief of his tribe, told him that it was time that he tried to dream. After his sweat-bath, the boy followed his father without speaking, because the postulant must not converse or associate with other humans between the taking of the bath and the finished attempt to dream. On and on into the dark forest the father led, followed by the naked boy, till at last the father stopped on a high hill, at the foot of a giant pine-tree.

By signs the father told the boy to climb the tree and to get into an eagle's nest that was on the topmost boughs. Then the old man went away, in order that the boy might reach the nest without coming too close to his human conductor.

Obediently the boy climbed the tree and sat upon the eagle's nest on the top. "I could see very far from that nest," he told me. "The day was warm and I hoped to dream that night, but the wind rocked the tree top, and the darkness made me so much afraid that I did not sleep.

"On the fourth night there came a terrible thunder-storm, with lightning and much wind. The great pine groaned and shook until I was sure it must fall. All about it, equally strong trees went down with loud crashings, and in the dark there were many awful sounds— sounds that I sometimes hear yet. Rain came, and I grew cold and more afraid. I had eaten nothing, of course, and I was weak—so weak and tired, that at last I slept, in the nest. I dreamed; yes, it was a wonderful dream that came to me, and it has most all come to pass. Part is yet to come. But come it surely will.

"First I saw my own people in three wars. Then I saw the Buffalo disappear in a hole in the ground, followed by many of my people. Then I saw the whole world at war, and many flags of white men were in this land of ours. It was a terrible war, and the fighting and the blood made me sick in my dream. Then, last of all, I saw a 'person' coming—coming across what seemed the plains. There were deep shadows all about him as he approached. This 'person' kept beckoning me to come to him, and at last I did go to him.

"'Do you know who I am,' he asked me.

"'No, "person," I do not know you. Who are you, and where is your country?'

"'If you will listen to me, boy, you shall be a great chief and your people shall love you. If you do not listen, then I shall turn against you. My name is "Reason."'

"As the 'person' spoke this last, he struck the ground with a stick he carried, and the blow set the grass afire. I have always tried to know that 'person.' I think I know him wherever he may be, and in any camp. He has helped me all my life, and I shall never turn against him—never."

That was the old chief's dream and now a word about the sweat-bath. A small lodge is made of willows, by bending them and sticking the ends in the ground. A completed sweat-lodge is shaped like an inverted bowl, and in the center is a small hole in the ground. The lodge is covered with robes, bark, and dirt, or anything that will make it reasonably tight. Then a fire is built outside and near the sweat-lodge in which stones are heated. When the stones are ready, the bather crawls inside the sweat-lodge, and an assistant rolls the hot stones from the fire, and into the lodge. They are then rolled into the hole in the lodge and sprinkled with water. One cannot imagine a hotter vapor bath than this system produces, and when the bather has satisfied himself inside, he darts from the sweat-lodge into the river, winter or summer. This treatment killed thousands of Indians when the smallpox was brought to them from Saint Louis, in the early days.

That night in the lodge War Eagle told a queer yarn. I shall modify it somewhat, but in our own sacred history there is a similar tale, well known to all. He said:

"Once, a long time ago, two 'thunders' were traveling in the air. They came over a village of our people, and there stopped to look about.

"In this village there was one fine, painted lodge, and in it there was an old man, an aged woman, and a beautiful young woman with wonderful hair. Of course the 'thunders' could look through the lodge skin and see all that was inside. One of them said to the other:

'Let us marry that young woman, and never tell her about it.'

"'All right,' replied the other 'thunder.' 'I am willing, for she is the finest young woman in all the village. She is good in her heart, and she is honest.'

"So they married her, without telling her about it, and she became the mother of twin boys. When these boys were born, they sat up and told their mother and the other people that they were not people, but were 'thunders,' and that they would grow up quickly.

"'When we shall have been on earth a while, we shall marry, and stay until we each have four sons of our own, then we shall go away and again become "thunders,"' they said.

"It all came to pass, just as they said it would. When they had married good women and each had four sons, they told the people one day that it was time for them to go away forever.

"There was much sorrow among the people, for the twins were good men and taught many good things which we have never forgotten, but everybody knew it had to be as they said. While they lived with us, these twins could heal the sick and tell just what was going to happen on earth.

"One day at noon the twins dressed themselves in their finest clothes and went out to a park in the forest. All the people followed them and saw them lie down on the ground in the park. The people stayed in the timber that grew about the edge of the park, and watched them until clouds and mists gathered about and hid them from view.

"It thundered loudly and the winds blew; trees fell down; and when the mists and clouds cleared away, they were gone—gone forever. But the people have never forgotten them, and my grandfather, who is in the ground near Rocker, was a descendant from one of the sons of the 'thunders.' Ho!"

Retrospection

It was evening in the badlands, and the red sun had slipped behind the far-off hills. The sundown breeze bent the grasses in the coulees and curled tiny dust-clouds on the barren knolls. Down in a gulch a clear, cool creek dallied its way toward the Missouri, where its water, bitter as gall, would be lost in the great stream. Here, where Nature forbids man to work his will, and where the she wolf dens and kills to feed her litter, an aged Indian stood near the scattered bones of two great buffalo-bulls. Time had bleached the skulls and whitened the old warrior's hair, but in the solitude he spoke to the bones as to a boyhood friend:

"Ho! Buffalo, the years are long since you died, and your tribe, like mine, was even then shrinking fast, but you did not know it; would not believe it; though the signs did not lie. My father and his father knew your people, and when one night you went away, we thought you did but hide and would soon come back. The snows have come and gone many times since then, and still your people stay away. The young-men say that the great herds have gone to the Sand Hills, and that my father still has meat. They have told me that the white man, in his greed, has killed—and not for meat—all the Buffalo that our people knew. They have said that the great herds that made the ground tremble as they ran were slain in a few short years by those who needed not. Can this be true, whenever since there was a world, our people killed your kind, and still left herds that grew in numbers until they often blocked the rivers when they passed? Our people killed your kind that they them-selves might live, but never did they go to war against you. Tell me, do your people hide, or are the young-men speaking truth, and have your people gone with mine to Sand Hill shadows to come back no more?"

"Ho! red man—my people all have gone. The young-men tell the truth and all my tribe have gone to feed among the shadow-hills, and your father still has meat. My people suffer from his arrows and his lance, yet there the herds increase as they did here, until the white man came and made his war upon us without cause or need. I was one of the last to die, and with my brother here fled to this forbidding country that I might hide; but one day when the snow was on the world, a white murderer followed on our trail, and with his noisy weapon sent our spirits to join the great shadow-herds. Meat? No, he took no meat, but from our quivering flesh he tore away the robes that Napa gave to make us warm, and left us for the Wolves. That night they came, and quarrelling, fighting, snapping among themselves, left but our bones to greet the morning sun. These bones the Coyotes and the weaker ones did drag and scrape, and scrape again, until the last of flesh or muscle disappeared. Then the winds came and sang—and all was done."

MYTHS AND LEGENDS
OF THE SIOUX

The Forgotten Ear Of Corn

An Arikara woman was once gathering corn from the field to store away for winter use. She passed from stalk to stalk, tearing off the ears and dropping them into her folded robe. When all was gathered she started to go, when she heard a faint voice, like a child's, weeping and calling:

"Oh, do not leave me! Do not go away without me."

The woman was astonished. "What child can that be?" she asked herself. "What babe can be lost in the cornfield?"

She set down her robe in which she had tied up her corn, and went back to search; but she found nothing.

As she started away she heard the voice again:

"Oh, do not leave me. Do not go away without me."

She searched for a long time. At last in one corner of the field, hidden under the leaves of the stalks, she found one little ear of corn. This it was that had been crying, and this is why all Indian women have since garnered their corn crop very carefully, so that the succulent food product should not even to the last small nubbin be neglected or wasted, and thus displease the Great Mystery.

The Little Mice

Once upon a time a prairie mouse busied herself all fall storing away a cache of beans. Every morning she was out early with her empty cast-off snake skin, which she filled with ground beans and dragged home with her teeth.

The little mouse had a cousin who was fond of dancing and talk, but who did not like to work. She was not careful to get her cache of beans and the season was already well gone before she thought to bestir herself. When she came to realize her need, she found she had no packing bag. So she went to her hardworking cousin and said:

"Cousin, I have no beans stored for winter and the season is nearly gone. But I have no snake skin to gather the beans in. Will you lend me one?"

"But why have you no packing bag? Where were you in the moon when the snakes cast off their skins?"

"I was here."

"What were you doing?"

"I was busy talking and dancing."

"And now you are punished," said the other. "It is always so with lazy, careless people. But I will let you have the snake skin. And now go, and by hard work and industry, try to recover your wasted time."

The Pet Rabbit

A little girl owned a pet rabbit which she loved dearly. She carried it on her back like a babe, made for it a little pair of moccasins, and at night shared with it her own robe.

Now the little girl had a cousin who loved her very dearly and wished to do her honor; so her cousin said to herself:

"I love my little cousin well and will ask her to let me carry her pet rabbit around;" (for thus do Indian women when they wish to honor a friend; they ask permission to carry about the friend's babe).

She then went to the little girl and said:

"Cousin, let me carry your pet rabbit about on my back. Thus shall I show you how I love you."

Her mother, too, said to her: "Oh no, do not let our little grandchild go away from our *tepee*."

But the cousin answered: "Oh, do let me carry it. I do so want to show my cousin honor." At last they let her go away with the pet rabbit on her back.

When the little girl's cousin came home to her *tepee*, some rough boys who were playing about began to make sport of her. To tease the little girl they threw stones and sticks at the pet rabbit. At last a stick struck the little rabbit upon the head and killed it.

When her pet was brought home dead, the little rabbit's adopted mother wept bitterly. She cut off her hair for mourning and all her little girl friends wailed with her. Her mother, too, mourned with them.

"Alas!" they cried, "alas, for the little rabbit. He was always kind and gentle. Now your child is dead and you will be lonesome."

The little girl's mother called in her little friends and made a great mourning feast for the little rabbit. As he lay in the *tepee* his adopted mother's little friends brought many precious things and covered his body. At the feast were given away robes and kettles and blankets and knives and great wealth in honor of the little rabbit. Him they wrapped in a robe with his little moccasins on and buried him in a high place upon a scaffold.

The Pet Donkey

There was a chief's daughter once who had a great many relations so that everybody knew she belonged to a great family.

When she grew up she married and there were born to her twin sons. This caused great rejoicing in her father's camp, and all the village women came to see the babes. She was very happy.

As the babes grew older, their grandmother made for them two saddle bags and brought out a donkey.

"My two grandchildren," said the old lady, "shall ride as is becoming to children having so many relations. Here is this donkey. He is patient and surefooted. He shall carry the babes in the saddle bags, one on either side of his back."

It happened one day that the chief's daughter and her husband were making ready to go on a camping journey. The father, who was quite proud of his children, brought out his finest pony, and put the saddle bags on the pony's back.

"There," he said, "my sons shall ride on the pony, not on a donkey; let the donkey carry the pots and kettles."

So his wife loaded the donkey with the household things. She tied the *tepee* poles into two great bundles, one on either side of the donkey's back; across them she put the travois net and threw into it the pots and kettles and laid the skin tent across the donkey's back.

But no sooner done than the donkey began to rear and bray and kick. He broke the tent poles and kicked the pots and kettles into bits and tore the skin tent. The more he was beaten the more he kicked.

At last they told the grandmother. She laughed. "Did I not tell you the donkey was for the children," she cried. "He knows the babies are the chief's children. Think you he will be dishonored with pots and kettles?" and she fetched the children and slung them over the donkey's back, when he became at once quiet again.

The camping party left the village and went on their journey. But the next day as they passed by a place overgrown with bushes, a band of enemies rushed out, lashing their ponies and sounding their war whoop. All was excitement. The men bent their bows and seized their lances. After a long battle the enemy fled. But when the camping party came together again—where were the donkey and the two babes? No one knew. For a long time they searched, but in vain. At last they turned to go back to the village, the father mournful, the mother wailing. When they came to the grandmother's *tepee*, there stood the good donkey with the two babes in the saddle bags.

The Rabbit And The Elk

The little rabbit lived with his old grandmother, who needed a new dress. "I will go out and trap a deer or an elk for you," he said. "Then you shall have a new dress."

When he went out hunting he laid down his bow in the path while he looked at his snares. An elk coming by saw the bow.

"I will play a joke on the rabbit," said the elk to himself. "I will make him think I have been caught in his bow string." He then put one foot on the string and lay down as if dead.

By and by the rabbit returned. When he saw the elk he was filled with joy and ran home crying: "Grandmother, I have trapped a fine elk. You shall have a new dress from his skin. Throw the old one in the fire!"

This the old grandmother did.

The elk now sprang to his feet laughing. "Ho, friend rabbit," he called, "You thought to trap me; now I have mocked you." And he ran away into the thicket.

The rabbit who had come back to skin the elk now ran home again. "Grandmother, don't throw your dress in the fire," he cried. But it was too late. The old dress was burned.

The Rabbit And The Grouse Girls

The rabbit once went out on the prairie in winter time. On the side of a hill away from the wind he found a great company of girls all with grey and speckled blankets over their backs. They were the grouse girls and they were coasting down hill on a board. When the rabbit saw them, he called out:

"Oh, maidens, that is not a good way to coast down hill. Let me get you a fine skin with bangles on it that tinkle as you slide." And away he ran to the *tepee* and brought a skin bag. It had red stripes on it and bangles that tinkled. "Come and get inside," he said to the grouse girls. "Oh, no, we are afraid," they answered. "Don't be afraid, I can't hurt you. Come, one of you," said the rabbit. Then as each hung back he added coaxingly: "If each is afraid alone, come all together. I can't hurt you *all*." And so he coaxed the whole flock into the bag. This done, the rabbit closed the mouth of the bag, slung it over his back and came home. "Grandmother," said he, as he came to the *tepee*, "here is a bag full of game. Watch it while I go for willow sticks to make spits."

But as soon as the rabbit had gone out of the tent, the grouse girls began to cry out:

"Grandmother, let us out."

"Who are you?" asked the old woman.

"Your dear grandchildren," they answered.

"But how came you in the bag?" asked the old woman.

"Oh, our cousin was jesting with us. He coaxed us in the bag for a joke. Please let us out."

"Certainly, dear grandchildren, I will let you out," said the old woman as she untied the bag: and lo, the grouse flock with a chuck-a-chuck-a-chuck flew up, knocking over the old grandmother and flew out of the square smoke opening of the winter lodge. The old woman caught only one grouse as it flew up and held it, grasping a leg with each hand.

When the rabbit came home with the spits she called out to him:

"Grandson, come quick. They got out but I have caught two."

When he saw what had happened he was quite angry, yet could not keep from laughing.

"Grandmother, you have but one grouse," he cried, and it is a very skinny one at that."

The Faithful Lovers

There once lived a chief's daughter who had many relations. All the young men in the village wanted to have her for wife, and were all eager to fill her skin bucket when she went to the brook for water.

There was a young man in the village who was industrious and a good hunter; but he was poor and of a mean family. He loved the maiden and when she went for water, he threw his robe over her head while he whispered in her ear:

"Be my wife. I have little but I am young and strong. I will treat you well, for I love you."

For a long time the maiden did not answer, but one day she whispered back.

"Yes, you may ask my father's leave to marry me. But first you must do something noble. I belong to a great family and have many relations. You must go on a war party and bring back the scalp of an enemy."

The young man answered modestly, "I will try to do as you bid me. I am only a hunter, not a warrior. Whether I shall be brave or not I do not know. But I will try to take a scalp for your sake."

So he made a war party of seven, himself and six other young men. They wandered through the enemy's country, hoping to get a chance to strike a blow. But none came, for they found no one of the enemy.

"Our medicine is unfavorable," said their leader at last. "We shall have to return home."

Before they started they sat down to smoke and rest beside a beautiful lake at the foot of a green knoll that rose from its shore. The knoll was covered with green grass and somehow as they looked at it they had a feeling that there was something about it that was mysterious or uncanny.

But there was a young man in the party named the jester, for he was venturesome and full of fun. Gazing at the knoll he said: "Let's run and jump on its top."

"No," said the young lover, "it looks mysterious. Sit still and finish your smoke."

"Oh, come on, who's afraid," said the jester, laughing. "Come on you — come on!" and springing to his feet he ran up the side of the knoll.

Four of the young men followed. Having reached the top of the knoll all five began to jump and stamp about in sport, calling, "Come on, come on," to the others. Suddenly they stopped — the knoll had begun to move toward the water. It was a gigantic turtle. The five men cried out in alarm and tried to run — too late! Their feet by some power were held fast to the monster's back.

"Help us — drag us away," they cried; but the others could do nothing. In a few moments the waves had closed over them.

The other two men, the lover and his friend, went on, but with heavy hearts, for they had forebodings of evil. After some days, they came to a river. Worn with fatigue the lover threw himself down on the bank.

"I will sleep awhile," he said, "for I am wearied and worn out."

"And I will go down to the water and see if I can chance upon a dead fish. At this time of the year the high water may have left one stranded on the seashore," said his friend.

And as he had said, he found a fish which he cleaned, and then called to the lover.

"Come and eat the fish with me. I have cleaned it and made a fire and it is now cooking."

"No, you eat it; let me rest," said the lover.

"Oh, come on."

"No, let me rest."

"But you are my friend. I will not eat unless you share it with me."

"Very well," said the lover, "I will eat the fish with you, but you must first make me a promise. If I eat the fish, you must promise, pledge yourself, to fetch me all the water that I can drink."

"I promise," said the other, and the two ate the fish out of their war-kettle. For there had been but one kettle for the party.

When they had eaten, the kettle was rinsed out and the lover's friend brought it back full of water. This the lover drank at a draught.

"Bring me more," he said.

Again his friend filled the kettle at the river and again the lover drank it dry.

"More!" he cried.

"Oh, I am tired. Cannot you go to the river and drink your fill from the stream?" asked his friend.

"Remember your promise."

"Yes, but I am weary. Go now and drink."

"Ek-hey, I feared it would be so. Now trouble is coming upon us," said the lover sadly. He walked to the river, sprang in, and lying down in the water with his head toward land, drank greedily. By and by he called to his friend.

"Come hither, you who have been my sworn friend. See what comes of your broken promise."

The friend came and was amazed to see that the lover was now a fish from his feet to his middle.

Sick at heart he ran off a little way and threw himself upon the ground in grief. By and by he returned. The lover was now a fish to his neck.

"Cannot I cut off the part and restore you by a sweat bath?" the friend asked.

"No, it is too late. But tell the chief's daughter that I loved her to the last and that I die for her sake. Take this belt and give it to her. She gave it to me as a pledge of her love for me," and he being then turned to a great fish, swam to the middle of the river and there remained, only his great fin remaining above the water.

The friend went home and told his story. There was great mourning over the death of the five young men, and for the lost lover. In the river the great fish remained, its fin just above the surface, and was called by the Indians "Fish that Bars," because it bar'd navigation. Canoes had to be portaged at great labor around the obstruction.

The chief's daughter mourned for her lover as for a husband, nor would she be comforted. "He was lost for love of me, and I shall remain as his widow," she wailed.

In her mother's *tepee* she sat, with her head covered with her robe, silent, working, working. "What is my daughter doing," her mother asked. But the maiden did not reply.

The days lengthened into moons until a year had passed. And then the maiden arose. In her hands were beautiful articles of clothing, enough for three men. There were three pairs of moccasins, three pairs of leggings, three belts, three shirts, three head dresses with beautiful feathers, and sweet smelling tobacco.

"Make a new canoe of bark," she said, which was made for her.

Into the canoe she stepped and floated slowly down the river toward the great fish.

"Come back my daughter," her mother cried in agony. "Come back. The great fish will eat you."

She answered nothing. Her canoe came to the place where the great fin arose and stopped, its prow grating on the monster's back. The maiden stepped out boldly. One by one she laid her presents on the fish's back, scattering the feathers and tobacco over his broad spine.

"Oh, fish," she cried, "Oh, fish, you who were my lover, I shall not forget you. Because you were lost for love of me, I shall never marry. All my life I shall remain a widow. Take these presents. And now leave the river, and let the waters run free, so my people may once more descend in their canoes."

She stepped into her canoe and waited. Slowly the great fish sank, his broad fin disappeared, and the waters of the St. Croix (Stillwater) were free.

The Artichoke And The Muskrat

On the shore of a lake stood an artichoke with its green leaves waving in the sun. Very proud of itself it was, and well satisfied with the world. In the lake below lived a muskrat in his *tepee*, and in the evening as the sun set he would come out upon the shore and wander over the bank. One evening he came near the place where the artichoke stood.

"Ho, friend," he said, "you seem rather proud of yourself. Who are you?"

"I am the artichoke," answered the other, "and I have many handsome cousins. But who are you?"

"I am the muskrat, and I, too, belong to a large family. I live in the water. I don't stand all day in one place like a stone."

"If I stand in one place all day," retorted the artichoke, "at least I don't swim around in stagnant water, and build my lodge in the mud."

"You are jealous of my fine fur," sneered the muskrat. "I may build my lodge in the mud, but I always have a clean coat. But you are half buried in the ground, and when men dig you up, you are never clean."

"And your fine coat always smells of musk," jeered the artichoke.

"That is true," said the muskrat. "But men think well of me, nevertheless. They trap me for the fine sinew in my tail; and handsome young women bite off my tail with their white teeth and make it into thread."

"That's nothing," laughed the artichoke. "Handsome young warriors, painted and splendid with feathers, dig me up, brush me off with their shapely hands and eat me without even taking the trouble to wash me off."

The Rabbit And The Bear With The Flint Body

The Rabbit and his grandmother were in dire straits, because the rabbit was out of arrows. The fall hunt would soon be on and his quiver was all but empty. Arrow sticks he could cut in plenty, but he had nothing with which to make arrowheads.

"You must make some flint arrowheads," said his grandmother. "Then you will be able to kill game."

"Where shall I get the flint?" asked the rabbit.

"From the old bear chief," said his old grandmother. For at that time all the flint in the world was in the bear's body.

So the rabbit set out for the village of the Bears. It was winter time and the lodges of the bears were set under the shelter of a hill where the cold wind would not blow on them and where they had shelter among the trees and bushes.

He came at one end of the village to a hut where lived an old woman. He pushed open the door and entered. Everybody who came for flint always stopped there because it was the first lodge on the edge of the village. Strangers were therefore not unusual in the old woman's hut, and she welcomed the rabbit. She gave him a seat and at night he lay with his feet to the fire.

The next morning the rabbit went to the lodge of the bear chief. They sat together awhile and smoked. At last the bear chief spoke.

"What do you want, my grandson?"

"I have come for some flint to make arrows," answered the rabbit.

The bear chief grunted, and laid aside his pipe. Leaning back he pulled off his robe and, sure enough, one half of his body was flesh and the other half hard flint.

"Bring a stone hammer and give it to our guest," he bade his wife. Then as the rabbit took the hammer he said: "Do not strike too hard."

"Grandfather, I shall be careful," said the rabbit. With a stroke he struck off a little flake of flint from the bear's body.

"*Ni-sko-ke-cha*? So big?" he asked.

"Harder, grandson; strike off bigger pieces," said the bear.

The rabbit struck a little harder.

"*Ni-sko-ke-cha*? So big?" he asked.

The bear grew impatient. "No, no, strike off bigger pieces. I can't be here all day. *Tanka kaksa wo*! Break off a big piece."

The rabbit struck again—hard! "*Ni-sko-ke-cha*?" he cried, as the hammer fell. But even as he spoke the bear's body broke in two, the flesh part fell away and only the flint part remained. Like a flash the rabbit darted out of the hut.

There was a great outcry in the village. Openmouthed, all the bears gave chase. But as he ran the rabbit cried: "*Wa-hin-han-yo* (snow, snow) *Ota-po, Ota-po*—lots more, lots more," and a great storm of snow swept down from the sky.

The rabbit, light of foot, bounded over the top of the snow. The bears sunk in and floundered about helpless. Seeing this, the rabbit turned back and killed them one by one with his club. That is why we now have so few bears.

Story Of The Lost Wife

A Dakota girl married a man who promised to treat her kindly, but he did not keep his word. He was unreasonable, fault-finding, and often beat her. Frantic with his cruelty, she ran away. The whole village turned out to search for her, but no trace of the missing wife was to be found.

Meanwhile, the fleeing woman had wandered about all that day and the next night. The next day she met a man, who asked her who she was. She did not know it, but he was not really a man, but the chief of the wolves.

"Come with me," he said, and he led her to a large village. She was amazed to see here many wolves—gray and black, timber wolves and coyotes. It seemed as if all the wolves in the world were there.

The wolf chief led the young woman to a great *tepee* and invited her in. He asked her what she ate for food.

"Buffalo meat," she answered.

He called two coyotes and bade them bring what the young woman wanted. They bounded away and soon returned with the shoulder of a fresh-killed buffalo calf.

"How do you prepare it for eating?" asked the wolf chief.

"By boiling," answered the young woman.

Again he called the two coyotes. Away they bounded and soon brought into the tent a small bundle. In it were punk, flint and steel — stolen, it may be, from some camp of men.

"How do you make the meat ready?" asked the wolf chief.

"I cut it into slices," answered the young woman.

The coyotes were called and in a short time fetched in a knife in its sheath. The young woman cut up the calf's shoulder into slices and ate it.

Thus she lived for a year, all the wolves being very kind to her. At the end of that time the wolf chief said to her:

"Your people are going off on a buffalo hunt. Tomorrow at noon they will be here. You must then go out and meet them or they will fall on us and kill us."

The next day at about noon the young woman went to the top of a neighboring knoll. Coming toward her were some young men riding on their ponies. She stood up and held her hands so that they could see her. They wondered who she was, and when they were close by gazed at her closely.

"A year ago we lost a young woman; if you are she, where have you been," they asked.

"I have been in the wolves' village. Do not harm them," she answered.

"We will ride back and tell the people," they said. "Tomorrow again at noon, we shall meet you."

The young woman went back to the wolf village, and the next day went again to a neighboring knoll, though to a different one. Soon she saw the camp coming in a long line over the prairie. First were the warriors, then the women and tents.

The young woman's father and mother were overjoyed to see her. But when they came near her the young woman fainted, for she could not now bear the smell of human kind. When she came to herself she said:

"You must go on a buffalo hunt, my father and all the hunters. Tomorrow you must come again, bringing with you the tongues and choice pieces of the kill."

This he promised to do; and all the men of the camp mounted their ponies and they had a great hunt. The next day they returned with their ponies laden with the buffalo meat. The young woman bade them pile the meat in a great heap between two hills which she pointed out to them. There was so much meat that the tops of the two hills were bridged level between by the meat pile. In the center of the pile the young woman planted a pole with a red flag. She then began to howl like a wolf, loudly.

In a moment the earth seemed covered with wolves. They fell greedily on the meat pile and in a short time had eaten the last scrap.

The young woman then joined her own people.

Her husband wanted her to come and live with him again. For a long time she refused. However, at last they became reconciled.

The Raccoon And The Crawfish

Sharp and cunning is the raccoon, say the Indians, by whom he is named Spotted Face.

A crawfish one evening wandered along a river bank, looking for something dead to feast upon. A raccoon was also out looking for something to eat. He spied the crawfish and formed a plan to catch him.

He lay down on the bank and feigned to be dead. By and by the crawfish came near by. "Ho," he thought, "here is a feast indeed; but is he really dead. I will go near and pinch him with my claws and find out."

So he went near and pinched the raccoon on the nose and then on his soft paws. The raccoon never moved. The crawfish then pinched him on the ribs and tickled him so that the raccoon could hardly keep from laughing. The crawfish at last left him. "The raccoon is surely dead," he thought. And he hurried back to the crawfish village and reported his find to the chief.

All the villagers were called to go down to the feast. The chief bade the warriors and young men to paint their faces and dress in their gayest for a dance.

So they marched in a long line—first the warriors, with their weapons in hand, then the women with their babies and children—to the place where the raccoon lay. They formed a great circle about him and danced, singing:

"We shall have a great feast

"On the spotted-faced beast, with soft smooth paws:
"He is dead!
"He is dead!
"We shall dance!
"We shall have a good time;
"We shall feast on his flesh."

But as they danced, the raccoon suddenly sprang to his feet.

"Who is that you say you are going to eat? He has a spotted face, has he? He has soft, smooth paws, has he? I'll break your ugly backs. I'll break your rough bones. I'll crunch your ugly, rough paws." And he rushed among the crawfish, killing them by scores. The crawfish warriors fought bravely and the women ran screaming, all to no purpose. They did not feast on the raccoon; the raccoon feasted on *them*!

Legend Of Standing Rock

A Dakota had married an Arikara woman, and by her had one child. By and by he took another wife. The first wife was jealous and pouted. When time came for the village to break camp she refused to move from her place on the tent floor. The tent was taken down but she sat on the ground with her babe on her back. The rest of the camp with her husband went on.

At noon her husband halted the line. "Go back to your sister-in-law," he said to his two brothers. "Tell her to come on and we will await you here. But hasten, for I fear she may grow desperate and kill herself."

The two rode off and arrived at their former camping place in the evening. The woman still sat on the ground. The elder spoke:

"Sister-in-law, get up. We have come for you. The camp awaits you."

She did not answer, and he put out his hand and touched her head. She had turned to stone!

The two brothers lashed their ponies and came back to camp. They told their story, but were not believed. "The woman has killed herself and my brothers will not tell me," said the husband. However, the whole village broke camp and came back to the place where they had left the woman. Sure enough, she sat there still, a block of stone.

The Indians were greatly excited. They chose out a handsome pony, made a new travois and placed the stone in the carrying net.

Pony and travois were both beautifully painted and decorated with streamers and colors. The stone was thought *"wakan"* (holy), and was given a place of honor in the center of the camp. Whenever the camp moved the stone and travois were taken along. Thus the stone woman was carried for years, and finally brought to Standing Rock Agency, and now rests upon a brick pedestal in front of the Agency office. From this stone Standing Rock Agency derives its name.

Story Of The Peace Pipe

Two young men were out strolling one night talking of love affairs. They passed around a hill and came to a little ravine or coulee. Suddenly they saw coming up from the ravine a beautiful woman. She was painted and her dress was of the very finest material.

"What a beautiful girl!" said one of the young men. "Already I love her. I will steal her and make her my wife."

"No," said the other. "Don't harm her. She may be holy."

The young woman approached and held out a pipe which she first offered to the sky, then to the earth and then advanced, holding it out in her extended hands.

"I know what you young men have been saying; one of you is good; the other is wicked," she said.

She laid down the pipe on the ground and at once became a buffalo cow. The cow pawed the ground, stuck her tail straight out behind her and then lifted the pipe from the ground again in her hoofs; immediately she became a young woman again.

"I am come to give you this gift," she said. "It is the peace pipe. Hereafter all treaties and ceremonies shall be performed after smoking it. It shall bring peaceful thoughts into your minds. You shall offer it to the Great Mystery and to mother earth."

The two young men ran to the village and told what they had seen and heard. All the village came out where the young woman was.

She repeated to them what she had already told the young men and added:

"When you set free the ghost (the spirit of deceased persons) you must have a white buffalo cow skin."

She gave the pipe to the medicine men of the village, turned again to a buffalo cow and fled away to the land of buffaloes.

A Bashful Courtship

A young man lived with his grandmother. He was a good hunter and wished to marry. He knew a girl who was a good moccasin maker, but she belonged to a great family. He wondered how he could win her.

One day she passed the tent on her way to get water at the river. His grandmother was at work in the *tepee* with a pair of old worn-out sloppy moccasins. The young man sprang to his feet. "Quick, grandmother—let me have those old sloppy moccasins you have on your feet!" he cried.

"My old moccasins, what do you want of them?" cried the astonished woman.

"Never mind! Quick! I can't stop to talk," answered the grandson as he caught up the old moccasins the old lady had doffed, and put them on. He threw a robe over his shoulders, slipped through the door, and hastened to the watering place. The girl had just arrived with her bucket.

"Let me fill your bucket for you," said the young man.

"Oh, no, I can do it."

"Oh, let me, I can go in the mud. You surely don't want to soil your moccasins," and taking the bucket he slipped in the mud, taking care to push his sloppy old moccasins out so the girl could see them. She giggled outright.

"My, what old moccasins you have," she cried.

"Yes, I have nobody to make me a new pair," he answered.

"Why don't you get your grandmother to make you a new pair?"

"She's old and blind and can't make them any longer. That's why I want you," he answered.

"Oh, you're fooling me. You aren't speaking the truth."

"Yes, I am. If you don't believe—come with me now!"

The girl looked down; so did the youth. At last he said softly:

"Well, which is it? Shall I take up your bucket, or will you go with me?"

And she answered, still more softly: "I guess I'll go with you!"

The girl's aunt came down to the river, wondering what kept her niece so long. In the mud she found two pairs of moccasin tracks close together; at the edge of the water stood an empty keg.

The Simpleton's Wisdom

There was a man and his wife who had one daughter. Mother and daughter were deeply attached to one another, and when the latter died the mother was disconsolate. She cut off her hair, cut gashes in her cheeks and sat before the corpse with her robe drawn over her head, mourning for her dead. Nor would she let them touch the body to take it to a burying scaffold. She had a knife in her hand, and if anyone offered to come near the body the mother would wail:

"I am weary of life. I do not care to live. I will stab myself with this knife and join my daughter in the land of spirits."

Her husband and relatives tried to get the knife from her, but could not. They feared to use force lest she kill herself. They came together to see what they could do.

"We must get the knife away from her," they said.

At last they called a boy, a kind of simpleton, yet with a good deal of natural shrewdness. He was an orphan and very poor. His moccasins were out at the sole and he was dressed in *wei-zi* (coarse buffalo skin, smoked).

"Go to the *tepee* of the mourning mother," they told the simpleton, "and in some way contrive to make her laugh and forget her grief. Then try to get the knife away from her."

The boy went to the tent and sat down at the door as if waiting to be given something. The corpse lay in the place of honor where the dead girl had slept in life. The body was wrapped in a rich robe and wrapped about with ropes. Friends had covered it with rich offerings out of respect to the dead.

As the mother sat on the ground with her head covered she did not at first see the boy, who sat silent. But when his reserve had worn away a little he began at first lightly, then more heavily, to drum on the floor with his hands. After a while he began to sing a comic song. Louder and louder he sang until carried away with his own singing he sprang up and began to dance, at the same time gesturing and making all manner of contortions with his body, still singing the comic song. As he approached the corpse he waved his hands over it in blessing. The mother put her head out of the blanket and when she saw the poor simpleton with his strange grimaces trying to do honor to the corpse by his solemn waving, and at the same time keeping up his comic song, she burst out laughing. Then she reached over and handed her knife to the simpleton.

"Take this knife," she said. "You have taught me to forget my grief. If while I mourn for the dead I can still be mirthful, there is no reason for me to despair. I no longer care to die. I will live for my husband."

The simpleton left the *tepee* and brought the knife to the astonished husband and relatives.

"How did you get it? Did you force it away from her, or did you steal it?" they said.

"She gave it to me. How could I force it from her or steal it when she held it in her hand, blade uppermost? I sang and danced for her and she burst out laughing. Then she gave it to me," he answered.

When the old men of the village heard the orphan's story they were very silent. It was a strange thing for a lad to dance in a *tepee* where there was mourning. It was stranger that a mother should laugh in a *tepee* before the corpse of her dead daughter. The old men gathered at last in a council. They sat a long time without saying anything, for they did not want to decide hastily. The pipe was filled and passed many times. At last an old man spoke.

"We have a hard question. A mother has laughed before the corpse of her daughter, and many think she has done foolishly, but I think the woman did wisely. The lad was simple and of no training, and we cannot expect him to know how to do as well as one with good home and parents to teach him. Besides, he did the best that he knew. He danced to make the mother forget her grief, and he tried to honor the corpse by waving over it his hands."

"The mother did right to laugh, for when one does try to do us good, even if what he does causes us discomfort, we should always remember rather the motive than the deed. And besides, the simpleton's dancing saved the woman's life, for she gave up her knife. In this, too, she did well, for it is always better to live for the living than to die for the dead."

A Little Brave And The Medicine Woman

A village of Indians moved out of winter camp and pitched their tents in a circle on high land overlooking a lake. A little way down the declivity was a grave. Choke cherries had grown up, hiding the grave from view. But as the ground had sunk somewhat, the grave was marked by a slight hollow.

One of the villagers going out to hunt took a short cut through the choke cherry bushes. As he pushed them aside he saw the hollow grave, but thought it was a washout made by the rains. But as he essayed to step over it, to his great surprise he stumbled and fell. Made curious by his mishap, he drew back and tried again; but again he fell. When he came back to the village he told the old men what had happened to him. They remembered then that a long time before there had been buried there a medicine woman or conjurer. Doubtless it was her medicine that made him stumble.

The story of the villager's adventure spread thru the camp and made many curious to see the grave. Among others were six little boys who were, however, rather timid, for they were in great awe of the dead medicine woman. But they had a little playmate named Brave, a mischievous little rogue, whose hair was always unkempt and tossed about and who was never quiet for a moment.

"Let us ask Brave to go with us," they said; and they went in a body to see him.

"All right," said Brave; "I will go with you. But I have something to do first. You go on around the hill *that* way, and I will hasten around *this* way, and meet you a little later near the grave."

So the six little boys went on as bidden until they came to a place near the grave. There they halted.

"Where is Brave?" they asked.

Now Brave, full of mischief, had thought to play a jest on his little friends. As soon as they were well out of sight he had sped around the hill to the shore of the lake and sticking his hands in the mud had rubbed it over his face, plastered it in his hair, and soiled his hands until he looked like a new risen corpse with the flesh rotting from his bones. He then went and lay down in the grave and awaited the boys.

When the six little boys came they were more timid than ever when they did not find Brave; but they feared to go back to the village without seeing the grave, for fear the old men would call them cowards.

So they slowly approached the grave and one of them timidly called out:

"Please, grandmother, we won't disturb your grave. We only want to see where you lie. Don't be angry."

At once a thin quavering voice, like an old woman's, called out:

"*Han, han, takoja, hechetuya, hechetuya*! Yes, yes, that's right, that's right."

The boys were frightened out of their senses, believing the old woman had come to life.

"Oh, grandmother," they gasped, "don't hurt us; please don't, we'll go."

Just then Brave raised his muddy face and hands up thru the choke cherry bushes. With the oozy mud dripping from his features he looked like some very witch just raised from the grave. The boys screamed outright. One fainted. The rest ran yelling up the hill to the village, where each broke at once for his mother's *tepee*.

As all the tents in a Dakota camping circle face the center, the boys as they came tearing into camp were in plain view from the *tepees*. Hearing the screaming, every woman in camp ran to her *tepee* door to see what had happened. Just then little Brave, as badly scared as the rest, came rushing in after them, his hair on end and covered with mud and crying out, all forgetful of his appearance:

"It's me, it's me!"

The women yelped and bolted in terror from the village. Brave dashed into his mother's *tepee*, scaring her out of her wits. Dropping pots and kettles, she tumbled out of the tent to run screaming with the rest. Nor would a single villager come near poor little Brave until he had gone down to the lake and washed himself.

The Bound Children

There once lived a widow with two children—the elder a daughter and the younger a son. The widow went in mourning for her husband a long time. She cut off her hair, let her dress lie untidy on her body and kept her face unpainted and unwashed.

There lived in the same village a great chief. He had one son just come old enough to marry. The chief had it known that he wished his son to take a wife, and all of the young women in the village were eager to marry the young man. However, he was pleased with none of them.

Now the widow thought, "I am tired of mourning for my husband and caring for my children. Perhaps if I lay aside my mourning and paint myself red, the chief's son may marry me."

So she slipped away from her two children, stole down to the river and made a bathing place thru the ice. When she had washed away all signs of mourning, she painted and decked herself and went to the chief's *tepee*. When his son saw her, he loved her, and a feast was made in honor of her wedding.

When the widow's daughter found herself forsaken, she wept bitterly. After a day or two she took her little brother in her arms and went to the *tepee* of an old woman who lived at one end of the village. The old woman's tumble down *tepee* was of bark and her dress and clothing was of old smoke-dried tent cover. But she was kind to the two waifs and took them in willingly.

The little girl was eager to find her mother. The old woman said to her: "I suspect your mother has painted her face red. Do not try to find her. If the chief's son marries her she will not want to be burdened with you."

The old woman was right. The girl went down to the river, and sure enough found a hole cut in the ice and about it lay the filth that the mother had washed from her body. The girl gathered up the filth and went on. By and by she came to a second hole in the ice. Here too was filth, but not so much as at the previous place. At the third hole the ice was clean.

The girl knew now that her mother had painted her face red. She went at once to the chief's *tepee*, raised the door flap and went in. There sat her mother with the chief's son at their wedding feast.

The girl walked up to her mother and hurled the filth in her mother's face.

"There," she cried, "you who forsake your helpless children and forget your husband, take that!"

And at once her mother became a hideous old woman.

The girl then went back to the lodge of the old woman, leaving the camp in an uproar. The chief soon sent some young warriors to seize the girl and her brother, and they were brought to his tent. He was furious with anger.

"Let the children be bound with lariats wrapped about their bodies and let them be left to starve. Our camp will move on," he said. The chief's son did not put away his wife, hoping she might be cured in some way and grow young again.

Everybody in camp now got ready to move; but the old woman came close to the girl and said:

"In my old *tepee* I have dug a hole and buried a pot with punk and steel and flint and packs of dried meat. They will tie you up like a corpse. But before we go I will come with a knife and pretend to stab you, but I will really cut the rope that binds you so that you can unwind it from your body as soon as the camp is out of sight and hearing."

And so, before the camp started, the old woman came to the place where the two children were bound. She had in her hand a knife bound to the end of a stick which she used as a lance. She stood over the children and cried aloud:

"You wicked girl, who have shamed your own mother, you deserve all the punishment that is given you. But after all I do not want to let you lie and starve. Far better kill you at once and have done with it!" and with her stick she stabbed many times, as if to kill, but she was really cutting the rope.

The camp moved on; but the children lay on the ground until noon the next day. Then they began to squirm about. Soon the girl was free, and she then set loose her little brother. They went at once to the old woman's hut where they found the flint and steel and the packs of dried meat.

The girl made her brother a bow and arrows and with these he killed birds and other small game.

The boy grew up a great hunter. They became rich. They built three great *tepees*, in one of which were stored rows upon rows of *parfleche* bags of dried meat.

One day as the brother went out to hunt, he met a handsome young stranger who greeted him and said to him:

"I know you are a good hunter, for I have been watching you; your sister, too, is industrious. Let me have her for a wife. Then you and I will be brothers and hunt together."

The girl's brother went home and told her what the young stranger had said.

"Brother, I do not care to marry," she answered. "I am now happy with you."

"But you will be yet happier married," he answered, "and the young stranger is of no mean family, as one can see by his dress and manners."

"Very well, I will do as you wish," she said. So the stranger came into the *tepee* and was the girl's husband.

One day as they were in their tent, a crow flew overhead, calling out loudly,

"Kaw, Kaw,

They who forsook the children have no meat."

The girl and her husband and brother looked up at one another.

"What can it mean?" they asked. "Let us send for Unktomi (the spider). He is a good judge and he will know."

"And I will get ready a good dinner for him, for Unktomi is always hungry," added the young wife.

When Unktomi came, his yellow mouth opened with delight at the fine feast spread for him. After he had eaten he was told what the crow had said.

"The crow means," said Unktomi, "that the villagers and chief who bound and deserted you are in sad plight. They have hardly anything to eat and are starving."

When the girl heard this she made a bundle of choicest meat and called the crow.

"Take this to the starving villagers," she bade him.

He took the bundle in his beak, flew away to the starving village and dropped the bundle before the chief's *tepee*. The chief came out and the crow called loudly:

"Kaw, Kaw!

The children who were forsaken have much meat; those who forsook them have none."

"What can he mean," cried the astonished villagers.

"Let us send for Unktomi," said one, "he is a great judge; he will tell us."

They divided the bundle of meat among the starving people, saving the biggest piece for Unktomi.

When Unktomi had come and eaten, the villagers told him of the crow and asked what the bird's words meant.

"He means," said Unktomi, "that the two children whom you forsook have *tepees* full of dried meat enough for all the village."

The villagers were filled with astonishment at this news. To find whether or not it was true, the chief called seven young men and sent them out to see. They came to the three *tepees* and there met the girl's brother and husband just going out to hunt (which they did now only for sport).

The girl's brother invited the seven young men into the third or sacred lodge, and after they had smoked a pipe and knocked out the ashes on a buffalo bone the brother gave them meat to eat, which the seven devoured greedily.

The next day he loaded all seven with packs of meat, saying:

"Take this meat to the villagers and lead them hither."

While they awaited the return of the young men with the villagers, the girl made two bundles of meat, one of the best and choicest pieces, and the other of liver, very dry and hard to eat. After a few days the camp arrived. The young woman's mother opened the door and ran in crying: "Oh, my dear daughter, how glad I am to see you." But the daughter received her coldly and gave her the bundle of dried liver to eat. But when the old woman who had saved the children's lives came in, the young girl received her gladly, called her grandmother, and gave her the package of choice meat with marrow.

Then the whole village camped and ate of the stores of meat all the winter until spring came; and withal they were so many, there was such abundance of stores that there was still much left.

The Signs Of Corn

When corn is to be planted by the Indians, it is the work of the women folk to see to the sorting and cleaning of the best seed. It is also the women's work to see to the planting. (This was in olden times.)

After the best seed has been selected, the planter measures the corn, lays down a layer of hay, then a layer of corn. Over this corn they sprinkle warm water and cover it with another layer of hay, then bind hay about the bundle and hang it up in a spot where the warm rays of the sun can strike it.

While the corn is hanging in the sun, the ground is being prepared to receive it. Having finished the task of preparing the ground, the woman takes down her seed corn which has by this time sprouted. Then she proceeds to plant the corn.

Before she plants the first hill, she extends her hoe heavenwards and asks the Great Spirit to bless her work, that she may have a good yield. After her prayer she takes four kernels and plants one at the north, one at the south, one at the east and one at the west sides of the first hill. This is asking the Great Spirit to give summer rain and sunshine to bring forth a good crop.

For different growths of the corn, the women have an interpretation as to the character of the one who planted it.

1st. Where the corn grows in straight rows and the cob is full of kernels to the end, this signifies that the planter of this corn is of an exemplary character, and is very truthful and thoughtful.

2nd. If the rows on the ears of corn are irregular and broken, the planter is considered careless and unthoughtful. Also disorderly and slovenly about her house and person.

3rd. When an ear of corn bears a few scattering kernels with spaces producing no corn, it is said that is a good sign that the planter will live to a ripe old age. So old will they be that like the corn, their teeth will be few and far between.

4th. When a stalk bears a great many nubbins, or small ears growing around the large one, it is a sign that the planter is from a large and respectable family.

After the corn is gathered, it is boiled into sweet corn and made into hominy; parched and mixed with buffalo tallow and rolled into round balls, and used at feasts, or carried by the warriors on the warpath as food.

When there has been a good crop of corn, an ear is always tied at the top of the medicine pole, of the sun dance, in thanks to the Great Spirit for his goodness to them in sending a bountiful crop.

Story Of The Rabbits

The Rabbit nation were very much depressed in spirits on account of being run over by all other nations. They, being very obedient to their chief, obeyed all his orders to the letter. One of his orders was that upon the approach of any other nation that they should follow the example of their chief and run up among the rocks and down into their burrows, and not show themselves until the strangers had passed.

This they always did. Even the chirp of a little cricket would send them all scampering to their dens.

One day they held a great council, and after talking over everything for some time, finally left it to their medicine man to decide. The medicine man arose and said:

"My friends, we are of no use on this earth. There isn't a nation on earth that fears us, and we are so timid that we cannot defend ourselves, so the best thing for us to do is to rid the earth of our nation, by all going over to the big lake and drowning ourselves."

This they decided to do; so going to the lake they were about to jump in, when they heard a splashing in the water. Looking, they saw a lot of frogs jumping into the lake.

"We will not drown ourselves," said the medicine man, "we have found a nation who are afraid of us. It is the frog nation." Had it not been for the frogs we would have had no rabbits, as the whole nation would have drowned themselves and the rabbit race would have been extinct.

How The Rabbit Lost His Tail

Once upon a time there were two brothers, one a great Genie and the other a rabbit. Like all genie, the older could change himself into any kind of an animal, bird, fish, cloud, thunder and lightning, or in fact anything that he desired.

The younger brother (the rabbit) was very mischievous and was continually getting into all kinds of trouble. His older brother was kept busy getting Rabbit out of all kinds of scrapes.

When Rabbit had attained his full growth he wanted to travel around and see something of the world. When he told his brother what he intended to do, the brother said: "Now, Rabbit, you are *Witkotko* (mischievous), so be very careful, and keep out of trouble as much as possible. In case you get into any serious trouble, and can't get out by yourself, just call on me for assistance, and no matter where you are, I will come to you."

Rabbit started out and the first day he came to a very high house, outside of which stood a very high pine tree. So high was the tree that Rabbit could hardly see the top. Outside the door, on an enormous stool, sat a very large giant fast asleep. Rabbit (having his bow and arrows with him) strung up his bow, and, taking an arrow from his quiver, said:

"I want to see how big this man is, so I guess I will wake him up." So saying he moved over to one side and took good aim, and shot the giant upon the nose. This stung like fire and awoke the giant, who jumped up, crying: "Who had the audacity to shoot me on the nose?" "I did," said Rabbit.

The giant, hearing a voice, looked all around, but saw nothing, until he looked down at the corner of the house, and there sat a rabbit.

"I had hiccoughs this morning and thought that I was going to have a good big meal, and here is nothing but a toothful."

"I guess you won't make a toothful of me," said Rabbit, "I am as strong as you, though I am little." "We will see," said the giant. He went into the house and came out, bringing a hammer that weighed many tons.

"Now, Mr. Rabbit, we will see who can throw this hammer over the top of that tree."

"Get something harder to do," said Rabbit.

"Well, we will try this first," said the giant. With that he grasped the hammer in both hands, swung it three times around his head and sent it spinning thru the air. Up, up, it went, skimming the top of the tree, and came down, shaking the ground and burying itself deep into the earth.

"Now," said the giant, "if you don't accomplish this same feat, I am going to swallow you at one mouthful." Rabbit said, "I always sing to my brother before I attempt things like this." So he commenced singing and calling his brother. "*Cinye! Cinye!*" (brother, brother) he sang. The giant grew nervous, and said: "Boy, why do you call your brother?"

Pointing to a small black cloud that was approaching very swiftly, Rabbit said: "That is my brother; he can destroy you, your house, and pine tree in one breath."

"Stop him and you can go free," said the giant. Rabbit waved his paws and the cloud disappeared.

From this place Rabbit continued on his trip towards the west. The next day, while passing thru a deep forest, he thought he heard some one moaning, as though in pain. He stopped and listened; soon the wind blew and the moaning grew louder. Following the direction from whence came the sound, he soon discovered a man stripped of his clothing, and caught between two limbs of a tall elm tree. When the wind blew the limbs would rub together and squeeze the man, who would give forth the mournful groans.

"My, you have a fine place up there. Let us change. You can come down and I will take your place." (Now this man had been placed up there for punishment, by Rabbit's brother, and he could not get down unless some one came along and proposed to take his place on the tree). "Very well," said the man. "Take off your clothes and come up. I will fasten you in the limbs and you can have all the fun you want."

Rabbit disrobed and climbed up. The man placed him between the limbs and slid down the tree. He hurriedly got into Rabbit's clothes, and just as he had completed his toilet, the wind blew very hard. Rabbit was nearly crazy with pain, and screamed and cried. Then he began to cry "*Cinye, Cinye*" (brother, brother). "Call your brother as much as you like, he can never find me." So saying the man disappeared in the forest.

Scarcely had he disappeared, when the brother arrived, and seeing Rabbit in the tree, said: "Which way did he go?" Rabbit pointed the direction taken by the man. The brother flew over the top of the trees, soon found the man and brought him back, making him take his old place between the limbs, and causing a heavy wind to blow and continue all afternoon and night, for punishment to the man for having placed his brother up there.

After Rabbit got his clothes back on, his brother gave him a good scolding, and wound up by saying: "I want you to be more careful in the future. I have plenty of work to keep me as busy as I want to be, and I can't be stopping every little while to be making trips to get you out of some foolish scrape. It was only yesterday that I came five hundred miles to help you from the giant, and today I have had to come a thousand miles, so be more careful from this time on."

Several days after this the Rabbit was traveling along the banks of a small river, when he came to a small clearing in the woods, and in the center of the clearing stood a nice little log hut. Rabbit was wondering who could be living here when the door slowly opened and an old man appeared in the doorway, bearing a tripe water pail in his right hand. In his left hand he held a string which was fastened to the inside of the house. He kept hold of the string and came slowly down to the river. When he got to the water he stooped down and dipped the pail into it and returned to the house, still holding the string for guidance.

Soon he reappeared holding on to another string, and, following this one, went to a large pile of wood and returned to the house with it. Rabbit wanted to see if the old man would come out again, but he came out no more. Seeing smoke ascending from the mud chimney, he thought he would go over and see what the old man was doing. He knocked at the door, and a weak voice bade him enter. He noticed that the old man was cooking dinner.

"Hello *Tunkasina* (grandfather), you must have a nice time, living here alone. I see that you have everything handy. You can get wood and water, and that is all you have to do. How do you get your provisions?"

"The wolves bring my meat, the mice my rice and ground beans, and the birds bring me the cherry leaves for my tea. Yet it is a hard life, as I am all alone most of the time and have no one to talk to, and besides, I am blind."

"Say, grandfather," said Rabbit, "let us change places. I think I would like to live here."

"If we exchange clothes," said the other, "you will become old and blind, while I will assume your youth and good looks." (Now, this old man was placed here for punishment by Rabbit's brother. He had killed his wife, so the genie made him old and blind, and he would remain so until some one came who would exchange places with him).

"I don't care for youth and good looks," said Rabbit, "let us make the change."

They changed clothes, and Rabbit became old and blind, whilst the old man became young and handsome.

"Well, I must go," said the man. He went out and cutting the strings close to the door, ran off laughing. "You will get enough of your living alone, you crazy boy," and saying this he ran into the woods.

Rabbit thought he would like to get some fresh water and try the string paths so that he would get accustomed to it. He bumped around the room and finally found the tripe water bucket. He took hold of the string and started out. When he had gotten a short distance from the door he came to the end of the string so suddenly, that he lost the end which he had in his hand, and he wandered about, bumping against the trees, and tangling himself up in plum bushes and thorns, scratching his face and hands so badly that the blood ran from them. Then it was that he commenced again to cry, "*Cinye! Cinye!*" (brother, brother). Soon his brother arrived, and asked which way the old man had gone.

"I don't know," said Rabbit, "I couldn't see which path he took, as I was blind."

The genie called the birds, and they came flying from every direction. As fast as they arrived the brother asked them if they had seen the man whom he had placed here for punishment, but none had seen him. The owl came last, and when asked if he had seen the man, he said "hoo-hoo."

"The man who lived here," said the brother.

"Last night I was hunting mice in the woods south of here and I saw a man sleeping beneath a plum tree. I thought it was your brother, Rabbit, so I didn't awaken him," said the owl.

"Good for you, owl," said the brother, "for this good news, you shall hereafter roam around only at night, and I will fix your eyes, so the darker the night the better you will be able to see. You will always have the fine cool nights to hunt your food. You other birds can hunt your food during the hot daylight." (Since then the owl has been the night bird).

The brother flew to the woods and brought the man back and cut the strings short, and said to him: "Now you can get a taste of what you gave my brother."

To Rabbit he said: "I ought not to have helped you this time. Anyone who is so crazy as to change places with a blind man should be left without help, so be careful, as I am getting tired of your foolishness, and will not help you again if you do anything as foolish as you did this time."

Rabbit started to return to his home. When he had nearly completed his journey he came to a little creek, and being thirsty took a good long drink. While he was drinking he heard a noise as though a wolf or cat was scratching the earth. Looking up to a hill which overhung the creek, he saw four wolves, with their tails intertwined, pulling with all their might. As Rabbit came up to them one pulled loose, and Rabbit saw that his tail was broken.

"Let me pull tails with you. My tail is long and strong," said Rabbit, and the wolves assenting, Rabbit interlocked his long tail with those of the three wolves and commenced pulling and the wolves pulled so hard that they pulled Rabbit's tail off at the second joint. The wolves disappeared.

"*Cinye! Cinye!* (Brother, brother.) I have lost my tail," cried Rabbit. The genie came and seeing his brother Rabbit's tail missing, said: "You look better without a tail anyway."

From that time on rabbits have had no tails.

Unktomi And The Arrowheads

There were once upon a time two young men who were very great friends, and were constantly together. One was a very thoughtful young man, the other very impulsive, who never stopped to think before he committed an act.

One day these two friends were walking along, telling each other of their experiences in love making. They ascended a high hill, and on reaching the top, heard a ticking noise as if small stones or pebbles were being struck together.

Looking around they discovered a large spider sitting in the midst of a great many flint arrowheads. The spider was busily engaged making the flint rocks into arrow heads. They looked at the spider, but he never moved, but continued hammering away on a piece of flint which he had nearly completed into another arrowhead.

"Let's hit him," said the thoughtless one. "No," said the other, "he is not harming anyone; in fact, he is doing a great good, as he is making the flint arrowheads which we use to point our arrows."

"Oh, you are afraid," said the first young man. "He can't harm you. Just watch me hit him." So saying, he picked up an arrowhead and throwing it at Unktomi, hit him on the side. As Unktomi rolled over on his side, got up and stood looking at them, the young man laughed and said: "Well, let us be going, as your grandfather, Unktomi, doesn't seem to like our company." They started down the hill, when suddenly the one who had hit Unktomi took a severe fit of coughing. He coughed and coughed, and finally small particles of blood came from his mouth. The blood kept coming thicker and in great gushes. Finally it came so thick and fast that the man could not get his breath and fell upon the ground dead.

The thoughtful young man, seeing that his friend was no more, hurried to the village and reported what had happened. The relatives and friends hurried to the hill, and sure enough, there lay the thoughtless young man still and cold in death. They held a council and sent for the chief of the Unktomi tribe. When he heard what had happened, he told the council that he could do nothing to his Unktomi, as it had only defended itself.

Said he: "My friends, seeing that your tribe was running short of arrowheads, I set a great many of my tribe to work making flint arrowheads for you. When my men are thus engaged they do not wish to be disturbed, and your young man not only disturbed my man, but grossly insulted him by striking him with one of the arrowheads which he had worked so hard to make. My man could not sit and take this insult, so as the young man walked away the Unktomi shot him with a very tiny arrowhead. This produced a hemorrhage, which caused his death. So now, my friends, if you will fill and pass the peace pipe, we will part good friends and my tribe shall always furnish you with plenty of flint arrowheads." So saying, Unktomi Tanka finished his peace smoke and returned to his tribe.

Ever after that, when the Indians heard a ticking in the grass, they would go out of their way to get around the sound, saying, Unktomi is making arrowheads; we must not disturb him.

Thus it was that *Unktomi Tanka* (Big Spider) had the respect of this tribe, and was never after disturbed in his work of making arrowheads.

The Bear And The Rabbit Hunt Buffalo

Once upon a time there lived as neighbors, a bear and a rabbit. The rabbit was a good shot, and the bear being very clumsy could not use the arrow to good advantage. The bear was very unkind to the rabbit. Every morning, the bear would call over to the rabbit and say: "Take your bow and arrows and come with me to the other side of the hill. A large herd of buffalo are grazing there, and I want you to shoot some of them for me, as my children are crying for meat."

The rabbit, fearing to arouse the bear's anger by refusing, consented, and went with the bear, and shot enough buffalo to satisfy the hungry family. Indeed, he shot and killed so many that there was lots of meat left after the bear and his family had loaded themselves, and packed all they could carry home. The bear being very gluttonous, and not wanting the rabbit to get any of the meat, said: "Rabbit, you come along home with us and we will return and get the remainder of the meat."

The poor rabbit could not even taste the blood from the butchering, as the bear would throw earth on the blood and dry it up. Poor Rabbit would have to go home hungry after his hard day's work.

The bear was the father of five children. The youngest boy was very kind to the rabbit. The mother bear, knowing that her youngest was a very hearty eater, always gave him an extra large piece of meat. What the baby bear did not eat, he would take outside with him and pretend to play ball with it, kicking it toward the rabbit's house, and when he got close to the door he would give the meat such a great kick, that it would fly into the rabbit's house, and in this way poor Rabbit would get his meal unknown to the papa bear.

Baby bear never forgot his friend Rabbit. Papa bear often wondered why his baby would go outside after each meal. He grew suspicious and asked the baby where he had been. "Oh, I always play ball outside, around the house, and when I get tired playing I eat up my meat ball and then come in."

The baby bear was too cunning to let papa bear know that he was keeping his friend rabbit from starving to death. Nevertheless, papa bear suspected baby and said: "Baby, I think you go over to the rabbit's after every meal."

The four older brothers were very handsome, but baby bear was a little puny fellow, whose coat couldn't keep out much cold, as it was short and shaggy, and of a dirty brown color. The three older brothers were very unkind to baby bear, but the fourth one always took baby's part, and was always kind to his baby brother.

Rabbit was getting tired of being ordered and bullied around by papa bear. He puzzled his brain to scheme some way of getting even with Mr. Bear for abusing him so much. He studied all night long, but no scheme worth trying presented itself. Early one morning Mr. Bear presented himself at Rabbit's door.

"Say, Rabbit, my meat is all used up, and there is a fine herd of buffalo grazing on the hillside. Get your bow and arrows and come with me. I want you to shoot some of them for me."

"Very well," said Rabbit, and he went and killed six buffalo for Bear. Bear got busy butchering and poor Rabbit, thinking he would get a chance to lick up one mouthful of blood, stayed very close to the bear while he was cutting up the meat. The bear was very watchful lest the rabbit get something to eat. Despite bear's watchfulness, a small clot of blood rolled past and behind the bear's feet. At once Rabbit seized the clot and hid it in his bosom. By the time Rabbit got home, the blood clot was hardened from the warmth of his body, so, being hungry, it put Mr. Rabbit out of sorts to think that after all his trouble he could not eat the blood.

Very badly disappointed, he lay down on his floor and gazed up into the chimney hole. Disgusted with the way things had turned out, he grabbed up the blood clot and threw it up through the hole. Scarcely had it hit the ground when he heard the voice of a baby crying, "*Ate! Ate!*" (father, father). He went outside and there he found a big baby boy. He took the baby into his house and threw him out through the hole again. This time the boy was large enough to say "*Ate, Ate, he-cun-sin-lo.*" (Father, father, don't do that). But nevertheless, he threw him up and out again. On going out the third time, there stood a handsome youth smiling at him. Rabbit at once adopted the youth and took him into his house, seating him in the seat of honor (which is directly opposite the entrance), and saying:

"My son, I want you to be a good, honest, straightforward man. Now, I have in my possession a fine outfit, and you, my son, shall wear it."

Suiting his action to his words, he drew out a bag from a hollow tree and on opening it, drew out a fine buckskin shirt (tanned white as snow), worked with porcupine quills. Also a pair of red leggings worked with beads. Moccasins worked with colored hair. A fine otter skin robe. White weasel skins to intertwine with his beautiful long black locks. A magnificent center eagle feather. A rawhide covered bow, accompanied by a quiver full of flint arrowheads.

The rabbit, having dressed his son in all the latest finery, sat back and gazed long and lovingly at his handsome son. Instinctively Rabbit felt that his son had been sent him for the purpose of being instrumental in the downfall of Mr. Bear. Events will show.

The morning following the arrival of Rabbit's son, Mr. Bear again presents himself at the door, crying out: "You lazy, ugly rabbit, get up and come out here. I want you to shoot some more buffalo for me."

"Who is this, who speaks so insultingly to you, father?" asked the son.

"It is a bear who lives near here, and makes me kill buffalo for his family, and he won't let me take even one little drop of blood from the killing, and consequently, my son, I have nothing in my house for you to eat."

The young man was anxious to meet Mr. Bear but Rabbit advised him to wait a little until he and Bear had gone to the hunt. So the son obeyed, and when he thought it time that the killing was done, he started out and arrived on the scene just as Mr. Bear was about to proceed with his butchering.

Seeing a strange shadow on the ground beside him, Mr. Bear looked up and gazed into the fearless eyes of rabbit's handsome son.

"Who is this?" asked Mr. Bear of poor little Rabbit.

"I don't know," answered Rabbit.

"Who are you?" asked the bear of Rabbit's son. "Where did you come from?"

The rabbit's son not replying, the bear spoke thus to him: "Get out of here, and get out quick, too."

At this speech the rabbit's son became angered, and fastened an arrow to his bow and drove the arrow through the bear's heart. Then he turned on Mrs. Bear and served her likewise. During the melee, Rabbit shouted: "My son, my son, don't kill the two youngest. The baby has kept me from starving and the other one is good and kind to his baby brother."

So the three older brothers who were unkind to their baby brother met a similar fate to that of their selfish parents.

This (the story goes) is the reason that bears travel only in pairs.

The Brave Who Went On The Warpath Alone And Won The Name Of The Lone Warrior

There was once a young man whose parents were not overburdened with the riches of this world, and consequently could not dress their only son in as rich a costume as the other young men of the tribe, and on account of not being so richly clad as they, he was looked down upon and shunned by them. He was never invited to take part in any of their sports; nor was he ever asked to join any of the war parties.

In the village lived an old man with an only daughter. Like the other family, they were poor, but the daughter was the belle of the tribe. She was the most sought after by the young men of the village, and warriors from tribes far distant came to press their suit at winning her for their bride. All to no purpose; she had the same answer for them as she had for the young men of the village.

The poor young man was also very handsome despite his poor clothes, but having never killed an enemy nor brought home any enemies' horses he was not (according to Indian rules) allowed to make love to any young or old woman. He tried in vain to join some of the war parties, that he might get the chance to win his spurs as a warrior. To all his pleadings, came the same answer: "You are not fit to join a war party. You have no horses, and if you should get killed our tribe would be laughed at and be made fun of as you have such poor clothes, and we don't want the enemy to know that we have any one of our tribe who dresses so poorly as you do."

Again, and again, he tried different parties, only to be made fun of and insulted.

One night he sat in the poor *tepee* of his parents. He was in deep study and had nothing to say. His father, noticing his melancholy mood, asked him what had happened to cause him to be so quiet, as he was always of a jolly disposition. The son answered and said:

"Father, I am going on the warpath alone. In vain I have tried to be a member of one of the war parties. To all of my pleadings I have got nothing but insults in return."

"But my son, you have no gun nor ammunition. Where can you get any and how can you get it? We have nothing to buy one for you with," said the father.

"I don't need any weapons. I am going to bring back some of the enemies' horses, and I don't need a gun for that."

Early the next morning (regardless of the old couple's pleadings not to go unarmed) the young man left the village and headed northwest, the direction always taken by the war parties.

For ten days he traveled without seeing any signs of a camp. The evening of the tenth day, he reached a very high butte, thickly wooded at the summit. He ascended this butte, and as he sat there between two large boulders, watching the beautiful rays of the setting sun, he was suddenly startled to hear the neigh of a horse. Looking down into the beautiful valley which was threaded by a beautiful creek fringed with timber, he noticed close to the base of the butte upon which he sat, a large drove of horses grazing peacefully and quietly. Looking closer, he noticed at a little distance from the main drove, a horse with a saddle on his back. This was the one that had neighed, as the drove drifted further away from him. He was tied by a long lariat to a large sage bush.

Where could the rider be, he said to himself. As if in answer to his question, there appeared not more than twenty paces from him a middle aged man coming up through a deep ravine. The man was evidently in search of some kind of game, as he held his gun in readiness for instant use, and kept his eyes directed at every crevice and clump of bush. So intent was he on locating the game he was trailing, that he never noticed the young man who sat like a statue not twenty paces away. Slowly and cautiously the man approached, and when he had advanced to within a few paces of the young man he stopped and turning around, stood looking down into the valley. This was the only chance that our brave young friend had. Being unarmed, he would stand no show if the enemy ever got a glimpse of him. Slowly and noiselessly he drew his hunting knife (which his father had given him on his departure from home) and holding it securely in his right hand, gathered himself and gave a leap which landed him upon the unsuspecting enemy's shoulders. The force with which he landed on the enemy caused him (the enemy) to lose his hold on his gun, and it went rattling down into the chasm, forty feet below.

Down they came together, the young man on top. No sooner had they struck the ground than the enemy had out his knife, and then commenced a hand to hand duel. The enemy, having more experience, was getting the best of our young friend. Already our young friend had two ugly cuts, one across his chest and the other through his forearm.

He was becoming weak from the loss of blood, and could not stand the killing pace much longer. Summoning all his strength for one more trial to overcome his antagonist, he rushed him toward the chasm, and in his hurry to get away from this fierce attack, the enemy stepped back one step too far, and down they both went into the chasm. Interlocked in each other's arms, the young man drove his knife into the enemy's side and when they struck the bottom the enemy relaxed his hold and straightened out stiff and dead.

Securing his scalp and gun, the young man proceeded down to where the horse was tied to the sage bush, and then gathering the drove of horses proceeded on his return to his own village. Being wounded severely he had to ride very slowly. All the long hours of the night he drove the horses towards his home village.

In the meantime, those at the enemies' camp wondered at the long absence of the herder who was watching their drove of horses, and finally seven young men went to search for the missing herder. All night long they searched the hillsides for the horses and herder, and when it had grown light enough in the morning they saw by the ground where there had been a fierce struggle.

Following the tracks in the sand and leaves, they came to the chasm where the combatants had fallen over, and there, lying on his back staring up at them in death, was their herder. They hastened to the camp and told what they had found. Immediately the warriors mounted their war ponies (these ponies are never turned loose, but kept tied close to the *tepee* of the owner), and striking the trail of the herd driven off by our young friend, they urged forth their ponies and were soon far from their camp on the trail of our young friend. All day long they traveled on his trail, and just as the sun was sinking they caught sight of him driving the drove ahead over a high hill. Again they urged forth their tired ponies. The young man, looking back along the trail, saw some dark objects coming along, and, catching a fresh horse, drove the rest ahead at a great rate. Again all night he drove them, and when daylight came he looked back (from a high butte) over his trail and saw coming over a distant raise, two horsemen. These two undoubtedly rode the best ponies, as he saw nothing of the others. Driving the horses into a thick belt of timber, he concealed himself close to the trail made by the drove of horses, and lay in ambush for the two daring horsemen who had followed him so far. Finally they appeared on the butte from where he had looked back and saw them following him. For a long time they sat there scouring the country before them in hopes that they might see some signs of their stolen horses. Nothing could they see. Had they but known, their horses were but a few hundred yards from them, but the thick timber securely hid them from view. Finally one of them arose and pointed to the timber. Then leaving his horse in charge of his friend, he descended the butte and followed the trail of the drove to where they had entered the timber. Little did he think that he was standing on the brink of eternity. The young man hiding not more than a hundred yards from him could have shot him there where he stood, but wanting to play fair, he stepped into sight. When he did, the enemy took quick aim and fired. He was too hasty. Had he taken more careful aim he might have killed our young friend, but his bullet whizzed harmlessly over the young man's head and buried itself in a tree. The young man took good aim and fired. The enemy threw up both hands and fell forward on his face. The other one on the hill, seeing his friend killed, hastily mounted his horse and leading his friend's horse, made rapidly off down the butte in the direction from whence he had come. Waiting for some time to be sure the one who was alive did not come up and take a shot at him, he finally advanced upon the fallen enemy and securing his gun, ammunition and scalp, went to his horse and drove the herd on through the woods and crossing a long flat prairie, ascended a long chain of hills and sat looking back along his trail in search of any of the enemy who might continue to follow him.

Thus he sat until the long shadows of the hills reminded him that it would soon be sunset, and as he must get some sleep, he wanted to find some creek bend where he could drive the bunch of ponies and feel safe as to their not straying off during the night. He found a good place for the herd, and catching a fresh horse, he picketed him close to where he was going to sleep, and wrapping himself in his blanket, was soon fast asleep. So tired and sleepy was he that a heavy rain which had come up, during the night, soaked him through and through, but he never awakened until the sun was high in the east.

He awoke and going to the place where he had left the herd, he was glad to find them all there. He mounted his horse and started his herd homeward again. For two days he drove them, and on the evening of the second day he came in sight of the village.

The older warriors, hearing of the young man going on this trip alone and unarmed, told the parents to go in mourning for their son, as he would never come back alive. When the people of the village saw this large drove of horses advancing towards them, they at first thought it was a war party of the enemy, and so the head men called the young warriors together and fully prepared for a great battle. They advanced upon the supposed enemy. When they got close enough to discern a lone horseman driving this large herd, they surrounded the horses and lone warrior, and brought him triumphantly into camp. On arriving in the camp (or village) the horses were counted and the number counted up to one hundred and ten head.

The chief and his criers (or heralds) announced through the whole village that there would be a great war dance given in honor of the Lone Warrior.

The whole village turned out and had a great war dance that was kept up three days and three nights. The two scalps which the young man had taken were tied to a pole which was placed in the center of the dance circle. At this dance, the Lone Warrior gave to each poor family five head of horses.

Being considered eligible now to pay his respects to any girl who took his fancy, he at once went to the camp of the beautiful girl of the tribe, and as he was always her choice, she at once consented to marry him.

The news spread through the village that Lone Warrior had won the belle of the nation for his bride, and this with the great feat which he had accomplished alone in killing two enemies and bringing home a great herd of horses, raised him to the rank of chief, which he faithfully filled to the end of his days. And many times he had to tell his grandchildren the story of how he got the name of the Lone Warrior.

The Sioux Who Married The Crow Chief's Daughter

A war party of seven young men, seeing a lone *tepee* standing on the edge of a heavy belt of timber, stopped and waited for darkness, in order to send one of their scouts ahead to ascertain whether the camp which they had seen was the camp of friend or enemy.

When darkness had settled down on them, and they felt secure in not being detected, they chose one of their scouts to go on alone and find out what would be the best direction for them to advance upon the camp, should it prove to be an enemy.

Among the scouts was one who was noted for his bravery, and many were the brave acts he had performed. His name was Big Eagle. This man they selected to go to the lone camp and obtain the information for which they were waiting.

Big Eagle was told to look carefully over the ground and select the best direction from which they should make the attack. The other six would await his return. He started on his mission, being careful not to make any noise. He stealthily approached the camp. As he drew near to the tent he was surprised to note the absence of any dogs, as these animals are always kept by the Sioux to notify the owners by their barking of the approach of anyone. He crawled up to the *tepee* door, and peeping through a small aperture, he saw three persons sitting inside. An elderly man and woman were sitting at the right of the fireplace, and a young woman at the seat of honor, opposite the door.

Big Eagle had been married and his wife had died five winters previous to the time of this episode. He had never thought of marrying again, but when he looked upon this young woman he thought he was looking upon the face of his dead wife. He removed his cartridge belts and knife, and placing them, along with his rifle, at the side of the tent, he at once boldly stepped inside the *tepee*, and going over to the man, extended his hand and shook first the man's hand, then the old woman's, and lastly the young woman's. Then he seated himself by the side of the girl, and thus they sat, no one speaking.

Finally, Big Eagle made signs to the man, explaining as well as possible by signs, that his wife had died long ago, and when he saw the girl she so strongly resembled his dead wife that he wished to marry her, and he would go back to the enemy's camp and live with them, if they would consent to the marriage of their daughter.

The old man seemed to understand, and Big Eagle again made signs to him that a party were lying in wait just a short distance from his camp. Noiselessly they brought in the horses, and taking down the tent, they at once moved off in the direction from whence they had come. The war party waited all night, and when the first rays of dawn disclosed to them the absence of the *tepee*, they at once concluded that Big Eagle had been discovered and killed, so they hurriedly started on their trail for home.

In the meantime, the hunting party, for this it was that Big Eagle had joined, made very good time in putting a good distance between themselves and the war party. All day they traveled, and when evening came they ascended a high hill, looking down into the valley on the other side. There stretched for two miles, along the banks of a small stream, an immense camp. The old man made signs for Big Eagle to remain with the two women where he was, until he could go to the camp and prepare them to receive an enemy into their village.

The old man rode through the camp and drew up at the largest *tepee* in the village. Soon Big Eagle could see men gathering around the *tepee*. The crowd grew larger and larger, until the whole village had assembled at the large *tepee*. Finally they dispersed, and catching their horses, mounted and advanced to the hill on which Big Eagle and the two women were waiting. They formed a circle around them and slowly they returned to the village, singing and riding in a circle around them.

When they arrived at the village they advanced to the large *tepee*, and motioned Big Eagle to the seat of honor in the *tepee*. In the village was a man who understood and spoke the Sioux language. He was sent for, and through him the oath of allegiance to the Crow tribe was taken by Big Eagle. This done he was presented with the girl to wife, and also with many spotted ponies.

Big Eagle lived with his wife among her people for two years, and during this time he joined in four different battles between his own people (the Sioux) and the Crow people, to whom his wife belonged.

In no battle with his own people would he carry any weapons, only a long willow coup-stick, with which he struck the fallen Sioux.

At the expiration of two years he concluded to pay a visit to his own tribe, and his father-in-law, being a chief of high standing, at once had it heralded through the village that his son-in-law would visit his own people, and for them to show their good will and respect for him by bringing ponies for his son-in-law to take back to his people.

Hearing this, the herds were all driven in and all day long horses were brought to the tent of Big Eagle, and when he was ready to start on his homeward trip, twenty young men were elected to accompany him to within a safe distance of his village. The twenty young men drove the gift horses, amounting to two hundred and twenty head, to within one day's journey of the village of Big Eagle, and fearing for their safety from his people, Big Eagle sent them back to their own village.

On his arrival at his home village, they received him as one returned from the dead, as they were sure he had been killed the night he had been sent to reconnoiter the lone camp. There was great feasting and dancing in honor of his return, and the horses were distributed among the needy ones of the village.

Remaining at his home village for a year, he one day made up his mind to return to his wife's people. A great many fancy robes, dresses, war bonnets, moccasins, and a great drove of horses were given him, and his wife, and he bade farewell to his people for good, saying, "I will never return to you again, as I have decided to live the remainder of my days with my wife's people."

On his arrival at the village of the Crows, he found his father-in-law at the point of death. A few days later the old man died, and Big Eagle was appointed to fill the vacancy of chief made by the death of his father-in-law.

Subsequently he took part in battles against his own people, and in the third battle was killed on the field. Tenderly the Crow warriors bore him back to their camp, and great was the mourning in the Crow village for the brave man who always went into battle unarmed, save only the willow wand which he carried.

Thus ended the career of one of the bravest of Sioux warriors who ever took the scalp of an enemy, and who for the love of his dead wife, gave up home, parents, and friends, to be killed on the field of battle by his own tribe.

The Boy And The Turtles

A boy went on a turtle hunt, and after following the different streams for hours, finally came to the conclusion that the only place he would find any turtles would be at the little lake, where the tribe always hunted them.

So, leaving the stream he had been following, he cut across country to the lake. On drawing near the lake he crawled on his hands and knees in order not to be seen by the turtles, who were very watchful, as they had been hunted so much. Peeping over the rock he saw a great many out on the shore sunning themselves, so he very cautiously undressed, so he could leap into the water and catch them before they secreted themselves. But on pulling off his shirt one of his hands was held up so high that the turtles saw it and jumped into the lake with a great splash.

The boy ran to the shore, but saw only bubbles coming up from the bottom. Directly the boy saw something coming to the surface, and soon it came up into sight. It was a little man, and soon others, by the hundreds, came up and swam about, splashing the water up into the air to a great height. So scared was the boy that he never stopped to gather up his clothes but ran home naked and fell into his grandmother's tent door.

"What is the trouble, grandchild," cried the old woman. But the boy could not answer. "Did you see anything unnatural?" He shook his head, "no." He made signs to the grandmother that his lungs were pressing so hard against his sides that he could not talk. He kept beating his side with his clenched hands. The grandmother got out her medicine bag, made a prayer to the Great Spirit to drive out the evil spirit that had entered her grandson's body, and after she had applied the medicine, the prayer must have been heard and answered, as the boy commenced telling her what he had heard and seen.

The grandmother went to the chief's tent and told what her grandson had seen. The chief sent two brave warriors to the lake to ascertain whether it was true or not. The two warriors crept to the little hill close to the lake, and there, sure enough, the lake was swarming with little men swimming about, splashing the water high up into the air. The warriors, too, were scared and hurried home, and in the council called on their return told what they had seen. The boy was brought to the council and given the seat of honor (opposite the door), and was named "*Wakan Wanyanka*" (sees holy).

The lake had formerly borne the name of Truth Lake, but from this time on was called "*Wicasa-bde*" — Man Lake.

The Hermit, Or The Gift Of Corn

In a deep forest, far from the villages of his people, lived a hermit. His tent was made of buffalo skins, and his dress was made of deer skin. Far from the haunts of any human being this old hermit was content to spend his days.

All day long he would wander through the forest studying the different plants of nature and collecting precious roots, which he used as medicine. At long intervals some warrior would arrive at the tent of the old hermit and get medicine roots from him for the tribe, the old hermit's medicine being considered far superior to all others.

After a long day's ramble in the woods, the hermit came home late, and being very tired, at once lay down on his bed and was just dozing off to sleep, when he felt something rub against his foot. Awakening with a start, he noticed a dark object and an arm was extended to him, holding in its hand a flint pointed arrow.

The hermit thought, "This must be a spirit, as there is no human being around here but myself!" A voice then said: "Hermit, I have come to invite you to my home." "*How* (yes), I will come," said the old hermit. Wherewith he arose, wrapped his robe about him and followed.

Outside the door he stopped and looked around, but could see no signs of the dark object.

"Whoever you are, or whatever you be, wait for me, as I don't know where to go to find your house," said the hermit. Not an answer did he receive, nor could he hear any noises as though anyone was walking through the brush. Re-entering his tent he retired and was soon fast asleep. The next night the same thing occurred again, and the hermit followed the object out, only to be left as before.

He was very angry to think that anyone should be trying to make sport of him, and he determined to find out who this could be who was disturbing his night's rest.

The next evening he cut a hole in the tent large enough to stick an arrow through, and stood by the door watching. Soon the dark object came and stopped outside of the door, and said: "Grandfather, I came to--," but he never finished the sentence, for the old man let go his arrow, and he heard the arrow strike something which produced a sound as though he had shot into a sack of pebbles. He did not go out that night to see what his arrow had struck, but early next morning he went out and looked at the spot about where he thought the object had stood. There on the ground lay a little heap of corn, and from this little heap a small line of corn lay scattered along a path. This he followed far into the woods. When he came to a very small knoll the trail ended. At the end of the trail was a large circle, from which the grass had been scraped off clean.

"The corn trail stops at the edge of this circle," said the old man, "so this must be the home of whoever it was that invited me." He took his bone knife and hatchet and proceeded to dig down into the center of the circle. When he had got down to the length of his arm, he came to a sack of dried meat. Next he found a sack of Indian turnips, then a sack of dried cherries; then a sack of corn, and last of all another sack, empty except that there was about a cupful of corn in one corner of it, and that the sack had a hole in the other corner where his arrow had pierced it. From this hole in the sack the corn was scattered along the trail, which guided the old man to the cache.

From this the hermit taught the tribes how to keep their provisions when traveling and were overloaded. He explained to them how they should dig a pit and put their provisions into it and cover them with earth. By this method the Indians used to keep provisions all summer, and when fall came they would return to their cache, and on opening it would find everything as fresh as the day they were placed there.

The old hermit was also thanked as the discoverer of corn, which had never been known to the Indians until discovered by the old hermit.

The Mysterious Butte

A young man was once hunting and came to a steep hill. The east side of the hill suddenly dropped off to a very steep bank. He stood on this bank, and at the base he noticed a small opening. On going down to examine it more closely, he found it was large enough to admit a horse or buffalo. On either side of the door were figures of different animals engraved into the wall.

He entered the opening and there, scattered about on the floor, lay many bracelets, pipes and many other things of ornament, as though they had been offerings to some great spirit. He passed through this first room and on entering the second it was so dark that he could not see his hands before his face, so becoming scared, he hurriedly left the place, and returning home told what he had seen.

Upon hearing this the chief selected four of his most daring warriors to go with this young man and investigate and ascertain whether the young man was telling the truth or not. The five proceeded to the butte, and at the entrance the young man refused to go inside, as the figures on either side of the entrance had been changed.

The four entered and seeing that all in the first chamber was as the young man had told, they went on to the next chamber and found it so dark that they could not see anything. They continued on, however, feeling their way along the walls. They finally found an entrance that was so narrow that they had to squeeze into it sideways. They felt their way around the walls and found another entrance, so low down that they had to crawl on their hands and knees to go through into the next chamber.

On entering the last chamber they found a very sweet odor coming from the opposite direction. Feeling around and crawling on their hands and knees, they discovered a hole in the floor leading downward. From this hole came up the sweet odor. They hurriedly held a council, and decided to go no further, but return to the camp and report what they had found. On getting to the first chamber one of the young men said: "I am going to take these bracelets to show that we are telling the truth." "No," said the other three, "this being the abode of some Great Spirit, you may have some accident befall you for taking what is not yours." "Ah! You fellows are like old women," said he, taking a fine bracelet and encircling his left wrist with it.

When they reached the village they reported what they had seen. The young man exhibited the bracelet to prove that it was the truth they had told.

Shortly after this, these four young men were out fixing up traps for wolves. They would raise one end of a heavy log and place a stick under, bracing up the log. A large piece of meat was placed about five feet away from the log and this space covered with poles and willows. At the place where the upright stick was put, a hole was left open, large enough to admit the body of a wolf. The wolf, scenting the meat and unable to get at it through the poles and willows, would crowd into the hole and working his body forward, in order to get the meat, would push down the brace and the log thus released would hold the wolf fast under its weight.

The young man with the bracelet was placing his bait under the log when he released the log by knocking down the brace, and the log caught his wrist on which he wore the bracelet. He could not release himself and called loud and long for assistance. His friends, hearing his call, came to his assistance, and on lifting the log found the young man's wrist broken. "Now," said they, "you have been punished for taking the wristlet out of the chamber of the mysterious butte."

Some time after this a young man went to the butte and saw engraved on the wall a woman holding in her hand a pole, with which she was holding up a large amount of beef which had been laid across another pole, which had broken in two from the weight of so much meat.

He returned to the camp and reported what he had seen. All around the figure he saw marks of buffalo hoofs, also marked upon the wall.

The next day an enormous herd of buffalo came near to the village, and a great many were killed. The women were busy cutting up and drying the meat. At one camp was more meat than at any other. The woman was hanging meat upon a long tent pole, when the pole broke in two and she was obliged to hold the meat up with another pole, just as the young man saw on the mysterious butte.

Ever after that the Indians paid weekly visits to this butte, and thereon would read the signs that were to govern their plans.

This butte was always considered the prophet of the tribe.

The Wonderful Turtle

Near to a Chippewa village lay a large lake, and in this lake there lived an enormous turtle. This was no ordinary turtle, as he would often come out of his home in the lake and visit with his Indian neighbors. He paid the most of his visits to the head chief, and on these occasions would stay for hours, smoking and talking with him.

The chief, seeing that the turtle was very smart and showed great wisdom in his talk, took a great fancy to him, and whenever any puzzling subject came up before the chief, he generally sent for Mr. Turtle to help him decide.

One day there came a great misunderstanding between different parties of the tribe, and so excited became both sides that it threatened to cause bloodshed. The chief was unable to decide for either faction, so he said, "I will call Mr. Turtle. He will judge for you."

Sending for the turtle, the chief vacated his seat for the time being, until the turtle should hear both sides, and decide which was in the right. The turtle came, and taking the chief's seat, listened very attentively to both sides, and thought long before he gave his decision. After thinking long and studying each side carefully, he came to the conclusion to decide in favor of both. This would not cause any hard feelings. So he gave them a lengthy speech and showed them where they were both in the right, and wound up by saying:

"You are both in the right in some ways and wrong in others. Therefore, I will say that you both are equally in the right."

When they heard this decision, they saw that the turtle was right, and gave him a long cheer for the wisdom displayed by him. The whole tribe saw that had it not been for this wise decision there would have been a great shedding of blood in the tribe. So they voted him as their judge, and the chief, being so well pleased with him, gave to him his only daughter in marriage.

The daughter of the chief was the most beautiful maiden of the Chippewa nation, and young men from other tribes traveled hundreds of miles for an opportunity to make love to her, and try to win her for a wife. It was all to no purpose. She would accept no one, only him whom her father would select for her. The turtle was very homely, but as he was prudent and wise, the father chose him, and she accepted him.

The young men of the tribe were very jealous, but their jealousy was all to no purpose. She married the turtle. The young men would make sport of the chief's son-in-law. They would say to him: "How did you come to have so flat a stomach?" The turtle answered them, saying:

"My friends, had you been in my place, you too would have flat stomachs. I came by my flat stomach in this way: The Chippewas and Sioux had a great battle, and the Sioux, too numerous for the Chippewas, were killing them off so fast that they had to run for their lives. I was on the Chippewa side and some of the Sioux were pressing five of us, and were gaining on us very fast. Coming to some high grass, I threw myself down flat on my face, and pressed my stomach close to the ground, so the pursuers could not see me. They passed me and killed the four I was with. After they had gone back, I arose and lo! my stomach was as you see it now. So hard had I pressed to the ground that it would not assume its original shape again."

After he had explained the cause of his deformity to them, they said: "The Turtle is brave. We will bother him no more." Shortly after this the Sioux made an attack upon the Chippewas, and every one deserted the village. The Turtle could not travel as fast as the rest and was left behind. It being an unusually hot day in the fall, the Turtle grew very thirsty and sleepy. Finally scenting water, he crawled towards the point from whence the scent came, and coming to a large lake jumped in and had a bath, after which he swam towards the center and dived down, and finding some fine large rocks at the bottom, he crawled in among them and fell asleep. He had his sleep out and arose to the top.

Swimming to shore he found it was summer. He had slept all winter. The birds were singing, and the green grass and leaves gave forth a sweet odor.

He crawled out and started out looking for the Chippewa camp. He came upon the camp several days after he had left his winter quarters, and going around in search of his wife, found her at the extreme edge of the village. She was nursing her baby, and as he asked to see it, she showed it to him. When he saw that it was a lovely baby and did not resemble him in any respect, he got angry and went off to a large lake, where he contented himself with catching flies and insects and living on seaweed the remainder of his life.

The Man And The Oak

There once lived a Sioux couple who had two children, a boy and a girl. Every fall this family would move away from the main camp and take up their winter quarters in a grove of timber some distance from the principal village. The reason they did this was that he was a great hunter and where a village was located for the winter the game was usually very scarce. Therefore, he always camped by himself in order to have an abundance of game adjacent to his camp.

All summer he had roamed around following the tribe to wherever their fancy might take them. During their travels this particular year there came to the village a strange girl who had no relatives there. No one seemed very anxious to take her into their family, so the great hunter's daughter, taking a fancy to the poor girl, took her to their home and kept her. She addressed her as sister, and the parents, on account of their daughter, addressed her as daughter.

This strange girl became desperately in love with the young man of the family, but being addressed as daughter by the parents, she could not openly show her feelings as the young man was considered her brother.

In the fall when the main village moved into a large belt of timber for their winter quarters, the hunter moved on to another place two days' travel from the main winter camp, where he would not be disturbed by any other hunters.

The young man had a tent by himself, and it was always kept nice and clean by his sister, who was very much attached to him. After a long day's hunt in the woods, he would go into his tent and lie down to rest, and when his supper was ready his sister would say, "My brother is so tired. I will carry his supper to him."

Her friend, whom she addressed as sister, would never go into the young man's tent. Along towards spring there came one night into the young man's tent a woman. She sat down by the door and kept her face covered so that it was hidden from view. She sat there a long time and finally arose and went away. The young man could not imagine who this could be. He knew that it was a long distance from the village and could not make out where the woman could have come from. The next night the woman came again and this time she came a little nearer to where the young man lay. She sat down and kept her face covered as before. Neither spoke a word. She sat there for a long time and then arose and departed. He was very much puzzled over the actions of this woman and decided to ascertain on her next visit who she was.

He kindled a small fire in his tent and had some ash wood laid on it so as to keep fire a long time, as ash burns very slowly and holds fire a long time.

The third night the woman came again and sat down still nearer his bed. She held her blanket open just a trifle, and he, catching up one of the embers, flashed it in her face; jumping up she ran hurriedly out of the tent. The next morning he noticed that his adopted sister kept her face hidden with her blanket. She chanced to drop her blanket while in the act of pouring out some soup, and when she did so he noticed a large burned spot on her cheek.

He felt so sorry for what he had done that he could eat no breakfast, but went outside and lay down under an oak tree. All day long he lay there gazing up into the tree, and when he was called for supper he refused, saying that he was not hungry, and for them not to bother him, as he would soon get up and go to bed. Far into the night he lay thus, and when he tried to arise he could not, as a small oak tree grew through the center of his body and held him fast to the ground.

In the morning when the family awoke they found the girl had disappeared, and on going outside the sister discovered her brother held fast to the earth by an oak tree which grew very rapidly. In vain were the best medicine men of the tribe sent for. Their medicine was of no avail. They said: "If the tree is cut down the young man will die."

The sister was wild with grief, and extending her hands to the sun, she cried: "Great Spirit, relieve my suffering brother. Any one who releases him I will marry, be he young, old, homely or deformed."

Several days after the young man had met with the mishap, there came to the tent a very tall man, who had a bright light encircling his body. "Where is the girl who promised to marry any one who would release her brother?" "I am the one," said the young man's sister. "I am the all-powerful lightning and thunder. I see all things and can kill at one stroke a whole tribe. When I make my voice heard the rocks shake loose and go rattling down the hillsides. The brave warriors cower shivering under some shelter at the sound of my voice. The girl whom you had adopted as your sister was a sorceress. She bewitched your brother because he would not let her make love to him. On my way here I met her traveling towards the west, and knowing what she had done, I struck her with one of my blazing swords, and she lies there now a heap of ashes. I will now release your brother."

So saying he placed his hand on the tree and instantly it crumbled to ashes. The young man arose, and thanked his deliverer.

Then they saw a great black cloud approaching, and the man said: "Make ready, we shall go home on that cloud." As the cloud approached near to the man who stood with his bride, it suddenly lowered and enveloped them and with a great roar and amidst flashes of lightning and loud peals of thunder the girl ascended and disappeared into the west with her Thunder and Lightning husband.

Story Of The Two Young Friends

There were once in a very large Indian camp two little boys who were fast friends. One of the boys, "*Chaske*" (meaning first born), was the son of a very rich family, and was always dressed in the finest of clothes of Indian costume. The other boy, "*Hake*" (meaning last born), was an orphan and lived with his old grandmother, who was very destitute, and consequently could not dress the boy in fine raiment. So poorly was the boy dressed that the boys who had good clothes always tormented him and would not play in his company.

Chaske did not look at the clothes of any boy whom he chose as a friend, but mingled with all boys regardless of how they were clad, and would study their dispositions. The well dressed he found were vain and conceited. The fairly well dressed he found selfish and spiteful. The poorly clad he found to be generous and truthful, and from all of them he chose Hake for his "*Koda*" (friend). As Chaske was the son of the leading war chief he was very much sought after by the rest of the boys, each one trying to gain the honor of being chosen for the friend and companion of the great chief's son; but, as I have before said, Chaske carefully studied them all and finally chose the orphan Hake.

It was a lucky day for Hake when he was chosen for the friend and companion of Chaske. The orphan boy was taken to the lodge of his friend's parents and dressed up in fine clothes and moccasins. (When the Indians' sons claim any one as their friend, the friend thus chosen is adopted into the family as their own son).

Chaske and Hake were inseparable. Where one was seen the other was not far distant. They played, hunted, trapped, ate and slept together. They would spend most of the long summer days hunting in the forests.

Time went on and these two fast friends grew up to be fine specimens of their tribe. When they became the age to select a sweetheart they would go together and make love to a girl, each helping the other to win the affection of the one of his choice. Chaske loved a girl who was the daughter of an old medicine man. She was very much courted by the other young men of the tribe, and many a horse loaded with robes and fine porcupine work was tied at the medicine man's *tepee* in offering for the hand of his daughter, but the horses, laden as when tied there, were turned loose, signifying that the offer was not accepted.

The girl's choice was Chaske's friend Hake. Although he had never made love to her for himself, he had always used honeyed words to her and was always loud in his praises for his friend Chaske. One night the two friends had been to see the girl, and on their return Chaske was very quiet, having nothing to say and seemingly in deep study. Always of a bright, jolly and amiable disposition, his silence and moody spell grieved his friend very much, and he finally spoke to Chaske, saying: "*Koda*, what has come over you? You who were always so jolly and full of fun? Your silence makes me grieve for you and I do not know what you are feeling so downhearted about. Has the girl said anything to you to make you feel thus?"

"Wait, friend," said Chaske, "until morning, and then I will know how to answer your inquiry. Don't ask me anything more tonight, as my heart is having a great battle with my brain."

Hake bothered his friend no more that night, but he could not sleep. He kept wondering what "Pretty Feather" (the girl whom his friend loved) could have said to Chaske to bring such a change over him. Hake never suspected that he himself was the cause of his friend's sorrow, for never did he have a thought that it was himself that Pretty Feather loved.

The next morning after they had eaten breakfast, Chaske proposed that they should go out on the prairies, and see if they would have the good luck to kill an antelope. Hake went out and got the band of horses, of which there were over a hundred. They selected the fleetest two in the herd, and taking their bows and arrows, mounted and rode away towards the south.

Hake was overjoyed to note the change in his friend. His oldtime jollity had returned. They rode out about five miles, and scaring up a drove of antelope they started in hot pursuit, and as their horses were very fleet of foot soon caught up to the drove, and each singling out his choice quickly dispatched him with an arrow. They could easily have killed more of the antelope, but did not want to kill them just for sport, but for food, and knowing that they had now all that their horses could pack home, they dismounted and proceeded to dress their kill.

After each had finished packing the kill on his horse, Chaske said: "Let us sit down and have a smoke before we start back. Besides, I have something to tell you which I can tell better sitting still than I can riding along." Hake came and sat down opposite his friend, and while they smoked Chaske said:

"My friend, we have been together for the last twenty years and I have yet the first time to deceive you in any way, and I know I can truthfully say the same of you. Never have I known you to deceive me nor tell me an untruth. I have no brothers or sisters. The only brother's love I know is yours. The only sister's love I will know will be Pretty Feather's, for brother, last night she told me she loved none but you and would marry you and you only. So, brother, I am going to take my antelope to my sister-in-law's tent and deposit it at her door. Then she will know that her wish will be fulfilled. I thought at first that you had been playing traitor to me and had been making love to her for yourself, but when she explained it all to me and begged me to intercede for her to you, I then knew that I had judged you wrongfully, and that, together with my lost love, made me so quiet and sorrowful last night. So now, brother, take the flower of the nation for your wife, and I will be content to continue through life a lonely bachelor, as never again can I give any woman the place which Pretty Feather had in my heart."

Their pipes being smoked out they mounted their ponies and Chaske started up in a clear, deep voice the beautiful love song of Pretty Feather and his friend Hake.

Such is the love between two friends, who claim to be as brothers among the Indians. Chaske gave up his love of a beautiful woman for a man who was in fact no relation to him.

Hake said, "I will do as you say, my friend, but before I can marry the medicine man's daughter, I will have to go on the warpath and do some brave deed, and will start in ten days." They rode towards home, planning which direction they would travel, and as it was to be their first experience on the warpath, they would seek advice from the old warriors of the tribe.

On their arrival at the village Hake took his kill to their own tent, while Chaske took his to the tent of the Medicine Man, and deposited it at the door and rode off towards home.

The mother of Pretty Feather did not know whether to take the offering or not, but Pretty Feather, seeing by this offering that her most cherished wish was to be granted, told her mother to take the meat and cook it and invite the old women of the camp to a feast in honor of the son-in-law who was soon to keep them furnished with plenty of meat. Hake and his friend sought out all of the old warriors and gained all the information they desired. Every evening Hake visited his intended wife and many happy evenings they spent together.

The morning of the tenth day the two friends left the village and turned their faces toward the west where the camps of the enemy are more numerous than in any other direction. They were not mounted and therefore traveled slowly, so it took about ten days of walking before they saw any signs of the enemy. The old warriors had told them of a thickly wooded creek within the enemies' bounds. The old men said, "That creek looks the ideal place to camp, but don't camp there by any means, because there is a ghost who haunts that creek, and any one who camps there is disturbed all through the night, and besides they never return, because the ghost is *Wakan* (holy), and the enemies conquer the travelers every time." The friends had extra moccasins with them and one extra blanket, as it was late in the fall and the nights were very cold.

They broke camp early one morning and walked all day. Along towards evening, the clouds which had been threatening all day, hurriedly opened their doors and down came the snowflakes thick and fast. Just before it started snowing the friends had noticed a dark line about two miles in advance of them. Chaske spoke to his friend and said: "If this storm continues we will be obliged to stay overnight at Ghost Creek, as I noticed it not far ahead of us, just before the storm set in."

"I noticed it also," said Hake. "We might as well entertain a ghost all night as to lie out on these open prairies and freeze to death." So they decided to run the risk and stay in the sheltering woods of Ghost Creek.

When they got to the creek it seemed as if they had stepped inside a big *tepee*, so thick was the brush and timber that the wind could not be felt at all. They hunted and found a place where the brush was very thick and the grass very tall. They quickly pulled the tops of the nearest willows together and by intertwining the ends made them fast, and throwing their tent robe over this, soon had a cozy *tepee* in which to sleep. They started their fire and cooked some dried buffalo meat and buffalo tallow, and were just about to eat their supper when a figure of a man came slowly in through the door and sat down near where he had entered. Hake, being the one who was doing the cooking, poured out some tea into his own cup, and putting a piece of pounded meat and marrow into a small plate, placed it before the stranger, saying: "Eat, my friend, we are on the warpath and do not carry much of a variety of food with us, but I give you the best we have."

The stranger drew the plate towards him, and commenced eating ravenously. He soon finished his meal and handed the dish and cup back. He had not uttered a word so far. Chaske filled the pipe and handed it to him. He smoked for a few minutes, took one last draw from the pipe and handed it back to Chaske, and then he said: "Now, my friends, I am not a living man, but the wandering spirit of a once great warrior, who was killed in these woods by the enemy whom you two brave young men are now seeking to make war upon. For years I have been roaming these woods in hopes that I might find someone brave enough to stop and listen to me, but all who have camped here in the past have run away at my approach or fired guns or shot arrows at me. For such cowards as these I have always found a grave. They never returned to their homes. Now I have found two brave men whom I can tell what I want done, and if you accomplish what I tell you to do, you will return home with many horses and some scalps dangling from your belts. Just over this range of hills north of us, a large village is encamped for the winter. In that camp is the man who laid in ambush and shot me, killing me before I could get a chance to defend myself. I want that man's scalp, because he has been the cause of my wanderings for a great many years. Had he killed me on the battlefield my spirit would have at once joined my brothers in the happy hunting grounds, but being killed by a coward, my spirit is doomed to roam until I can find some brave man who will kill this coward and bring me his scalp. This is why I have tried every party who have camped here to listen to me, but as I have said before, they were all cowards. Now, I ask you two brave young men, will you do this for me?"

"We will," said the friends in one voice. "Thank you, my boys. Now, I know why you came here, and that one of you came to earn his feathers by killing an enemy, before he would marry; the girl he is to marry is my granddaughter, as I am the father of the great Medicine Man. In the morning there will pass by in plain sight of here a large party. They will chase the buffalo over on that flat. After they have passed an old man leading a black horse and riding a white one will come by on the trail left by the hunting party. He will be driving about a hundred horses, which he will leave over in the next ravine. He will then proceed to the hunting grounds and get meat from the different hunters. After the hunters have all gone home he will come last, singing the praises of the ones who gave him the meat. This man you must kill and scalp, as he is the one I want killed. Then take the white and black horse and each mount and go to the hunting grounds. There you will see two of the enemy riding about picking up empty shells. Kill and scalp these two and each take a scalp and come over to the high knoll and I will show you where the horses are, and as soon as you hand me the old man's scalp I will disappear and you will see me no more. As soon as I disappear, it will start in snowing. Don't be afraid as the snow will cover your trail, but nevertheless, don't stop traveling for three days and nights, as these people will suspect that some of your tribe have done this, and they will follow you until you cross your own boundary lines."

When morning came, the two friends sat in the thick brush and watched a large party pass by their hiding place. So near were they that the friends could hear them laughing and talking. After the hunting party had passed, as the spirit had told them, along came the old man, driving a large band of horses and leading a fine looking coal black horse. The horse the old man was riding was as white as snow. The friends crawled to a little brush covered hill and watched the chase after the shooting had ceased. The friends knew it would not be long before the return of the party, so they crawled back to their camp and hurriedly ate some pounded meat and drank some cherry tea. Then they took down their robe and rolled it up and got everything in readiness for a hurried flight with the horses. Scarcely had they got everything in readiness when the party came by, singing their song of the chase. When they had all gone the friends crawled down to the trail and lay waiting for the old man. Soon they heard him singing. Nearer and nearer came the sounds of the song until at last at a bend in the road, the old man came into view. The two friends arose and advanced to meet him. On he came still singing. No doubt he mistook them for some of his own people. When he was very close to them they each stepped to either side of him and before he could make an outcry they pierced his cowardly old heart with two arrows. He had hardly touched the ground when they both struck him with their bows, winning first and second honors by striking an enemy after he has fallen. Chaske having won first honors, asked his friend to perform the scalping deed, which he did. And wanting to be sure that the spirit would get full revenge, took the whole scalp, ears and all, and tied it to his belt. The buffalo beef which the old man had packed upon the black horse, they threw on the top of the old man. Quickly mounting the two horses, they hastened out across the long flat towards the hunting grounds. When they came in sight of the grounds there they saw two men riding about from place to place. Chaske took after the one on the right, Hake the one on the left. When the two men saw these two strange men riding like the wind towards them, they turned their horses to retreat towards the hills, but the white and the black were the swiftest of the tribe's horses, and quickly overtook the two fleeing men. When they came close to the enemy they strung their arrows onto the bowstring and drove them through the two fleeing hunters. As they were falling they tried to shoot, but being greatly exhausted, their bullets whistled harmlessly over the heads of the two friends. They scalped the two enemies and took their guns and ammunition, also secured the two horses and started for the high knoll. When they arrived at the place, there stood the spirit. Hake presented him with the old man's scalp and then the spirit showed them the large band of horses, and saying, "Ride hard and long," disappeared and was seen no more by any war parties, as he was thus enabled to join his forefathers in the happy hunting grounds.

The friends did as the spirit had told them. For three days and three nights they rode steadily. On the fourth morning they came into their own boundary. From there on they rode more slowly, and let the band of horses rest and crop the tops of long grass. They would stop occasionally, and while one slept the other kept watch. Thus they got fairly well rested before they came in sight of where their camp had stood when they had left. All that they could see of the once large village was the lone tent of the great Medicine Man. They rode up on to a high hill and farther on towards the east they saw smoke from a great many *tepees*. They then knew that something had happened and that the village had moved away.

"My friend," said Chaske, "I am afraid something has happened to the Medicine Man's lodge, and rather than have you go there, I will go alone and you follow the trail of our party and go on ahead with the horses. I will take the black and the white horses with me and I will follow on later, after I have seen what the trouble is."

"Very well, my friend, I will do as you say, but I am afraid something has happened to Pretty Feather." Hake started on with the horses, driving them along the broad trail left by the hundreds of travois. Chaske made slowly towards the *tepee*, and stopping outside, stood and listened. Not a sound could he hear. The only living thing he saw was Pretty Feather's spotted horse tied to the side of the tent. Then he knew that she must be dead. He rode off into the thick brush and tied his two horses securely. Then he came back and entered the *tepee*. There on a bed of robes lay someone apparently dead. The body was wrapped in blankets and robes and bound around and around with *parfleche* ropes. These he carefully untied and unwound. Then he unwrapped the robes and blankets and when he uncovered the face, he saw, as he had expected to, the face of his lost love, Pretty Feather. As he sat gazing on her beautiful young face, his heart ached for his poor friend. He himself had loved and lost this beautiful maiden, and now his friend who had won her would have to suffer the untold grief which he had suffered.

What was that? Could it have been a slight quivering of the nostrils that he had seen, or was it mad fancy playing a trick on him? Closer he drew to her face, watching intently for another sign. There it was again, only this time it was a long, deep drawn breath. He arose, got some water and taking a small stick slowly forced open her mouth and poured some into it. Then he took some sage, dipped it into the water and sprinkled a little on her head and face. There were many *parfleche* bags piled around the *tepee*, and thinking he might find some kind of medicine roots which he could use to revive her he started opening them one after the other. He had opened three and was just opening the fourth, when a voice behind him asked: "What are you looking for?" Turning quickly, he saw Pretty Feather looking at him. Overjoyed, he cried, "What can I do so that you can get up and ride to the village with me? My friend and I just returned with a large band of horses and two scalps. We saw this tent and recognized it. My friend wanted to come, but I would not let him, as I feared if he found anything had happened to you he would do harm to himself, but now he will be anxious for my return, so if you will tell me what you need in order to revive you, I will get it, and we can then go to my friend in the village."

"At the foot of my bed you will find a piece of eagle fat. Build a fire and melt it for me. I will drink it and then we can go."

Chaske quickly started a fire, got out the piece of fat and melted it. She drank it at one draught, and was about to arise when she suddenly said: "Roll me up quick and take the buffalo hair rope and tie it about my spotted horse's neck; tie his tail in a knot and tie him to the door. Then run and hide behind the trees. There are two of the enemy coming this way."

Chaske hurriedly obeyed her orders, and had barely concealed himself behind the trees, when there came into view two of the enemy. They saw the horse tied to the door of the deserted tent, and knew that some dead person occupied the *tepee,* so through respect for the dead, they turned out and started to go through the brush and trees, so as not to pass the door. (The Indians consider it a bad omen to pass by the door of a *tepee* occupied by a dead body, that is, while in the enemy's country). So by making this detour they traveled directly towards where Chaske was concealed behind the tree. Knowing that he would be discovered, and there being two of them, he knew the only chance he had was for him to kill one of them before they discovered him, then he stood a better chance at an even combat. On they came, little thinking that one of them would in a few minutes be with his forefathers.

Chaske noiselessly slipped a cartridge into the chamber of his gun, threw it into action and took deliberate aim at the smaller one's breast. A loud report rang out and the one he had aimed at threw up his arms and fell heavily forward, shot through the heart.

Reloading quickly Chaske stepped out from behind the tree. He could easily have killed the other from his concealed position, but, being a brave young man, he wanted to give his opponent a fair chance. The other had unslung his gun and a duel was then fought between the two lone combatants. They would spring from side to side like two great cats. Then advance one or two steps and fire. Retreat a few steps, spring to one side and fire again. The bullets whistled past their heads, tore up the earth beneath their feet, and occasionally one would hit its mark, only to cause a flesh wound.

Suddenly the enemy aimed his gun and threw it upon the ground. His ammunition was exhausted, and slowly folding his arms he stood facing his opponent, with a fearless smile upon his face, expecting the next moment to fall dead from a bullet from the rifle of Chaske. Not so. Chaske was too honorable and noble to kill an unarmed man, and especially one who had put up such a brave fight as had this man. Chaske advanced and picked up the empty gun. The *Toka* (enemy) drew from a scabbard at his belt a long bowie knife, and taking it by the point handed it, handle first, to Chaske. This signified surrender. Chaske scalped the dead *Toka* and motioned for his prisoner to follow him. In the meantime Pretty Feather had gotten up and stood looking at the duel. When she heard the first shot she jumped up and cut a small slit in the tent from which she saw the whole proceedings.

Knowing that one or both of them must be wounded, she hurriedly got water and medicine roots, and when they came to the tent she was prepared to dress their wounds.

Chaske had a bullet through his shoulder and one through his hand. They were very painful but not dangerous. The prisoner had a bullet through his leg, also one through the muscle of his left arm. Pretty Feather washed and dressed their wounds, and Chaske went and brought the black and white horses and mounting Pretty Feather upon the white horse, and the prisoner on her spotted one, the three soon rode into the village, and there was a great cry of joy when it was known that Pretty Feather had come back to them again.

Hake, who was in his tent grieving, was told that his friend had returned and with him Pretty Feather. Hearing this good news he at once went to the Medicine Man's tent and found the Medicine Man busily dressing the wounds of his friend and a stranger. The old Medicine Man turned to Hake and said:

"Son-in-law, take your wife home with you. It was from grief at your absence that she went into a trance, and we, thinking she was dead, left her for such. Hadn't it been for your friend here, she would surely have been a corpse now. So take her and keep her with you always, and take as a present from me fifty of my best horses."

Hake and his beautiful bride went home, where his adopted mother had a fine large tent put up for them. Presents of cooking utensils, horses, robes and finely worked shawls and moccasins came from every direction, and last of all Chaske gave as a present to his friend the *Toka* man whom he had taken as prisoner. On presenting him with this gift, Chaske spoke thus:

"My friend, I present to you, that you may have him as a servant to look after your large band of horses, this man with whom I fought a two hours' duel, and had his ammunition lasted he would probably have conquered me, and who gave me the second hardest fight of my life.

The hardest fight of my life was when I gave up Pretty Feather. You have them both. To the *Toka* (enemy) be kind, and he will do all your biddings. To Pretty Feather be a good husband."

So saying, Chaske left them, and true to his word, lived the remainder of his days a confirmed bachelor.

The Story Of The Pet Crow

Once upon a time there came to a large village a plague of crows. So thick were they that the poor women were sorely tried keeping them out of their *tepees* and driving them away from their lines of jerked buffalo meat. Indeed they got so numerous and were such a great nuisance that the Chief finally gave orders to his camp criers or heralds to go out among the different camps and announce the orders of their Chief, that war should be made upon the crows to extermination; that their nests were to be destroyed and all eggs broken. The war of extermination was to continue until not a crow remained, except the youngest found was to be brought to him alive.

For a week the war on the crows continued. Thousands of dead crows were brought in daily, and at the end of the week not a bird of that species could be seen in the neighborhood. Those that escaped the deadly arrow of the warriors, flew away, never to return to those parts again.

At the end of the war made upon the crows, there was brought to the Chief's *tepee* the youngest found. Indeed, so young was the bird that it was only the great medicine of the Chief that kept him alive until he could hop about and find his own food. The Chief spent most of his time in his lodge teaching the young crow to understand and talk the language of the tribe. After the crow had mastered this, the Chief then taught him the languages of the neighboring tribes. When the crow had mastered these different languages the chief would send him on long journeys to ascertain the location of the camps of the different enemies.

When the crow would find a large Indian camp he would alight and hop about, pretending to be picking up scraps, but really keeping his ears open for anything he might hear. He would hang around all day, and at night when they would all gather in the large council tent (which always stood in the center of the village) to determine upon their next raid, and plan for a horse stealing trip, Mr. Crow was always nearby to hear all their plans discussed. He would then fly away to his master (the Chief) and tell him all that he had learned.

The Chief would then send a band of his warriors to lie in ambush for the raiding party, and, as the enemy would not suspect anything they would go blindly into the pitfall of death thus set for them. Thus the crow was the scout of this chief, whose reputation as a *Wakan* (Holy man) soon reached all of the different tribes. The Chief's warriors would intercept, ambush and annihilate every war party headed for his camp.

So, finally learning that they could not make war on this chief's people unbeknown to them, they gave up making war on this particular band. When meat was running low in the camp this chief would send the crow out to look for buffalo. When he discovered a herd he would return and report to his master; then the chief would order out the hunters and they would return laden with meat. Thus the crow kept the camp all the time informed of everything that would be of benefit to them.

One day the crow disappeared, over which there was great grief among the tribe. A week had passed away, when Mr. Crow reappeared. There was great rejoicing upon his return, but the crow was downcast and would not speak, but sat with a drooping head perched at the top of the chief's *tepee*, and refused all food that was offered to him.

In vain did the chief try to get the crow to tell him the cause of his silence and seeming grief. The crow would not speak until the chief said: "Well, I will take a few of my warriors and go out and try to ascertain what has happened to cause you to act as you do."

Upon hearing this, the crow said: "Don't go. I dreaded to tell you what I know to be a fact, as I have heard it from some great medicine men. I was traveling over the mountains west of here, when I spied three old men sitting at the top of the highest peak. I very cautiously dropped down behind a rock and listened to their talk. I heard your name mentioned by one of them, then your brother's name was mentioned. Then the third, who was the oldest, said: 'in three days from today the lightning will kill those two brothers whom all the nations fear.'"

Upon hearing what the crow stated the tribe became grief stricken. On the morning of the third day the chief ordered a nice *tepee* placed upon the highest point, far enough away from the village, so that the peals of thunder would not alarm the babies of the camp.

A great feast was given, and after the feasting was over there came in six young maidens leading the war horses of the two brothers. The horses were painted and decorated as if for a charge on the enemy. One maiden walked ahead of the chief's horse bearing in her hands the bow and arrows of the great warrior. Next came two maidens, one on either side of the prancing war steed, each holding a rein. Behind the chief's horse came the fourth maiden. Like the first, she bore in her hands the bow and arrows of the chief's brother. Then the fifth and sixth maidens each holding a rein, walked on either side of the prancing horse of the chief's brother. They advanced and circled the large gathering and finally stopped directly in front of the two brothers, who immediately arose and taking their bows and arrows vaulted lightly upon their war steeds, and singing their death song, galloped off amid a great cry of grief from the people who loved them most dearly.

Heading straight for the *tepee* that had been placed upon the highest point, adjacent to the village, they soon arrived at their destination and, dismounting from their horses, turned, waved their hands to their band, and disappeared within the *tepee*. Scarcely had they entered the lodge when the rumblings of distant thunder could be heard. Nearer, and nearer, came the sound, until at last the storm overspread the locality in all its fury. Flash upon flash of lightning burst forth from the heavens. Deafening peals of thunder followed each flash. Finally, one flash brighter than any of the others, one peal more deafening than those preceding it, and the storm had passed.

Sadly the warriors gathered together, mounted their horses and slowly rode to the *tepee* on the high point. Arriving there they looked inside the lodge and saw the two brothers lying cold and still in death, each holding the lariat of his favorite war horse. The horses also lay dead side by side in front of the tent. (From this came the custom of killing the favorite horse of a dead warrior at the burial of the owner).

As the Indians sadly left the hill to return home, they heard a noise at the top of the *tepee*, and looking up they saw the crow sitting on one of the splintered *tepee* poles. He was crying most pitifully, and as they rode off he flew up high in the air and his pitiful "caw" became fainter and fainter till at last they heard it no more. And from that day, the story goes, no crow ever goes near the village of that band of Indians.

The "*Wasna*" (Pemmican) Man And The Unktomi (Spider)

Once upon a time there appeared from out of a large belt of timber a man attired in the fat of the buffalo. On his head he wore the honeycomb part of the stomach. To this was attached small pieces of fat. The fat which covered the stomach he wore as a cloak. The large intestines he wore as leggings, and the kidney fat as his moccasins.

As he appeared he had the misfortune to meet "*Unktomi*" (spider) with his hundreds of starving children. Upon seeing the fat, Unktomi and his large family at once attacked the man, who, in order to save his life, started to run away, but so closely did Unktomi and his family pursue him that in order to make better time and also get a little better start, he threw off his head covering, which the Unktomi family hastily devoured, and were again closing in upon him. He then threw off his cloak and they devoured that, and were close upon him again, when he threw off his leggings. These were hastily eaten up, and, as they drew near to a lake, the man threw off the kidney fat, and, running to the edge of the lake, dived down into the water and kept beneath the surface, swimming to the opposite shore. After the Unktomi family had eaten the kidney fat they came to the water's edge, and the grease was floating on the surface of the water which they lapped up, until there was not a grease spot left floating on the surface.

The small morsels had only sharpened their appetites, and as they saw the man sitting on the opposite shore, Unktomi and his family proceeded around the lake and came upon two men sitting on the shore. Unktomi saw that the other man was "*Wakupupi*" (pounded beef). The family surrounded the two and Unktomi ordered them to fight. Fearing Unktomi and his large family, they at once commenced to fight and Pounded Meat was soon killed. The hungry family at once fell to eating him. So busy were they that none noticed the fat man sneak off and disappear.

When they had finished the pounded beef man they looked around to fall upon the fat man, but nowhere could he be seen. Unktomi said, "I will track him and when I find him, I will return for you, so stay here and await my return."

He followed the fat man's tracks until farther east on the shore of the lake he found the fat man in the act of skinning a deer, which he had killed. (He had held on to his bow and arrows when he jumped into the lake). "My," said Unktomi, "this will make a fine meal for my hungry children. I will go after them, so hurry and cut the meat up into small pieces so they each can have a piece."

"All right, go ahead and get your family," said Fat Man. During Unktomi's absence, the fat man hurriedly cut the meat up into small pieces and carried them up into a tree that stood near to the shore. When he had carried it all up he threw sand and dirt upon the blood, and so left no trace of the deer.

On the arrival of Unktomi and his family, no signs of the fat man or the deer could be found. They wandered about the spot looking for tracks which might lead them to where the fat man had cached the meat, as Unktomi said he could not have carried it very far. Now the fat man was up in the tree and sat watching them. The reflection of the tree was in the water, and some of the children going close to the shore, discovered it as they looked at the reflection. The fat man cut a piece of meat and extending it towards them, drew back his hand and put the meat into his mouth.

"Come quick, father, here he is eating the meat," said the children. Unktomi came and seeing the reflection, thought the fat man was down in the lake. "Wait, I will bring him up for you." So saying, he dived down, but soon arose without anything. Again and again he tried, but could not reach the bottom. He told the children to gather rock for him. These he tied around his neck and body, and dived down for the last time. The last the children saw of their father was the bubbles which arose to the surface of the lake. The rocks being too heavy for him, held him fast to the bottom, and some hungry fish soon made a feast out of the body of poor "*Unktomi.*"

The Resuscitation Of The Only Daughter

There once lived an old couple who had an only daughter. She was a beautiful girl, and was very much courted by the young men of the tribe, but she said that she preferred single life, and to all their heart-touching tales of deep affection for her she always had one answer. That was "No."

One day this maiden fell ill and day after day grew worse. All the best medicine men were called in, but their medicines were of no avail, and in two weeks from the day that she was taken ill she lay a corpse. Of course there was great mourning in the camp. They took her body several miles from camp and rolled it in fine robes and blankets, then they laid her on a scaffold which they had erected. (This was the custom of burial among the Indians). They placed four forked posts into the ground and then lashed strong poles lengthwise and across the ends and made a bed of willows and stout ash brush. This scaffold was from five to seven feet from the ground. After the funeral the parents gave away all of their horses, fine robes and blankets and all of the belongings of the dead girl. Then they cut their hair off close to their heads, and attired themselves in the poorest apparel they could secure.

When a year had passed the friends and relatives of the old couple tried in vain to have them set aside their mourning. "You have mourned long enough," they would say. "Put aside your mourning and try and enjoy a few more pleasures of this life while you live. You are both growing old and can't live very many more years, so make the best of your time." The old couple would listen to their advice and then shake their heads and answer: "We have nothing to live for. Nothing we could join in would be any amusement to us, since we have lost the light of our lives."

So the old couple continued their mourning for their lost idol. Two years had passed since the death of the beautiful girl, when one evening a hunter and his wife passed by the scaffold which held the dead girl. They were on their return trip and were heavily loaded down with game, and therefore could not travel very fast. About half a mile from the scaffold a clear spring burst forth from the side of a bank, and from this trickled a small stream of water, moistening the roots of the vegetation bordering its banks, and causing a growth of sweet green grass. At this spring the hunter camped and tethering his horses, at once set about helping his wife to erect the small *tepee* which they carried for convenience in traveling.

When it became quite dark, the hunter's dogs set up a great barking and growling. "Look out and see what the dogs are barking at," said the hunter to his wife. She looked out through the door and then drew back saying: "There is the figure of a woman advancing from the direction of the girl's scaffold."

"I expect it is the dead girl; let her come, and don't act as if you were afraid," said the hunter. Soon they heard footsteps advancing and the steps ceased at the door. Looking down at the lower part of the door the hunter noticed a pair of small moccasins, and knowing that it was the visitor, said: "Whoever you are, come in and have something to eat."

At this invitation the figure came slowly in and sat down by the door with head covered and with a fine robe drawn tightly over the face. The woman dished up a fine supper and placing it before the visitor, said: "Eat, my friend, you must be hungry." The figure never moved, nor would it uncover to eat. "Let us turn our back towards the door and our visitor may eat the food," said the hunter. So his wife turned her back towards the visitor and made herself very busy cleaning the small pieces of meat that were hanging to the back sinews of the deer which had been killed. (This the Indians use as thread.) The hunter, filling his pipe, turned away and smoked in silence. Finally the dish was pushed back to the woman, who took it and after washing it, put it away. The figure still sat at the door, not a sound coming from it, neither was it breathing. The hunter at last said: "Are you the girl that was placed upon that scaffold two years ago?" It bowed its head two or three times in assent.

"Are you going to sleep here tonight; if you are, my wife will make down a bed for you." The figure shook its head.

"Are you going to come again tomorrow night to us?" It nodded assent.

For three nights in succession the figure visited the hunter's camp. The third night the hunter noticed that the figure was breathing. He saw one of the hands protruding from the robe. The skin was perfectly black and was stuck fast to the bones of the hand. On seeing this the hunter arose and going over to his medicine sack which hung on a pole, took down the sack and, opening it, took out some roots and mixing them with skunk oil and vermillion, said to the figure:

"If you will let us rub your face and hands with this medicine it will put new life into the skin and you will assume your complexion again and it will put flesh on you." The figure assented and the hunter rubbed the medicine on her hands and face. Then she arose and walked back to the scaffold. The next day the hunter moved camp towards the home village. That night he camped within a few miles of the village. When night came, the dogs, as usual, set up a great barking, and looking out, the wife saw the girl approaching.

When the girl had entered and sat down, the hunter noticed that the girl did not keep her robe so closely together over her face. When the wife gave her something to eat, the girl reached out and took the dish, thus exposing her hands, which they at once noticed were again natural. After she had finished her meal, the hunter said: "Did my medicine help you?" She nodded assent. "Do you want my medicine rubbed all over your body?" Again she nodded. "I will mix enough to rub your entire body, and I will go outside and let my wife rub it on for you." He mixed a good supply and going out left his wife to rub the girl. When his wife had completed the task she called to her husband to come in, and when he came in he sat down and said to the girl: "Tomorrow we will reach the village. Do you want to go with us?" She shook her head. "Will you come again to our camp tomorrow night after we have camped in the village?" She nodded her head in assent. "Then do you want to see your parents?" She nodded again, and arose and disappeared into the darkness.

Early the next morning the hunter broke camp and traveled far into the afternoon, when he arrived at the village. He instructed his wife to go at once and inform the old couple of what had happened. The wife did so and at sunset the old couple came to the hunter's *tepee*. They were invited to enter and a fine supper was served them. Soon after they had finished their supper the dogs of the camp set up a great barking. "Now she is coming, so be brave and you will soon see your lost daughter," said the hunter. Hardly had he finished speaking when she entered the tent as natural as ever she was in life. Her parents clung to her and smothered her with kisses.

They wanted her to return home with them, but she would stay with the hunter who had brought her back to life, and she married him, becoming his second wife. A short time after taking the girl for his wife, the hunter joined a war party and never returned, as he was killed on the battlefield.

A year after her husband's death she married again. This husband was also killed by a band of enemies whom the warriors were pursuing for stealing some of their horses. The third husband also met a similar fate to the first. He was killed on the field of battle.

She was still a handsome woman at the time of the third husband's death, but never again married, as the men feared her, saying she was holy, and that any one who married her would be sure to be killed by the enemy.

So she took to doctoring the sick and gained the reputation of being the most skilled doctor in the nation. She lived to a ripe old age and when she felt death approaching she had them take her to where she had rested once before, and crawling to the top of the newly erected scaffold, wrapped her blankets and robes about her, covered her face carefully, and fell into that sleep from which there is no more awakening.

The Story Of The Pet Crane

There was once upon a time a man who did not care to live with his tribe in a crowded village, but preferred a secluded spot in the deep forest, there to live with his wife and family of five children. The oldest of the children (a boy) was twelve years of age, and being the son of a distinguished hunter, soon took to roaming through the forest in search of small game.

One day during his ramblings, he discovered a crane's nest, with only one young crane occupying it. No doubt some fox or traveling weasel had eaten the rest of the crane's brothers and sisters. The boy said to himself, "I will take this poor little crane home and will raise him as a pet for our baby. If I leave him here some hungry fox will be sure to eat the poor little fellow." He carried the young crane home and it grew to be nearly as tall as the boy's five-year-old sister.

Being brought up in a human circle, it soon grew to understand all the family said. Although it could not speak it took part in all the games played by the children. The father of the family was, as I have before mentioned, a great hunter. He always had a plentiful supply of deer, antelope, buffalo and beaver meats on hand, but there came a change. The game migrated to some other locality, where no deadly shot like *"Kutesan"* (Never Miss) would be around to annihilate their fast decreasing droves. The hunter started out early one morning in hopes of discovering some of the game which had disappeared as suddenly as though the earth had swallowed them. The hunter traveled the whole day, all to no purpose. It was late in the evening when he staggered into camp. He was nearly dead with fatigue. Hastily swallowing a cup of cherry bark tea (the only article of food they had in store), he at once retired and was soon in the sweet land of dreams. The children soon joined their father and the poor woman sat thinking how they could save their dear children from starvation. Suddenly out upon the night air rang the cry of a crane. Instantly the pet crane awoke, stepped outside and answered the call. The crane which had given the cry was the father of the pet crane, and learning from Mr. Fox of the starving condition of his son and his friends, he flew to the hunting grounds of the tribe, and as there had been a good kill that day, the crane found no trouble in securing a great quantity of fat. This he carried to the tent of the hunter and, hovering over the tent he suddenly let the fat drop to the earth and at once the pet crane picked it up and carried it to the woman.

Wishing to surprise the family on their awakening in the morning she got a good stick for a light, heaped up sticks on the dying embers, and started up a rousing fire and proceeded to melt or try out the fat, as melted fat is considered a favorite dish. Although busily occupied she kept her ears open for any strange noises coming out of the forest, there being usually some enemies lurking around. She held her pan in such a position that after the fat started to melt and quite a lot of the hot grease accumulated in the pan, she could plainly see the tent door reflected in the hot grease, as though she used a mirror.

When she had nearly completed her task, she heard a noise as though some footsteps were approaching. Instantly her heart began to beat a tattoo on her ribs, but she sat perfectly quiet, calling all her self-control into play to keep from making an outcry. This smart woman had already studied out a way in which to best this enemy, in case an enemy it should be. The footsteps, or noise, continued to advance, until at last the woman saw reflected in the pan of grease a hand slowly protruding through the tent door, and the finger pointed, as if counting, to the sleeping father, then to each one of the sleeping children, then to her who sat at the fire. Little did Mr. Enemy suppose that the brave woman who sat so composed at her fire, was watching every motion he was making. The hand slowly withdrew, and as the footsteps slowly died away, there rang out on the still night air the deep fierce howl of the prairie wolf. (This imitation of a prairie wolf is the signal to the war party that an enemy has been discovered by the scout whom they have sent out in advance). At once she aroused her husband and children. Annoyed at being so unceremoniously disturbed from his deep sleep, the husband crossly asked why she had awakened him so roughly. The wife explained what she had seen and heard. She at once pinned an old blanket around the crane's shoulders and an old piece of buffalo hide on his head for a hat or head covering. Heaping piles of wood onto the fire she instructed him to run around outside of the hut until the family returned, as they were going to see if they could find some roots to mix up with the fat. Hurriedly she tied her blanket around her middle, put her baby inside of it, and then grabbed her three year old son and packed him on her back. The father also hurriedly packed the next two and the older boy took care of himself.

Immediately upon leaving the tent they took three different directions, to meet again on the high hill west of their home. The reflection from the fire in the tent disclosed to them the poor pet crane running around the tent. It looked exactly like a child with its blanket and hat on.

Suddenly there rang out a score of shots and war whoops of the dreaded Crow Indians. Finding the tent deserted they disgustedly filed off and were swallowed up in the darkness of the deep forest.

The next morning the family returned to see what had become of their pet crane. There, riddled to pieces, lay the poor bird who had given up his life to save his dear friends.

White Plume

There once lived a young couple who were very happy. The young man was noted throughout the whole nation for his accuracy with the bow and arrow, and was given the title of "Dead Shot," or "He who never misses his mark," and the young woman, noted for her beauty, was named Beautiful Dove.

One day a stork paid this happy couple a visit and left them a fine big boy. The boy cried "*Ina, ina*" (mother, mother). "Listen to our son," said the mother, "he can speak, and hasn't he a sweet voice?" "Yes," said the father, "it will not be long before he will be able to walk." He set to work making some arrows and a fine hickory bow for his son. One of the arrows he painted red, one blue, and another yellow. The rest he left the natural color of the wood. When he had completed them, the mother placed them in a fine quiver, all worked in porcupine quills, and hung them up over where the boy slept in his fine hammock of painted moose hide.

At times when the mother would be nursing her son, she would look up at the bow and arrows and talk to her baby, saying: "My son, hurry up and grow fast so you can use your bow and arrows. You will grow up to be as fine a marksman as your father." The baby would coo and stretch his little arms up towards the bright colored quiver as though he understood every word his mother had uttered. Time passed and the boy grew up to a good size, when one day his father said: "Wife, give our son the bow and arrows so that he may learn how to use them." The father taught his son how to string and unstring the bow, and also how to attach the arrow to the string. The red, blue and yellow arrows, he told the boy, were to be used only whenever there was any extra good shooting to be done, so the boy never used these three until he became a master of the art. Then he would practice on eagles and hawks, and never an eagle or hawk continued his flight when the boy shot one of the arrows after him.

One day the boy came running into the tent, exclaiming: "Mother, mother, I have shot and killed the most beautiful bird I ever saw." "Bring it in, my son, and let me look at it." He brought the bird and upon examining it she pronounced it a different type of bird from any she had ever seen. Its feathers were of variegated colors and on its head was a topknot of pure white feathers. The father, returning, asked the boy with which arrow he had killed the bird. "With the red one," answered the boy. "I was so anxious to secure the pretty bird that, although I know I could have killed it with one of my common arrows, I wanted to be certain, so I used the red one."

"That is right, my son," said the father. "When you have the least doubt of your aim, always use one of the painted arrows, and you will never miss your mark."

The parents decided to give a big feast in honor of their son killing the strange, beautiful bird. So a great many elderly women were called to the tent of Pretty Dove to assist her in making ready for the big feast. For ten days these women cooked and pounded beef and cherries, and got ready the choicest dishes known to the Indians. Of buffalo, beaver, deer, antelope, moose, bear, quail, grouse, duck of all kinds, geese and plover meats there was an abundance. Fish of all kinds, and every kind of wild fruit were cooked, and when all was in readiness, the heralds went through the different villages, crying out: "*Ho-po, ho-po*" (now all, now all), Dead Shot and his wife, Beautiful Dove, invite all of you, young and old, to their *tepee* to partake of a great feast, given by them in honor of a great bird which their son has killed, and also to select for their son some good name which he will bear through life. So all bring your cups and wooden dishes along with your horn spoons, as there will be plenty to eat. Come, all you council men and chiefs, as they have also a great tent erected for you in which you hold your council."

Thus crying, the heralds made the circle of the village. The guests soon arrived. In front of the tent was a pole stuck in the ground and painted red, and at the top of the pole was fastened the bird of variegated colors; its wings stretched out to their full length and the beautiful white waving so beautifully from its topknot, it was the center of attraction. Half way up the pole was tied the bow and arrow of the young marksman. Long streamers of fine bead and porcupine work waved from the pole and presented a very striking appearance. The bird was faced towards the setting sun. The great chief and medicine men pronounced the bird "*Wakan*" (something holy).

When the people had finished eating they all fell in line and marched in single file beneath the bird, in order to get a close view of it. By the time this vast crowd had fully viewed the wonderful bird, the sun was just setting clear in the west, when directly over the rays of the sun appeared a cloud in the shape of a bird of variegated colors. The councilmen were called out to look at the cloud, and the head medicine man said that it was a sign that the boy would grow up to be a great chief and hunter, and would have a great many friends and followers.

This ended the feast, but before dispersing, the chief and councilmen bestowed upon the boy the title of White Plume.

One day a stranger came to the village, who was very thin and nearly starved. So weak was he that he could not speak, but made signs for something to eat. Luckily the stranger came to Dead Shot's tent, and as there was always a plentiful supply in his lodge, the stranger soon had a good meal served him. After he had eaten and rested he told his story.

"I came from a very great distance," said he. "The nations where I came from are in a starving condition. No place can they find any buffalo, deer nor antelope. A witch or evil spirit in the shape of a white buffalo has driven all the large game out of the country. Every day this white buffalo comes circling the village, and anyone caught outside of their tent is carried away on its horns. In vain have the best marksmen of the tribe tried to shoot it. Their arrows fly wide off the mark, and they have given up trying to kill it as it bears a charmed life. Another evil spirit in the form of a red eagle has driven all the birds of the air out of our country. Every day this eagle circles above the village, and so powerful is it that anyone being caught outside of his tent is descended upon and his skull split open to the brain by the sharp breastbone of the Eagle. Many a marksman has tried his skill on this bird, all to no purpose.

"Another evil spirit in the form of a white rabbit has driven out all the animals which inhabit the ground, and destroyed the fields of corn and turnips, so the nation is starving, as the arrows of the marksmen have also failed to touch the white rabbit. Anyone who can kill these three witches will receive as his reward, the choice of two of the most beautiful maidens of our nation. The younger one is the handsomer of the two and has also the sweetest disposition. Many young, and even old men, hearing of this (our chief's) offer, have traveled many miles to try their arrows on the witches, but all to no purpose. Our chief, hearing of your great marksmanship, sent me to try and secure your services to have you come and rid us of these three witches."

Thus spoke the stranger to the hunter. The hunter gazed long and thoughtfully into the dying embers of the camp fire. Then slowly his eyes raised and looked lovingly on his wife who sat opposite to him. Gazing on her beautiful features for a full minute he slowly dropped his gaze back to the dying embers and thus answered his visitor:

"My friend, I feel very much honored by your chief having sent such a great distance for me, and also for the kind offer of his lovely daughter in marriage, if I should succeed, but I must reject the great offer, as I can spare none of my affections to any other woman than to my queen whom you see sitting there."

White Plume had been listening to the conversation and when his father had finished speaking, said: "Father, I am a child no more. I have arrived at manhood. I am not so good a marksman as you, but I will go to this suffering tribe and try to rid them of their three enemies. If this man will rest for a few days and return to his village and inform them of my coming, I will travel along slowly on his trail and arrive at the village a day or two after he reaches there."

"Very well, my son," said the father, "I am sure you will succeed, as you fear nothing, and as to your marksmanship, it is far superior to mine, as your sight is much clearer and aim quicker than mine."

The man rested a few days and one morning started off, after having instructed White Plume as to the trail. White Plume got together what he would need on the trip and was ready for an early start the next morning. That night Dead Shot and his wife sat up away into the night instructing their son how to travel and warning him as to the different kinds of people he must avoid in order to keep out of trouble. "Above all," said the father, "keep a good look out for Unktomi (spider); he is the most tricky of all, and will get you into trouble if you associate with him."

White Plume left early, his father accompanying him for several miles. On parting, the father's last words were: "Look out for Unktomi, my son, he is deceitful and treacherous."

"I'll look out for him, father;" so saying he disappeared over a hill. On the way he tried his skill on several hawks and eagles and he did not need to use his painted arrows to kill them, but so skillful was he with the bow and arrows that he could bring down anything that flew with his common arrows. He was drawing near to the end of his destination when he had a large tract of timber to pass through. When he had nearly gotten through the timber he saw an old man sitting on a log, looking wistfully up into a big tree, where sat a number of prairie chickens.

"Hello, grandfather, why are you sitting there looking so downhearted?" asked White Plume. "I am nearly starved, and was just wishing someone would shoot one of those chickens for me, so I could make a good meal on it," said the old man. "I will shoot one for you," said the young man. He strung his bow, placed an arrow on the string, simply seemed to raise the arrow in the direction of the chicken (taking no aim). Twang went out the bow, zip went the arrow and a chicken fell off the limb, only to get caught on another in its descent. "There is your chicken, grandfather."

"Oh, my grandson, I am too weak to climb up and get it. Can't you climb up and get it for me?" The young man, pitying the old fellow, proceeded to climb the tree, when the old man stopped him, saying: "Grandson, you have on such fine clothes, it is a pity to spoil them; you had better take them off so as not to spoil the fine porcupine work on them." The young man took off his fine clothes and climbed up into the tree, and securing the chicken, threw it down to the old man. As the young man was scaling down the tree, the old man said: "*Iyashkapa, iyashkapa,*" (stick fast, stick fast). Hearing him say something, he asked, "What did you say, old man?" He answered, "I was only talking to myself." The young man proceeded to descend, but he could not move. His body was stuck fast to the bark of the tree. In vain did he beg the old man to release him. The old Unktomi, for he it was, only laughed and said: "I will go now and kill the evil spirits, I have your wonderful bow and arrows and I cannot miss them. I will marry the chief's daughter, and you can stay up in that tree and die there."

So saying, he put on White Plume's fine clothes, took his bow and arrows and went to the village. As White Plume was expected at any minute, the whole village was watching for him, and when Unktomi came into sight the young men ran to him with a painted robe, sat him down on it and slowly raising him up they carried him to the tent of the chief. So certain were they that he would kill the evil spirits that the chief told him to choose one of the daughters at once for his wife. (Before the arrival of White Plume, hearing of him being so handsome, the two girls had quarreled over which should marry him, but upon seeing him the younger was not anxious to become his wife.) So Unktomi chose the older one of the sisters, and was given a large tent in which to live. The younger sister went to her mother's tent to live, and the older was very proud, as she was married to the man who would save the nation from starvation. The next morning there was a great commotion in camp, and there came the cry that the white buffalo was coming. "Get ready, son-in-law, and kill the buffalo," said the chief.

Unktomi took the bow and arrows and shot as the buffalo passed, but the arrow went wide off its mark. Next came the eagle, and again he shot and missed. Then came the rabbit, and again he missed.

"Wait until tomorrow, I will kill them all. My blanket caught in my bow and spoiled my aim." The people were very much disappointed, and the chief, suspecting that all was not right, sent for the young man who had visited Dead Shot's *tepee*. When the young man arrived, the chief asked: "Did you see White Plume when you went to Dead Shot's camp?" "Yes, I did, and ate with him many times. I stayed at his father's *tepee* all the time I was there," said the young man. "Would you recognize him if you saw him again?" asked the chief. "Anyone who had but one glimpse of White Plume would surely recognize him when he saw him again, as he is the most handsome man I ever saw," said the young man.

"Come with me to the tent of my son-in-law and take a good look at him, but don't say what you think until we come away." The two went to the tent of Unktomi, and when the young man saw him he knew it was not White Plume, although it was White Plume's bow and arrows that hung at the head of the bed, and he also recognized the clothes as belonging to White Plume. When they had returned to the chief's tent, the young man told what he knew and what he thought. "I think this is some Unktomi who has played some trick on White Plume and has taken his bow and arrows and also his clothes, and hearing of your offer, is here impersonating White Plume. Had White Plume drawn the bow on the buffalo, eagle and rabbit today, we would have been rid of them, so I think we had better scare this Unktomi into telling us where White Plume is," said the young man.

"Wait until he tries to kill the witches again tomorrow," said the chief.

In the meantime the younger daughter had taken an axe and gone into the woods in search of dry wood. She went quite a little distance into the wood and was chopping a dry log. Stopping to rest a little she heard someone saying: "Whoever you are, come over here and chop this tree down so that I may get loose." Going to where the big tree stood, she saw a man stuck onto the side of the tree. "If I chop it down the fall will kill you," said the girl. "No, chop it on the opposite side from me, and the tree will fall that way. If the fall kills me, it will be better than hanging up here and starving to death," said White Plume, for it was he.

The girl chopped the tree down and when she saw that it had not killed the man, she said: "What shall I do now?" "Loosen the bark from the tree and then get some stones and heat them. Get some water and sage and put your blanket over me." She did as told and when the steam arose from the water being poured upon the heated rocks, the bark loosened from his body and he arose. When he stood up, she saw how handsome he was. "You have saved my life," said he. "Will you be my wife?" "I will," said she. He then told her how the old man had fooled him into this trap and took his bow and arrows, also his fine porcupine worked clothes, and had gone off, leaving him to die. She, in turn, told him all that had happened in camp since a man, calling himself White Plume, came there and married her sister before he shot at the witches, and when he came to shoot at them, missed every shot. "Let us make haste, as the bad Unktomi may ruin my arrows."

They approached the camp and whilst White Plume waited outside, his promised wife entered Unktomi's tent and said: "Unktomi, White Plume is standing outside and he wants his clothes and bow and arrows."

"Oh, yes, I borrowed them and forgot to return them; make haste and give them to him."

Upon receiving his clothes, he was very much provoked to find his fine clothes wrinkled and his bow twisted, while the arrows were twisted out of shape. He laid the clothes down, also the bows and arrows, and passing his hand over them, they assumed their right shapes again. The daughter took White Plume to her father's tent and upon hearing the story he at once sent for his warriors and had them form a circle around Unktomi's tent, and if he attempted to escape to catch him and tie him to a tree, as he (the chief) had determined to settle accounts with him for his treatment of White Plume, and the deception employed in winning the chief's eldest daughter. About midnight the guard noticed something crawling along close to the ground, and seizing him found it was Unktomi trying to make his escape before daylight, whereupon they tied him to a tree. "Why do you treat me thus," cried Unktomi, "I was just going out in search of medicine to rub on my arrows, so I can kill the witches."

"You will need medicine to rub on yourself when the chief gets through with you," said the young man who had discovered that Unktomi was impersonating White Plume.

In the morning the herald announced that the real White Plume had arrived, and the chief desired the whole nation to witness his marksmanship. Then came the cry: "The White Buffalo comes." Taking his red arrow, White Plume stood ready. When the buffalo got about opposite him, he let his arrow fly. The buffalo bounded high in the air and came down with all four feet drawn together under its body, the red arrow having passed clear through the animal, piercing the buffalo's heart. A loud cheer went up from the village.

"You shall use the hide for your bed," said the chief to White Plume. Next came a cry, "the eagle, the eagle." From the north came an enormous red eagle. So strong was he, that as he soared through the air his wings made a humming sound as the rumble of distant thunder. On he came, and just as he circled the tent of the chief, White Plume bent his bow, with all his strength drew the arrow back to the flint point, and sent the blue arrow on its mission of death. So swiftly had the arrow passed through the eagle's body that, thinking White Plume had missed, a great wail went up from the crowd, but when they saw the eagle stop in his flight, give a few flaps of his wings, and then fall with a heavy thud into the center of the village, there was a greater cheer than before. "The red eagle shall be used to decorate the seat of honor in your *tepee*," said the chief to White Plume. Last came the white rabbit. "Aim good, aim good, son-in-law," said the chief. "If you kill him you will have his skin for a rug." Along came the white rabbit, and White Plume sent his arrow in search of rabbit's heart, which it found, and stopped Mr. Rabbit's tricks forever.

The chief then called all of the people together and before them all took a hundred willows and broke them one at a time over Unktomi's back. Then he turned him loose. Unktomi, being so ashamed, ran off into the woods and hid in the deepest and darkest corner he could find. This is why Unktomis (spiders) are always found in dark corners, and anyone who is deceitful or untruthful is called a descendant of the Unktomi tribe.

Story Of Pretty Feathered Forehead

There was once a baby boy who came into the world with a small cluster of different colored feathers grown fast to his forehead. From this he derived his name, "Pretty Feathered Forehead." He was a very pleasant boy as well as handsome, and he had the respect of the whole tribe. When he had grown up to be a young man, he never, like other young men, made love to any of the tribe's beauties. Although they were madly in love with him, he never noticed any of them. There were many handsome girls in the different camps, but he passed them by.

One day he said: "Father, I am going on a visit to the Buffalo nation." The father gave his consent, and away went the son. The father and mother suspected the object of their son's visit to the Buffalo nation, and forthwith commenced preparing a fine reception for their intended daughter-in-law. The mother sewed together ten buffalo hides and painted the brave deeds of her husband on them. This she made into a commodious tent, and had work bags and fine robes and blankets put inside. This was to be the tent of their son and daughter-in-law. In a few weeks the son returned, bringing with him a beautiful Buffalo girl. The parents of the boy gave a big feast in honor of the occasion, and the son and his wife lived very happily together.

In the course of time a son came to the young couple, and the father was very proud of his boy. When the boy became a year old, the father said to his wife: "I am going for a visit to the Elk nation." The mother was very sad, as she knew her husband was going after another wife. He returned, bringing with him a very beautiful elk girl. When the Buffalo woman saw the elk girl she was very downcast and sad, but the husband said: "Don't be sad; she will do all the heavy work for you."

They lived quite happily together for a long time. The Elk girl also became the mother of a fine boy. The two boys had grown up large enough to play around. One day the Elk woman was tanning hides outside and the two boys were playing around near their mothers, when all at once the buffalo boy ran across the robe, leaving his tracks on the white robe which his step-mother had nearly completed. This provoked the elk woman and she gave vent to her feelings by scolding the boy: "You clumsy flat mouth, why couldn't you run around my work, instead of across it?" The buffalo cow standing in the door, heard every word that the elk woman had said, and when she heard her son called flat mouth it made her very angry, although she did not say a word to any one. She hurriedly gathered some of her belongings and, calling her son, she started off in a westerly direction.

The husband being absent on a hunting expedition did not return until late in the afternoon. Upon his return his oldest boy always ran out to meet him, but this time as the boy did not put in an appearance, the father feared that something had happened to the boy. So hurriedly going to his tent he looked around, but failing to see the boy or his mother, he asked his elk wife, where the boy and his mother were. The elk wife answered: "She took her boy on her back and started off in that direction," (pointing towards the west).

"How long has she been gone?"

"Since early morning." The husband hurriedly caught a fresh horse and, without eating anything, rode off in the direction taken by his buffalo wife and boy. Near dark he ascended a high hill and noticed a small tent down in the valley. It was a long distance down to the tent, so it was very late when he arrived there. He tethered his horse and went into the tent and found the boy and his mother fast asleep. Upon lying down beside them the boy awoke, and upon seeing his father, motioned to him to go outside with him.

On going outside the boy told his father that it would be useless for him to try and coax his mother to return, as she was too highly insulted by the elk wife to ever return. Then the boy told about what the elk wife had said and that she had called him flat mouth. "My mother is determined to return to her people, but if you want to follow us you may, and perhaps, after she has visited with her relatives a little while, you may induce her to return with you. In the morning we are going to start very early, and as the country we will travel through is very hard soil, I will stamp my feet hard so as to leave my tracks imprinted in the softest places, then you will be able to follow the direction we will take."

The two went into the tent and were soon fast asleep. The father, being very much fatigued, slept very soundly, and when he awoke the sun was beating down upon him. The mother and boy were nowhere to be seen. The tent had been taken down from over him so carefully that he had not been awakened. Getting his horse, he mounted and rode after the two who had left him sleeping. He had no trouble in following the trail, as the boy had stamped his feet hard and left his little tracks in the soft places.

That evening he spied the little tent again and on getting to it found them both asleep. The boy awoke and motioned for his father to go outside. He again told his father that the next day's travel would be the hardest of all. "We will cross a great plain, but before we get there we will cross a sandy hollow. When you get to the hollow, look at my tracks; they will be deep into the sand, and in each track you will see little pools of water. Drink as much as you can, as this is the only chance you will get to have a drink, there being no water from there to the big ridge, and it will be dark by the time you get to the ridge. The relations of my mother live at that ridge and I will come and talk to you once more, before I leave you to join my mother's people."

Next morning, as before, he awoke to find himself alone. They had left him and proceeded on their journey. He mounted again and when he arrived at the sandy hollow, sure enough, there, deep in the sand, were the tracks of his son filled to the top with water. He drank and drank until he had drained the last one. Then he arose and continued on the trail, and near sundown he came in sight of their little tent away up on the side of the ridge. His horse suddenly staggered and fell forward dead, having died of thirst.

From there he proceeded on foot. When he got to where the tent stood he entered, only to find it empty. "I guess my son intends to come here and have his last talk with me," thought the father. He had eaten nothing for three days, and was nearly famished. He lay down, but the pangs of hunger kept sleep away. He heard footsteps outside and lay in readiness, thinking it might be an enemy. Slowly opening the covering of the door, his son looked in and seeing his father lying awake, drew back and ran off up the ridge, but soon returned bringing a small parcel with him. When he entered he gave the parcel to his father and said: "Eat, father; I stole this food for you, so I could not get very much." The father soon ate what his son had brought. When he had finished, the son said: "Tomorrow morning the relatives of my mother will come over here and take you down to the village. My mother has three sisters who have their work bags made identically the same as mother's. Were they to mix them up they could not each pick out her own without looking inside so as to identify them by what they have in them. You will be asked to pick out mother's work bag, and if you fail they will trample you to death. Next they will tell you to pick out my mother from among her sisters, and you will be unable to distinguish her from the other three, and if you fail they will bury you alive. The last they will try you on, in case you meet the first and second tests successfully, will be to require you to pick me out from my three cousins, who are as much like me as my reflection in the water. The bags you can tell by a little pebble I will place on my mother's. You can pick my mother out by a small piece of grass which I will put in her hair, and you can pick me out from my cousins, for when we commence to dance, I will shake my head, flop my ears and switch my tail. You must choose quickly, as they will be very angry at your success, and if you lose any time they will make the excuse that you did not know, that they may have an excuse to trample you to death."

The boy then left, after admonishing his father to remember all that he had told him. Early next morning the father heard a great rumbling noise, and going outside, he saw the whole hillside covered with buffalo. When he appeared they set up a loud bellowing and circled around him. One old bull came up and giving a loud snort, passed on by, looking back every few steps. The man, thinking he was to follow this one, did so, and the whole herd, forming a half circle around him, escorted him down the west side of the range out on to a large plain, where there stood a lone tree. To this tree the old bull led him and stopped when he reached the tree. A large rock at the foot of the tree served as a seat for the man. As soon as he was seated there came four female buffaloes, each bearing a large work box. They set the boxes down in a row in front of the man, and the herd crowded around closer in order to get a good view. The old bull came to the front and stood close to the bags, which had been taken out of the four boxes.

The man stood up, and looking at the bags, noticed a small pebble resting on the one next to the left end. Stepping over he pulled the bag towards him and secretly pushed the little pebble off the bag, so that no one would notice it. When they saw that he had selected the right one, they set up a terrific bellow.

Then came the four sisters and stood in a line before the man. Glancing along from the one on the right to the last one on the left, he stepped forward and placed his hand on the one next to the right. Thanks to his boy, if he hadn't put that little stem of grass on his mother's hair, the father could never have picked out his wife, as the four looked as much alike as four peas. Next came the four boy calves, and as they advanced they commenced dancing, and his son was shaking his head and flopping his ears and switching his tail. The father was going to pick out his boy, when a fainting spell took him, and as he sank to the ground the old bull sprang forward on top of him, and instantly they rushed upon him and he was soon trampled to a jelly. The herd then moved to other parts.

The elk wife concluded that something had happened to her husband and determined upon going in search of him. As she was very fleet of foot it did not take her long to arrive at the lone tree. She noticed the blood splashed on the base of the tree, and small pieces of flesh stamped into the earth. Looking closer, she noticed something white in the dust. Stooping and picking it out of the dust, she drew forth the cluster of different colored feathers which had been fastened to her husband's forehead. She at once took the cluster of feathers, and going to the east side of the ridge, heated stones and erected a *wickieup*, placed the feathers inside, and getting water, she sprinkled the stones, and this caused a thick vapor in the *wickieup*. She continued this for a long time, when she heard something moving inside the *wickieup*. Then a voice spoke up, saying: "Whoever you are, pour some more water on and I will be all right." So the woman got more water and poured it on the rocks. "That will do now, I want to dry off." She plucked a pile of sage and in handing it in to him, he recognized his elk wife's hand.

They went back home and shortly after the buffalo, hearing about him coming back to life, decided to make war on him and kill him and his wife, she being the one who brought him back to life. The woman, hearing of this, had posts set in the ground and a strong platform placed on top. When the buffalo came, her husband, her son and herself, were seated upon the bough platform, and the buffalo could not reach them. She flouted her red blanket in their faces, which made the buffalo wild with rage. The hunter's friends came to his rescue, and so fast were they killing the buffalo that they took flight and rushed away, never more to bother Pretty Feather Forehead.

The Four Brothers Or *Inyanhoksila* (Stone Boy)

Alone and apart from their tribe dwelt four orphan brothers. They had erected a very comfortable hut, although the materials used were only willows, hay, birch bark, and adobe mud. After the completion of their hut, the oldest brother laid out the different kinds of work to be done by the four of them. He and the second and third brothers were to do all the hunting, and the youngest brother was to do the house work, cook the meals, and keep plenty of wood on hand at all times.

As his older brothers would leave for their hunting very early every morning, and would not return till late at night, the little fellow always found plenty of spare time to gather into little piles fine dry wood for their winter use.

Thus the four brothers lived happily for a long time. One day while out gathering and piling up wood, the boy heard a rustling in the leaves and looking around he saw a young woman standing in the cherry bushes, smiling at him.

"Who are you, and where did you come from?" asked the boy, in surprise. "I am an orphan girl and have no relatives living. I came from the village west of here. I learned from rabbit that there were four orphan brothers living here all alone, and that the youngest was keeping house for his older brothers, so I thought I would come over and see if I couldn't have them adopt me as their sister, so that I might keep house for them, as I am very poor and have no relations, neither have I a home."

She looked so pitiful and sad that the boy thought to himself, "I will take her home with me, poor girl, no matter what my brothers think or say." Then he said to her: "Come on, *tanke* (sister). You may go home with me; I am sure my older brothers will be glad to have you for our sister."

When they arrived at the hut, the girl hustled about and cooked up a fine hot supper, and when the brothers returned they were surprised to see a girl sitting by the fire in their hut. After they had entered the youngest brother got up and walked outside, and a short time after the oldest brother followed him out. "Who is that girl, and where did she come from?" he asked his brother. Whereupon the brother told him the whole story. Upon hearing this the oldest brother felt very sorry for the poor orphan girl and going back into the hut he spoke to the girl, saying: "Sister, you are an orphan, the same as we; you have no relatives, no home. We will be your brothers, and our poor hut shall be your home. Henceforth call us brothers, and you will be our sister."

"Oh, how happy I am now that you take me as your sister. I will be to you all as though we were of the same father and mother," said the girl. And true to her word, she looked after everything of her brothers and kept the house in such fine shape that the brothers blessed the day that she came to their poor little hut. She always had an extra buckskin suit and two pairs of moccasins hanging at the head of each one's bed. Buffalo, deer, antelope, bear, wolf, wildcat, mountain lion and beaver skins she tanned by the dozen, and piled nicely in one corner of the hut.

When the Indians have walked a great distance and are very tired, they have great faith in painting their feet, claiming that paint eases the pain and rests their feet.

After their return from a long day's journey, when they would be lying down resting, the sister would get her paint and mix it with the deer tallow and rub the paint on her brother's feet, painting them up to their ankles. The gentle touch of her hands, and the soothing qualities of the tallow and paint soon put them into a deep, dreamless steep.

Many such kind actions on her part won the hearts of the brothers, and never was a full blood sister loved more than was this poor orphan girl, who had been taken as their adopted sister. In the morning when they arose, the sister always combed their long black silken scalp locks and painted the circle around the scalp lock a bright vermillion.

When the hunters would return with a goodly supply of beef, the sister would hurry and relieve them of their packs, hanging each one high enough from the ground so the prowling dogs and coyotes could not reach them. The hunters each had a post on which to hang his bow and flint head arrows. (Good hunters never laid their arrows on the ground, as it was considered unlucky to the hunter who let his arrows touch the earth after they had been out of the quiver). They were all perfectly happy, until one day the older brother surprised them all by saying: "We have a plentiful supply of meat on hand at present to last us for a week or so. I am going for a visit to the village west of us, so you boys all stay at home and help sister. Also gather as much wood as you can and I will be back again in four days. On my return we will resume our hunting and commence getting our year's supply of meat."

He left the next morning, and the last they saw of him was while he stood at the top of the long range of hills west of their home. Four days had come and gone and no sign of the oldest brother.

"I am afraid that our brother has met with some accident," said the sister. "I am afraid so, too," said the next oldest. "I must go and search for him; he may be in some trouble where a little help would get him out." The second brother followed the direction his brother had taken, and when he came to the top of the long range of hills he sat down and gazed long and steadily down into the long valley with a beautiful creek winding through it. Across the valley was a long plain stretching for miles beyond and finally ending at the foot of another range of hills, the counterpart of the one upon which he sat.

After noting the different landmarks carefully, he arose and slowly started down the slope and soon came to the creek he had seen from the top of the range. Great was his surprise on arriving at the creek to find what a difference there was in the appearance of it from the range and where he stood. From the range it appeared to be a quiet, harmless, laughing stream. Now he saw it to be a muddy, boiling, bubbling torrent, with high perpendicular banks. For a long time he stood, thinking which way to go, up or down stream. He had just decided to go down stream, when, on chancing to look up, he noticed a thin column of smoke slowly ascending from a little knoll. He approached the place cautiously and noticed a door placed into the creek bank on the opposite side of the stream. As he stood looking at the door, wondering who could be living in a place like that, it suddenly opened and a very old appearing woman came out and stood looking around her. Soon she spied the young man, and said to him: "My grandchild, where did you come from and whither are you bound?" The young man answered: "I came from east of this ridge and am in search of my oldest brother, who came over in this direction five days ago and who has not yet returned."

"Your brother stopped here and ate his dinner with me, and then left, traveling towards the west," said the old witch, for such she was. "Now, grandson, come across on that little log bridge up the stream there and have your dinner with me. I have it all cooked now and just stepped outside to see if there might not be some hungry traveler about, whom I could invite in to eat dinner with me." The young man went up the stream a little distance and found a couple of small logs which had been placed across the stream to serve as a bridge. He crossed over and went down to the old woman's dugout hut. "Come in grandson, and eat. I know you must be hungry."

The young man sat down and ate a real hearty meal. On finishing he arose and said: "Grandmother, I thank you for your meal and kindness to me. I would stay and visit with you awhile, as I know it must be very lonely here for you, but I am very anxious to find my brother, so I must be going. On my return I will stop with my brother and we will pay you a little visit."

"Very well, grandson, but before you go, I wish you would do me a little favor. Your brother did it for me before he left, and cured me, but it has come back on me again. I am subject to very severe pains along the left side of my backbone, all the way from my shoulder blade down to where my ribs attach to my backbone, and the only way I get any relief from the pain is to have someone kick me along the side." (She was a witch, and concealed in her robe a long sharp steel spike. It was placed so that the last kick they would give her, their foot would hit the spike and they would instantly drop off into a swoon, as if dead.)

"If I won't hurt you too much, grandmother, I certainly will be glad to do it for you," said the young man, little thinking he would be the one to get hurt.

"No, grandson, don't be afraid of hurting me; the harder you kick the longer the pain stays away." She laid down on the floor and rolled over on to her right side, so he could get a good chance to kick the left side where she said the pain was located.

As he moved back to give the first kick, he glanced along the floor and he noticed a long object wrapped in a blanket, lying against the opposite wall. He thought it looked strange and was going to stop and investigate, but just then the witch cried out as if in pain. "Hurry up, grandson, I am going to die if you don't hurry and start in kicking."

"I can investigate after I get through with her," thought he, so he started in kicking and every kick he would give her she would cry: "Harder, kick harder." He had to kick seven times before he would get to the end of the pain, so he let out as hard as he could drive, and when he came to the last kick he hit the spike, and driving it through his foot, fell down in a dead swoon, and was rolled up in a blanket by the witch and placed beside his brother at the opposite side of the room.

When the second brother failed to return, the third went in search of the two missing ones. He fared no better than the second one, as he met the old witch who served him in a similar manner as she had his two brothers.

"Ha! Ha!" she laughed, when she caught the third, "I have only one more of them to catch, and when I get them I will keep them all here a year, and then I will turn them into horses and sell them back to their sister. I hate her, for I was going to try and keep house for them and marry the oldest one, but she got ahead of me and became their sister, so now I will get my revenge on her. Next year she will be riding and driving her brothers and she won't know it."

When the third brother failed to return, the sister cried and begged the last one not to venture out in search of them. But go he must, and go he did, only to do as his three brothers had done.

Now the poor sister was nearly distracted. Day and night she wandered over hills and through woods in hopes she might find or hear of some trace of them. Her wanderings were in vain. The hawks had not seen them after they had crossed the little stream. The wolves and coyotes told her that they had seen nothing of her brothers out on the broad plains, and she had given them up for dead.

One day, as she was sitting by the little stream that flowed past their hut, throwing pebbles into the water and wondering what she should do, she picked up a pure white pebble, smooth and round, and after looking at it for a long time, threw it into the water. No sooner had it hit the water than she saw it grow larger. She took it out and looked at it and threw it in again. This time it had assumed the form of a baby. She took it out and threw it in the third time and the form took life and began to cry: "*Ina, ina*" (mother, mother). She took the baby home and fed it soup, and it being an unnatural baby, quickly grew up to a good sized boy. At the end of three months he was a good big, stout youth. One day he said: "Mother, why are you living here alone? To whom do all these fine clothes and moccasins belong?" She then told him the story of her lost brothers. "Oh, I know now where they are. You make me lots of arrows. I am going to find my uncles." She tried to dissuade him from going, but he was determined and said: "My father sent me to you so that I could find my uncles for you, and nothing can harm me, because I am stone and my name is Stone Boy."

The mother, seeing that he was determined to go, made a whole quiver full of arrows for him, and off he started. When he came to the old witch's hut, she was nowhere to be seen, so he pushed the door in and entered. The witch was busily engaged cooking dinner.

"Why, my dear grandchild, you are just in time for dinner. Sit down and we will eat before you continue your journey." Stone Boy sat down and ate dinner with the old witch. She watched him very closely, but when she would be drinking her soup he would glance hastily around the room. Finally he saw the four bundles on the opposite side of the room, and he guessed at once that there lay his four uncles. When he had finished eating he took out his little pipe and filled it with "*kini-kinic*," and commenced to smoke, wondering how the old woman had managed to fool his smart uncles. He couldn't study it out, so when he had finished his smoke he arose to pretend to go. When the old woman saw him preparing to leave, she said: "Grandson, will you kick me on the left side of my backbone. I am nearly dead with pain and if you kick me good and hard it will cure me."

"All right, grandma," said the boy. The old witch lay down on the floor and the boy started in to kick. At the first kick he barely touched her. "Kick as hard as you can, grandson; don't be afraid you will hurt me, because you can't." With that Stone Boy let drive and broke two ribs. She commenced to yell and beg him to stop, but he kept on kicking until he had kicked both sides of her ribs loose from the backbone. Then he jumped on her backbone and broke it and killed the old witch.

He built a big fire outside and dragged her body to it, and threw her into the fire. Thus ended the old woman who was going to turn his uncles into horses.

Next he cut willows and stuck them into the ground in a circle. The tops he pulled together, making a *wickieup*. He then took the old woman's robes and blankets and covered the *wickieup* so that no air could get inside. He then gathered sage brush and covered the floor with a good thick bed of sage; got nice round stones and got them red hot in the fire, and placed them in the *wickieup* and proceeded to carry his uncles out of the hut and lay them down on the soft bed of sage. Having completed carrying and depositing them around the pile of rocks, he got a bucket of water and poured it on the hot rocks, which caused a great vapor in the little *wickieup*. He waited a little while and then listened and heard some breathing inside, so he got another bucket and poured that on also. After awhile he could hear noises inside as though some one were moving about. He went again and got the third bucket and after he had poured that on the rocks, one of the men inside said: "Whoever you are, good friend, don't bring us to life only to scald us to death again." Stone Boy then said: "Are all of you alive?"

"Yes," said the voice.

"Well, come out," said the boy. And with that he threw off the robes and blankets, and a great cloud of vapor arose and settled around the top of the highest peak on the long range, and from that did Smoky Range derive its name.

The uncles, when they heard who the boy was, were very happy, and they all returned together to the anxiously waiting sister. As soon as they got home, the brothers worked hard to gather enough wood to last them all winter. Game they could get at all times of the year, but the heavy fall of snow covered most of the dry wood and also made it very difficult to drag wood through the deep snow. So they took advantage of the nice fall weather and by the time the snow commenced falling they had enough wood gathered to last them throughout the winter. After the snow fell a party of boys swiftly coasted down the big hill west of the brothers' hut. The Stone Boy used to stand and watch them for hours at a time. His youngest uncle said: "Why don't you go up and coast with them?" The boy said: "They may be afraid of me, but I guess I will try once, anyway." So the next morning when the crowd came coasting, Stone Boy started for the hill. When he had nearly reached the bottom of the coasting hill all of the boys ran off excepting two little fellows who had a large coaster painted in different colors and had little bells tied around the edges, so when the coaster was in motion the bells made a cheerful tinkling sound. As Stone Boy started up the hill the two little fellows started down and went past him as though shot from a hickory bow.

When they got to the end of their slide, they got off and started back up the hill. It being pretty steep, Stone Boy waited for them, so as to lend a hand to pull the big coaster up the hill. As the two little fellows came up with him he knew at once that they were twins, as they looked so much alike that the only way one could be distinguished from the other was by the scarfs they wore. One wore red, the other black. He at once offered to help them drag their coaster to the top of the hill. When they got to the top the twins offered their coaster to him to try a ride. At first he refused, but they insisted on his taking it, as they said they would sooner rest until he came back. So he got on the coaster and flew down the hill, only he was such an expert he made a zigzag course going down and also jumped the coaster off a bank about four feet high, which none of the other coasters dared to tackle. Being very heavy, however, he nearly smashed the coaster. Upon seeing this wonderful jump, and the zigzag course he had taken going down, the twins went wild with excitement and decided that they would have him take them down when he got back. So upon his arrival at the starting point, they both asked him at once to give them the pleasure of the same kind of a ride he had taken. He refused, saying: "We will break your coaster. I alone nearly smashed it, and if we all get on and make the same kind of a jump, I am afraid you will have to go home without your coaster."

"Well, take us down anyway, and if we break it our father will make us another one." So he finally consented. When they were all seated ready to start, he told them that when the coaster made the jump they must look straight ahead. "By no means look down, because if you do we will go over the cut bank and land in a heap at the bottom of the gulch."

They said they would obey what he said, so off they started swifter than ever, on account of the extra weight, and so swiftly did the sleigh glide over the packed, frozen snow, that it nearly took the twins' breath away. Like an arrow they approached the jump. The twins began to get a little nervous. "Sit steady and look straight ahead," yelled Stone Boy. The twin next to Stone Boy, who was steering behind, sat upright and looked far ahead, but the one in front crouched down and looked into the coulee. Of course, Stone Boy, being behind, fell on top of the twins, and being so heavy, killed both of them instantly, crushing them to a jelly.

The rest of the boys, seeing what had happened, hastened to the edge of the bank, and looking down, saw the twins laying dead, and Stone Boy himself knocked senseless, lying quite a little distance from the twins. The boys, thinking that all three were killed, and that Stone Boy had purposely steered the sleigh over the bank in such a way that it would tip and kill the twins, returned to the village with this report. Now, these twins were the sons of the head chief of the Buffalo Nation. So at once the chief and his scouts went over to the hill to see if the boys had told the truth.

When they arrived at the bank they saw the twins lying dead, but where was Stone Boy? They looked high and low through the gulch, but not a sign of him could they find. Tenderly they picked up the dead twins and carried them home, then held a big council and put away the bodies of the dead in Buffalo custom.

A few days after this the uncles were returning from a long journey. When they drew near their home they noticed large droves of buffalo gathered on their side of the range. Hardly any buffalo ever ranged on this east side of the range before, and the brothers thought it strange that so many should so suddenly appear there now.

When they arrived at home their sister told them what had happened to the chief's twins, as her son had told her the whole story upon his arrival at home after the accident.

"Well, probably all the buffalo we saw were here for the council and funeral," said the older brother. "But where is my nephew?"

(Stone Boy) he asked his sister. "He said he had noticed a great many buffalo around lately and he was going to learn, if possible, what their object was," said the sister. "Well, we will wait until his return."

When Stone Boy left on his trip that morning, before the return of his uncles, he was determined to ascertain what might be the meaning of so many buffalo so near the home of himself and uncles. He approached several bunches of young buffalo, but upon seeing him approaching they would scamper over the hills. Thus he wandered from bunch to bunch, scattering them all. Finally he grew tired of their cowardice and started for home. When he had come to within a half mile or so of home he saw an old shaggy buffalo standing by a large boulder, rubbing on it first one horn and then the other. On coming up close to him, the boy saw that the bull was so old he could hardly see, and his horns so blunt that he could have rubbed them for a year on that boulder and not sharpened them so as to hurt anyone.

"What are you doing here, grandfather?" asked the boy.

"I am sharpening my horns for the war," said the bull.

"What war?" asked the boy.

"Haven't you heard," said the old bull, who was so near sighted he did not recognize Stone Boy. "The chief's twins were killed by Stone Boy, who ran them over a cut bank purposely, and the chief has ordered all of his buffalo to gather here, and when they arrive we are going to kill Stone Boy and his mother and his uncles."

"Is that so? When is the war to commence?"

"In five days from now we will march upon the uncles and trample and gore them all to death."

"Well, grandfather, I thank you for your information, and in return will do you a favor that will save you so much hard work on your blunt horns." So saying he drew a long arrow from his quiver and strung his bow, attached the arrow to the string and drew the arrow half way back. The old bull, not seeing what was going on, and half expecting some kind of assistance in his horn sharpening process, stood perfectly still. Thus spoke Stone Boy:

"Grandfather, you are too old to join in a war now, and besides if you got mixed up in that big war party you might step in a hole or stumble and fall and be trampled to death. That would be a horrible death, so I will save you all that suffering by just giving you this." At this word he pulled the arrow back to the flint head and let it fly. True to his aim, the arrow went in behind the old bull's foreleg, and with such force was it sent that it went clear through the bull and stuck into a tree two hundred feet away.

Walking over to the tree, he pulled out his arrow. Coolly straightening his arrow between his teeth and sighting it for accuracy, he shoved it back into the quiver with its brothers, exclaiming: "I guess, grandpa, you won't need to sharpen your horns for Stone Boy and his uncles."

Upon his arrival home he told his uncles to get to work building three stockades with ditches between and make the ditches wide and deep so they will hold plenty of buffalo. "The fourth fence I will build myself," he said.

The brothers got to work early and worked until very late at night. They built three corrals and dug three ditches around the hut, and it took them three days to complete the work. Stone Boy hadn't done a thing towards building his fence yet, and there were only two days more left before the charge of the buffalo would commence. Still the boy didn't seem to bother himself about the fence. Instead he had his mother continually cutting arrow sticks, and as fast as she could bring them he would shape them, feather and head them. So by the time his uncles had their fences and corrals finished he had a thousand arrows finished for each of his uncles. The last two days they had to wait, the uncles joined him and they finished several thousand more arrows. The evening before the fifth day he told his uncles to put up four posts, so they could use them as seats from which to shoot.

While they were doing this, Stone Boy went out to scout and see how things looked. At daylight he came hurriedly in saying, "You had better get to the first corral; they are coming."

"You haven't built your fence, nephew." Whereupon Stone Boy said: "I will build it in time; don't worry, uncle."

The dust on the hillsides rose as great clouds of smoke from a forest fire. Soon the leaders of the charge came in sight, and upon seeing the timber stockade they gave forth a great snort or roar that fairly shook the earth. Thousands upon thousands of mad buffalo charged upon the little fort. The leaders hit the first stockade and it soon gave way. The maddened buffalo pushed forward by the thousands behind them; plunged forward, only to fall into the first ditch and be trampled to death by those behind them. The brothers were not slow in using their arrows, and many a noble beast went down before their deadly aim with a little flint pointed arrow buried deep in his heart.

The second stockade stood their charge a little longer than did the first, but finally this gave way, and the leaders pushed on through, only to fall into the second ditch and meet a similar fate to those in the first. The brothers commenced to look anxiously towards their nephew, as there was only one more stockade left, and the second ditch was nearly bridged over with dead buffalo, with the now thrice maddened buffalo attacking the last stockade more furiously than before, as they could see the little hut through the openings in the corral.

"Come in, uncles," shouted Stone Boy. They obeyed him, and stepping to the center he said: "Watch me build my fence." Suiting the words, he took from his belt an arrow with a white stone fastened to the point and fastening it to his bow, he shot it high in the air. Straight up into the air it went, for two or three thousand feet, then seemed to stop suddenly and turned with point down and descended as swiftly as it had ascended. Upon striking the ground a high stone wall arose, enclosing the hut and all who were inside. Just then the buffalo broke the last stockade only to fill the last ditch up again. In vain did the leaders butt the stone wall. They hurt themselves, broke their horns and mashed their snouts, but could not even scar the wall.

The uncles and Stone Boy in the meantime rained arrows of death into their ranks.

When the buffalo chief saw what they had to contend with, he ordered the fight off. The crier or herald sang out: "Come away, come away, Stone Boy and his uncles will kill all of us."

So the buffalo withdrew, leaving over two thousand of their dead and wounded on the field, only to be skinned and put away for the feasts of Stone Boy and his uncles, who lived to be great chiefs of their own tribe, and whose many relations soon joined them on the banks of Stone Boy Creek.

The Unktomi (Spider), Two Widows, And The Red Plums

There once lived, in a remote part of a great forest, two widowed sisters, with their little babies. One day there came to their tent a visitor who was called Unktomi (spider). He had found some nice red plums during his wanderings in the forest, and he said to himself, "I will keep these plums and fool the two widows with them." After the widows had bidden him be seated, he presented them with the plums.

On seeing them they exclaimed "*hi nu, hi nu* (an exclamation of surprise), where did you get those fine plums?" Unktomi arose and pointing to a crimson tipped cloud, said: "You see that red cloud? Directly underneath it is a patch of plums. So large is the patch and so red and beautiful are the plums that it is the reflection of them on the cloud that you see."

"Oh, how we wish someone would take care of our babies, while we go over there and pick some," said the sisters.

"Why, I am not in any particular hurry, so if you want to go I will take care of my little nephews until you return." (Unktomi always claimed relationship with everyone he met).

"Well brother," said the older widow, "take good care of them and we will be back as soon as possible."

The two then took a sack in which to gather the plums, and started off towards the cloud with the crimson lining. Scarcely had they gone from Unktomi's sight when he took the babies out of their swinging hammocks and cut off first one head and then the other. He then took some old blankets and rolled them in the shape of a baby body and laid one in each hammock. Then he took the heads and put them in place in their different hammocks. The bodies he cut up and threw into a large kettle. This he placed over a rousing fire. Then he mixed Indian turnips and Arikara squash with the baby meat and soon had a kettle of soup. Just about the time the soup was ready to serve the widows returned. They were tired and hungry and not a plum had they. Unktomi, hearing the approach of the two, hurriedly dished out the baby soup in two wooden dishes and then seated himself near the door so that he could get out easily. Upon the entrance of the widows, Unktomi exclaimed: "Sisters, I had brought some meat with me and I cooked some turnips and squash with it and made a pot of fine soup. The babies have just fallen asleep, so don't waken them until you have finished eating, for I know that you are nearly starved." The two fell to at once and after they had somewhat appeased their appetites, one of them arose and went over to see how her baby was resting. Noting an unnatural color on her baby's face, she raised him up only to have his head roll off from the bundle of blankets. "'My son! my son!" she cried out. At once the other hastened to her baby and grabbed it up, only to have the same thing happen. At once they surmised who had done this, and caught up sticks from the fire with which to beat Unktomi to death. He, expecting something like this to happen, lost very little time in getting outside and down into a hole at the roots of a large tree. The two widows not being able to follow Unktomi down into the hole, had to give up trying to get him out, and passed the rest of the day and night crying for their beloved babies. In the meantime Unktomi had gotten out by another opening, and fixing himself up in an entirely different style, and painting his face in a manner that they would not recognize him, he cautiously approached the weeping women and inquired the cause of their tears.

Thus they answered him: "Unktomi came here and fooled us about some plums, and while we were absent killed our babies and made soup out of their bodies. Then he gave us the soup to eat, which we did, and when we found out what he had done we tried to kill him, but he crawled down into that hole and we could not get him out."

"I will get him out," said the mock stranger, and with that he crawled down into the hole and scratched his own face all over to make the widows believe he had been fighting with Unktomi. "I have killed him, and that you may see him I have enlarged the hole so you can crawl in and see for yourselves, also to take some revenge on his dead body." The two foolish widows, believing him, crawled into the hole, only to be blocked up by Unktomi, who at once gathered great piles of wood and stuffing it into the hole, set it on fire, and thus ended the last of the family who were foolish enough to let Unktomi tempt them with a few red plums.

MYTHS AND LEGENDS OF CALIFORNIA AND THE OLD SOUTHWEST

The Beginning of Newness
Zuni (New Mexico)
Before the beginning of the New-making, the All-father Father alone had being. Through ages there was nothing else except black darkness. In the beginning of the New-making, the All-father Father thought outward in space, and mists were created and up-lifted. Thus through his knowledge he made himself the Sun who was thus created and is the great Father. The dark spaces brightened with light. The cloud mists thickened and became water.

From his flesh, the Sun-father created the Seed-stuff of worlds, and he himself rested upon the waters. And these two, the Four-fold-containing Earth-mother and the All-covering Sky-father, the surpassing beings, with power of changing their forms even as smoke changes in the wind, were the father and mother of the soul beings.

Then as man and woman spoke these two together. "Behold!" said Earth-mother, as a great terraced bowl appeared at hand, and within it water, "This shall be the home of my tiny children. On the rim of each world-country in which they wander, terraced mountains shall stand, making in one region many mountains by which one country shall be known from another."

Then she spat on the water and struck it and stirred it with her fingers. Foam gathered about the terraced rim, mounting higher and higher. Then with her warm breath she blew across the terraces. White flecks of foam broke away and floated over the water. But the cold breath of Sky-father shattered the foam and it fell downward in fine mist and spray.

Then Earth-mother spoke:

"Even so shall white clouds float up from the great waters at the borders of the world, and clustering about the mountain terraces of the horizon, shall be broken and hardened by thy cold. Then will they shed downward, in rain-spray, the water of life, even into the hollow places of my lap. For in my lap shall nestle our children, man-kind and creature-kind, for warmth in thy coldness."

So even now the trees on high mountains near the clouds and Sky-father, crouch low toward Earth mother for warmth and protection. Warm is Earth-mother, cold our Sky-father.

Then Sky-father said, "Even so. Yet I, too, will be helpful to our children." Then he spread his hand out with the palm downward and into all the wrinkles of his hand he set the semblance of shining yellow corn-grains; in the dark of the early world-dawn they gleamed like sparks of fire.

"See," he said, pointing to the seven grains between his thumb and four fingers, "our children shall be guided by these when the Sun-father is not near and thy terraces are as darkness itself. Then shall our children be guided by lights." So Sky-father created the stars. Then he said, "And even as these grains gleam up from the water, so shall seed grain like them spring up from the earth when touched by water, to nourish our children." And thus they created the seed-corn. And in many other ways they devised for their children, the soul-beings.

But the first children, in a cave of the earth, were unfinished. The cave was of sooty blackness, black as a chimney at night time, and foul. Loud became their murmurings and lamentations, until many sought to escape, growing wiser and more man-like.

But the earth was not then as we now see it. Then Sun-father sent down two sons (sons also of the Foam-cap), the Beloved Twain, Twin

Brothers of Light, yet Elder and Younger, the Right and the Left, like to question and answer in deciding and doing. To them the Sun-father imparted his own wisdom. He gave them the great cloud-bow, and for arrows the thunderbolts of the four quarters. For buckler, they had the fog-making shield, spun and woven of the floating clouds and spray. The shield supports its bearer, as clouds are supported by the wind, yet hides its bearer also. And he gave to them the fathership and control of men and of all creatures. Then the Beloved Twain, with their great cloud-bow lifted the Sky-father into the vault of the skies, that the earth might become warm and fitter for men and creatures. Then along the sun-seeking trail, they sped to the mountains westward. With magic knives they spread open the depths of the mountain and uncovered the cave in which dwelt the unfinished men and creatures. So they dwelt with men, learning to know them, and seeking to lead them out.

Now there were growing things in the depths, like grasses and vines. So the Beloved Twain breathed on the stems, growing tall toward the light as grass is wont to do, making them stronger, and twisting them upward until they formed a great ladder by which men and creatures ascended to a second cave.

Up the ladder into the second cave-world, men and the beings crowded, following closely the Two Little but Mighty Ones. Yet many fell back and were lost in the darkness. They peopled the under-world from which they escaped in after time, amid terrible earth shakings.

In this second cave it was as dark as the night of a stormy season, but larger of space and higher. Here again men and the beings increased, and their complainings grew loud. So the Twain again increased the growth of the ladder, and again led men upward, not all at once, but in six bands, to become the fathers of the six kinds of men, the yellow, the tawny gray, the red, the white, the black, and the mingled. And this time also many were lost or left behind.

Now the third great cave was larger and lighter, like a valley in starlight. And again they increased in number. And again the Two led them out into a fourth cave. Here it was light like dawning, and men began to perceive and to learn variously, according to their natures, wherefore the Twain taught them first to seek the Sun-father.

Then as the last cave became filled and men learned to understand, the Two led them forth again into the great upper world, which is the World of Knowing Seeing.

The Men of the Early Times
Zuni (New Mexico)

Eight years was but four days and four nights when the world was new. It was while such days and nights continued that men were led out, in the night-shine of the World of Seeing. For even when they saw the great star, they thought it the Sun-father himself, it so burned their eye-balls. Men and creatures were more alike then than now. Our fathers were black, like the caves they came from; their skins were cold and scaly like those of mud creatures; their eyes were goggled like an owl's; their ears were like those of cave bats; their feet were webbed like those of walkers in wet and soft places; they had tails, long or short, as they were old or young. Men crouched when they walked, or crawled along the ground like lizards. They feared to walk straight, but crouched as before time they had in their cave worlds, that they might not stumble or fall in the uncertain light.

When the morning star arose, they blinked excessively when they beheld its brightness and cried out that now surely the Father was coming. But it was only the elder of the Bright Ones, heralding with his shield of flame the approach of the Sun-father. And when, low down in the east, the Sun-father himself appeared, though shrouded in the mist of the world-waters, they were blinded and heated by his light and glory. They fell down wallowing and covered their eyes with their hands and arms, yet ever as they looked toward the light, they struggled toward the Sun as moths and other night creatures seek the light of a camp fire. Thus they became used to the light. But when they rose and walked straight, no longer bending, and looked upon each other, they sought to clothe themselves with girdles and garments of bark and rushes. And when by walking only upon their hinder feet they were bruised by stone and sand, they plaited sandals of yucca fiber.

Creation and Longevity
Achomawi (Pit River, Cal.)

Coyote began the creation of the earth, but Eagle completed it. Coyote scratched it up with his paws out of nothingness, but Eagle complained there were no mountains for him to perch on. So Coyote made hills, but they were not high enough. Therefore Eagle scratched up great ridges. When Eagle flew over them, his feathers dropped down, took root, and became trees. The pin feathers became bushes and plants.

Coyote and Fox together created man. They quarreled as to whether they should let men live always or not. Coyote said, "If they want to die, let them die." Fox said, "If they want to come back, let them come back." But Coyote's medicine was stronger, and nobody ever came back. Coyote also brought fire into the world, for the Indians were freezing. He journeyed far to the west, to a place where there was fire, stole some of it, and brought it home in his ears. He kindled a fire in the mountains, and the Indians saw the smoke of it, and went up and got fire.

Old Mole's Creation
Shastika (Cal.)

Long, long ago, before there was any earth, Old Mole burrowed underneath Somewhere, and threw up the earth which forms the world. Then Great Man created the people. But the Indians were cold.

Now in the cast gleamed the white Fire Stone. Therefore Coyote journeyed eastward, and brought back the Fire Stone for the Indians. So people had fire.

In the beginning, Sun had nine brothers, all flaming hot like himself. But Coyote killed the nine brothers and so saved the world from burning up. But Moon also had nine brothers all made of ice, like himself, and the Night People almost froze to death. Therefore Coyote went away out on the eastern edge of the world with his flint-stone knife. He heated stones to keep his hands warm, and as the Moons arose, he killed one after another with his flint-stone knife, until he had slain nine of them. Thus the people were saved from freezing at night.

When it rains, some Indian, sick in heaven, is weeping. Long, long ago, there was a good young Indian on earth. When he died the Indians wept so that a flood came upon the earth, and drowned all people except one couple.

The Creation of the World
Pima (Arizona)

In the beginning there was nothing at all except darkness. All was darkness and emptiness. For a long, long while, the darkness gathered until it became a great mass. Over this the spirit of Earth Doctor drifted to and fro like a fluffy bit of cotton in the breeze. Then Earth Doctor decided to make for himself an abiding place. So he thought within himself, "Come forth, some kind of plant," and there appeared the creosote bush. He placed this before him and set it upright. But it at once fell over. He set it upright again; again it fell. So it fell until the fourth time it remained upright. Then Earth Doctor took from his breast a little dust and flattened it into a cake. When the dust cake was still, he danced upon it, singing a magic song.

Next he created some black insects which made black gum on the creosote bush. Then he made a termite which worked with the small earth cake until it grew very large. As he sang and danced upon it, the flat World stretched out on all sides until it was as large as it is now. Then he made a round sky-cover to fit over it, round like the houses of the Pimas. But the earth shook and stretched, so that it was unsafe. So Earth Doctor made a gray spider which was to spin a web around the edges of the earth and sky, fastening them together. When this was done, the earth grew firm and solid.

Earth Doctor made water, mountains, trees, grass, and weeds-made everything as we see it now. But all was still inky blackness. Then he made a dish, poured water into it, and it became ice. He threw this round block of ice far to the north, and it fell at the place where the earth and sky were woven together. At once the ice began to gleam and shine. We call it now the sun. It rose from the ground in the north up into the sky and then fell back. Earth Doctor took it and threw it to the west where the earth and sky were sewn together. It rose into the sky and again slid back to the earth. Then he threw it to the far south, but it slid back again to the flat earth. Then at last he threw it to the east. It rose higher and higher in the sky until it reached the highest point in the round blue cover and began to slide down on the other side. And so the sun does even yet.

Then Earth Doctor poured more water into the dish and it became ice. He sang a magic song, and threw the round ball of ice to the north where the earth and sky are woven together. It gleamed and shone, but not so brightly as the sun. It became the moon, and it rose in the sky, but fell back again, just as the sun had done. So he threw the ball to the west, and then to the south, but it slid back each time to the earth. Then he threw it to the east, and it rose to the highest point in the sky-cover and began to slide down on the other side. And so it does even today, following the sun.

But Earth Doctor saw that when the sun and moon were not in the sky, all was inky darkness. So he sang a magic song, and took some water into his mouth and blew it into the sky, in a spray, to make little stars. Then he took his magic crystal and broke it into pieces and threw them into the sky, to make the larger stars. Next he took his walking stick and placed ashes on the end of it. Then he drew it across the sky to form the Milky Way. So Earth Doctor made all the stars.

Spider's Creation
Sia (New Mexico)

In the beginning, long, long ago, there was but one being in the lower world. This was the spider, Sussistinnako. At that time there were no other insects, no birds, animals, or any other living creature.

The spider drew a line of meal from north to south and then crossed it with another line running east and west. On each side of the first line, north of the second, he placed two small parcels. They were precious but no one knows what was in them except Spider. Then he sat down near the parcels and began to sing. The music was low and sweet and the two parcels accompanied him, by shaking like rattles. Then two women appeared, one from each parcel.

In a short time people appeared and began walking around. Then animals, birds, and insects appeared, and the spider continued to sing until his creation was complete.

But there was no light, and as there were many people, they did not pass about much for fear of treading upon each other. The two women first created were the mothers of all. One was named Utset and she as the mother of all Indians. The other was Now-utset, and she was the mother of all other nations. While it was still dark, the spider divided the people into clans, saying to some, "You are of the Corn clan, and you are the first of all." To others he said, "You belong to the Coyote clan." So he divided them into their clans, the clans of the Bear, the Eagle, and other clans.

After Spider had nearly created the earth, Ha-arts, he thought it would be well to have rain to water it, so he created the Cloud People, the Lightning People, the Thunder People, and the Rainbow People, to work for the people of Ha-arts, the earth. He divided this creation into six parts, and each had its home in a spring in the heart of a great mountain upon whose summit was a giant tree. One was in the spruce tree on the Mountain of the North; another in the pine tree on the Mountain of the West; another in the oak tree on the Mountain of the South; and another in the aspen tree on the Mountain of the East; the fifth was on the cedar tree on the Mountain of the Zenith; and the last in an oak on the Mountain of the Nadir.

The spider divided the world into three parts: Ha-arts, the earth; Tinia, the middle plain; and Hu-wa-ka, the upper plain. Then the spider gave to these People of the Clouds and to the rainbow, Tinia, the middle plain.

Now it was still dark, but the people of Ha-arts made houses for themselves by digging in the rocks and the earth. They could not build houses as they do now, because they could not see. In a short time Utset and Now-utset talked much to each other, saying,

"We will make light, that our people may see. We cannot tell the people now, but tomorrow will be a good day and the day after tomorrow will be a good day," meaning that their thoughts were good. So they spoke with one tongue. They said, "Now all is covered with darkness, but after a while we will have light."

Then these two mothers, being inspired by Sussistinnako, the spider, made the sun from white shell, turkis, red stone, and abalone shell. After making the sun, they carried him to the east and camped there, since there were no houses. The next morning they climbed to the top of a high mountain and dropped the sun down behind it. After a time he began to ascend. When the people saw the light they were happy.

When the sun was far off, his face was blue; as he came nearer, the face grew brighter. Yet they did not see the sun himself, but only a large mask which covered his whole body.

The people saw that the world was large and the country beautiful. When the two mothers returned to the village, they said to the people, "We are the mothers of all."

The sun lighted the world during the day, but there was no light at night. So the two mothers created the moon from a slightly black stone, many kinds of yellow stone, turkis, and a red stone, that the world might be lighted at night. But the moon traveled slowly and did not always give light. Then the two mothers created the Star People and made their eyes of sparkling white crystal that they might twinkle and brighten the world at night. When the Star People lived in the lower world they were gathered into beautiful groups; they were not scattered about as they are in the upper world.

The Gods and the Six Regions

In ancient times, Po-shai-an-ki-a, the father of the sacred bands, or tribes, lived with his followers in the City of Mists, the Middle Place, guarded by six warriors, the prey gods. Toward the North, he was guarded by Long Tail, the mountain lion; West by Clumsy Foot, the bear; South by Black-Mark Face, the badger; East by Hang Tail, the wolf; above by White Cap, the eagle; below by Mole.

So when he was about to go forth into the world, he divided the earth into six regions: North, the Direction of the Swept or Barren Plains; West, the Direction of the Home of the Waters; South, the Place of the Beautiful Red; East, the Direction of the Home of Day; upper regions, the Direction of the Home of the High; lower regions, the Direction of the Home of the Low.

How Old Man Above Created the World
Shastika (Cal.)

Long, long ago, when the world was so new that even the stars were dark, it was very, very flat. Chareya, Old Man Above, could not see through the dark to the new, flat earth. Neither could he step down to it because it was so far below him. With a large stone he bored a hole in the sky. Then through the hole he pushed down masses of ice and snow, until a great pyramid rose from the plain. Old Man Above climbed down through the hole he had made in the sky, stepping from cloud to cloud, until he could put his foot on top the mass of ice and snow. Then with one long step he reached the earth.

The sun shone through the hole in the sky and began to melt the ice and snow. It made holes in the ice and snow. When it was soft, Chareya bored with his finger into the earth, here and there, and planted the first trees. Streams from the melting snow watered the new trees and made them grow. Then he gathered the leaves which fell from the trees and blew upon them. They became birds. He took a stick and broke it into pieces. Out of the small end he made fishes and placed them in the mountain streams. Of the middle of the stick, he made all the animals except the grizzly bear. From the big end of the stick came the grizzly bear, who was made master of all. Grizzly was large and strong and cunning. When the earth was new he walked upon two feet and carried a large club. So strong was Grizzly that Old Man Above feared the creature he had made. Therefore, so that he might be safe, Chareya hollowed out the pyramid of ice and snow as a *tepee*. There he lived for thousands of snows. The Indians knew he lived there because they could see the smoke curling from the smoke hole of his *tepee*. When the pale-face came, Old Man Above went away. There is no longer any smoke from the smoke hole. White men call the *tepee* Mount Shasta.

The Search for the Middle and the Hardening of the World
Zuni (New Mexico)

As it was with the first men and creatures, so it was with the world. It was young and unripe. Earthquakes shook the world and rent it. Demons and monsters of the under-world fled forth. Creatures became fierce, beasts of prey, and others turned timid, becoming their quarry.

Wretchedness and hunger abounded and black magic. Fear was everywhere among them, so the people, in dread of their precious possessions, became wanderers, living on the seeds of grass, eaters of dead and slain things. Yet, guided by the Beloved Twain, they sought in the light and under the pathway of the Sun, the Middle of the world, over which alone they could find the earth at rest.

When the tremblings grew still for a time, the people paused at the First of Sitting Places. Yet they were still poor and defenseless and unskilled, and the world still moist and unstable. Demons and monsters fled from the earth in times of shaking, and threatened wanderers. Then the Two took counsel of each other. The Elder said the earth must be made more stable for men and the valleys where their children rested. If they sent down their fire bolts of thunder, aimed to all the four regions, the earth would heave up and down, fire would, belch over the world and burn it, floods of hot water would sweep over it, smoke would blacken the daylight, but the earth would at last be safer for men. So the Beloved Twain let fly the thunderbolts.

The mountains shook and trembled, the plains cracked and crackled under the floods and fires, and the hollow places, the only refuge of men and creatures, grew black and awful. At last thick rain fell, putting out the fires. Then water flooded the world, cutting deep trails through the mountains, and burying or uncovering the bodies of things and beings. Where they huddled together and were blasted thus, their blood gushed forth and flowed deeply, here in rivers, there in floods, for gigantic were they. But the blood was charred and blistered and blackened by the fires into the black rocks of the lower mesas. There were vast plains of dust, ashes, and cinders, reddened like the mud of the hearth place. Yet many places behind and between the mountain terraces were unharmed by the fires, and even then green grew the trees and grasses and even flowers bloomed. Then the earth became more stable, and drier, and its lone places less fearsome since monsters of prey were changed to rock. But ever and again the earth trembled and the people were troubled.

"Let us again seek the Middle," they said. So they traveled far eastward to their second stopping place, the Place of Bare Mountains. Again the world rumbled, and they traveled into a country to a place called Where-tree-boles-stand-in-the-midst-of-waters. There they remained long, saying, "This is the Middle." They built homes there. At times they met people who had gone before, and thus they learned war. And many strange things happened there, as told in speeches of the ancient talk.

Then when the earth groaned again, the Twain bade them go forth, and they murmured. Many refused and perished miserably in their own homes, as do rats in falling trees, or flies in forbidden food.

But the greater number went forward until they came to Steam-mist-in-the-midst-of-waters. And they saw the smoke of men's hearth fires and many houses scattered over the hills before them. When they came nearer, they challenged the people rudely, demanding who they were and why there, for in their last standing-place they had had touch of war.

"We are the People of the Seed," said the men of the hearth-fires, "born elder brothers of ye, and led of the gods."

"No," said our fathers, "we are led of the gods and we are the Seed People . . . "

Long lived the people in the town on the sunrise slope of the mountains of Kahluelawan, until the earth began to groan warningly again. Loath were they to leave the place of the Kaka and the lake of their dead. But the rumbling grew louder and the Twain Beloved called, and all together they journeyed eastward, seeking once more the Place of the Middle. But they grumbled amongst themselves, so when they came to a place of great promise, they said, "Let us stay here. Perhaps it may be the Place of the Middle."

So they built houses there, larger and stronger than ever before, and more perfect, for they were strong in numbers and wiser, though yet unperfected as men. They called the place "The Place of Sacred Stealing."

Long they dwelt there, happily, but growing wiser and stronger, so that, with their tails and dressed in the skins of animals, they saw they were rude and ugly.

In chase or in war, they were at a disadvantage, for they met older nations of men with whom they fought. No longer they feared the gods and monsters, but only their own kind. So therefore the gods called a council.

Changed shall ye be, oh our children, "cried the Twain." Ye shall walk straight in the pathways, clothed in garments, and without tails, that ye may sit more straight in council, and without webs to your feet, or talons on your hands."

So the people were arranged in procession like dancers. And the Twain with their weapons and fires of lightning shored off the forelocks hanging down over their faces, severed the talons, and slitted the webbed fingers and toes. Sore was the wounding and loud cried the foolish, when lastly the people were arranged in procession for the razing of their tails.

But those who stood at the end of the line, shrinking farther and farther, fled in their terror, climbing trees and high places, with loud chatter. Wandering far, sleeping ever in tree tops, in the far-away Summerland, they are sometimes seen of far-walkers, long of tail and long handed, like wizened men-children.

But the people grew in strength, and became more perfect, and more than ever went to war. They grew vain. They had reached the Place of the Middle. They said, "Let us not wearily wander forth again even though the earth tremble and the Twain bid us forth."

And even as they spoke, the mountain trembled and shook, though far-sounding.

But as the people changed, changed also were the Twain, small and misshapen, hard-favored and unyielding of will, strong of spirit, evil and bad. They taught the people to war, and led them far to the eastward.

At last the people neared, in the midst of the plains to the eastward, great towns built in the heights. Great were the fields and possessions of this people, for they knew how to command and carry the waters, bringing new soil. And this, too, without hail or rain. So our ancients, hungry with long wandering for new food, were the more greedy and often gave battle.

It was here that the Ancient Woman of the Elder People, who carried her heart in her rattle and was deathless of wounds in the body, led the enemy, crying out shrilly. So it fell out ill for our fathers. For, moreover, thunder raged and confused their warriors, rain descended and blinded them, stretching their bow strings of sinew and quenching the flight of their arrows as the flight of bees is quenched by the sprinkling plume of the honey-hunter. But they devised bow strings of yucca and the Two Little Ones sought counsel of the Sun-father who revealed the life-secret of the Ancient Woman and the magic powers over the under-fires of the dwellers of the mountains, so that our enemy in the mountain town was overmastered. And because our people found in that great town some hidden deep in the cellars, and pulled them out as rats are pulled from a hollow cedar, and found them blackened by the fumes of their war magic, yet wiser than the common people, they spared them and received them into their next of kin of the Black Corn. . . .

But the tremblings and warnings still sounded, and the people searched for the stable Middle.

Now they called a great council of men and the beasts, birds, and insects of all kinds. After a long council it was said, "Where is Water-skate? He has six legs, all very long. Perhaps he can feel with them to the uttermost of the six regions, and point out the very Middle."

So Water-skate was summoned. But lo! It was the Sun-father in his likeness which appeared. And he lifted himself to the zenith and extended his fingerfeet to all the six regions, so that they touched the north, the great waters; the west, and the south, and the east, the great waters; and to the northeast the waters above. and to the southwest the waters below. But to the north his finger foot grew cold, so he drew it in. Then gradually he settled down upon the earth and said, "Where my heart rests, mark a spot, and build a town of the Mid-most, for there shall be the Mid-most Place of the Earth-mother." And his heart rested over the middle of the plain and valley of Zuni. And when he drew in his finger-legs, lo! there were the trail-roads leading out and in like stays of a spider's nest, into and from the mid-most place he had covered.

Here because of their good fortune in finding the stable Middle, the priest father called the town the Abiding-place-of-happy-fortune.

Origin of Light
Gallinomero (Russian River, Cal.)

In the earliest beginning, the darkness was thick and deep. There was no light. The animals ran here and there, always bumping into each other. The birds flew here and there, but continually knocked against each other.

Hawk and Coyote thought a long time about the darkness. Then Coyote felt his way into a swamp and found a large number of dry tule reeds. He made a ball of them. He gave the ball to Hawk, with some flints, and Hawk flew up into the sky, where he touched off the tule reeds and sent the bundle whirling around the world. But still the nights were dark, so Coyote made another bundle of tule reeds, and Hawk flew into the air with them, and touched them off with the flints. But these reeds were damp and did not burn so well. That is why the moon does not give so much light as the sun.

Pokoh, the Old Man
Pai Ute (near Kern River, Cal.)

Pokoh, Old Man, they say, created the world. Pokoh had many thoughts. He had many blankets in which he carried around gifts for men. He created every tribe out of the soil where they used to live. That is why an Indian wants to live and die in his native place. He was made of the same soil. Pokoh did not wish men to wander and travel, but to remain in their birthplace.

Long ago, Sun was a man, and was bad. Moon was good. Sun had a quiver full of arrows, and they are deadly. Sun wishes to kill all things. Sun has two daughters (Venus and Mercury) and twenty men kill them; but after fifty days, they return to life again.

Rainbow is the sister of Pokoh, and her breast is covered with flowers. Lightning strikes the ground and fills the flint with fire. That is the origin of fire. Some say the beaver brought fire from the east, hauling it on his broad, flat tail. That is why the beaver's tail has no hair on it, even to this day. It was burned off.

There are many worlds. Some have passed and some are still to come. In one world the Indians all creep; in another they all walk; in another they all fly. Perhaps in a world to come, Indians may walk on four legs; or they may crawl like snakes; or they may swim in the water like fish.

Thunder and Lightning
Maidu (near Sacramento Valley, Cal.)

Great-Man created the world and all the people. At first the earth was very hot, so hot it was melted, and that is why even today there is fire in the trunk and branches of trees, and in the stones.

Lightning is Great-Man himself coming down swiftly from his world above, and tearing apart the trees with his flaming arm.

Thunder and Lightning are two great spirits who try to destroy mankind. But Rainbow is a good spirit who speaks gently to them, and persuades them to let the Indians live a little longer.

Creation of Man
Miwok (San Joaquin Valley, Cal.)

After Coyote had completed making the world, he began to think about creating man. He called a council of all the animals. The animals sat in a circle, just as the Indians do, with Lion at the head, in an open space in the forest. On Lion's right was Grizzly Bear; next Cinnamon Bear; and so on to Mouse, who sat at Lion's left.

Lion spoke first. Lion said he wished man to have a terrible voice, like himself, so that he could frighten all animals. He wanted man also to be well covered with hair, with fangs in his claws, and very strong teeth. Grizzly Bear laughed. He said it was ridiculous for any one to have such a voice as Lion, because when he roared he frightened away the very prey for which he was searching. But he said man should have very great strength; that he should move silently, but very swiftly; and he should be able to seize his prey without noise.

Buck said man would look foolish without antlers. And a terrible voice was absurd, but man should have ears like a spider's web, and eyes like fire.

Mountain Sheep said the branching antlers would bother man if he got caught in a thicket. If man had horns rolled up, so that they were like a stone on each side of his head, it would give his head weight enough to butt very hard.

When it came Coyote's turn, he said the other animals were foolish because they each wanted man to be just like themselves. Coyote was sure he could make a man who would look better than Coyote himself, or any other animal. Of course he would have to have four legs, with five fingers. Man should have a strong voice, but he need not roar all the time with it. And he should have feet nearly like Grizzly Bear's, because he could then stand erect when he needed to. Grizzly Bear had no tail, and man should not have any. The eyes and ears of Buck were good, and perhaps man should have those. Then there was Fish, which had no hair, and hair was a burden much of the year. So Coyote thought man should not wear fur. And his claws should be as long as the Eagle's, so that he could hold things in them. But no animal was as cunning and crafty as Coyote, so man should have the wit of Coyote.

Then Beaver talked. Beaver said man would have to have a tail, but it should be broad and flat, so he could haul mud and sand on it. Not a furry tail, because they were troublesome on account of fleas. Owl said man would be useless without wings.

But Mole said wings would be folly. Man would be sure to bump against the sky. Besides, if he had wings and eyes both, he would get his eyes burned out by flying too near the sun. But without eyes, he could burrow in the soft, cool earth where he could be happy.

Mouse said man needed eyes so he could see what he was eating. And nobody wanted to burrow in the damp earth. So the council broke up in a quarrel.

Then every animal set to work to make a man according to his own ideas. Each one took a lump of earth and modeled it just like himself. All but Coyote, for Coyote began to make the kind of man he had talked of in the council.

It was late when the animals stopped work and fell asleep. All but Coyote, for Coyote was the cunningest of all the animals, and he stayed awake until he had finished his model. He worked hard all night. When the other animals were fast asleep he threw water on the lumps of earth, and so spoiled the models of the other animals. But in the morning he finished his own, and gave it life long before the others could finish theirs. Thus man was made by Coyote.

The First Man And Woman
Nishinam (near Bear River, Cal.)

The first man created by Coyote was called Aikut. His wife was Yototowi. But the woman grew sick and died. Aikut dug a grave for her close beside his camp fire, for the Nishinam did not burn their dead then. All the light was gone from his life. He wanted to die, so that he could follow Yototowi, and he fell into a deep sleep.

There was a rumbling sound and the spirit of Yototowi arose from the earth and stood beside him. He would have spoken to her, but she forbade him, for when an Indian speaks to a ghost he dies. Then she turned away and set out for the dance-house of ghosts. Aikut followed her. Together they journeyed through a great, dark country, until they came to a river which separated them from the Ghost-land. Over the river there was a bridge of but one small rope, so small that hardly Spider could crawl across it. Here the woman started off alone, but when Aikut stretched out his arms, she returned. Then she started again over the bridge of thread. And Aikut spoke to her, so that he died. Thus together they journeyed to the Spirit-land.

Old Man Above and the Grizzlies
Shastika (Cal.)

Along time ago, while smoke still curled from the smoke hole of the *tepee*, a great storm arose. The storm shook the *tepee*. Wind blew the smoke down the smoke hole. Old Man Above said to Little Daughter: "Climb up to the smoke hole. Tell Wind to be quiet. Stick your arm out of the smoke hole before you tell him." Little Daughter climbed up to the smoke hole and put out her arm. But Little Daughter put out her head also. She wanted to see the world. Little Daughter wanted to see the rivers and trees, and the white foam on the Bitter Waters. Wind caught Little Daughter by the hair. Wind pulled her out of the smoke hole and blew her down the mountain. Wind blew Little Daughter over the smooth ice and the great forests, down to the land of the Grizzlies. Wind tangled her hair and then left her cold and shivering near the *tepees* of the Grizzlies. Soon Grizzly came home. In those days Grizzly walked on two feet, and carried a big stick. Grizzly could talk as people do. Grizzly laid down the young elk he had killed and picked up Little Daughter. He took Little Daughter to his *tepee*. Then Mother Grizzly warmed her by the fire. Mother Grizzly gave her food to eat.

Soon Little Daughter married the son of Grizzly. Their children were not Grizzlies. They were men. So the Grizzlies built a *tepee* for Little Daughter and her children. White men call the *tepee* Little Shasta.

At last Mother Grizzly sent a son to Old Man Above. Mother Grizzly knew that Little Daughter was the child of Old Man Above, but she was afraid. She said: "Tell Old Man Above that Little Daughter is alive."

Old Man Above climbed out of the smoke hole. He ran down the mountain side to the land of the Grizzlies. Old Man Above ran very quickly. Wherever he set his foot the snow melted. The snow melted very quickly and made streams of water. Now Grizzlies stood in line to welcome Old Man Above. They stood on two feet and carried clubs. Then Old Man Above saw his daughter and her children. He saw the new race of men. Then Old Man Above became very angry. He said to Grizzlies:

"Never speak again. Be silent. Neither shall ye stand upright. Ye shall use your hands as feet. Ye shall look downward."

Then Old Man Above put out the fire in the *tepee*. Smoke no longer curls from the smoke hole. He fastened the door of the *tepee*. The new race of men he drove out. Then Old Man Above took Little Daughter back to his *tepee*.

That is why grizzlies walk on four feet and look downward. Only when fighting they stand on two feet and use their fists like men.

The Creation of Man-Kind and the Flood
Pima (Arizona)

After the world was ready, Earth Doctor made all kinds of animals and creeping things. Then he made images of clay, and told them to be people. After a while there were so many people that there was not food and water enough for all. They were never sick and none died. At last there grew to be so many they were obliged to eat each other. Then Earth Doctor, because he could not give them food and water enough, killed them all. He caught the hook of his staff into the sky and pulled it down so that it crushed all the people and all the animals, until there was nothing living on the earth. Earth Doctor made a hole through the earth with his stick, and through that he went, coming out safe, but alone, on the other side.

He called upon the sun and moon to come out of the wreck of the world and sky, and they did so. But there was no sky for them to travel through, no stars, and no Milky Way. So Earth Doctor made these all over again. Then he created another race of men and animals.

Then Coyote was born. Moon was his mother. When Coyote was large and strong he came to the land where the Pima Indians lived.

Then Elder Brother was born. Earth was his mother, and Sky his father. He was so powerful that he spoke roughly to Earth Doctor, who trembled before him. The people began to increase in numbers, just as they had done before, but Elder Brother shortened their lives, so the earth did not become so crowded. But Elder Brother did not like the people created by Earth Doctor, so he planned to destroy them again. So Elder Brother planned to create a magic baby.

The screams of the baby shook the earth. They could be heard for a great distance. Then Earth Doctor called all the people together, and told them there would be a great flood. He sang a magic song and then bored a hole through the flat earth-plain through to the other side. Some of the people went into the hole to escape the flood that was coming, but not very many got through. Some of the people asked Elder Brother to help them, but he did not answer. Only Coyote he answered. He told Coyote to find a big log and sit on it, so that he would float on the surface of the water with the driftwood. Elder Brother got into a big olla which he had made, and closed it tight. So he rolled along on the ground under the olla. He sang a magic song as he climbed into his olla.

A young man went to the place where the baby was screaming. Its tears were a great torrent which cut gorges in the earth before it. The water was rising all over the earth. He bent over the child to pick it up, and immediately both became birds and flew above the flood. Only five birds were saved from the flood. One was a flicker and one a vulture. They clung by their beaks to the sky to keep themselves above the waters, but the tail of the flicker was washed by the waves and that is why it is stiff to this day. At last a god took pity on them and gave them power to make "nests of down" from their own breasts on which they floated on the water. One of these birds was the vipisimal, and if any one injures it to this day, the flood may come again.

Now South Doctor called his people to him and told them that a flood was coming. He sang a magic song and he bored a hole in the ground with a cane so that people might go through to the other side. Others he sent to Earth Doctor, but Earth Doctor told them they were too late. So they sent the people to the top of a high mountain called Crooked Mountain. South Doctor sang a magic song and traced his cane around the mountain, but that held back the waters only for a short time. Four times he sang and traced a line around the mountain, yet the flood rose again each time. There was only one thing more to do.

He held his magic crystals in his left hand and sang a song. Then he struck it with his cane. A thunder peal rang through the mountains. He threw his staff into the water and it cracked with a loud noise. Turning, he saw a dog near him. He said, "How high is the tide?" The dog said, "It is very near the top." He looked at the people as he said it. When they heard his voice they all turned to stone. They stood just as they were, and they are there to this day in groups: some of the men talking, some of the women cooking, and some crying.

But Earth Doctor escaped by enclosing himself in his reed staff, which floated upon the water. Elder Brother rolled along in his olla until he came near the mouth of the Colorado River. The olla is now called Black Mountain. After the flood he came out and visited all parts of the land. When he met Coyote and Earth Doctor, each claimed to have been the first to appear after the flood, but at last they admitted Elder Brother was the first, so he became ruler of the world.

The Birds and the Flood
Pima (Arizona)

Once upon a time, when all the earth was flooded, two birds were hanging above the water. They were clinging to the sky with their beaks. The larger bird was gray with a long tail and beak, but the smaller one was the tiny bird that builds a nest shaped like an olla, with only a very small opening at the top. The birds were tired and frightened. The larger one cried and cried, but the little bird held on tight and said, "Don't cry. I'm littler than you are, but I'm very brave."

Legend of the Flood
Ashochimi (Coast Indians, Cal.)

Long ago there was a great flood which destroyed all the people in the world. Only Coyote was saved. When the waters subsided, the earth was empty. Coyote thought about it a long time.

Then Coyote collected a great bundle of tail feathers from owls, hawks, eagles, and buzzards. He journeyed over the whole earth and carefully located the site of each Indian village. Where the *tepees* had stood, he planted a feather in the ground and scraped up the dirt around it. The feathers sprouted like trees, and grew up and branched. At last they turned into men and women. So the world was inhabited with people again.

The Great Flood
Sia (New Mexico)
For a long time after the fight, the people were very happy, but the ninth year was very bad. The whole earth was filled with water. The water did not fall in rain, but came in as rivers between the mesas. It continued to flow in from all sides until the people and the animals fled to the mesa tops. The water continued to rise until nearly level with the tops of the mesas. Then Sussistinnako cried, "Where shall my people go? Where is the road to the north?" He looked to the north. "Where is the road to the west? Where is the road to the east? Where is the road to the south?" He looked in each direction. He said, "I see the waters are everywhere."

All of the medicine men sang four days and four nights, but still the waters continued to rise.

Then Spider placed a huge reed upon the top of the mesa. He said, "My people will pass up through this to the world above."

Utset led the way, carrying a sack in which were many of the Star people. The medicine men followed, carrying sacred things in sacred blankets on their backs. Then came the people, and the animals, and the snakes, and birds. The turkey was far behind and the foam of the water rose and reached the tip ends of his feathers. You may know that is true because even to this day they bear the mark of the waters.

When they reached the top of the great reed, the earth which formed the floor of the world above, barred their way. Utset called to Locust, "Man, come here." Locust went to her. She said, "You know best how to pass through the earth. Go and make a door for us."

"Very well, mother," said Locust. "I think I can make a way."

He began working with his feet and after a while he passed through the earthy floor, entering the upper world. As soon as he saw it, he said to Utset, "It is good above."

Utset called Badger, and said, "Make a door for us. Sika, the Locust has made one, but it is very small."

"Very well, mother, I will," said Badger.

After much work he passed into the world above, and said, "Mother, I have opened the way." Badger also said, "Father-mother, the world above is good."

Utset then called Deer. She said, "You go through first. If you can get your head through, others may pass."

The deer returned saying, "Father, it is all right. I passed without trouble."

Utset called Elk. She said, "You pass through. If you can get your head and horns through the door, all may pass."

Elk returned saying, "Father, it is good. I passed without trouble."

Then Utset told the buffalo to try, and he returned saying, "Father-mother, the door is good. I passed without trouble."

Utset called the scarab beetle and gave him the sack of stars, telling him to pass out first with them. Scarab did not know what the sack contained, but he was very small and grew tired carrying it. He wondered what could be in the sack. After entering the new world he was so tired he laid down the sack and peeped into it. He cut only a tiny hole, but at once the Star People flew out and filled the heavens everywhere.

Then Utset and all the people came, and after Turkey passed, the door was closed with a great rock so that the waters from below could not follow them.

Then Utset looked for the sack with the Star People. She found it nearly empty and could not tell where the stars had gone. The little beetle sat by, very much frightened and very sad. But Utset was angry and said, "You are bad and disobedient. From this time forth, you shall be blind." That is the reason the scarabaeus has no eyes, so the old ones say. But the little fellow had saved a few of the stars by grasping the sack and holding it fast. Utset placed these in the heavens. In one group she placed seven—the great bear. In another, three. In another group she placed the Pleiades, and threw the others far off into the sky.

The Flood and the Theft of Fire
Tolowa (Del Norte Co., Cal.)

Along time ago there came a great rain. It lasted a long time and the water kept rising till all the valleys were submerged, and the Indian tribes fled to the high lands. But the water rose, and though the Indians fled to the highest point, all were swept away and drowned-all but one man and one woman. They reached the very highest peak and were saved. These two Indians ate the fish from the waters around them. Then the waters subsided. All the game was gone, and all the animals. But the children of these two Indians, when they died, became the spirits of deer and bear and insects, and so the animals and insects came back to the earth again.

The Indians had no fire. The flood had put out all the fires in the world. They looked at the moon and wished they could secure fire from it. Then the Spider Indians and the Snake Indians formed a plan to steal fire. The Spiders wove a very light balloon, and fastened it by a long rope to the earth. Then they climbed into the balloon and started for the moon. But the Indians of the Moon were suspicious of the Earth Indians. The Spiders said, "We came to gamble." The Moon Indians were much pleased and all the Spider Indians began to gamble with them. They sat by the fire.

Then the Snake Indians sent a man to climb up the long rope from the earth to the moon. He climbed the rope, and darted through the fire before the Moon Indians understood what he had done. Then he slid down the rope to earth again. As soon as he touched the earth he traveled over the rocks, the trees, and the dry sticks lying upon the ground, giving fire to each. Everything he touched contained fire. So the world became bright again, as it was before the flood.

When the Spider Indians came down to earth again, they were immediately put to death, for the tribes were afraid the Moon Indians might want revenge.

Legend of the Flood in Sacramento Valley
Maidu (near Sacramento Valley, Cal.)

Long, long ago the Indians living in Sacramento Valley were happy. Suddenly there came the swift sound of rushing waters, and the valley became like Big Waters, which no man can measure. The Indians fled, but many slept beneath the waves. Also the frogs and the salmon pursued them and they ate many Indians. Only two who fled into the foothills escaped.

To these two, Great Man gave many children, and many tribes arose. But one great chief ruled all the nation. The chief went out upon a wide knoll overlooking Big Waters, and he knew that the plains of his people were beneath the waves. Nine sleeps he lay on the knoll, thinking thoughts of these great waters. Nine sleeps he lay without food, and his mind was thinking always of one thing: How did this deep water cover the plains of the world?

At the end of nine sleeps he was changed. He was not like himself. No arrow could wound him. He was like Great Man for no Indian could slay him. Then he spoke to Great Man and commanded him to banish the waters from the plains of his ancestors. Great Man tore a hole in the mountain side, so that the waters on the plains flowed into Big Waters. Thus the Sacramento River was formed.

The Fable of the Animals
Karok (near Klamath River, Cal.)

A great many hundred snows ago, Kareya, sitting on the Sacred Stool, created the world. First, he made the fishes in the Big Water, then the animals on the green land, and last of all, Man! But at first the animals were all alike in power. No one knew which animals should be food for others, and which should be food for man. Then Kareya ordered them all to meet in one place, that Man might give each his rank and his power. So the animals all met together one evening, when the sun was set, to wait overnight for the coming of Man on the next morning. Kareya also commanded Man to make bows and arrows, as many as there were animals, and to give the longest one to the animal which was to have the most power, and the shortest to the one which should have least power. So he did, and after nine sleeps his work was ended, and the bows and arrows which he had made were very many.

Now the animals, being all together, went to sleep, so they might be ready to meet Man on the next morning. But Coyote was exceedingly cunning—he was cunning above all the beasts. Coyote wanted the longest bow and the greatest power, so he could have all the other animals for his meat. He decided to stay awake all night, so that he would be first to meet Man in the morning. So he laughed to himself and stretched his nose out on his paw and pretended to sleep.

About midnight he began to be sleepy. He had to walk around the camp and scratch his eyes to keep them open. He grew more sleepy, so that he had to skip and jump about to keep awake. But he made so much noise, he awakened some of the other animals. When the morning star came up, he was too sleepy to keep his eyes open any longer. So he took two little sticks, and sharpened them at the ends, and propped open his eyelids. Then he felt safe. He watched the morning star, with his nose stretched along his paws, and fell asleep. The sharp sticks pinned his eyelids fast together.

The morning star rose rapidly into the sky. The birds began to sing. The animals woke up and stretched themselves, but still Coyote lay fast asleep. When the sun rose, the animals went to meet Man. He gave the longest bow to Cougar, so he had greatest power; the second longest he gave to Bear; others he gave to the other animals, giving all but the last to Frog. But the shortest one was left. Man cried out, "What animal have I missed?" Then the animals began to look about and found Coyote fast asleep, with his eyelids pinned together. All the animals began to laugh, and they jumped upon Coyote and danced upon him. Then they led him to Man, still blinded, and Man pulled out the sharp sticks and gave him the shortest bow of all. It would hardly shoot an arrow farther than a foot. All the animals laughed.

But Man took pity on Coyote, because he was now weaker even than Frog. So at his request, Kareya gave him cunning, ten times more than before, so that he was cunning above all the animals of the wood. Therefore Coyote was friendly to Man and his children, and did many things for them.

Coyote and Sun
Pai Ute (near Kern River, Cal.)

Along time ago, Coyote wanted to go to the sun. He asked Pokoh, Old Man, to show him the trail. Coyote went straight out on this trail and he traveled it all day. But Sun went round so that Coyote came back at night to the place from which he started in the morning.

The next morning, Coyote asked Pokoh to show him the trail. Pokoh showed him, and Coyote traveled all day and came back at night to the same place again.

But the third day, Coyote started early and went out on the trail to the edge of the world and sat down on the hole where the sun came up. While waiting for the sun he pointed with his bow and arrow at different places and pretended to shoot. He also pretended not to see the sun.

When Sun came up, he told Coyote to get out of his way. Coyote told him to go around; that it was his trail. But Sun came up under him and he had to hitch forward a little. After Sun came up a little farther, it began to get hot on Coyote's shoulder, so he spit on his paw and rubbed his shoulder. Then he wanted to ride up with the sun. Sun said, "Oh, no"; but Coyote insisted. So Coyote climbed up on Sun, and Sun started up the trail in the sky. The trail was marked off into steps like a ladder. As Sun went up he counted "one, two, three," and so on. By and by Coyote became very thirsty, and he asked Sun for a drink of water. Sun gave him an acorn-cup full. Coyote asked him why he had no more. About noontime, Coyote became very impatient. It was very hot. Sun told him to shut his eyes. Coyote shut them, but opened them again. He kept opening and shutting them all the afternoon. At night, when Sun came down, Coyote took hold of a tree. Then he clambered off Sun and climbed down to the earth.

The Course of the Sun
Sia (New Mexico)

Sussistinnako, the spider, said to the sun, "My son, you will ascend and pass over the world above. You will go from north to south. Return and tell me what you think of it."

The sun said, on his return, "Mother, I did as you bade me, and I did not like the road."

Spider told him to ascend and pass over the world from west to the east. On his return, the sun said,

"It may be good for some, mother, but I did not like it."

Spider said, "You will again ascend and pass over the straight road from the east to the west. Return and tell me what you think of it."

That night the sun said, "I am much contented. I like that road much."

Sussistinnako said, "My son, you will ascend each day and pass over the world from east to west."

Upon each day's journey the sun stops midway from the east to the center of the world to eat his breakfast. In the center he stops to eat his dinner. Halfway from the center to the west he stops to eat his supper. He never fails to eat these three meals each day, and always stops at the same points.

The sun wears a shirt of dressed deerskin, with leggings of the same reaching to his thighs. The shirt and leggings are fringed. His moccasins are also of deerskin and embroidered in yellow, red, and turkis beads. He wears a kilt of deerskin, having a snake painted upon it. He carries a bow and arrows, the quiver being of cougar skin, hanging over his shoulder, and he holds his bow in his left hand and an arrow in his right. He always wears the mask which protects him from the sight of the people of Ha-arts.

At the top of the mask is an eagle plume with parrot plumes; an eagle plume is at each side, and one at the bottom of the mask. The hair around the head and face is red like fire, and when it moves and shakes people cannot look closely at the mask. It is not intended that they should observe closely, else they would know that instead of seeing the sun they see only his mask.

The moon came to the upper world with the sun and he also wears a mask. Each night the sun passes by the house of Sussistinnako, the spider, who asks him, "How are my children above? How many have died today? How many have been born today?" The sun lingers only long enough to answer his questions. He then passes on to his house in the east.

The Foxes and the Sun
Yurok (near Klamath River, Cal.)
Once upon a time, the Foxes were angry with Sun. They held a council about the matter. Then twelve Foxes were selected — twelve of the bravest to catch Sun and tie him down. They made ropes of sinew; then the twelve watched until the Sun, as he followed the downward trail in the sky, touched the top of a certain hill. Then the Foxes caught Sun, and tied him fast to the hill. But the Indians saw them, and they killed the Foxes with arrows. Then they cut the sinews. But the Sun had burned a great hole in the ground. The Indians know the story is true, because they can see the hole which Sun burned.

The Theft of Fire
Karok (near Klamath River, Cal.)

There was no fire on earth and the Karoks were cold and miserable. Far away to the east, hidden in a treasure box, was fire which Kareya had made and given to two old hags, lest the Karoks should steal it. So Coyote decided to steal fire for the Indians.

Coyote called a great council of the animals. After the council he stationed a line from the land of the Karoks to the distant land where the fire was kept. Lion was nearest the Fire Land, and Frog was nearest the Karok land. Lion was strongest and Frog was weakest, and the other animals took their places, according to the power given them by Man. Then Coyote took an Indian with him and went to the hill top, but he hid the Indian under the hill. Coyote went to the *tepee* of the hags. He said, "Good-evening." They replied, "Good-evening."

Coyote said, "It is cold out here. Can you let me sit by the fire?" So they let him sit by the fire. He was only a coyote. He stretched his nose out along his forepaws and pretended to go to sleep, but he kept the corner of one eye open watching. So he spent all night watching and thinking, but he had no chance to get a piece of the fire.

The next morning Coyote held a council with the Indian. He told him when he, Coyote, was within the *tepee*, to attack it. Then Coyote went back to the fire. The hags let him in again. He was only a Coyote. But Coyote stood close by the casket of fire. The Indian made a dash at the *tepee*. The hags rushed out after him, and Coyote seized a fire brand in his teeth and flew over the ground. The hags saw the sparks flying and gave chase. But Coyote reached Lion, who ran with it to Grizzly Bear. Grizzly Bear ran with it to Cinnamon Bear; he ran with it to Wolf, and at last the fire came to Ground- Squirrel. Squirrel took the brand and ran so fast that his tail caught fire. He curled it up over his back, and burned the black spot in his shoulders. You can see it even today.

Squirrel came to Frog, but Frog couldn't run. He opened his mouth wide and swallowed the fire. Then he jumped but the hags caught his tail. Frog jumped again, but the hags kept his tail. That is why Frogs have no tail, even to this day. Frog swam under water, and came up on a pile of driftwood. He spat out the fire into the dry wood, and that is why there is fire in dry wood even today. When an Indian rubs two pieces together, the fire comes out.

The Theft of Fire
Sia (New Mexico)

A long, long time ago, the people became tired of feeding on grass, like deer and wild animals, and they talked together how fire might be found. The Ti-amoni said, "Coyote is the best man to steal fire from the world below," so he sent for Coyote.

When Coyote came, the Ti-amoni said, "The people wish for fire. We are tired of feeding on grass. You must go to the world below and bring the fire."

Coyote said, "It is well, father. I will go."

So Coyote slipped stealthily to the house of Sussistinnako. It was the middle of the night. Snake, who guarded the first door, was asleep, and he slipped quickly and quietly by. Cougar, who guarded the second door, was asleep, and Coyote slipped by. Bear, who guarded the third door, was also sleeping. At the fourth door, Coyote found the guardian of the fire asleep. Slipping through into the room of Sussistinnako, he found him also sleeping.

Coyote quickly lighted the cedar brand which was attached to his tail and hurried out. Spider awoke, just enough to know some one was leaving the room. "Who is there?" he cried. Then he called, "Some one has been here." But before he could waken the sleeping Bear and Cougar and Snake, Coyote had almost reached the upper world.

The Earth-Hardening After the Flood
Sia (New Mexico)

After the flood, the Sia returned to Ha-arts, the earth. They came through an opening in the far north. After they had remained at their first village a year, they wished to pass on, but the earth was very moist and Utset was puzzled how to harden it.

Utset called Cougar. She said, "Have you any medicine to harden the road so that we may pass over it?" Cougar replied, "I will try, mother." But after going a short distance over the road, he sank to his shoulders in the wet earth. He returned much afraid and told Utset that he could go no farther.

Then she sent for Bear. She said, "Have you any medicine to harden the road?" Bear started out, but he sank to his shoulders, and returned saying, "I can do nothing."

Then Utset called Badger, and he tried. She called Shrew, and he failed. She called Wolf, and he failed.

Then Utset returned to the lower world and asked Sussistinnako what she could do to harden the earth so that her people might travel over it. He asked, "Have you no medicine to make the earth firm? Have you asked Cougar and Wolf, Bear and Badger and Wolf to use their medicines to harden the earth?"

Utset said, "I have tried all these."

Then Sussistinnako said, "Others will understand." He told her to have a woman of the Kapina (spider) clan try to harden the earth.

When the woman arrived, Utset said, "My mother, Sussistinnako tells me the Kapina society understand how to harden the earth."

The woman said, "I do not know how to make the earth hard."

Three times Utset asked the woman about hardening the earth, and three times the woman said, "I do not know." The fourth time the woman said, "Well, I guess I know. I will try."

So she called together the members of the Spider society, the Kapina, and said,

"Our mother, Sussistinnako, bids us work for her and harden the earth so that the people may pass over it." The spider woman first made a road of fine cotton which she produced from her own body, and suspended it a few feet above the earth. Then she told the people they could travel on that. But the people were afraid to trust themselves to such a frail road.

Then Utset said, "I wish a man and not a woman of the Spider society to work for me."

Then he came. He threw out a charm of wood, latticed so it could be expanded or contracted. When it was extended it reached to the middle of the earth. He threw it to the south, to the east, and to the west; then he threw it toward the people in the north.

So the earth was made firm that the people might travel upon it. Soon after Utset said, "I will soon leave you. I will, return to the home from which I came."

Then she selected a man of the Corn clan. She said to him, "You will be known as Ti-amoni (arch-ruler). You will be to my people as myself. You will pass with them over the straight road. I give to you all my wisdom, my thoughts, my heart, and all. I fill your mind with my mind." He replied: "It is well, mother. I will do as you say."

The Origins of the Totems and of Names
Zuni (New Mexico)

Now the Twain Beloved and the priest-fathers gathered in council for the naming and selection of man-groups and creature-kinds, and things. So they called the people of the southern space the Children of Summer, and those who loved the sun most became the Sun people. Others who loved the water became the Toad people, or Turtle people, or Frog people. Others loved the seeds of the earth and became the Seed people, or the people of the First-growing grass, or of the Tobacco. Those who loved warmth were the Fire or Badger people. According to their natures they chose their totems.

And so also did the People of Winter, or the People of the North. Some were known as the Bear people, or the Coyote people, or Deer people; others as the Crane people, Turkey people, or Grouse people. So the Badger people dwelt in a warm place, even as the badgers on the sunny side of hills burrow, finding a dwelling amongst the dry roots whence is fire.

Traditions of Wanderings
Hopi (Arizona)

After the Hopi had been taught to build stone houses, they took separate ways. My people were the Snake people. They lived in snake skins, each family occupying a separate snake skin bag. All were hung on the end of a rainbow which swung around until the end touched Navajo Mountain. Then the bags dropped from it. Wherever a bag dropped, there was their house. After they arranged their bags they came out from them as men and women, and they then built a stone house which had five sides. Then a brilliant star arose in the southeast. It would shine for a while and disappear.

The old men said, "'Beneath that star there must be people." They decided to travel to it. They cut a staff and set it in the ground and watched until the star reached its top. Then they started and traveled as long as the star shone. When it disappeared they halted. But the star did not shine every night. Sometimes many years passed before it appeared again. When this occurred, the people built houses during their halt. They built round houses and square houses, and all the ruins between here and Navajo Mountain mark the places where our people lived. They waited until the star came to the top of the staff again, but when they moved on, many people remained in those houses.

When our people reached Waipho (a spring a few miles from Walpi) the star vanished. It has never been seen since. They built a house there, but Masauwu, the God of the Face of the Earth, came and compelled the people to move about halfway between the East Mesa and the Middle Mesa and there they stayed many plantings. One time when the old men were assembled, the god came among them, looking like a horrible skeleton and rattling his bones. But he could not frighten them. So he said, "I have lost my wager. All that I have is yours. Ask for anything you want and I will give it to you."

At that time, our people's house was beside the water course. The god said, "Why do you sit there in the mud? Go up yonder where it is dry." So they went across to the west side of the mesa near the point and built a house and lived there.

Again when the old men assembled two demons came among them, but the old men took the great Baho and chased them away.

Other Hopi (Hopituh) came into this country from time to time and old people said, "Build here," or "Build there," and portioned the land among the newcomers.

The Migration of the Water People
Walpi (Arizona)

In the long ago, the Snake, Horn, and Eagle people lived here (in Tusayan) but their corn grew only a span high and when they sang for rain, the Cloud god sent only a thin mist. My people lived then in the distant Pa-lat Kwa-bi in the South. There was a very bad old man there. When he met any one he would spit in their faces. . . . He did all manner of evil. Baholihonga got angry at this and turned the world upside down. Water spouted up through the kivas and through the fire places in the houses. The earth was rent in great chasms, and water covered everything except one narrow ridge of mud. Across this the Serpent-god told all the people to travel. As they journeyed across, the feet of the bad slipped and they fell into the dark water. The good people, after many days, reached dry land.

While the water was rising around the village, the old people got on top of the houses. They thought they could not struggle across with the younger people. But Baholihonga clothed them with the skins of turkeys. They spread their wings out and floated in the air just above the surface of the water, and in this way they got across. There were saved of us, the Water people, the Corn people, the Lizard, Horned-toad, and Sand peoples, two families of Rabbit, and the Tobacco people. The turkey tail dragged in the water. That is why there is white on the turkey's tail now. This is also the reason why old people use turkey-feathers at the religious ceremonies.

Coyote and the Mesquite Beans
Pima (Arizona)

After the waters of the flood had gone down, Elder Brother said to Coyote, "Do not touch that black bug; and do not eat the mesquite beans. It is dangerous to harm anything that came safe through the flood." So Coyote went on, but presently he came to the black bug. He stopped and ate it up. Then he went on to the mesquite beans. He stopped and looked at them a while, and then said, "I will just taste one and that will be all." But he stood there and ate and ate until he had eaten them all up. And the bug and the beans swelled up in his stomach and killed him.

Origin of the Sierra Nevadas and Coast Range
Yokuts (near Fresno, Cal.)

Once there was a time when there was nothing in the world but water. About the place where Tulare Lake is now, there was a pole standing far up out of the water, and on this pole perched Hawk and Crow. First Hawk would sit on the pole a while, then Crow would knock him off and sit on it himself. Thus they sat on the top of the pole above the water for many ages. At last they created the birds which prey on fish. They created Kingfisher, Eagle, Pelican, and others. They created also Duck. Duck was very small but she dived to the bottom of the water, took a beakful of mud, and then died in coming to the top of the water. Duck lay dead floating on the water. Then Hawk and Crow took the mud from Duck's beak, and began making the mountains.

They began at the place now known as Ta-hi-cha-pa Pass, and Hawk made the east range. Crow made the west one. They pushed the mud down hard into the water and then piled it high. They worked toward the north. At last Hawk and Crow met at Mount Shasta. Then their work was done. But when they looked at their mountains, Crow's range was much larger than Hawk's.

Hawk said to Crow, "How did this happen, you rascal? You have been stealing earth from my bill. That is why your mountains are the biggest." Crow laughed.

Then Hawk chewed some Indian tobacco. That made him wise. At once he took hold of the mountains and turned them around almost in a circle. He put his range where Crow's had been. That is why the Sierra Nevada Range is larger than the Coast Range.

Legend of Tu-Tok-A-Nu'-La (El Capitan)
Yosemite Valley

Here were once two little boys living in the valley who went down to the river to swim. After paddling and splashing about to their hearts' content, they went on shore and crept up on a huge boulder which stood beside the water. They lay down in the warm sunshine to dry themselves, but fell asleep. They slept so soundly that they knew nothing, though the great boulder grew day by day, and rose night by night, until it lifted them up beyond the sight of their tribe, who looked for them everywhere.

The rock grew until the boys were lifted high into the heaven, even far up above the blue sky, until they scraped their faces against the moon. And still, year after year, among the clouds they slept.

Then there was held a great council of all the animals to bring the boys down from the top of the great rock. Every animal leaped as high as he could up the face of the rocky wall. Mouse could only jump as high as one's hand; Rat, twice as high. Then Raccoon tried; he could jump a little farther. One after another of the animals tried, and Grizzly Bear made a great leap far up the wall, but fell back. Last of all Lion tried, and he jumped farther than any other animal, but fell down upon his back. Then came tiny Measuring-Worm, and began to creep up the rock. Soon he reached as high as Raccoon had jumped, then as high as Bear, then as high as Lion's leap, and by and by he was out of sight, climbing up the face of the rock. For one whole snow, Measuring-Worm climbed the rock, and at last he reached the top. Then he wakened the boys, and came down the same way he went up, and brought them down safely to the ground. Therefore the rock is called Tutokanula, the measuring worm. But white men call it El Capitan.

Legend of Tis-Se'-Yak (South Dome and North Dome)
Yosemite Valley

Tisseyak and her husband journeyed from a country very far off, and entered the valley of the Yosemite foot-sore from travel. She bore a great heavy conical basket, strapped across her head. Tisseyak came first. Her husband followed with a rude staff and a light roll of skins on his back. They were thirsty after their long journey across the mountains. They hurried forward to drink of the waters, and the woman was still in advance when she reached Lake Awaia. Then she dipped up the water in her basket and drank of it. She drank up all the water. The lake was dry before her husband reached it. And because the woman drank all the water, there came a drought. The earth dried tip. There was no grass, nor any green thing.

But the man was angry because he had no water to drink. He beat the woman with his staff and she fled, but he followed and beat her even more. Then the woman wept. In her anger she turned and flung her basket at the man. And even then they were changed into stone. The woman's basket lies upturned beside the man. The woman's face is tear-stained, with long dark lines trailing down.

South Dome is the woman and North Dome is the husband. The Indian woman cuts her hair straight across the forehead, and allows the sides to drop along her cheeks, forming a square face.

California Big Trees
Pai Utes (near Kern River, Cal.)

The California big trees are sacred to the Monos, who call them "woh-woh-nau," a word formed in imitation of the hoot of the owl. The owl is the guardian spirit and the god of the big trees. Bad luck comes to those who cut down the big trees, or shoot at an owl, or shoot in the presence of the owl.

In old days the Indians tried to persuade the white men not to cut down the big trees. When they see the trees cut down they call after the white men. They say the owl will bring them evil.

The Children of Cloud
Pima (Arizona)

When the Hohokam dwelt on the Gila River and tilled their farms around the great temple which we call Casa Grande, there was a beautiful young woman in the pueblo who had two twin sons. Their father was Cloud, and he lived far away.

One day the boys came to their mother, as she was weaving mats. "Who is our father?" they asked. "We have no one to run to when he returns from the hunt, or from war, to shout to him."

The mother answered: "In the morning, look toward the sunrise and you will see a white Cloud standing upright. He is your father."

"Can we visit our father?" they asked.

"Yes," said their mother. You may visit him, but you must make the journey without stopping. First you will reach Wind, who is your father's eldest brother. Behind him you will find your father."

The boys traveled four days and came to the house of Wind.

"Are you our father?" they asked.

"No, I am your Uncle," answered Wind." Your father lives in the next house. Go on to him."

They traveled on to Cloud. But Cloud drove them away. He said, "Go to your uncle Wind. He will tell you something." But Wind sent them back to Cloud again. Thus the boys were driven away from each house four times. Then Cloud said to them, "Prove to me you are my sons. If you are, you can do what I do."

The younger boy sent chain lightning across the sky with sharp, crackling thunder. The elder boy sent the heat lightning with its distant rumble of thunder.

"You are my children," said Cloud. "You have power like mine."

But again he tested them. He took them to a house near by where a flood of rain had drowned the people. "If I they are my sons," he said, "they will not be harmed."

Then Cloud sent the rain and the storm. The water rose higher and higher, but the two boys were not harmed. The water could not drown them. Then Cloud took them to his home and there they stayed a long, long time.

But after a long time, the boys wished to see their mother again. Then Cloud made them some bows and arrows differing from any they had ever seen, and sent them to their mother. He told them he would watch over them as they traveled but they must speak to no one they met on their way.

So the boys traveled to the setting sun. First they met Raven. They remembered their father's command and turned aside so as not to meet him. Then they met Roadrunner, and turned aside to avoid him. Next came Hawk and Eagle.

Eagle said, "Let's scare those boys." So he swooped down over their heads until they cried from fright.

"We were just teasing you," said Eagle. "We will not do you any harm." Then Eagle flew on.

Next they met Coyote. They tried to avoid him, but Coyote ran around and put himself in their way. Cloud was watching and he sent down thunder and lightning. And the boys sent out their magic thunder and lightning also, until Coyote was frightened and ran away.

Now this happened on the mountain top, and one boy was standing on each side of the trail. After Coyote ran away, they were changed into mescal—the very largest mescal ever known. The place was near Tucson. This is the reason why mescal grows on the mountains, and why thunder and lightning go from place to place—because the children did. That is why it rains when we gather mescal.

The Cloud People
Sia (New Mexico)

Now all the Cloud People, the Lightning People, the Thunder and Rainbow Peoples followed the Sia into the upper world. But all the people of Tinia, the middle world, did not leave the lower world. Only a portion were sent by the Spider to work for the people of the upper world. The Cloud People are so many that, although the demands of the earth people are so great, there are always many passing about over Tinia for pleasure. These Cloud People ride on wheels, small wheels being used by the little Cloud children and large wheels by the older ones.

The Cloud People keep always behind their masks. The shape of the mask depends upon the number of the people and the work being done. The Henati are the floating white clouds behind which the Cloud People pass for pleasure. The Heash are clouds like the plains and behind these the Cloud People are laboring to water the earth. Water is brought by the Cloud People, from the springs at the base of the mountains, in gourds and jugs and vases by the men, women, and children. They rise from the springs and pass through the trunk of the tree to its top, which reaches Tinia. They pass on to the point to be sprinkled.

The priest of the Cloud People is above even the priests of the Thunder, Lightning, and Rainbow Peoples. The Cloud People have ceremonials, just like those of the Sia. On the altars of the Sia may be seen figures arranged just as the Cloud People sit in their ceremonials.

When a priest of the Cloud People wishes assistance from the Thunder and Lightning Peoples, he notifies their priests, but keeps a supervision of all things himself.

Then the Lightning People shoot their arrows to make it rain the harder. The smaller flashes come from the bows of the children. The Thunder People have human forms, with wings of knives, and by flapping these wings they make a great noise. Thus they frighten the Cloud and Lightning People into working the harder.

The Rainbow People were created to work in Tinia to make it more beautiful for the people of Ha-arts, the earth, to look upon. The elders make the beautiful rainbows, but the children assist. The Sia have no idea of what or how these bows are made. They do know, however, that war heroes always travel upon the rainbows.

Rain Song
Sia (New Mexico)

We, the ancient ones, ascended from the middle of the world below, through the door of the entrance to the lower world, we hold our songs to the Cloud, Lightning, and Thunder Peoples as we hold our own hearts. Our medicine is precious.

(Addressing the people of Tinia:)

We entreat you to send your thoughts to us so that we may sing your songs straight, so that they will pass over the straight road to the Cloud priests that they may cover the earth with water, so that she may bear all that is good for us.

Lightning People, send your arrows to the middle of the earth. Hear the echo! Who is it? The People of the Spruce of the North. All your people and your thoughts come to us. Who is it? People of the white floating Clouds. Your thoughts come to us. All your people and your thoughts come to us. Who is it? The Lightning People. Your thoughts come to us. Who is it? Cloud People at the horizon. All your people and your thoughts come to us.

Rain Song
White floating clouds. Clouds, like the plains, come and water the earth. Sun, embrace the earth that she may be fruitful. Moon, lion of the north, bear of the west, badger of the south, wolf of the east, eagle of the heavens, shrew of the earth, elder war hero, younger war hero, warriors of the six mountains of the world, intercede with the Cloud People for us that they may water the earth. Medicine bowl, cloud bowl, and water vase give us your hearts, that the earth may be watered. I make the ancient road of meal that my song may pass straight over it—the ancient road. White shell bead woman who lives where the sun goes down, mother whirlwind, father Sussistinnako, mother Yaya, creator of good thoughts, yellow woman of the north, blue woman of the west, red woman of the south, white woman of the east, slightly yellow woman of the zenith, and dark woman of the nadir, I ask your intercession with the Cloud People.

Rain Song
Sia (New Mexico)
Let the white floating clouds—the clouds like the plains—the lightning, thunder, rainbow, and cloud peoples, water the earth. Let the people of the white floating clouds,- the people of the clouds like the plains—the lightning, thunder, rain bow, and cloud peoples - come and work for us, and water the earth.

The Corn Maidens
Zuni (New Mexico)
After long ages of wandering, the precious Seed-things rested over the Middle at Zuni, and men turned their hearts to the cherishing of their corn and the Corn Maidens instead of warring with strange men. But there was complaint by the people of the customs followed. Some said the music was not that of the olden time. Far better was that which of nights they often heard as they wandered up and down the river trail. Wonderful music, as of liquid voices in

caverns, or the echo of women's laughter in water-vases. And the music was timed with a deep-toned drum from the Mountain of Thunder. Others thought the music was that of the ghosts of ancient men, but it was far more beautiful than the music when danced the Corn Maidens. Others said light clouds rolled upward from the grotto in Thunder Mountain like to the mists that leave behind them the dew, but lo! even as they faded the bright garments of the Rainbow women might be seen fluttering, and the broidery and paintings of these dancers of the mist were more beautiful than the costumes of the Corn Maidens.

Then the priests of the people said, "It may well be Paiyatuma, the liquid voices his flute and the flutes of his players."

Now when the time of ripening corn was near, the fathers ordered preparation for the dance of the Corn Maidens. They sent the two Master-Priests of the Bow to the grotto at Thunder Mountains, saying., "If you behold Paiyatuma, and his maidens, perhaps they will give us the help of their customs."

Then up the river trail, the priests heard the sound of a drum and strains of song. It was Paiyatuma and his seven maidens, the Maidens of the House of Stars, sisters of the Corn Maidens.

The God of Dawn and Music lifted his flute and took his place in the line of dancers. The drum sounded until the cavern shook as with thunder. The flutes sang and sighed as the wind in a wooded canon while still the storm is distant. White mists floated up from the wands of the Maidens, above which fluttered the butterflies of Summer-land about the dress of the Rainbows in the strange blue light of the night.

Then Paiyatuma, smiling, said, "Go the way before, telling the fathers of our custom, and straightway we will follow."

Soon the sound of music was heard, coming from up the river, and soon the Flute People and singers and maidens of the Flute dance. Up rose the fathers and all the watching people, greeting the God of Dawn with outstretched hand and offering of prayer meal. Then the singers took their places and sounded their drum, flutes, and song of clear waters, while the Maidens of the Dew danced their Flute dance. Greatly marveled the people, when from the wands they bore forth came white clouds, and fine cool mists descended.

Now when the dance was ended and the Dew Maidens had retired, out came the beautiful Mothers of Corn. And when the players of the flutes saw them, they were enamored of their beauty and gazed upon them so intently that the Maidens let fall their hair and cast down their eyes.

And jealous and bolder grew the mortal youths, and in the morning dawn, in rivalry, the dancers sought all too freely the presence of the Corn Maidens, no longer holding them so precious as in the olden time. And the matrons, intent on the new dance, heeded naught else. But behold! The mists increased greatly, surrounding dancers and watchers alike, until within them, the Maidens of Corn, all in white garments, became invisible. Then sadly and noiselessly they stole in amongst the people and laid their corn wands down amongst the trays, and laid their white broidered garments thereupon, as mothers lay soft kilting over their babes. Then even as the mists became they, and with the mists drifting, fled away, to the far south Summer-land.

The Search for the Corn Maidens
Zuni (New Mexico)

Then the people in their trouble called the two Master-Priests and said: "Who, now, think ye, should journey to seek our precious Maidens? Bethink ye! Who amongst the Beings is even as ye are, strong of will and good of eyes? There is our great elder brother and father, Eagle, he of the floating down and of the terraced tail-fan. Surely he is enduring of will and surpassing of sight."

"Yea. Most surely," said the fathers. "Go ye forth and beseech him."

Then the two sped north to Twin Mountain, where in a grotto high up among the crags, with his mate and his young, dwelt the Eagle of the White Bonnet.

They climbed the mountain, but behold! Only the eaglets were there. They screamed lustily and tried to hide themselves in the dark recesses.

"Pull not our feathers, ye of hurtful touch, but wait. When we are older we will drop them for you even from the clouds."

"Hush," said the warriors. "Wait in peace. We seek not ye but thy father."

Then from afar, with a frown, came old Eagle. "Why disturb ye my featherlings?" he cried.

"Behold! Father and elder brother, we come seeking only the light of thy favor. Listen!"

Then they told him of the lost Maidens of the Corn, and begged him to search for them.

"Be it well with thy wishes," said Eagle. "Go ye before contentedly."

So the warriors returned to the council. But Eagle winged his way high into the sky. High, high, he rose, until he circled among the clouds, small-seeming and swift, like seed-down in a whirlwind. Through all the heights, to the north, to the west, to the south, and to the east, he circled and sailed. Yet nowhere saw he trace of the Corn Maidens. Then he flew lower, returning. Before the warriors were rested, people heard the roar of his wings. As he alighted, the fathers said, "Enter thou and sit, oh brother, and say to us what thou hast to say." And they offered him the cigarette of the space relations.

When they had puffed the smoke toward the four points of the compass, and Eagle had purified his breath with smoke, and had blown smoke over sacred things, he spoke.

"Far have I journeyed, scanning all the regions. Neither bluebird nor woodrat can hide from my seeing," he said, snapping his beak. "Neither of them, unless they hide under bushes. Yet I have failed to see anything of the Maidens ye seek for. Send for my younger brother, the Falcon. Strong of flight is he, yet not so strong as I, and nearer the ground he takes his way ere sunrise."

Then the Eagle spread his wings and flew away to Twin Mountain. The Warrior-Priests of the Bow sped again fleetly over the plain to the westward for his younger brother, Falcon.

Sitting on an ant hill, so the warriors found Falcon. He paused as they approached, crying, "If ye have snare strings, I will be off like the flight of an arrow well plumed of our feathers! "

"No," said the priests. "Thy elder brother hath bidden us seek thee."

Then they told Falcon what had happened, and how Eagle had failed to find the Corn Maidens, so white and beautiful.

"Failed!" said Falcon. "Of course he failed. He climbs aloft to the clouds and thinks he can see under every bush and into every shadow, as sees the Sunfather who sees not with eyes. Go ye before."

Before the Warrior-Priests had turned toward the town, the Falcon had spread his sharp wings and was skimming off over the tops of the trees and bushes as though verily seeking for field mice or birds' nests. And the Warriors returned to tell the fathers and to await his coming.

But after Falcon had searched over the world, to the north and west, to the east and south, he too returned and was received as had been Eagle. He settled on the edge of a tray before the altar, as on the ant hill he settles today. When he had smoked and had been smoked, as had been Eagle, he told the sorrowing fathers and mothers that he had looked behind every copse and cliff shadow, but of the Maidens he had found no trace.

"They are hidden more closely than ever sparrow hid," he said. Then he, too, flew away to his hills in the west.

"Our beautiful Maiden Mothers," cried the matrons. "Lost, lost as the dead are they!"

"Yes," said the others. "Where now shall we seek them? The far-seeing Eagle and the close-searching Falcon alike have failed to find them."

"Stay now your feet with patience," said the fathers. Some of them had heard Raven, who sought food in the refuse and dirt at the edge of town, at daybreak.

"Look now," they said. "There is Heavy-nose, whose beak never fails to find the substance of seed itself, however little or well hidden it be. He surely must know of the Corn Maidens. Let us call him."

So the warriors went to the river side. When they found Raven, they raised their hands, all weaponless.

"We carry no pricking quills," they called. "Blackbanded father, we seek your aid. Look now! The Mother-maidens of Seed whose substance is the food alike of thy people and our people, have fled away. Neither our grandfather the Eagle, nor his younger brother the Falcon, can trace them. We beg you to aid us or counsel us."

"Ka! ka!" cried the Raven. "Too hungry am I to go abroad fasting on business for ye. Ye are stingy! Here have I been since perching time, trying to find a throatful, but ye pick thy bones and lick thy bowls too clean for that, be sure."

"Come in, then, poor grandfather. We will give thee food to cat. Yea, and a cigarette to smoke, with all the ceremony."

"Say ye so?" said the Raven. He ruffled his collar and opened his mouth so wide with a lusty kaw-la-ka- that he might well have swallowed his own head. "Go ye before," he said, and followed them into the court of the dancers.

He was not ill to look upon. Upon his shoulders were bands of white cotton, and his back was blue, gleaming like the hair of a maiden dancer in the sunlight. The Master-Priest greeted Raven, bidding him sit and smoke.

"Ha! There is corn in this, else why the stalk of it?" said the Raven, when he took the cane cigarette of the far spaces and noticed the joint of it. Then he did as he had seen the Master-Priest do, only more greedily. He sucked in such a throatful of the smoke, fire and all, that it almost strangled him. He coughed and grew giddy, and the smoke all hot and stinging went through every part of him. It filled all his feathers, making even his brown eyes bluer and blacker, in rings. It is not to be wondered at, the blueness of flesh, blackness of dress, and skinniness, yes, and tearfulness of eye which we see in the Raven today. And they are all as greedy of corn food as ever, for behold! No sooner had the old Raven recovered than he espied one of the ears of corn half hidden under the mantle-covers of the trays. He leaped from his place laughing. They always laugh when they find anything, these ravens. Then he caught up the ear of corn and made off with it over the heads of the people and the tops of the houses, crying.

"Ha! ha! In this wise and in no other will ye find thy Seed Maidens." But after a while he came back, saying, "A sharp eye have I for the flesh of the Maidens. But who might see their breathing-beings, ye dolts, except by the help of the Father of Dawn-Mist himself, whose breath makes breath of others seem as itself." Then he flew away cawing. Then the elders said to each other, "It is our fault, so how dare we prevail on our father Paiyatuma to aid us? He warned us of this in the old time."

Suddenly, for the sun was rising, they heard Paiyatuma in his daylight mood and transformation. Thoughtless and loud, uncouth in speech, he walked along the outskirts of the village. He joked fearlessly even of fearful things, for all his words and deeds were the reverse of his sacred being. He sat down on a heap of vile refuse, saying he would have a feast.

"My poor little children," he said. But he spoke to aged priests and white-haired matrons.

"Good-night to you all," he said, though it was in full dawning. So he perplexed them with his speeches.

"We beseech thy favor, oh father, and thy aid, in finding our beautiful Maidens." So the priests mourned.

"Oh, that is all, is it? But why find that which is not lost, or summon those who will not come?"

Then he reproached them for not preparing the sacred plumes, and picked up the very plumes he had said were not there.

Then the wise Pekwinna, the Speaker of the Sun, took two plumes and the banded wing-tips of the turkey, and approaching Paiyatuma stroked him with the tips of the feathers and then laid the feathers upon his lips. . . .

Then Paiyatuma became aged and grand and straight, as is a tall tree shorn by lightning. He said to the father:

"Thou are wise of thought and good of heart. Therefore I will summon from Summer-land the beautiful Maidens that ye may look upon them once more and make offering of plumes in sacrifice for them, but they are lost as dwellers amongst ye."

Then he told them of the song lines and the sacred speeches and of the offering of the sacred plume wands, and then turned him about and sped away so fleetly that none saw him.

Beyond the first valley of the high plain to the southward Paiyatuma planted the four plume wands. First he planted the yellow, bending over it and watching it. When it ceased to flutter, the soft down on it leaned northward but moved not. Then he set the blue wand and watched it; then the white wand. The eagle down on them leaned to right and left and still northward, yet moved not. Then farther on he planted the red wand, and bending low, without breathing, watched it closely. The soft down plumes began to wave as though blown by the breath of some small creature. Backward and forward, northward and southward they swayed, as if in time to the breath of one resting.

"'T is the breath of my Maidens in Summer-land, for the plumes of the southland sway soft to their gentle breathing. So shall it ever be. When I set the down of my mists on the plains and scatter my bright beads in the northland, summer shall go thither from afar, borne on the breath of the Seed Maidens. Where they breathe, warmth, showers, and fertility shall follow with the birds of Summer-land, and the butterflies, northward over the world."

Then Paiyatuma arose and sped by the magic of his knowledge into the countries of Summer-land, fled swiftly and silently as the soft breath he sought for, bearing his painted flute before him. And when he paused to rest, he played on his painted flute and the butterflies and birds sought him. So he sent them to seek the Maidens, following swiftly, and long before he found them he greeted them with the music of his songsound, even as the People of the Seed now greet them in the song of the dancers.

When the Maidens heard his music and saw his tall form in their great fields of corn, they plucked ears, each of her own kind, and with them filled their colored trays and over all spread embroidered mantles—embroidered in all the bright colors and with the creature-songs of Summer-land. So they sallied forth to meet him and welcome him. Then he greeted them, each with the touch of his hands and the breath of his flute, and bade them follow him to the northland home of their deserted children.

So by the magic of their knowledge they sped back as the stars speed over the world at night time, toward the home of our ancients. Only at night and dawn they journeyed, as the dead do, and the stars also. So they came at evening in the full of the last moon to the Place of the Middle, bearing their trays of seed.

Glorious was Paiyatuma, as he walked into the courts of the dancers in the dusk of the evening and stood with folded arms at the foot of the bow-fringed ladder of priestly council, he and his follower Shutsukya. He was tall and beautiful and banded with his own mists, and carried the banded wings of the turkeys with which he had winged his flight from afar, leading the Maidens, and followed as by his own shadow by the black being of the corn-soot, Shutsukya, who cries with the voice of the frost wind when the corn has grown aged and the harvest is taken away. And surpassingly beautiful were the Maidens clothed in the white cotton and embroidered garments of Summer-land.

Then after long praying and chanting by the priests, the fathers of the people, and those of the Seed and Water, and the keepers of sacred things, the Maiden-mother of the North advanced to the foot of the ladder. She lifted from her head the beautiful tray of yellow corn and Paiyatama took it. He pointed it to the regions, each in turn, and the Priest of the North came and received the tray of sacred seed.

Then the Maiden of the West advanced and gave up her tray of blue corn. So each in turn the Maidens gave up their trays of precious seed. The Maiden of the South, the red seed; the Maiden of the East, the white seed; then the Maiden with the black seed, and lastly, the tray of all-color seed which the Priestess of Seed-and-All herself received. And now, behold! The Maidens stood as before, she of the North at the northern end, but with her face southward far looking;

she of the West, next, and lo! so all of them, with the seventh and last, looking southward. And standing thus, the darkness of the night fell around them. As shadows in deep night, so these Maidens of the Seed of Corn, the beloved and beautiful, were seen no more of men. And Paiyatuma stood alone, for Shutsukya walked now behind the Maidens, whistling shrilly, as the frost wind whistles when the corn is gathered away, among the lone canes and dry leaves of a gleaned field.

Hasjelti and Hostjoghon
Navajo (New Mexico)

Hasjelti was the son of the white corn, and Hostjoghon the son of the yellow corn. They were born on the mountains where the fogs meet. These two became the great song-makers of the world.

To the mountain where they were born (Henry Mountain, Utah), they gave two songs and two prayers. Then they went to Sierra Blanca (Colorado) and made two songs and prayers and dressed the mountain in clothing of white shell with two eagle plumes upon its head. They visited San Mateo Mountain (New Mexico) and gave to it two songs and prayers, and dressed it in turquoise, even to leggings and moccasins, and placed two eagle plumes upon its head. Then they went to San Francisco Mountain (Arizona) and made two songs and prayers and dressed that mountain in abalone shells with two eagle plumes upon its head. They then visited Ute Mountain and gave to it two songs and prayers and dressed it in black beads. Then they returned to their own mountain where the fogs meet and said, "We two have made all these songs."

Other brothers were born of the white corn and yellow corn, and two brothers were placed on each mountain. They are the spirits of the mountains and to them the clouds come first. All the brothers together made game, the deer and elk and buffalo, and so game was created. Navajos pray for rain and snow to Hasjelti and Hostjoghon. They stand upon the mountain tops and call the clouds to gather around them. Hasjelti prays to the sun, for the Navajos.

"Father, give me the light of your mind that my mind may be strong. Give me your strength, that my arm may be strong. Give me your rays, that corn and other vegetation may grow."

The most important prayers are addressed to Hasjelti and the most valuable gifts made to him. He talks to the Navajos through the birds, and for this reason the choicest feathers and plumes are placed in the cigarettes and attached to the prayer sticks offered to him.

The Song-Hunter
Navajo (New Mexico)

A man sat thinking. "Let me see. My songs are too short. I want more songs. Where shall I go to find them?"

Hasjelti appeared and perceiving his thoughts, said, "I know where you can get more songs."

"Well, I want to get more. So I will follow you."

They went to a certain point in a box canon in the Big Colorado River and here they found four gods, the Hostjobokon, at work, hewing cottonwood logs.

Hasjelti said, "This will not do. Cottonwood becomes water-soaked. You must use pine instead of cottonwood."

The Hostjobokon began boring the pine with flint, but Hasjelti said, "That is slow work." He commanded a whirlwind to hollow the log. A cross, joining at the exact middle of each log, a solid one and the hollow one, was formed. The arms of the cross were equal.

The song-hunter entered the hollow log and Hasjelti closed the end with a cloud so that water would not enter when the logs were launched upon the great waters. The logs floated off. The Hostjobokon, accompanied by their wives, rode upon the logs, one couple sitting upon each arm.

Hasjelti, Hostjoghon, and the two Naaskiddi walked upon the banks to keep the logs off shore. Hasjelti carried a squirrel skin filled with tobacco, with which to supply the gods on their journey. Hostjoghon carried a staff ornamented with eagle and turkey plumes and a gaming ring with two humming birds tied to it with white cotton cord. The two Naaskiddi carried staffs of lightning. The Naaskiddi had clouds upon their backs in which the seeds of all corn and grasses were carried. After floating a long distance down the river, they came to waters that had a shore on one side only. Here they landed. Here they found a people like themselves. When these people learned of the Song-hunter, they gave him many songs and they painted pictures on a cotton blanket and said, "These pictures must go with the songs. If we give this blanket to you, you will lose it. We will give you white earth and black coals which you will grind together to make black paint, and we will give you white sand, yellow sand, and red sand. For the blue paint you will take white sand and black coals with a very little red and yellow sand. These will give you blue."

And so the Navajo people make blue, even to this day.

The Song-hunter remained with these people until the corn was ripe. There he learned to eat corn and he carried some back with him to the Navajos, who had not seen corn before, and he taught them how to raise it and how to eat it.

When he wished to return home, the logs would not float upstream. Four sunbeams attached themselves to the logs, one to each cross arm, and so drew the Song-hunter back to the box canon from which he had started. When he reached that point, he separated the logs. He placed the end of the solid log into the hollow end of the other and planted this great pole in the river. It may be seen there today by the venturesome. In early days many went there to pray and make offerings.

The Guiding Duck and the Lake of Death
Zuni (New Mexico)

Now K-yak-lu, the all-hearing and wise of speech, all alone had been journeying afar in the North Land of cold and white loneliness. He was lost, for the world in which he wandered was buried in the snow which lies spread there forever. So cold he was that his face became wan and white from the frozen mists of his own breath, white as become all creatures who dwell there. So cold at night and dreary of heart, so lost by day and blinded by the light was he that he wept, and died of heart and became transformed as are the gods. Yet his lips called continually and his voice grew shrill and dry-sounding, like the voice of far-flying water-fowl. As he cried, wandering blindly, the water birds flocking around him peered curiously at him, calling meanwhile to their comrades. But wise though he was of all speeches, and their meanings plain to him, yet none told him the way to his country and people.

Now the Duck heard his cry and it was like her own. She was of all regions the traveler and searcher, knowing all the ways, whether above or below the waters, whether in the north, the west, the south, or the east, and was the most knowing of all creatures. Thus the wisdom of the one understood the knowledge of the other.

And the All-wise cried to her, "The mountains are white and the valleys; all plains are like others in whiteness, and even the light of our Father the Sun, makes all ways more hidden of whiteness! In brightness my eyes see but darkness."

The Duck answered:

"Think no longer sad thoughts. Thou hearest all as I see all. Give me tinkling shells from thy girdle and place them on my neck and in my beak. I may guide thee with my seeing if thou hear and follow my trail. Well I know the way to thy country. Each year I lead thither the wild geese and the cranes who flee there as winter follows."

So the All-wise placed his talking shells on the neck of the Duck, and the singing shells in her beak, and though painfully and lamely, yet he followed the sound she made with the shells. From place to place with swift flight she sped, then awaiting him, ducking her head that the shells might call loudly. By and by they came to the country of thick rains and mists on the borders of the Snow World, and passed from water to water, until wider water lay in their path. In vain the Duck called and jingled the shells from the midst of the waters. K-yak-lu could neither swim nor fly as could the Duck.

Now the Rainbow-worm was near in that land of mists and waters and he heard the sound of the sacred shells.

"These be my grandchildren," he said, and called, "Why mourn ye? Give me plumes of the spaces. I will bear you on my shoulders."

Then the All-wise took two of the lightest plumewands, and the Duck her two strong feathers. And he fastened them together and breathed on them while the Rainbow-worm drew near. The Rainbow unbent himself that K-yak-lu might mount, then he arched himself high among the clouds. Like an arrow he straightened himself forward, and followed until his face looked into the Lake of the Ancients. And there the All-wise descended, and sat there alone, in the plain beyond the mountains. The Duck had spread her wings in flight to the south to take counsel of the gods.

Then the Duck, even as the gods had directed, prepared a litter of poles and reeds, and before the morning came, with the litter they went, singing a quaint and pleasant song, down the northern plain. And when they found the All-wise, he looked upon them in the starlight and wept. But the father of the gods stood over him and chanted the sad dirge rite. Then K-yak-lu sat down in the great soft litter they bore for him. They lifted it upon their shoulders, bearing it lightly, singing loudly as they went, to the shores of the deep black lake, where gleamed from the middle the lights of the dead.

Out over the magic ladder of rushes and canes which reared itself over the water, they bore him. And K-yak-lu, scattering sacred prayer meal before him, stepped down the way, slowly, like a blind man. No sooner had he taken four steps than the ladder lowered into the deep. And the All-wise entered the council room of the gods.

The gods sent out their runners, to summon all beings, and called in dancers for the Dance of Good. And with these came the little ones who had sunk beneath the waters, well and beautiful and all seemingly clad in cotton mantles and precious neck jewels.

The Boy Who Became A God
Navajo (New Mexico)

The Tolchini, a clan of the Navajos, lived at Wind Mountains. One of them used to take long visits into the country. His brothers thought he was crazy. The first time on his return, he brought with him a pine bough; the second time, corn. Each time he returned he brought something new and had a strange story to tell. His brothers said: "He is crazy. He does not know what he is talking about."

Now the Tolchini left Wind Mountains and went to a rocky foothill east of the San Mateo Mountain. They had nothing to eat but seed grass. The eldest brother said, "Let us go hunting," but they told the youngest brother not to leave camp. But five days and five nights passed, and there was no word. So he followed them.

After a day's travel he camped near a canon, in a cavelike place. There was much snow but no water so he made a fire and heated a rock, and made a hole in the ground. The hot rock heated the snow and gave him water to drink. Just then he heard a tumult over his head, like people passing. He went out to see what made the noise and saw many crows crossing back and forth over the canon. This was the home of the crow, but there were other feathered people there, and the chaparral cock. He saw many fires made by the crows on each side of the canyon. Two crows flew down near him and the youth listened to hear what was the matter.

The two crows cried out, "Somebody says. Somebody says."

The youth did not know what to make of this.

A crow on the opposite side called out, "What is the matter? Tell us! Tell us! What is wrong?"

The first two cried out, "Two of us got killed. We met two of our men who told us."

Then they told the crows how two men who were out hunting killed twelve deer, and a party of the Crow People went to the deer after they were shot. They said, "Two of us who went after the blood of the deer were shot."

The crows on the other side of the ca–on called, "Which men got killed?"

"The chaparral cock, who sat on the horn of the deer, and the crow who sat on its backbone."

The others called out, "We are not surprised they were killed. That is what we tell you all the time. If you go after dead deer you must expect to be killed."

"We will not think of them longer," so the two crows replied. "They are dead and gone. We are talking of things of long ago."

But the youth sat quietly below and listened to everything that was said.

After a while the crows on the other side of the canon made a great noise and began to dance. They had many songs at that time. The youth listened all the time. After the dance a great fire was made and he could see black objects moving, but he could not distinguish any people. He recognized the voice of Hasjelti. He remembered everything in his heart. He even remembered the words of the songs that continued all night. He remembered every word of every song. He said to himself, "I will listen until daylight."

The Crow People did not remain on the side of the canon where the fires were first built. They crossed and recrossed the canon in their dance. They danced back and forth until daylight. Then all the crows and the other birds flew away to the west. All that was left was the fires and the smoke.

Then the youth started for his brothers' camp. They saw him coming. They said, "He will have lots of stories to tell. He will say he saw something no one ever saw."

But the brother-in-law who was with them said, "Let him alone. When he comes into camp he will tell us all. I believe these things do happen for he could not make up these things all the time."

Now the camp was surrounded by pinon brush and a large fire was burning in the center. There was much meat roasting over the fire. When the youth reached the camp, he raked over the coals and said. "I feel cold." Brother-in-law replied, "It is cold. When people camp together, they tell stories to one another in the morning. We have told ours, now you tell yours."

The youth said, "Where I stopped last night was the worst camp I ever had." The brothers paid no attention but the brother-in-law listened. The youth said, "I never heard such a noise." Then he told his story. Brother-in-law asked what kind of people made the noise.

The youth said, "I do not know. They were strange people to me, but they danced all night back and forth across the canon and I heard them say my brothers killed twelve deer and afterwards killed two of their people who went for the blood of the deer. I heard them say, "'That is what must be expected. If you go to such places, you must expect to be killed.' "

The elder brother began thinking. He said, "How many deer did you say were killed?"

"Twelve."

Elder brother said, "I never believed you before, but this story I do believe. How do you find out all these things? What is the matter with you that you know them?"

The boy said, "I do not know. They come into my mind and to my eyes." Then they started homeward, carrying the meat. The youth helped them. As they were descending a mesa, they sat down on the edge to rest. Far down the mesa were four mountain sheep. The brothers told the youth to kill one.

The youth hid in the sage brush and when the sheep came directly toward him, he aimed his arrow at them. But his arm stiffened and became dead. The sheep passed by.

He headed them off again by hiding in the stalks of a large yucca. The sheep passed within five steps of him, but again his arm stiffened as he drew the bow.

He followed the sheep and got ahead of them and hid behind a birch tree in bloom. He had his bow ready, but as they neared him they became gods. The first was Hasjelti, the second was Hostjoghon, the third Naaskiddi, and the fourth Hadatchishi. Then the youth fell senseless to the ground. The four gods stood one on each side of him, each with a rattle. They traced with their rattles in the sand the figure of a man, drawing lines at his head and feet. Then the youth recovered and the gods again became sheep. They said, "Why did you try to shoot us? You see you are one of us." For the youth had become a sheep.

The gods said, "There is to be a dance, far off to the north beyond the Ute Mountain. We want you to go with us. We will dress you like ourselves and teach you to dance. Then we will wander over the world."

Now the brothers watched from the top of the mesa but they could not see what the trouble was. They saw the youth lying on the ground, but when they reached the place, all the sheep were gone. They began crying, saying, "For a long time we would not believe him, and now he has gone off with the sheep."

They tried to head off the sheep, but failed. They said, "If we had believed him, he would not have gone off with the sheep. But perhaps some day we will see him again."

At the dance, the five sheep found seven others. This made their number twelve. They journeyed all around the world. All people let them see their dances and learn their songs. Then the eleven talked together and said,

"There is no use keeping this youth with us longer. He has learned everything. He may as well go back to his people and teach them to do as we do."

So the youth was taught to have twelve in the dance, six gods and six goddesses, with Hasjelti to lead them. He was told to have his people make masks to represent the gods.

So the youth returned to his brothers, carrying with him all songs, all medicines, and clothing.

Origin of Clear Lake
Patwin (Sacramento Valley, Cal.)

Before anything was created at all, Old Frog and Old Badger lived alone together. Old Badger wanted to drink, so Old Frog gnawed into a tree, drew out all the sap and put it in a hollow place. Then he created Little Frogs to help him, and working together they dug out the lake. Then Old Frog made the little flat whitefish. Some of them lived in the lake, but others swam down Cache Creek, and turned into the salmon, pike, and sturgeon which swim in the Sacramento.

The Great Fire
Patwin (Sacramento Valley, Cal.)

Long ago a man loved two women and wished to marry both of them. But the women were magpies and they laughed at him. Therefore the man went to the north, and made for himself a tule boat. Then he set the world on fire, and himself escaped to sea in his boat.

But the fire burned with terrible speed. It ate its way into the south. It licked up all things on earth, men, trees, rocks, animals, water, and even the ground itself.

Now Old Coyote saw the burning and the smoke from his place far in the south, and he ran with all his might to put it out. He put two little boys in a sack and ran north like the wind. He took honey-dew into his mouth, chewed it up, spat on the fire, and so put it out. Now the fire was out, but there was no water and Coyote was thirsty. So he took Indian sugar again, chewed it up, dug a hole in the bottom of the creek, covered up the sugar in it, and it turned to water and filled the creek. So the earth had water again.

But the two little boys cried because they were lonesome, for there was nobody left on earth. Then Coyote made a sweat house, and split a number of sticks, and laid them in the sweat house over night. In the morning they had all turned into men and women.

Origin of the Raven and the Macaw
Zuni (New Mexico)

The priest who was named Yanauluha carried ever in his hand a staff which now in the daylight was plumed and covered with feathers—yellow, blue-green, red, white, black, and varied. Attached to it were shells, which made a song-like tinkle. The people when they saw it stretched out their hands and asked many questions.

Then the priest balanced it in his hand, and struck with it a hard place, and blew upon it. Amid the plumes appeared four round things-mere eggs they were. Two were blue like the sky and two dun-red like the flesh of the Earth-mother.

Then the people asked many questions.,

"These," said the priests, "are the seed of living beings. Choose which ye will follow. From two eggs shall come beings of beautiful plumage, colored like the grass and fruits of summer. Where they fly and ye follow, shall always be summer. Without toil, fields of food shall flourish. And from the other two eggs shall come evil beings, piebald, with white, without colors. And where these two shall fly and ye shall follow, winter strives with summer. Only by labor shall the fields yield fruit, and your children and theirs shall strive for the fruits. Which do ye choose?"

"The blue! The blue!" cried the people, and those who were strongest carried off the blue eggs, leaving the red eggs to those who waited. They laid the blue eggs with much gentleness in soft sand on the sunny side of a hill, watching day by day. They were precious of color; surely they would be the precious birds of the Summer-land. Then the eggs cracked and the birds came out, with open eyes and pin feathers under their skins.

"We chose wisely," said the people. "Yellow and blue, red and green, are their dresses, even seen through their skins." So they fed them freely of all the foods which men favor. Thus they taught them to eat all desirable food. But when the feathers appeared, they were black with white bandings. They were ravens. And they flew away croaking hoarse laughs and mocking our fathers.

But the other eggs became beautiful macaws, and were wafted by a toss of the priest's wand to the faraway Summer-land.

So those who had chosen the raven, became the Raven People. They were the Winter People and they were many and strong. But those who had chosen the macaw, became the Macaw People. They were the Summer People, and few in number, and less strong, but they were wiser because they were more deliberate. The priest Yanauluha, being wise, became their father, even as the Sun-father is among the little moons of the sky. He and his sisters were the ancestors of the priest-keepers of things.

Coyote and the Hare
Sia (New Mexico)

One day Coyote was passing about when he saw Hare sitting before his house. Coyote thought, "In a minute I will catch you," and he sprang and caught Hare.

Hare cried, "Man Coyote, do not eat me. Wait just a minute; I have something to tell you—something you will be glad to hear—something you must hear."

"Well," said Coyote, "I will wait."

"Let me sit at the entrance of my house," said Hare. "Then I can talk to you."

Coyote allowed Hare to take his seat at the entrance.

Hare said, What are you thinking of, Coyote?

"Nothing," said Coyote.

"Listen, then," said Hare. "I am a hare and I am very much afraid of people. When they come carrying arrows, I am afraid of them. When they see me they aim their arrows at me and I am afraid, and oh! how I tremble!"

Hare began trembling violently until he saw Coyote a little off his guard, then he began to run. It took Coyote a minute to think and then he ran after Hare, but always a little behind. Hare raced away and soon entered a house, just in time to escape Coyote. Coyote tried to enter the house but found it was hard stone. He became very angry.

Coyote cried, "I was very stupid! Why did I allow this Hare to fool me? I must have him. But this house is so strong, how can I open it?"

Coyote began to work, but after a while he said to himself, "The stone is so strong I cannot open it."

Presently Hare called, "Man Coyote, how are you going to kill me?"

"I know how," said Coyote. "I will kill you with fire."

"Where is the wood?" asked Hare, for he knew there was no wood at his house.

"I will bring grass," said Coyote, "and set fire to it. The fire will enter your house and kill you."

"Oh," said Hare, "but the grass is mine. It is my food; it will not kill me. It is my friend. The grass will not kill me."

"Then," said Coyote, "I will bring all the trees of the wood and set fire to them."

"All the trees know me," said Hare. "They are my friends. They will not kill me. They are my food." Coyote thought a minute. Then he said, "I will bring the gum of the0 pinon and set fire to that."

Hare said, "Now I am afraid. I do not eat that. It is not my friend."

Coyote rejoiced that he had thought of a plan for getting the hare. He hurried and brought all the gum he could carry and placed it at the door of Hare's house and set fire to it. In a short time the gum boiled like hot grease, and Hare cried, "Now I know I shall die! What shall I do?" Yet all the time he knew what he would do.

But Coyote was glad Hare was afraid. After a while Hare called, "The fire is entering my house," and Coyote answered, "'Blow it out!"

But Coyote drew nearer and blew with all his might to blow the flame into Hare's house.

Hare cried, "You are so close you are blowing the fire on me and I will soon be burned."

Coyote was so happy that he drew closer and blew harder, and drew still closer so that his face was very close to Hare's face. Then Hare suddenly threw the boiling gum into Coyote's face and escaped from his house.

It took Coyote a long time to remove the gum from his face, and he felt very sorrowful. He said, "I am very, very stupid."

Coyote and the Quails
Pima (Arizona)

Once upon a time, long ago, Coyote was sleeping so soundly that a covey of quails came along and cut pieces of fat meat out of his flesh without arousing him. Then they went on. After they had camped for the evening, and were cooking the meat, Coyote came up the trail.

Coyote said, "Where did you get that nice, fat meat? Give me some." Quails gave him all he wanted. Then he went farther up the trail. After he had gone a little way, Quails called to him,

"Coyote, you were eating your own flesh."

Coyote said, "What did you say?"

Quails said, "Oh, nothing. We heard something calling behind the mountains."

Soon the quails called again: "Coyote, you ate your own meat."

"What did you say?"

"Oh, nothing. We heard somebody pounding his grinding-stone. "

So Coyote went on. But at last he began to feel where he had been cut. Then he knew what the quails meant. He turned back down the trail and told Quails he would eat them up. He began to chase them. The quails flew above ground and Coyote ran about under them. At last they got tired, but Coyote did not because he was so angry.

By and by Quails came to a hole, and one of the keenest-witted picked up a piece of prickly cholla cactus and pushed it into the hole; then they all ran in after it. But Coyote dug out the hole and reached them. When he came to the first quail he said,

"Was it you who told me I ate my own flesh?"

Quail said, "No."

So Coyote let him go and he flew away. When Coyote came to the second quail, he asked the same question. Quail said, "No," and then flew away.

So Coyote asked every quail, until the last quail was gone, and then he came to the cactus branch. Now the prickly cactus branch was so covered with feathers that it looked just like a quail. Coyote asked it the same question, but the cactus branch did not answer. Then Coyote said, "I know it was you because you do not answer."

So Coyote bit very hard into the hard, prickly branch, and it killed him.

Coyote and the Fawns
Sia (New Mexico)

Another day when he was traveling around, Coyote met a deer with two fawns. The fawns were beautifully spotted, and he said to the deer, "How did you paint your children? They are so beautiful!"

Deer replied, "I painted them with fire from the cedar."

"And how did you do the work?" asked Coyote.

"I put my children into a cave and built a fire of cedar in front of it. Every time a spark flew from the fire it struck my children, making a beautiful spot."

"Oh," said Coyote, "I will do the same thing. Then I will make my children beautiful."

He hurried to his house and put his children in a cave. Then he built a fire of cedar in front of it and stood off to watch the fire. But the children cried because the fire was very hot. Coyote kept calling to them not to cry because they would be beautiful like the deer. After a time the crying ceased and Coyote was pleased. But when the fire died down, he found they were burned to death. Coyote expected to find them beautiful, but instead they were dead.

Then he was enraged with the deer and ran away to hunt her, but he could not find her anywhere. He was much distressed to think the deer had fooled him so easily.

How the Bluebird Got its Color
Pima (Arizona)

A long time ago, the bluebird was a very ugly color. But Bluebird knew of a lake where no river flowed in or out, and he bathed in this four times every morning for four mornings. Every morning he sang a magic song:

"There's a blue water. It lies there.

I went in.

I am all blue."

On the fourth morning Bluebird shed all his feathers and came out of the lake just in his skin. But the next morning when he came out of the lake he was covered with blue feathers.

Now all this while Coyote had been watching Bluebird. He wanted to jump in and get him to eat, but he was afraid of the water. But on that last morning Coyote said, "How is it you have lost all your ugly color, and now you are blue and gay and beautiful? You are more beautiful than anything that flies in the air. I want to be blue, too." Now Coyote at that time was a bright green.

"I only went in four times on four mornings," said Bluebird. He taught Coyote the magic song, and he went in four times, and the fifth time he came out as blue as the little bird.

Then Coyote was very, very proud because he was a blue coyote. He was so proud that as he walked along he looked around on every side to see if anybody was looking at him now that he was a blue coyote and so beautiful. He looked to see if his shadow was blue, too. But Coyote was so busy watching to see if others were noticing him that he did not watch the trail. By and by he ran into a stump so hard that it threw him down in the dirt and he was covered with dust all over. You may know this is true because even today coyotes are the color of dirt.

Coyote's Eyes
Pima (Arizona)

When Coyote was traveling about one day, he saw a small bird. The bird was hopping about contentedly and Coyote thought, "What a beautiful bird. It moves about so gracefully."

He drew nearer to the bird and asked, "What beautiful things are you working with?" but the bird could not understand Coyote. After a while the bird took out his two eyes and threw them straight up into the air, like two stones. It looked upward but had no eyes. Then the bird said, "Come, my eyes. Come quickly, down into my head." The eyes fell down into the bird's head, just where they belonged, but were much brighter than before.

Coyote thought he could brighten his eyes. He asked the bird to take out his eyes. The bird took out Coyote's eyes, held them for a moment in his hands, and threw them straight up into the air. Coyote looked up and called, "Come back, my eyes. Come quickly." They at once fell back into his head and were much brighter than before. Coyote wanted to try it again, but the bird did not wish to. But Coyote persisted. Then the bird said, "Why should I work for you, Coyote? No, I will work no more for you." But Coyote still persisted, and the bird took out his eyes and threw them up. Coyote cried, "Come, my eyes, come back to me."

But his eyes continued to rise into the air, and the bird began to go away. Coyote began to weep. But the bird was annoyed, and called back, "Go away now. I am tired of you. Go away and get other eyes."

But Coyote refused to go and entreated the bird to find eyes for him. At last the bird gathered gum from a pinon tree and rolled it between his hands and put it in Coyote's eye holes, so that he could see. But his eyes had been black and very bright. His new eyes were yellow.

"Now," said the bird, it "go away. You cannot stay here any longer."

Coyote and the Tortillas
Pima (Arizona)

Once upon a time, a river rose very high and spread all over the land. An Indian woman was going along the trail by the river side with a basket of tortillas on her head, but she was wading in water up to her waist. Now Coyote was afraid of the water, so he had climbed into a cottonwood tree. When the woman came up the trail, Coyote called, "Oh, come to this tree and give me some of those nice tortillas."

The woman said, "No. I can't give them to you; they are for somebody else."

"If you do not come here I will shoot you," said Coyote, and the woman really thought he had a bow. So she came to the tree and said, "You must come down and get them. I can't climb trees."

Coyote came down as far as he dared, but he was afraid of the deep water. The woman laughed at him. She said, "Just see how shallow it is. It's only up to my ankles." But she was standing on a big stump. Coyote looked at the water. It seemed shallow and safe enough, so he jumped. But the water was deep and he was drowned. Then the woman went on up the trail.

Coyote as a Hunter
Sia (New Mexico)

Coyote traveled a long distance and in the middle of the day it was very hot. He sat down and rested, and thought, as he looked up to Tinia, "How I wish the Cloud People would freshen my path and make it cool." In just a little while the Cloud People gathered over the trail Coyote was following and he was glad that his path was to be cool and shady. After he traveled some distance further, he sat down again and looking upward said, "I wish the Cloud People would send rain. My road would be cooler and fresher." In a little while a shower came and Coyote was contented.

But in a short time he again sat down and wished that the road could be very moist, that it would be fresh to his feet, and almost immediately the trail was as wet as though a river had passed over it. Again Coyote was contented.

But after a while he took his seat again. He said to himself, "I guess I will talk again to the Cloud People." Then he looked up and said to them,

"I wish for water over my road-water to my elbows, that I may travel on my hands and feet in the cool waters; then I shall be refreshed and happy."

In a short time his road was covered with water, and he moved on. But again he wished for something more, and said to the Cloud People, "I wish much for water to my shoulders. Then I will be happy and contented."

In a moment the waters arose as he wished, yet after a while he looked up and said, "If you will only give me water so high that my eyes, nose, mouth and ears are above it, I will be happy. Then indeed my road will be cool."

But even this did not satisfy him, and after traveling a while longer he implored the Cloud People to give him a river that he might float over the trail, and immediately a river appeared and Coyote floated down stream. Now be had been high in the mountains and wished to go to Hare Land.

After floating a long distance, he at last came to Hare Land and saw many Hares a little distance off, on both sides of the river. Coyote lay down in the mud as though he were dead and listened. Soon a woman ka-wate (mephitis) came along with a vase and a gourd for water. She said, "Here is a dead coyote. Where did he come from? I guess from the mountains above. I guess he fell into the water and died."

Coyote looked up and said, "Come here, woman."

She said, "What do you want?"

Coyote said, "I know the Hares and other small animals well. In a little while they will come here and think I am dead and be happy. What do you think about it?"

Ka-wate said, "I have no thoughts at all."

So Coyote explained his plan. . . .

So Coyote lay as dead, and all the Hares and small animals saw him lying in the river, and rejoiced that he was dead. The Hares decided to go in a body and see the dead Coyote. Rejoicing over his death, they struck him with their hands and kicked him. There were crowds of Hares and they decided to have a great dance. Now and then a dancing Hare would stamp upon Coyote who lay as if dead. During the dance the Hares clapped their hands over their mouth and gave a whoop like a war-whoop.

Then Coyote rose quickly and took two clubs which the ka-wate had given him, and together they killed all of the Hares. There was a great number and they were piled up like stones.

Coyote said, "Where shall I find fire to cook the hares? Ah," he said, pointing across to a high rock, "that rock gives good shade and it is cool. I will find fire and cook my meat in the shade of that rock."

So they carried all the hares to that point and Coyote made a large fire and threw them into it. When he had done this he was very warm and tired. He lay down close to the rock in the shade.

After a while he said to Ka-wate, "We will run a race. The one who wins will have all the hares."

She said, "How could I beat you? Your feet are so much larger than mine."

Coyote said, "I will allow you the start of me." He made a torch of the inner shreds of cedar bark and wrapped it with yucca thread and lighted it. Then he tied this torch to the end of his tail. He did this to see that the ka-wate did not escape him.

Ka-wate started first, but when out of sight of Coyote, she slipped into the house of Badger. Then Coyote started with the fire attached to his tail. Wherever he touched the grass, he set fire to it. But Ka-wate hurried back to the rock, carried all the hares on top except four tiny ones, and then climbed up on the rock.

Coyote was surprised not to overtake her. He said, "She must be very quick. How could she run so fast?" Then he returned to the rock, but did not see her.

He was tired and sat down in the shade of the rock. "Why doesn't she come?" he said. "Perhaps she will not come before night, her feet are so small."

Ka-wate sat on the rock above and heard all he said. She watched him take a stick and look into the mound for the hares. He pulled out a small one which he threw away. But the second was smaller than the first. Then a third and a fourth, each tiny, and all he threw away. "I do not care for the smaller ones," he said. "There are so many here, I will not eat the little ones." But he hunted and hunted in the mound of ashes for the hares. All were gone.

He said, "That woman has robbed me." Then he picked up the four little ones and ate them. He looked about for Ka-wate but did not see her because he did not look up. Then as he was tired and lay down to rest, he looked up and saw her, with the cooked hares piled beside her.

Coyote was hungry. He begged her to throw one down. She threw a very small one. Then Coyote became angry. And he was still more angry because he could not climb the rock. She had gone where he could not go.

How the Rattlesnake Learned to Bite
Pima (Arizona)
After people and the animals were created, they all lived together. Rattlesnake was there, and was called Soft Child because he was so

soft in his motions. The people liked to hear him rattle and little rest did he get because they continually poked and scratched him so that he would shake the rattles in his tail. At last Rattlesnake went to Elder Brother to ask help. Elder Brother pulled a hair from his own lip, cut it in short pieces, and made it into teeth for Soft Child.

"If any one bothers you," he said, "bite him."

That very evening Ta-api, Rabbit, came to Soft Child as he had done before and scratched him. Soft Child raised his head and bit Rabbit. Rabbit was angry and scratched again. Soft Child bit him again. Then Rabbit ran about saying that Soft Child was angry and had bitten him. Then he went to Rattlesnake again, and twice more he was bitten.

The bites made Rabbit very sick. He asked for a bed of cool sea sand. Coyote was sent to the sea for the cool, damp sand. Then Rabbit asked for the shade of bushes that he might feel the cool breeze. But at last Rabbit died. He was the first creature which had died in this new world. Then the people were troubled because they did not know what to do with the body of Rabbit. One said, "If we bury him, Coyote will surely dig him up."

Another said, "If we hide him, Coyote will surely find him."

And another said, "If we put him in a tree, Coyote will surely climb up."

So they decided to burn the body of Rabbit, and yet there was no fire on earth.

Blue Fly said, "Go to Sun and get some of the fire which he keeps in his house," So Coyote scampered away, but he was sure the people were trying to get rid of him so he kept looking back.

Then Blue Fly made the first fire drill. Taking a stick like an arrow he twirled it in his hands, letting the lower end rest on a flat stick that lay on the ground. Soon smoke began to arise, and then fire came. The people gathered fuel and began their duty.

But Coyote, looking back, saw fire ascending. He turned and ran back as fast as he could go. When the people saw him coming, they formed a ring, but he raced around the circle until he saw two short men standing together. He jumped over them, and seized the heart of Rabbit. But he burned his mouth doing it, and it is black to this day.

Coyote and the Rattlesnake
Sia (New Mexico)

Coyote's house was not far from Rattlesnake's home. One morning when they were out walking together, Coyote said to Rattlesnake, "Tomorrow come to my house."

In the morning Rattlesnake went to Coyote's house. He moved slowly along the floor, shaking his rattle. Coyote sat at one side, very much frightened. The movements of the snake and the rattle frightened him. Coyote had a pot of rabbit meat on the fire, which he placed in front of the snake, saying, "Companion, eat."

"I will not eat your meat. I do not understand your food," said Rattlesnake.

"What food do you eat?"

"I eat the yellow flowers of the corn."

Coyote at once began to search for the yellow corn flowers. When he found some, Rattlesnake said, "Put some on top of my head so that I may eat it."

Coyote stood as far off as he could and placed the pollen on the snake's head.

The snake said, "Come nearer and put enough on my head so that I may find it."

Coyote was very much afraid, but after a while he came nearer and did as he was told.

Then the snake went away, saying, "Companion, tomorrow you come to my house."

"All right," said Coyote. Tomorrow I will come."

Coyote sat down and thought about the morrow. He thought a good deal about what the snake might do. So he made a small rattle by placing tiny pebbles in a gourd and fastened it to the end of his tail. He shook it a while and was much pleased with it.

The next morning he started for the snake's house. He shook the rattle on the end of his tail and smiled, and said to himself, "This is good. When I go into Rattlesnake's house, he will be very much afraid of me."

Coyote did not walk into Snake's house, but moved like a snake. But Coyote could not shake his rattle as the snake shook his. He had to hold it in his hand. But when he shook his rattle, the snake seemed much afraid, and said,

"Companion, I am afraid of you."

Now Rattlesnake had a stew of rats on the fire, and he placed some before Coyote. But Coyote said, "I do not understand your food. I cannot eat it because I do not understand it."

Rattlesnake insisted upon his eating, but Coyote refused. He said, "If you put some of the flower of the corn on my head, I will eat. I understand that food."

The snake took some corn pollen, but he pretended to be afraid of Coyote and stood off some distance. Coyote said, "Come nearer and place it on top my head."

Snake replied, "I am afraid of you."

Coyote said, "Come nearer. I am not bad."

Then the snake came closer and put the pollen on top of Coyote's head. But Coyote did not have the long tongue of the snake and he could not get the pollen off the top of his head. He put out his tongue first on one side of his nose and then on the other, but he could only reach to the side of his nose. His efforts made the snake laugh, but the snake put his hand over his mouth so Coyote should not see him laugh. Really, the snake hid his head in his body.

At last Coyote went home. As he left the snake's house, he held his tail in his hand and shook the rattle.

Snake cried, "Oh, companion! I am so afraid of you!" but really the snake shook with laughter.

When Coyote reached his home he said to himself, "I was such a fool. Rattlesnake had much food to eat and I would not take it. Now I am very hungry."

Then he went out in search of food.

Origin of the Saguaro and Palo Verde Cacti
Pima (Arizona)

Once upon a time an old Indian woman had two grandchildren. Every day she ground wheat and corn between the grinding stones to make porridge for them. One day as she put the water-olla on the fire outside the house to heat the water, she told the children not to quarrel because they might upset the olla. But the children began to quarrel. They upset the olla and spilled the water and their grandmother spanked them.

Then the children were angry and ran away. They ran far away over the mountains. The grandmother heard them whistling and she ran after them and followed them from place to place. but she could not catch up with them.

At last the older boy said, "I will turn into a saguaro, so that I shall live forever and bear fruit every summer."

The younger said, "Then I will turn into a palo verde and stand there forever. These mountains are so bare and have nothing on them but rocks, I will make them green."

The old woman heard the cactus whistling and recognized the voice of her grandson. So she went up to it and tried to take the prickly thing into her arms, but the thorns killed her.

That is how the saguaro and the palo verde came to be on the mountains and the desert.

The Thirsty Quails
Pima (Arizona)

A Quail once had more than twenty children, and with them she wandered over the whole country in search of water and could not find it. It was very hot and they were all crying, "Where can we get some water? Where can we get some water?" but for a long time they could find none.

At last, way in the north, under a mesquite tree, the mother quail saw a pond of water, but it was very muddy and not fit to drink. But the little quails had been wandering so many days and were so tired they stopped under the shade of the mesquite tree, and by and by, one by one, they went down to the water and 'drank it. But the water was so bad they all died.

The Boy and the Beast
Pima (Arizona)

Once an old woman lived with her daughter and son-in-law and their little boy. They were following the trail of the Apache Indians. Now whenever a Pima Indian sees the trail of an Apache he draws a ring around it; then he can catch him sooner. And these Pimas drew circles around the trail of the Apaches they were following, but one night when they were asleep, the Apaches came down upon them. They took the man and younger woman by the hair and shook them out of their skins, just as one would shake corn out of a sack. So the boy and the old woman were left alone.

Now these two had to live on berries and anything they could find, and they wandered from place to place. In one place a strange beast, big enough to swallow people, camped in the bushes near them. The grand-mother told the boy not to go near these bushes. But the boy took some sharp stones in his hands, and went toward them. As he came near, the great monster began to breathe. He began to suck in his breath and he sucked the boy right into his stomach. But with his sharp stones the boy began to cut the beast, so that he died. Then the boy made a hole large enough to climb out of.

When his grandmother came to look for him, the boy met her and said, "I have killed that monster."

The grandmother said, "Oh, no. Such a little boy as you are to kill such a great monster!"

The boy said, "But I was inside of him. just look at the stones I cut him with."

Then the grandmother went softly up to the bushes, and looked at the monster. It was full of holes, just as the little boy had said.

Then they moved down among the berry bushes and had all they wanted to eat.

Why the Apaches are Fierce
Pima (Arizona)

Elder Brother, Coyote, and Earth Doctor, after the flood vanished, began to create people and animals. Coyote made all the animals, Elder Brother made the people, and Earth Doctor made queer creatures which had only one leg, or immense ears, or many fingers, and some having flames of fire in their knees.

Elder Brother divided his figures of people into four groups. One of the Apaches came to life first. He shivered and said, "Oh, it's very cold," and began to sway back and forth. Then Elder Brother said, "I didn't think you would be the first to awake," and he took all the Apaches up in his hand and threw them over the mountains. That made them angry, and that is why they have always been so fierce.

Speech on the Warpath
Pima (Arizona)

We have come thus far, my brothers. In the east there is White Gopher, who gnaws with his strong teeth. He was friendly and came to me. On his way he came to the surface from the underground four times. Looking in all four directions, he saw a magic whitish trail. Slowly following this, he neared the enemy, coming to the surface from the underground four times during the journey. Their power stood in their land like a mountain, but he bit it off short, and he sank their springs by biting them. He saw that the wind of the enemy was strong and he cut it up with his teeth. He gnawed in short pieces their clouds. They had good dreams and bright false-seeing, good bow strings and straight-flying reeds, but these he grasped and bit off short. The different belongings lying about he took with him, turning around homeward. On his way homeward over the whitish trail, he came to the surface four times, and magic fire appeared around the edges. Then he came to his bed. He felt that the land roared rejoicingly with him.

In the south was Blue Coyote and there I sent my cry. He was friendly and came to me from his blue darkness, circling around and shouting, four times, on his journey, making magic fire everywhere. When he arrived, he looked in four directions, then understood. A whitish magic trail lay before him. He cast his blue darkness upon the enemy and slowly approached them, circling around and shouting four times on the way. Like a mountain was their power in the land, and he sucked it in. The springs of water under the trees he sucked in. The wind that was blowing he inhaled. He sucked in the clouds. The people dreamed of a white thing, and their dreams he sucked in, with their best bow strings and the straight-flying reeds. All the different belongings which lay around he gathered and slowly turned back. Hidden in the blue darkness, he came to me, circling around, shouting, four times on his journey. Then he homeward took his way, circling, howling, four times, and shouting reached his bed. With pleasure he felt all directions thud. The east echoed.

In the sunset direction was Black Kangaroo Mouse, an expert robber. To him I sent my cry. He was friendly to me and came hidden in black darkness, sitting down four times upon his way. Magic fire covered the edges of his trail. When he reached me. he looked in all directions. The magic trail brightly lay before him. He threw black darkness around him and slowly reached the enemy, sitting down four times upon the trail. He found a bag of the enemy, with much prized possessions. It was tied one knot on top of another) but he bit them off. He took from it the blue necklaces, blue earrings, and the different belongings lying around gathered up with him. Then he slowly took his way back on the magic trail, with magic fire everywhere. Hidden in his yellow darkness, he returned to me. He left the others at the council and in darkness took his homeward way, resting four times. He sat on his bed and felt all directions of the earth rustling in the darkness. Darkness lay all around.

I called on Owl, the white blood-sucker. To him I sent my cry. He was friendly and came down to me with four thin flys (sailing) on the way. He looked in all directions. The magic trail brightly before him lay. He flew, with four thin flys, toward the enemy. The mountain of their power which stood in the land he bit off short. The springs he bit off, and their very good dreams. The best bow strings and the straight-flying reeds he grasped and cut very short. He bit off their flesh and made holes in their bones. From the things gathered, he made a belt from a bowstring. Then he returned. He came through the whitish mist of dawn in four flights. The people held a council. Leaving them there, he after four thin flys reached his bed in the gray dawn mist. Then in all directions he heard the darkness rattling, as he lay there.

The Spirit Land
Gallinomero (Russian River, Cal.)

When the flames burn low on the funeral pyres of the Gallinomero, Indian mourners gather up handfuls of ashes and scatter them high in air. Thus the good mount up into the air, or go to the Happy Western Land beyond the Big Water.

But the bad Indians go to an island in the Bitter Waters, an island naked and barren and desolate, covered only with brine-spattered stone, swept with cold winds and the biting sea-spray. Here they live always, breaking stone upon one another, with no food but the broken stones and no drink but the salt sea water.

Song of the Ghost Dance
Pai Ute (Kern River, Cal.)

The snow lies there—ro-rani!
The snow lies there—ro-rani!
The snow lies there—ro-rani!

The snow lies there — ro-rani!
The Milky Way lies there.
The Milky Way lies there.

"This is one of the favorite songs of the Paiute Ghost dance. . . . It must be remembered that the dance is held in the open air at night, with the stars shining down on the wide-extending plain walled in by the giant Sierras, fringed at the base with dark pines, and with their peaks white with eternal snows. Under such circumstances this song of the snow lying white upon the mountains, and the Milky Way stretching across the clear sky, brings up to the Paiute the same patriotic home love that comes from lyrics of singing birds and leafy trees and still waters to the people of more favored regions. . . . The Milky Way is the road of the dead to the spirit world."

CPSIA information can be obtained
at www.ICGtesting.com
Printed in the USA
LVOW12s0113230516

489455LV00001B/85/P